Para Azul

OUT IN THE COLD

By Stuart Johnstone

Out in the Cold
Into the Dark

OUT IN THE COLD

STUART JOHNSTONE

Allison & Busby Limited
11 Wardour Mews
London W1F 8AN
allisonandbusby.com

First published in Great Britain by Allison & Busby in 2020.
This paperback edition published by Allison & Busby in 2021.

A CIP catalogue record for this book is available from
the British Library.

10 9 8 7 6 5 4 3 2 1

ISBN 978-0-7490-2638-7

Typeset in 10.5/15.5 pt Sabon LT Pro by
Allison & Busby Ltd

MIX
Paper from
responsible sources
FSC® C020471

The paper used for this Allison & Busby publication
has been produced from trees that have been legally sourced
from well-managed and credibly certified forests.

Printed and bound by
CPI Group (UK) Ltd, Croydon, CR0 4YY

CHAPTER ONE

Gut Feeling

John tried the letterbox again. He let the flap fall, sending harsh metallic claps both inside the bare-sounding flat and all around the stairwell, knowing half the building had probably been awoken by our now-lengthy efforts.

Five seconds of silence. Ten. Nothing.

At John's request I held the flap open while he shone his torch through.

'No carpet,' he said, 'no light bulbs even; is this definitely the right address?'

I checked the message on my radio screen and confirmed it was.

'What do you think?' he said.

'You're asking me?' I laughed. He had been doing this more and more. I enjoyed the responsibility implied, though not so much the pressure that came with it.

John began rapping the butt-end of his torch against the door. The sound was piercing, and I resisted the urge to plug my ears with my fingers.

The door to the flat behind us juddered open, the scowl on the man's face turned to apologetic surprise and the door closed over.

John was sniffing through the letterbox now.

'What *are* you doing?' I asked.

'Just checking,' he said. 'I think we're going to have to put the door in.'

'I'll get it from the car,' I said. I made my way down the stairwell, watching my feet carefully as the orange haze from the buzzing communal stair-light failed to penetrate the gloom efficiently.

Three certainties in life, John would say often, too often to forget he'd said it to me before. *Death, taxes, and they're always on the top floor.* Today he was right enough. He had a lot of these little sayings. I wondered if they were his, or if he'd learnt them from *his* tutor and, if so, whether I was doomed to inherit them someday.

I held the ram out to John by its crude handles, my arms shaking with the weight of it. He just gave me a trademark look and I knew I was doing the swinging.

He was squat, middle-aged and out of shape, but his shoulders were better equipped for this sort of thing than my slight frame.

I pulled the ram up to chest height and opted for the pendulum approach. If John hadn't been there, I would probably have voiced the *and-a-one, and-a-two, and-a-threeee* out loud. When I reached the count of two, fingers burst from the letterbox, tiny fingers.

'Jesus!' John spluttered, drawing away from the wriggling digits. He shone his light through as the hand withdrew. 'Hello,' he said with a small voice, 'is your mummy or daddy there, can you get them? A wee girl,' he said to me 'can't be older than three. Where's your mummy? Can you open the door?' John continued with the girl. She said something in reply I couldn't hear. I crouched down next to John and saw the dark-haired girl shielding her eyes from the torchlight.

'Can you get Mummy to come to the door, sweetheart?' I asked.

'Asleepin',' she replied.

'Did *you* call us? Can you open the door?'

She tried and the handle turned but the door stayed shut, remaining firmly locked. 'Do you know where the key is? Does Mummy have it?' I asked, realising I was machine-gunning questions at the poor girl.

'Mummy asleepin',' she repeated.

'OK, honey, I need you to stand back away from the door now, can you do that?'

John gave me a nod and I lifted the ram once more. He held his hand up as I approached. 'Do you have a dolly, a baby?' he asked, a moment of inspiration. 'You do? Could I meet her, could you go get her for me?'

John's flat stop-hand turned to a go-point. I planted my feet and swung at the Yale lock and the ram battered through, taking part of the doorframe with it. The door crashed open, slammed against the wall and swung defeated on its hinge. Angry splinters jutted like fangs from the frame's edge.

John's torch lit the dark-haired girl standing in the carpetless hall in pyjama bottoms and a grubby vest top. A grim-looking doll wearing only a blue bonnet hung from her hand. The astonished look on her face quickly dropped, as did the doll, as she began to sob. I dumped the ram and approached cautiously, trying not to frighten her any further.

The smell from the flat was stifling. Nothing specific, just general filth and neglect. I flicked my sleeve over my hand and held it to my face, something I would learn in later years to be a mistake. Experience would teach me the best way to deal with smell is to just breathe normally; the nose becomes accustomed quickly. Any efforts to avoid the stench are futile and only serve to prolong the discomfort.

'What's your name, sweetheart?' My voice came out funny from my reluctance to breathe through my nose, so 'name' sounded more like 'dame'.

I pulled her hands from her tear-streaked face, but she didn't reply. I lifted her and asked again. Her hands moved to my shoulders, holding me at arm's length, though she didn't otherwise resist. She looked at me for the first time. Her wet eyes scanned my face in the gloom. They were quickly drawn to the yellow light beaconing from my radio. She ceased crying now that she had found this wondrous toy on my shoulder. I turned the radio off so she couldn't activate the emergency button and handed it to her to play with while I waited for John to search the flat with his too-small-for-the-job torch. Mine was no better and the large torch in the car hadn't been charged by whoever had used it last.

'My name's Don,' I said to her, 'and that funny man over there is John. What's your name?'

'Carly,' she said, more to the radio than to me.

'That's a pretty name. Where's your phone?' I was still hoping that this was to turn out as nine out of ten dropped calls did; an accidental or mischievous dialling of treble-nine, resulting in some finger wagging and corrective advice. This hope was growing thinner with every passing second.

'Mummy's room.'

'Is Mummy there too, can you show us?' I asked. She pointed down the hall where John's torchlight bobbed and spun.

'John, she's going to show us,' I called.

Carly pointed to the furthest away door, closed over.

'Better stay there,' said John. I nodded and began asking Carly about her nursery. Apparently her teacher was Miss McPake, and she was nice. She had yellow hair, and a blue car.

John returned to the hall. I raised my torch to see him shaking his head, a foreboding expression on his face. Mummy wasn't asleepin'.

John riffled through the contents of a purple purse he had found, looking for the woman's details. He reached for his radio, giving our call sign. Control acknowledged and I carried Carly back down the hall. She didn't need to hear what John had to say.

As we passed back along the hallway Carly tugged on the collar of my stab vest. 'Baby,' she said. I looked around the floor and spotted the dropped doll and handed it to her, swapping it for the return of my radio. I turned it back on and inserted my earpiece. John was passing the grim news.

'That's confirmed, Control, no suspicious circumstances, door was locked from the inside, no signs of struggle, no wounds.'

'That's received, Echo-Three-Three, I'll update supervisors. Do you require detectives?'

'Negative, I'll email them the incident for the morning meeting. Can you just confirm Social Services are en route? Oh, and we'll need a joiner to re-secure a wooden door.'

'Roger, Three-Three.'

Carly fell asleep in the car once it had warmed up. I had coddled her in my uniform fleece jacket and she was snoring gently. John had dabbed at her face with a sanitation wipe from the first-aid box, only succeeding in making her look grubbier with the streaks of clean skin standing out in contrasting hue to the rest.

'What did you find?' I asked John, now that I safely could.

'The mother in bed, stiff and cold. Some pill bottles and charred foil.'

'Such a shame,' I said.

'Shame? Selfish fucking wretch you mean.' This took me a little by surprise, and not just because of the sudden raising of his voice; it really wasn't like John. 'Sorry,' he said, 'I just don't get how someone could do that.' He turned to look at Carly. She hadn't stirred. John had a daughter of his own. I'd never met her, but he talked about her often and with obvious pride. She was studying to be a nurse and was only four years younger than me.

'Do you think she made the call?' I asked.

'The girl? Must have. Mum's been dead a while, at least a day.'

'What will happen to her?' I said, sending a nod towards the sleeping girl.

'I'm not sure,' said John, still looking at her. 'If there's no family to take her she'll be placed with a foster family; if she's really lucky, adopted.'

'And what if she's not lucky?'

John considered this for a moment. 'She'll be passed pillar to post between foster homes and institutions for her entire childhood. God only knows what she'll be when she comes out the other end.'

There was a period of silence as we both digested this. I wished dearly that I hadn't asked.

Everyone then seemed to arrive at once: the undertakers in their dark blue private ambulance, the joiner in his white van and a social worker looking bleary-eyed, clearly on call and asleep when they had summoned her. The priority was to get Carly out. Seeing your mother being removed in a black body bag is the kind of thing you can't unsee. John stood with the social worker, passing on as many details as he had been able to glean from the purse. I lifted Carly carefully, trying not to wake her, and brought her over. John was being told that neither Carly nor her mother were known to social work, which horrified me. I didn't comment; I didn't want to sound like I was attacking the social worker personally. It wasn't her fault the system had failed here. She was a middle-aged woman with a kind face, a useful advantage in her job, I guessed. I handed the half-sleeping girl over. Her small fist was again gripping the edge of my vest and she began to moan as I carefully prised her fingers. As I walked away, she began to cry, understanding dawning on her perhaps. My heart was breaking and the urge to return to her was overwhelming.

'Baby,' she called, her voice and lower lip trembling.

Oh shit, I thought and went to the car to retrieve her doll. I passed it to her and couldn't resist tucking a dark curl around her ear. I exchanged sympathetic smiles with the social worker.

Carly seemed to settle briefly, until the social worker began buckling her into a child seat in her car. I joined John, who was helping the undertakers remove equipment from their vehicle.

'Baby,' I could hear Carly screaming in the background. The social worker must have had to remove her doll to properly secure her in her seat. We waited until they had driven off before traipsing back to the flat, the five of us each lugging something necessary up the stairs. I had the body bag.

The two heavy-set undertakers were impressively dressed in black suits and equally sombre ties – impressive given that it was four in the morning and nobody would have blamed them for turning up in jeans. They hadn't brought a torch, clearly unaccustomed to having to do their job in a house without light bulbs. The torch the joiner had was no better than ours. Still, between us we managed to manoeuvre a stretcher into the bedroom.

She lay naked on her front, underneath a heavy half-pulled-back quilt.

She was, mercifully, facing away from me. Her arms were up above her head and must have been hugging the pillow her head had been resting on before John had removed it.

John double-checked the body with the aid of the extra torches.

I looked away as he checked for sexual injury.

I was still getting used to bodies and John hadn't yet put me in a lead position for this type of call. I knew I would be able to deal with it when I had to, but while I *didn't* have to, I took advantage.

Carly's mum was a large woman, twenty-eight according to her driving licence, though you'd have guessed older. The roots of her brilliant-blonde hair showed that she shared her daughter's natural colour and she sported an array of, frankly, grotesque tattoos: Tweety-Bird looking like he had walked into a hall of mirrors on one shoulder, 'Carly' written in a swirly font on a forearm, and 'Ewan' etched across a garish pink heart on her shoulder. The girl's dad perhaps; and where the hell was he?

The smell in the room was a concentrated version of the rest of the house. Massive piles of dirty clothing lay against one wall like a fabric snowdrift. Used dishes were stacked beside the bed, and coffee cups acting as Petri dishes lay mingled between empty vodka bottles and glasses.

There was a smell coming from the body too. Not of decomposing flesh, not yet, more like a smell from a butcher's shop. No longer a human odour, just meat.

The smell didn't seem to bother anyone else. They simply set about their tasks as if this was the most natural, pedestrian thing in the world. Perhaps, for them, it was.

I began noting down the long names on the labels of the pill bottles before bagging them. John assisted the undertakers in wrapping Carly's mum in the sheet she lay on. *Clever*, I thought, that wouldn't have occurred to me. It meant they could lift her easily while I slid the open body bag underneath and not have to touch her too much.

It was decided that the stretcher would only make things more difficult in the tight turns of the flat. The undertakers lifted her shoulders while I took hold of her feet and led the way, with John making a path with the torch.

My stomach lurched as we left the room. It took me by surprise. As much as the smell was unpleasant, it was unusual for it to induce a gag reflex. I hid it, or did my best to, and the others didn't seem to notice. If they had I would certainly have been subjected to well-meaning, but nevertheless tiresome, ridicule.

The joiner was finishing replacing the lock and drilling screws into the edge of the door frame to undo the damage I had done to it as we passed him.

'Always the top floor eh,' he said to John, as we started down the stairs.

'Three certainties in life . . .' I could hear John beginning.

We waited in the car for the joiner to finish. We would meet the others at the hospital morgue to book the body through once we had finished at the scene.

It was agreed I would write the report, or rather John told me I would. I was trying to recall all the information needed to complete it, hoping I wouldn't have to ask him later.

A vague pain was niggling at my lower stomach, either from the earlier lurch or from nightshifts generally, I thought. They played havoc with my system. Some of my colleagues, John included, could consume an entire evening meal at three or four in the morning, unthinkable to me.

A tap at the window startled me. The joiner passed in two sets of keys and John gave him a piece of paper with the incident number and we said our farewells. John wound his seat back to as horizontal a position as it would allow. He would get twenty minutes' sleep as I drove to the hospital, again something some of the team could do, but I could not.

I unhooked the keys from the antenna of my radio and immediately dropped them as my stomach twisted into spasm.

'You OK?' asked John, rolling his head towards me, his arms crossed on his chest, ready to nod off.

'Fine,' I lied. I fished the keys from the dirty floor under the pedals. The ache in my gut was constant, a film of sweat was creeping over me. I arched my back, trying to shift it and slipped the key into the ignition before another wave of shooting nausea and agony overcame me. I tried to stop the pain leaving me audibly, grinding my teeth and clenching my fists around the wheel, but a grunt escaped.

'You want me to drive?'

'I'm fine,' I said again, with depleting plausibility.

'You probably just need to fart,' said John, lying back again, eyes closed. 'It happens to me on the nightshift sometimes. Let her rip, just crack a window.' I smiled, and got the car started, taking advantage of a short reprieve.

I punched the gearstick into first and set off tentatively. I reached the end of the street without further cramps, and I put my foot down with more confidence.

I had just shifted into third when my stomach pitched once more. The pain that then flooded my abdomen made the other spasms feel utterly insignificant. In my panic I must have stamped on the brake. I shot forward, doubling over at a perfect height for the top of the wheel to connect with the bridge of my nose.

I felt it break. Not with a snap, but with a crunch. Light flooded my eyes as the two areas of pain waged a vicious war.

Blood was dripping into my cupped hands and John was saying something, but I didn't hear. I needed to get back to that bedroom.

I don't recall turning the engine off or applying the handbrake as I fled the car. I vaguely remember John calling after me, and the taste of blood. I do remember running, and the banging of doors, and the fishing of keys.

I entered the flat and immediately realised I had forgotten a torch. I fished my phone from my pocket and selected the torch function, which would deplete the battery in minutes. Some part of me expected to see Carly's mother when I reached the room, but I found only an empty bed, my mind painting a residual image of the woman as I'd just seen her.

I swept the light from the phone around the room and began tentatively kicking over piles of clothes and boxes. I reached the clothing, piled high on the far wall and my stomach churned.

I held the light high and began to remove items onto the bed, the odd drip from my still-bleeding nose falling onto them.

The snowdrift turned out to be more of a light dusting, I realised, as my hand hit something solid. I cleared a large blanket from the pile and was faced with thin wooden bars.

A child's cot.

I cleared the remaining garments from around it and raised the phone over the top.

He was eighteen months old, I would later learn. His name was Ewan, I knew even then.

The child's eyes were open, staring straight up. The sleeve and shoulder of his Babygro were thick with white vomit, long dried.

I could hear John wheezing from the hall, approaching.

My hand shook as I reached into the cot. I placed the back of my fingers on the boy's face expecting cold confirmation. But he was warm, hot even.

His eyes rolled towards me and I laughed. I'm not sure why.

CHAPTER TWO

Past on the Way

I feel sick again.

Saliva floods my mouth. The room feels like it's spinning. Since I can see nothing, I can't confirm that it's not, or even if this is, in fact, a room. The almost total darkness makes it impossible to get a fix on anything. I need a visual anchor to stop the carousel in my head.

I've dealt with far more grizzly incidents in my career than that night with Carly and her mum. Shocking incidents of violence, cruelty and horror, but that's the one I always go back to in the quiet moments. It's been what, eight? No, nine years now. I haven't seen or spoken to John in at least half that time. It's absurd how people who seem so important to you can slip out of your life entirely.

Before that night my nose was perfectly straight, now it has a certain boxer's angle about it. It adds character,

Karen had told me. You're my wee panda, *she had also said, chuckling at my twin black eyes and gently kissing the bridge of my knackered nose.*

I'm smiling, I can't help it. That was a sweet moment.

I'm considering standing again, but the last time I tried, I slammed my head off something, right on the spot where she hit me. My legs gave out instantly. I think I was unconscious again for a while.

I'll just stay seated for a while. I don't think I could take that pain a second time. The blow must have opened up the wound. There's what feels like dried blood on my face between my right eye and ear, and my collar is wet and sticky. A strong iron smell fills my nostrils. That and mould. Wherever I am must be full of it.

What the hell did that woman hit me with? And how did I not see it coming?

My hands are cuffed behind my back. They've been applied too tight; my fingers are swollen and slightly numb. I can spin my wrists for a little relief, but only just. I have to remember to do that every few minutes to try to swap the trapped blood in my fingers for some carrying oxygen.

The floor is covered in some bizarrely fluffy material. Under that is cold loose dirt.

I try to shake off the dream-like malaise. Is this what a concussion feels like?

I will have to try to take control of the situation, soon. Find my bearings, figure this out. Though not right at this second. Just give me a minute. Maybe a few.

Think.

There's time for that at least.

Now . . . if she wanted me dead, she had the perfect opportunity; why would she leave me here? Does that mean she'll be back?

Listen, *I tell myself. I hold my breath and really listen. But again nothing. Just a low ringing in my ears, and I'm pretty sure that's coming from me.*

I should get up.

Get up.

No wait, *I really am going to be sick.*

I heave, but there's nothing. Nothing but my abdomen wringing itself like a wet tea towel.

I spit.

I will get up. *Just need a minute.*

God, this job!

It doesn't matter where you work. If you've been a cop for any length of time, you've seen some horrible shit, pretty sure that's fact. That night with Carly's mum, it comes back to me again and again, because of what it could have been. This sense of what if . . .

I was such a green boy back then. Perpetually terrified. The first two years, working with John, were ceaselessly stressful. The constant feeling of inadequacy as you learn the job, the shifts, the very nature of the work. Still, those two years were also often fun. Or maybe it just feels that way because of how things went later.

Losing John, the way I did, the way it went down, I thought it couldn't get any worse, but that was only the start of the trouble. Stratharder was to be a fresh start.

I had mixed feelings about the move, but I couldn't stay where I was. Besides, what had I left to stay for?

Windows down and music cranked I left Oban behind, having stopped briefly to look at my old house and wishing I hadn't bothered. It was nothing like I remembered. Everything was so small and normal and not at all like the magical childhood photographs in my head.

I headed north on the A85, everything only vaguely familiar. I passed over the Connel Bridge and soon the small airport came into view.

Jamie, a friend from school, used to take me and some other guys up to one of the runways and let us have a shot of his Renault Clio. If the cops had turned up then, and caught me driving without a licence and insurance, then a career in the police would have been a non-starter. *Not about what you've done*, John would say, and he would report to me his own adolescent transgressions, some of which made mine look no more serious than chap door run. *It's about what you got caught for.*

The airport represented a geographical line in the sand. It was as far north as my knowledge took me; I was heading into uncharted Argyll.

I had forgotten just how beautiful the region was. The West Highlands of Scotland epitomise the idyllic depiction of the country, the shortbread tin fantasy. We don't tend to advertise that most of the country has as much concrete as any other, and that these picturesque parts are actually pretty awkward to get to.

Keeping only an irresponsible half-eye on the road, I took in the green views to my right and a tree-obscured look at Ardmucknish Bay to my left, stretching out in glittering silver-blue before it was lost from sight entirely.

I fished a fresh CD from the large rucksack keeping me company on the passenger seat. It was the only place left to put it. Every other inch of the car was crammed with suitcases and bags, much of it my work gear. It was a depressing realisation that I could pack my entire life into a Volkswagen Polo. It made me wonder if it was the barometer of a person; what size of car could contain you. If it was, I wasn't doing well.

The cyber-female voice of the satnav informed me I was five miles from my destination. The destination I had set was a random spot on the main road, where I guessed the turn off for Kirkmartin would be as it was nowhere to be found on Google Maps. Even Stratharder, a much larger town in comparison was somewhat elusive and just appeared as a patch of pixelated green. Loosely speaking, Stratharder is my neck of the woods – backwoods; but I was only vaguely aware of it as a town. Dad said much the same when I called and asked him about it.

I was so busy looking for a sign for Kirkmartin that I drove straight past one for Stratharder – 8 miles, it registered somewhere in my head after the fact. According to the letting information on the strangely amateurish estate agent website, Kirkmartin could be found on the road to Stratharder, a few miles out. It was as specific as that.

I found a U-turn opportunity and pulled onto the new

road, which was one of those not-really-designed-for-two-cars types. No white lines down the middle and verges that looked so soft that I wouldn't trust anything but a Land Rover to get out of them.

The route skirted the edge of a large rocky outcrop for a mile or so before heading into thick forest. I drove on for about ten minutes before realising the road had been, and for what I could see ahead, continued to be, completely straight. The trees on each side leant over to form a tunnel of nature. The low autumn sun beating down on the canopy sent regular deep shadows across the road that drummed a beat on my eyes. The effect was hypnotic and soporific. My speed dropped to forty with the view ahead difficult to make out through the constant strobe of sharp light and deep shadow. Another five minutes passed and still the way ahead maintained a seemingly perfect straight line. I had never experienced this before, not to my recollection at least. Even major roads rarely managed a straight stretch for long, with Scotland's abundance of natural features relentlessly requiring negotiation.

Just as I was beginning to think I may have taken a wrong turn, not that there had been any turns, another vehicle came into view. Something else on the road reintroduced a healthy sense of perspective. A small, bright yellow car was coming into increasing focus. I slowed further and pulled as far left as I could without risking the Polo's off-road ability. A terrific din buzzed from the approaching car, which was maintaining its middle-of-the-road position. Certain that it would start edging to the opposite side, I continued. The car's lights began to flash as it neared and was weaving side to side. I worried that whoever was behind the wheel might be in trouble.

It was charging towards me, the exhaust growling, then joined with the horn being pumped. There was no sign of it slowing as it weaved and screeched like a mad thing. I pulled the wheel hard to the left and was forced from the road, frantically finding a section of verge between the trees. I heard a deep clunk and felt it up through my arse as my own exhaust struck something solid. The left wheels sunk into the verge and I had to steer into a skid to right myself. The yellow car tore past me with two young-looking faces laughing and hurling obscenities out of the side windows of the hideously modified hatchback.

'Arseholes,' I spat, as I wrestled frantically with the wheel.

I managed to stop the Polo from sliding to a complete halt, knowing I'd never get it out without help if I did. I wheeled back onto the road, coming to a stop in the middle. I stepped out as the waspish buzz of the other car's exhaust faded into the distance. I was left in a serene silence interrupted only by birdsong and a light breeze cutting through the trees, which had thinned to reveal lush farmland on both sides. Far off to my left the rocky outcrop remained stubbled with fir trees and long sinuous lines of thin mist marking out the contours of its face.

I inspected the tyres: caked in mud, but otherwise fine. I tried to check the exhaust but could see little with the car having developed a tail of weeds and moss from the verge.

The way ahead stretched uphill where the trees grew thick again and swallowed the road out of sight. The farmland to my left also rose uphill and my eye was drawn to a section of stone brick jutting from an overgrown hedge. On closer inspection it was the ruin of some old building, too substantial and tall to be a cottage. Its one-time height was marked by a wall at the far side which looked ready to succumb to gravitational inevitability, simultaneously being held together and threatening to be ripped apart by ivy and moss.

I drove on, tentatively at first, listening for any damage to the car, though it seemed fine. At the top of the hill, finally was a bend. The road then sloped downhill to the left and I caught my first glimpse of Stratharder. Looking down on the town a battle was being waged between the grey of man and the green of nature. Smoke from chimneys and the odd steeple defiantly broke through the canopy. The thick green undergrowth lining the verge became a carefully coiffured hedge as I entered the limits of the town.

I was instantly charmed by the place. It was like stepping back in time and a quick check of the reception on my phone only compounded this assessment. The road continued gently downhill through the town centre in a long S-curve. Other than a Co-op supermarket, most of the shops were independent; cheesemonger, butcher, baker, even a few clothes shops. A crass yellow-fronted video store sat like a boil on the face of the high street, otherwise, yes, charming.

I slowed at the main crossroads in the town and inspected the sign posts. Back along from where I'd come, Oban was twenty-six miles, above that Kirkmartin at four miles. *Odd*, I thought, *I'm sure I hadn't passed any turnings*. In addition to these a tourist-info sign directed visitors to the town library and a blue police sign, ingeniously vandalised with

'FUK-DA' spray-painted above it, signalled to the south. *What the hell*, I thought, *while I'm here . . .*

The police station had a laughably enormous car park to the rear, pitted with potholes and circled by a corroded metal fence. The station itself was also ludicrously large for a town this size. It was of typical design for a cop shop, all cubic concrete and austere grey. An incongruously beautiful hanging basket draped from a bracket at the public entrance.

I entered and that same sense of time travel struck me. I'd visited county stations before, all of which, understandably, were a little outdated, but this place was something else. In place of a standard bulletproof-glass public window, an unprotected, well-chipped wooden bar met me. The one modern feature was the automated ceiling light which blinkered into life as the door closed behind me. The small waiting area was equipped with a few plastic chairs beside a single public toilet. On the far wall was a door, I assumed giving access to the station proper. It was locked by a number combination panel, which made me smile as there was nothing at all stopping me hopping over the bar and into the station beyond.

The rattle of a keyboard caught my attention. A small, middle-aged woman I had failed to see initially sat at a desk in the centre of the room. She was holding an outstretched hand and a single lofted be-with-you-in-a-minute finger. I waited, studying the public awareness posters, some from previous decades, on the wall. One, which promoted vigilance against leaving your mobile phone unguarded in the pub, displayed a picture of a Nokia phone I nostalgically recognised as a 3210, sitting beside a half-empty pint of lager. I snorted a laugh. I sent my first text message on one of those, my first sext message too, come to think of it. Diane Cowie, first year at uni. She had sent the first one. We had been on one date and neither of us were sure how it had gone. We had texted with pleasantries afterwards and agreed to 'do it again sometime', but contact then waned. Then out of the blue I get this *So . . . are u going to fck me or what???* text. Turns out she'd been at a party and been put up to it by a friend; or her friend had written it for her, I forget. God bless whoever she was, because two nights later, after much said sexting, we were indeed fcking.

'The two youths walked past the vehicle.'

'Pardon me?' I said, the woman's odd statement startling me.

'Is it S-T or E-D? The youths walked past the vehicle?' she called. I glanced behind, thinking perhaps someone had walked in behind me unnoticed, and it was they she was addressing. But no.

'Do you mean which version of the word "past"?' I said, guessing at a possible meaning. The woman, in her fifties at another guess, held one earpiece of her headphones away from her face. She was dictating reports, I decided. She looked at me expectantly.

'Yes, is it S-T or E-D? That word always gives me trouble.'

'Um . . . past; S-T,' I said. The woman tapped away before slapping the return key like a cymbal crash. She stepped out from behind her desk and approached the counter, smiling and pushing her silver-rimmed glasses up into her hair. Despite the warm weather she was dressed for the cold, in a heavy grey wool cardigan and slightly darker grey tweed skirt. Her hair, also grey to complete the theme, was pulled back into a tight bun making her eyes wide and intense. Despite this her manner was warm and inviting. I liked Margaret from the start.

'Are you lost, dear? You need some directions?' Evidently, this was the chief reason someone would have in Stratharder to visit the police station.

'No, well, actually yes, I could do with . . . Sorry, let me start again. My name is Don Colyear, I'm the new sergeant.'

'Oh,' she said, placing her glasses back on and tilting her head back to get a better view. 'Are you sure?' I didn't know if she was joking. I laughed anyway. 'It's just that you look so young.' She quickly held her hands up, to indicate no offence was intended.

'It's fine. I suppose thirty-three *is* young for promotion.'

'Well, you'd better come in then. You'll have tea?'

Tea? I thought. It was twenty-six degrees outside.

'That would be lovely, thank you,' I said.

There was a clunk from the adjacent security door as she unlocked it. The door swung open and I made to enter, but was stopped by an outstretched hand.

'Some identification please,' she said sternly.

'Oh, of course, I could be anyone.' I was fishing my wallet from my pocket when I saw the woman laughing.

'I'm just kidding. Who'd show up here claiming to be you if they weren't? Come on through. I'm Margaret by the way.'

'Nice to meet you, Margaret.'

'Make yourself at home. How do you take your tea?'

'Just milk, thanks,' I said, perusing my new workplace. Margaret disappeared down a hallway.

The station was orderly, nothing out of place, yet the beaten furniture, the drab decor and sheer volume of paperwork, as neatly stacked as it was, just made the place feel . . . ramshackle.

The only noise in the room came from the whirring fan of Margaret's computer. Her workstation was the only part of the station with some life about it. Framed photographs of young children were dotted jauntily along her desk. A sign which read 'Don't Ask Me, I Only Work Here!' and a jar of boiled sweets also inhabited her little corner. Her work tray, complete with three tiers, was labelled, from top to bottom: *In Mail, Out Mail, Shake it all about Mail.* A small television sitting on top of an ancient video recorder – seriously this thing might have been Betamax – was on, with the sound muted and subtitles playing. It was *EastEnders*, or *Corrie*, or . . . well, some soap opera.

'Oh, I'm sorry,' said Margaret, returning with two unfeasibly large mugs. 'If I'd know it was you, Sergeant, I would have turned it off. I just like to have it on when I'm doing my typing.'

'It doesn't bother me in the slightest, Margaret.' I was going to struggle with this new authority thing. Just hearing that title made my skin crawl. I felt like such an imposter. 'And it's Don, Margaret, I think we should dispense with the "sergeant", if that's OK with you?'

'Sounds good to me,' she said, handing me a mug

which read *I'd rather be golfing*. Someone's unwanted gift I assumed. 'I'm not sure the inspector would be keen, though.' She sat at her desk and swung round on her chair to face me, pulling another chair over with her foot.

'Inspector Wallace? I forgot to ask, is he here? I'd like to introduce myself.' I sat and sipped from my mug, which took both hands to hold comfortably.

'No, he's working from Oban today. He goes between here and there. He doesn't announce where he's going to be. He likes to keep people on their toes. It means nobody turns up here for a skive. They're terrified they'll get caught up here without an excuse.'

'What's he like?'

Margaret took a long sip of her tea, eyeing me. 'Ask me again when I know you better,' she said with a sardonic smile.

'Will do,' I said. I considered myself warned. 'When he's about, call me Sarge if you have to, otherwise it's Don.'

'Fair enough. Where are you staying then, in town?'

'Actually, that's why I needed directions. I'm staying in Kirkmartin?'

'Ah, you're staying at Hilda's?'

'Mrs Brownhill?'

'That's right. Hilda's lovely. You can't miss it; she's just about halfway along the Langie.' I didn't have to ask; my confused expression was sufficient. 'The Langie. The long straight road you took to get here?'

'Right, yes. Well, I'm afraid I did miss her. I was watching out for it too.'

'Did you see the old church? The crumbling building by the side of the road?'

I nodded and sipped.

'Well, you're not far from there. There's a wee road just beyond takes you down the hill, Hilda's place is on the right.'

'Thanks,' I said. I was about halfway through my cauldron of tea, and I knew I couldn't possibly drink any more. 'How long have you worked here, Margaret?'

'Oh, let's see, nearly twenty-eight years now? Yes, that's right. It'll be thirty years when I retire.'

'Oh, you don't look old enough, Margaret,' I said, trying to be charming. She looked entirely old enough.

'Not really my choice,' she said with a shrug. 'I don't drive, so when they close the station I would need to commute to Oban to stay on, so I'll just call it a day.'

'Closing the station? I don't understand. Why did they send me here if the station is being closed?'

Margaret looked suddenly disappointed. 'That's what I was building up to ask you. It seemed rude to just come out with it. But now you mention it, it's what we're all wondering. What the hell are you doing here?'

I shook my head. 'I'm not sure, Margaret. To fill in for the last sergeant, I guess.'

Margaret placed her mug down gently and turned her body to mirror mine exactly.

'That's just it though, Don, there's never been a sergeant here before. Not ever.'

CHAPTER THREE

Introductions

Stratharder Police Station was a very different place when I arrived the following day. It was as if someone had applied the paddles of a defibrillator and shocked it into life.

The first indication of this new pulse was in the car park; I left my car between two marked police vehicles, one small Vauxhall Astra, looking as if it had just been driven from the showroom, despite the licence plate indicating it was in fact four years old, and a larger, well-used Ford Focus estate, newer than the Astra but already longing for retirement.

I arrived early for my first shift and found the front door to the station propped open, presumably to allow air to circulate. It was another fine day, which would make it four in a row, I calculated. Another few and it might just break some kind of Scottish record.

As I entered the station, a young officer typing away on

one of the computers in the corner looked up. She smiled, but went back to her keyboard. She was somewhere in her late twenties. Her auburn hair was cut short, swept forward and across giving her an elfin, almost androgynous appearance. Her short, ever so slightly upturned nose, and ears peeking from her hair only heightened the effect.

I passed into the station and dropped my bags, unsure where I should take them.

'I wouldn't do that if I was you,' the elfin girl said, but her gaze remained on her screen.

'I'm sorry?'

'Your bags. If the inspector comes downstairs and sees them, he'll have a fit. There's a locker room down the hall, I'll show you.' She made the familiar rapid Ctrl-Alt-Del, triple-click to lock her workstation and strode towards me. She was astonishingly short. I hadn't noticed while she'd been seated, but her feet must have been dangling from the chair. If she was five feet, it was by a photo finish. She walked past me and I followed her down the hall.

'So, you're Sergeant Colyear?'

'Don,' I said. 'And you are?'

'Rowan Forbes. I'm pretty new here too.'

'New to the police or to the area?'

'Both. I've been in seven months, and I'm not from *here*,' she ended in a derisive tone. 'There's a male and a female locker room, but to be honest I don't think it really matters, you'll be the only one using it,' she said, stopping halfway down the hall and poking a thumb at a door.

I entered and threw my bags into one of the open lockers, of which there were perhaps two dozen or so. I was about to close the door behind me but Rowan nonchalantly followed me inside. A long bench sat between the two rows of lockers and I could see a shower room at the far end. I hung my jacket and pulled a T-shirt from my bag. Rowan had remained by the door and was eyeing me curiously; it was clear she wasn't about to give me any privacy and I didn't want to start our working relationship with an awkward exchange. As I swapped shirts she at least looked away, propping her back up against the wall. I hauled my body armour over my head, securing it with the side zips.

'Do you cover this area?' I asked.

'Supposed to, but spend most of my time down the road.'

'In Oban?'

'Yeah, it's OK, still pretty dull, but positively jumping compared to this place.'

I secured my belt and began placing my officer safety equipment into the corresponding clips and holsters. Cuffs to the right, baton to the left, clicking them into place without looking, so familiar was the routine.

'What brings you up to the office today? I thought the inspector didn't like the troops up here?'

'I'm working with PC Ritchie today, he's in with the inspector just now.'

'Is he your tutor?'

'Not exactly,' she said, chewing on the end of a finger in thought. 'I don't have a tutor as such, I kinda get passed around.'

'That doesn't seem right. Consistency is important at this stage.'

She held her hands up. 'Hey, you're preaching to the choir, brother.'

'Well, we'll see what we can do about that, Rowan.' I made to leave but she stood in the doorway with a pained expression on her face.

'Actually, could you not?' she said. 'I mean what you do is up to you, of course, Sarge.'

'Don.'

'Don, but please leave my name out of it, if you don't mind.'

'What do you mean?'

'Politics, you'll see. I just want to keep my head down and get through the rest of this year and next, and then I'll be posted somewhere else.'

I had no idea what she was talking about, but I agreed to whatever it was I was agreeing to and returned to the main office. A large, heavy-set officer watched as Rowan and I came back from the locker room. I could swear I heard an accusatory 'Oh aye' under his breath, but I let it go, in the spirit of not rocking boats on the first day. Instead I strode purposefully up to him and held out my hand.

'Don Colyear,' I said.

He looked at me squarely and gave my hand an overly firm shake.

'Brian Ritchie,' he said, then snatched his hand away before turning to Rowan. 'Right, short-stuff, see you later.'

'What do you mean?' said Rowan. 'I'm just updating a crime report. I'll only be a second.'

'You're staying. I'm leaving. The inspector wants you to show the new boy around,' said Brian. He was in his forties, his hair a salt and pepper side sweep. His beard only just about qualified as such, barely long enough to have moved out of the stubble category into something acceptable under appearance standards. He had a naturally powerful look about him but, somewhat untrained, his body armour no doubt girdling a stomach typical of middle-aged neglect.

'I'll just check my emails, Rowan,' I said as Brian departed. 'Then maybe you can show me around town?'

She agreed and I settled myself in front of the terminal next to hers. I knew the inbox would be depressingly full. My two weeks of annual leave ensured an ocean of information to wade through, mostly inconsequential bulletins, lookout requests, and Force news; but hidden amongst the police spam would be some important items. I sighed as the email loaded up and I saw over three hundred unread items waiting for me. Worse than I feared. I quickly scanned my mail, looking to see if anything in particular jumped out at me, and one did catch my eye. The brief subject line made it conspicuous: *Speak to me* it read. It was from Alyson. I thought she'd given up trying to get my attention. She was obviously doing well for herself. Her email prefix showed she was now Govan CID. Becoming a detective was something she'd aspired to from the beginning. We'd joined on the same intake and been assigned to the same station and shift. I was glad to have someone to trade notes with.

We were introduced to our tutor constables on day one. Alyson was paired with a solid, serious-looking guy, complete with cop-tash; the kind of facial hair abandoned several decades before by all but those in law enforcement. Still, he had an air of competency about him. I got John, as one gets the flu, or the shaft – or so I thought. He was a small, round man. Jolly as a dog with two tails and slovenly in appearance. What little hair he had, spiked electrically from the sides and back of his head. His uniform was more grey than black, having absorbed months, if not years, of dandruff, sweat and whatever else he had come into contact with in the course of the job. Everything sat at a sort of jaunty angle with him – the skin-dusted armour, his hat and of course his ever-present smile. Suffice to say I was not pleased with my allocated mentor. I felt I was at an immediate disadvantage and I was sure Alyson would find herself streets ahead of me.

However, very quickly the noises coming out of camp Alyson were not good. Her tutor, Phil, she told me at the first night out in Glasgow about a month after joining the shift, was a spectacular prick; her words. A misogynistic control freak with a short temper. In the first few weeks she hadn't been allowed to open her notebook once. Alyson had to laugh off his clumsy, unctuous advances on a daily basis. She told me this in the corner of the pub and had cried a little. It forced me to re-evaluate my working relationship with John.

While Phil did his best to keep Alyson sitting in the car, John had me talking and taking notes in almost every scenario. Unless it was clear the situation required a more experienced hand, he stood patiently aside while I learnt by doing. What I had misconstrued as laziness was actually good tutorship.

I hovered the cursor over Alyson's email for a moment, then clicked and read:

Don,

Will you please grow up?

At least tell me you're OK. If you don't, I'm going to visit your dad and make him tell me what's going on.

I won't send any more texts, or emails to your private address. The message has been received loud and clear, but ignoring me completely is just cruel.

There are only so many ways to say sorry, and I think I've used them all twice by now. I don't need forgiveness, at least not any more, but I do need to know you're all right.

I heard you had to have an operation; I felt sick when I was told. I wanted to come and see you, I really did.

I'm not trying to justify myself, here. What I did is utterly inexcusable, but you need to understand things from my side.

The email went on much further, but that's when I closed it. I hovered over the trash can icon for a moment, then clicked.

Gone.

'Sergeant Colyear?'

A deep, sonorous voice startled me. I stood and extended my hand to the inspector. He took it briefly, not shaking it, but holding it, holding me in place as his eyes scrutinised my face. He then took a step back and looked at me head to toe. The first thing that struck me about him was his black hair. It was entirely too black, particularly as his hawkish eyebrows were a far more natural combination of brown and grey.

'Would you make us both a tea and join me in my office?'

'Certainly, Inspector,' I said.

Margaret showed me to the small kitchen area and introduced me to the bureaucratic nightmare that was the tea fund.

I could neither knock nor open the door handle with my fingers straining to control the cups. I placed my own on the floor and chapped the inspector's door with a double tap. There was a pause of a few seconds before I was beckoned from the other side.

'First impressions?' he said, as I set his tea before him without a thank you.

'Of?' I said, settling myself into an uncomfortable plastic chair at the opposite side of the imposing desk.

'Stratharder, our little town.'

'Oh, very nice. I mean I haven't really had a chance to see much of it yet, but what I have has been very charming.'

'Charming,' he said, stretching the word, tasting it. He held his mug of tea in both hands, his gaze was to the window over my shoulder. 'I suppose it is, it's home.'

'I didn't realise you lived here, Inspector.'

'Yes, I stay up the hill. The house has been in my family for several generations. Stratharder may not be the most happening place' – his use of the word 'happening' made my skin crawl; that word hadn't been *happening* for a very long time – 'but that's how I like it. It's how most people round here like it. You're staying out at Hilda's? How are you settling in?'

'Fine, thank you. It's a nice apartment, and she's a lovely lady.'

'Oh, she is,' the inspector agreed, 'very . . . friendly. A little lonely of course, but friendly. I would lock your door at night if were you.' He wagged his finger at me and laughed to himself. The elusive road to Hilda's that Margaret had described had been there, right enough. In my own defence it was easy to miss. From the Stratharder side it was clear as day, there was even a little metal signpost on the opposite verge stating *Kirkmartin 2*. From my original approach, the adjacent bushes sat awkwardly, making the roadside look continuous. The road had taken me up over a hill and revealed a stunning view of a small glen; the backdrop of which was the daunting buttress of fir-lined rockfaces I'd admired on my drive in to Stratharder. The road plunged precariously downhill and narrowed, so that even a moderately sized vehicle would have filled it. Two deep troughs had gripped the wheels as I descended and I'd waited for my already battered exhaust to be finally ripped from the underside. However, miraculously, it had remained. The roadsides had risen quickly and submerged the track in near darkness. I had passed a row of cottages on my left, derelict and roofless, before reaching Hilda's. A driveway allowed for a couple of cars and I'd parked next to a small Suzuki jeep. Hilda had met me at the door with a welcoming smile, wearing a silk dressing gown in a colour somewhere between purple and pink. Her long grey hair hung in spider wisps across her shoulders and significant bosom.

'Do you have a family?' asked the inspector.

'You mean wife and kids? No.'

'Still sowing wild oats and all that?'

My skin crawled a little farther. 'Not exactly, no. I'm not long out of a relationship actually, Inspector.'

'Oh, I'm sorry to hear that, Don, I really am. It is all right if I call you Don?'

'Of course. In fact I'd prefer it.'

'I will address you as Sergeant in front of the subordinates of course, and I expect the same professional courtesy in return; but when we're chatting like this you may call me Stewart, if you like.'

I knew Inspector Stewart Wallace was always going to be *The Inspector* to me, but I said: 'That's fine, I understand. May I ask you something, Stewart?'

The inspector sat forward in his chair, his interest piqued. 'Yes, go ahead.'

'I've heard that my position here is, well . . . I didn't take over from a previous . . . Sorry. Let me put this another way. Am I the first sergeant at Stratharder?'

He smiled and sipped at his tea, and then stood. He walked to the window.

'Are we to speak candidly, Don? I mean are we to lay our cards on the table?'

I studied him for a minute trying to get a read on him, judge the level of hostility in his voice. 'If there are cards to be laid, Inspector, I think we ought to, don't you?'

He turned to face me. 'All right, here's where I'm at.' He folded his arms across his chest, sending signals of his discomfort but also his resolve. 'I didn't want you here. Actually, to be more precise, I *don't* want you here.

Stratharder neither needs nor wants a sergeant. Your presence here is as pointless as it is political.'

'Political, Inspector?'

'Listen, let's agree to this. You don't pretend to be naive, and I won't bullshit you.'

The back of my neck burned, partly from embarrassment and partly from an embryo of anger. I shifted in my chair so I could face him properly. I stopped myself from crossing my arms and forced a passive cross-legged stance. I let him continue.

'I'm sure you're a pleasant young man, Don, and I don't mean to get off on the wrong foot, but you see, I simply don't appreciate having others' dirty laundry being dumped on me, and my town. I protested at your placement here, although it clearly fell on deaf ears. An ace beats a king, I suppose. Still, it doesn't mean I have to like it, nor does it mean I have to bend over backwards to accommodate what is a selfish and poorly judged decision. Out of sight, out of mind, that's why you're here, only you're sitting right in front of me, aren't you? And I can see you just fine.'

He paused then, perhaps expecting a rebuttal, but all I had heard so far was complaint. I waited for him to reach some kind of point.

'Look,' he said with a tone of retraction, 'this is not a personal thing, and you should try not to take it as such. I'm not attacking you here. What happened at your last station is in the past, but it happened.'

'What is it you understand to have *happened*, Inspector?'

'Let's keep this friendly, Sergeant,' he warned, retaking his seat behind the desk. 'I'm not judging. There are two sides to every story, but if you haven't realised by now, let me explain. The police is a family. Even now that we have merged as a single force, it just means we are a larger family, and we look after our own. Trust is everything in this job, surely you know that?'

'I don't know which version of events has trickled its way up here, Inspector, so it's difficult to defend myself. But I *do* appreciate how important trust is. However, respect, responsibility, accountability, are these not also important virtues?'

A silence fell across us. I looked down and saw that my feet were planted and my arms were viced across my chest. I was also, I noticed, leaning partly over the desk. I reset myself and took a deep, cleansing breath. I knew exactly what he was getting at, but if he wasn't going to come out and say it, I wasn't going to concede that he had the tiniest of points. If I had been in his shoes, I would probably have been somewhere south of delighted with my appointment here.

'Perhaps this is something we should discuss another time,' he said. I knew all too well that this subject was never likely to be raised again. 'We've no choice but to make space for you, Don. I don't know if you're aware, but this station is to be closed in two years. It would probably have been sooner, but it just so happens that is when I'm due to retire, and I think I've been afforded a gesture of courtesy. You'll be glad to hear that I don't always work out of here, I'm often in Oban where I work with the other community officers. What precious little supervisory work there is will be shared between yourself and I. I will remain in charge of day to day rostering of the officers. I will organise their appraisals and annual leave, and I will oversee all missing persons and local warrants.'

'Fine. What does that leave for me?'

'Time, Sergeant, lots of time. You will look after crime reports generated in Stratharder only and I suppose since Constable Forbes is allocated here, you will oversee her probationary portfolio.'

'Fine,' I said again, deciding it best not to argue. 'What about incidents at this end? I can attend those, can't I?'

This brought back the smile to his face.

'Oh yes, by all means fill all that time dealing with the rampant crime wave we are plagued with in Stratharder.'

Stratharder's unseasonal autumn sunny spell had come to an abrupt and soggy end, much to Rowan's annoyance.

'The only thing that messes my hair up worse than the rain is this fecking hat. You do realise nobody wears them, don't you? And will you please slow down? I need to take three steps for your two. I don't want to be jogging all day,' she said, sliding a section of fringe gently under the brim of her hat.

'Sorry.' I slowed my pace. 'I don't like the hats either, but the inspector lives in this town, remember, and he's going to take any excuse to pressure me out of here.'

'Is that what he said?'

'Perhaps not in as many words. So, what does this town have to offer?'

Rowan puffed an amused breath. 'The real highlight is the road out. It's a must-see.'

'Come on, there must be some redeeming features?'

'Well, there's our cosmopolitan shopping precinct. Here, I'll show you. Prepare to be impressed.'

It could have been a different town altogether from the one I had driven through a few days before. The gloomy weather cast the place in, literally, a different light. It took ten minutes to reach the town centre from the station on foot. It might have taken six on my own. The quirky little independent shops had seemed quaint when I passed them the first time, but seeing them up close now, they looked dingy and outdated. The blue paintwork on the ornate wrought-iron canopy and shopfronts was in need of touching up, and in some places far more than that. Orange rust bruises appeared in the corners and bases while strips of loose paint on the long sections flapped in the wind. We passed a ladies' clothing shop. The mannequin in the window was topless and looked like she'd grown tired of the indignity, scuffed as she was around the pointy extremities. Argyle Rentals was the most occupied of the stores. The only one with a clientele under the age of fifty, although it was difficult to see exactly who was inside, due to the intimidating diagonal poster on the window, which read:

ALL DVDs £1
EVERYTHING MUST GO!

The slow march of death from streaming platforms that had seen the demise of video stores across the country had eventually found Stratharder. Its population would just have to illegally download their movies and games like the rest of us.

We headed for the crossroads in the centre of town. On the way I learnt Rowan was from Inverness. She had hoped to be posted closer to home, but the proviso of joining the force, especially since the eight individual Scottish forces joined to form the one, was that you could be posted anywhere you were required. Although the word 'required' and Stratharder seemed a poor fit. She was twenty-nine, shared a flat in Dumbarton with a fellow probationary officer she met at the Tulliallan Training College and was previously in banking.

A small cenotaph next to the crossroads celebrated the six Stratharder men who gave their lives in the First World War, a fresh wreath laid at its foot. An iron bench was set alongside it and a public phone box beside that. Rowan cleared the rain from a corner of the bench as well as she could and sat to adjust her footwear.

'Am I on the right channel with this radio?' I asked, confirming the LED display showed the settings I was given. 'Only, I haven't heard a thing out of it all day.'

'That's not unusual around here.' She leant up and checked my screen. 'Yeah that's right, I haven't heard anything either. What exactly are we patrolling here? Not that I'm complaining.' She pulled her entire boot from her foot and shook out a small stone.

'It's funny how much your "not complaining" sounds a lot like complaining. We're just flying the flag.' She gave me a slant-eyed, uncomprehending look. 'It's an expression; we're reassuring the community, public relations, that sort of thing.'

'Reassuring them that we're not afraid of the rain?'

'Exactly. We're big, tough law enforcers; nobody will

mess with you once they see you wring your socks out.'

'Funny.' She flicked the toe of her sock sending another stone falling to the earth.

'So, you're the guide here. Now, I know this road,' I said, pointing west, 'that's the long road back out. The highlight, as you put it.'

'The Langie.'

'Right, the Langie. The long straight road to freedom. And this road,' I pointed south the way we'd just come, 'this takes us to the station, and then where? What's beyond that?'

'Just some industrial units, a dead end.'

'See, you're blowing my mind here. Look at this idiot,' I said, and pointed at a large white van waiting to turn at the crossroads. The lights changed and the driver, holding a phone to his left ear with his right hand, spun the wheel with the heel of his free hand, manoeuvring into a right turn. Everything ridiculously crossed over.

'What a twat,' said Rowan. 'I have my tickets with me. Shame we missed him.'

I barely heard what she said. I was looking at the place where the van had turned. On the pavement at the far side of the crossroads a middle-aged woman was looking at me, staring, unblinking.

'Do you know her?' I asked.

'Who?'

'The woman in the long dark coat on the far side.' The woman was standing perfectly still. Her face was a blur from that distance, just a blank oval space. Her hands were pushed into her pockets.

Rowan squinted her eyes and shielded them from the first rays of sunshine trying to break through. 'She does seem familiar. I can't place her though.'

'I guess people aren't used to seeing us out on foot like this,' I said dismissively. 'OK, how about north, then, where does that lead?' I pointed up to where the white van had come from.

'Up the hill? Mostly houses, the hotel, the church, primary school and community hall. You know, usual town stuff.'

'*The* hotel?'

'The one and only, and the only place you'll get a drink round here.'

'And this one?' I nodded east, the continuation of the Langie, the road the white van had disappeared along. It ran downhill and was lined on both sides by squat but picturesque cottages.

'It heads out of town, eventually takes you to the Ogilvie estate.'

'A sporting estate?' I asked.

'Amongst other things, yes. It's pretty much the only reason you'd have a tourist pass through here. It has self-catering lodges, a small fishing loch and people with too much money.'

'What's beyond that?'

'The great Scottish wilderness, another dead end.' She pulled her boot back on and yanked the laces tight.

'So, let me get this right. There's one road into this town and one road out?'

Rowan considered this for a moment. 'Yeah, I guess so.'

'Sergeant?' said a voice from behind us. Rowan let out a squeak of fright as we both jumped and turned. A tall girl with a mane of dark red hair stood holding the hand of a young boy. She wore a grin on her handsome face. She turned to the boy who sported the same red hair. 'Aren't you going to say hello to Sergeant Colyear, Connor?'

The boy looked at me sheepishly, hiding as well as he could around the flank of the woman. 'Hello,' he said after a hefty nudge.

'Hello, Connor,' I replied, confused. 'Sorry, do I know you?' I asked the woman. She was striking to look at, athletic, with toned shoulders accentuated by her vest top and tight jeans, clearly not bothered by the rain. I was trying to make a quick assessment of the relationship. She could plausibly be mother or sister to the boy.

'Not yet, but it's a small town. News travels fast, and in a place as small as this you're big news, Sergeant.'

'Well, I don't know about that,' I laughed, realising I was blushing. I rubbed at my neck and said: 'So, you know my name, but you are?'

'Mhairi.'

She held out a semi-limp hand, palm down. I didn't know whether I was expected to shake it or kiss it. There was a moment's hesitation and I elected to shake. I looked again at the boy, bright-cheeked, still half hiding behind the woman and guessed his age at about ten.

'And this is . . . your little brother?'

'Oh, aren't you the charmer,' she said with a gentle slap of my shoulder. 'This is my wee man, my little monkey-boy.' She mauled him, teasingly, hugging him and mussing his hair.

'Mum, get off!' he said.

'Sorry, I just thought . . .'

'That I was far too young to have a boy this age? You're forgiven. It's been a while since I heard that.'

Her eyes drifted off over my shoulder, and I turned, following them. The woman in the long coat was approaching, fast.

'I see the fan club is gathering, Sergeant. I'll leave you to it. Right, Monkey-Boy, let's get you back to school. Just had him at the dentist. Nice to finally meet you, and you too, Constable.'

'Nice to meet you, Mhairi.'

She walked off across the road. There was a sway in her walk that looked affected, exaggerated. When I looked back at Rowan a smirk on her face made me realise I'd been watching Mhairi walk away just a little too long.

'Hello,' the thin woman in the long coat said. She almost skidded to a halt, snatched my hand and shook it enthusiastically. 'You're Sergeant Colyear.' There was no hint of a question in this. She peered back over her shoulder and continued, 'I just wanted to say hello.'

'Hello,' I said. 'And you are—?'

'You're new in town.'

'Um, yes. I'm sorry to ask,' I said, 'but was there some sort of community bulletin or something I'm not aware of?' This question I directed at Rowan, as well as the woman.

Rowan laughed. 'Welcome to Stratharder, Sarge. A community bulletin is snail mail compared to the gossip chain here.'

'I wondered, Sergeant, whether I might be able to, well, if we might be able to—'

'Katherine, that's where you got to.' A man, similarly thin to the enthusiastic woman, appeared seemingly from nowhere. 'I looked around for a second and you were gone.'

'Oh, I just spotted the new sergeant and I wanted to say hello.'

'Sarge, look,' said Rowan. 'He's back, and still on his bloody phone.' I switched my attention to the crossroads. The van was being held up by passing traffic. The man behind the wheel was having an animated conversation with the gadget by his ear. He hadn't spotted us at all.

'I'm sorry, we really do have to deal with this. It was nice to meet you both,' I said.

'Yes, sorry, we won't hold you up any long—' The man was cut short by the woman suddenly throwing her arms around me and giving me an awkward hug. 'Katherine, I don't think that's appropriate.'

'It's fine,' I said and patted her shoulder while prising her off. 'But we have to . . .'

'Yes, of course,' the woman said.

A break had appeared in the traffic and the van driver made to pull out. Rowan calmly and fearlessly stepped in front of it, her hand held out. The van lurched forward then backwards as it braked hard to a sudden stop. The startled driver pulled the phone from his ear and raised both hands with a look of incredulity. Rowan motioned for him to pull over and I joined her by the side of the road.

'We'll just have a word in his ear,' I said. 'Let's not upset the apple cart just yet.'

Rowan did not look pleased.

The van rolled halfway onto the pavement and came to a stop. I approached the driver's window, and, to my utter astonishment, he was still on his phone. The grubby-faced man in blue overalls looked straight ahead, as if I wasn't there. I stood patiently for a minute before tapping the window. His eyes flicked towards me, as if seeing me for the first time. He smiled, rolled down the window, held the phone to his chest and said, 'Be with you in a minute, officer.' The window rolled back up and he continued his conversation.

'Get your tickets,' I said to Rowan.

'Yes!' she said joyously, and produced a brand-new book from her trouser combat pocket.

'Have you given one of these before?'

'No, Brian says they're a waste of time, that they just annoy people so they don't talk to the police when you really need them to. Witness wasters, he calls them.'

'Well, handing them out indiscriminately I disagree with, but in instances like this they're justified.' I tapped on the window again, harder, and got a disgruntled glare and a palm to look at.

I started helping Rowan complete the ticket, filling in what we could without the driver's help, but he must have caught a glimpse of what we were doing and the door flew open.

'Woah, hold on.'

I ignored him and showed Rowan where to put the vehicle's registration.

'Look, I work for Mr Ogilvie. This is his van,' he said, leaning out of the cab.

'Is this East Main Street?' I asked Rowan. She confirmed it was. 'Right, well that goes in here, the time is . . . fourteen-fifteen hours, that goes there—'

'Look, I'm sorry, it was kind of an emergency, the wife's going into labour.' The man stepped out of the van and approached us, thickset with a belly tenting the form of his overalls. He held an open, apologetic stance, his phone still in his right hand.

'I'll be with you in a minute, sir. Just stay in the van.'

He mumbled some expletive under his breath and climbed back into the vehicle.

'Do you think his wife is in labour?' asked Rowan.

'Well, he's in his late forties, maybe even fifty, so unless his wife is way younger, then no. Plus, he was clearly arguing with whoever he was on the phone to, so he'd have to be the biggest prick who walked the earth to be shouting at his wife delivering his child.'

'Good point.'

I stepped up to the van. 'Right, sir, do you have your driving documents with you?'

'You're making a mistake.'

'Oh, no doubt. Documents?'

He reached into his wallet, brought out his licence and handed it over. I passed it on to Rowan and asked her to do a full check on it. She walked off, talking into the radio.

'It was a two-second call, come on. Look, Inspector Wallace knows me, just give him a call.'

'We won't keep you long, sir.'

'You're making a mistake.'

'I tell you what, give me your phone so I can check who

you were last talking to. If it was your wife, hell, if it was anyone female, I'll rip up this ticket here and now.'

He stood facing me. He glanced down at his phone and then back to me. 'You're just a smart arse, aren't you?'

'I have my moments.'

'Write the fucking ticket then, but you'll regret it, you interfering pig bastard.'

I presented as calm and confident an appearance as I could, but he was standing over me, and had a foot of height and at least three stone advantage. His words came out through his teeth. I continued to write, keeping half an eye on the pen, the other half on the clenched fists by his side.

Rowan returned. She had an excited glint in her eye. She whispered the result of the licence check in my ear. I took the licence from her and read it.

I took the ticket from the book and ripped it in two, then four, eight.

'At last, some sense,' Mr A. Hughes of 34 Conifer Lane, Stratharder said. 'Well, busy day, must get on,' he continued. He held out his hand for his licence.

'I'm afraid there are some issues with your licence, Mr Hughes, I'll need to keep hold of this for the time being. Oh, and you're under arrest.'

CHAPTER FOUR

Stick to Your Guns

'You did *not* say that to him,' said Rowan, open-mouthed but still managing to smile as she drove. The van we were in was surely just the beginning of the inspector's retaliations. He was duty-bound to secure me a vehicle from the Oban fleet and he'd outdone himself to find this thing. It was old, beaten, and something in the rear cell compartment had come loose and caused a tremendous rattle if you took the thing over sixty. Still, despite its geriatric appearance it could shift. There was nothing at all wrong with the engine. It was unloved and unwanted – I figured we would make a good team.

'I guess I just got sick of tiptoeing around him. Besides, he doesn't have a leg to stand on. I'm following procedure. What he was suggesting was unscrupulous, borderline illegal.'

I had received a call from Margaret that morning, imparting a request from the inspector for me to come in early 'for a little chat'. I knew it was going to prove awkward and I was prepared for a war of words, if it proved Mr Hughes was indeed a friend of his. What I wasn't prepared for was Mr Hughes sitting there in the inspector's office while he calmly tried to talk me out of procedures against Hughes and when that didn't work, bombarded me with overt threats. I might have relented – after all, it was a fairly minor thing and I had no burning desire to make life difficult for myself. What stopped me was the thought of Rowan losing her first case.

'That won't stop him coming for you,' Rowan warned with a small shake of her head.

'I'm well aware of the target on my back, thank you. I'll be fine; he's all mouth and no trousers. As long as I'm here I'll do things my way. I'm not going to be intimidated.'

'Famous last words . . .' she breathed.

We rolled through the town crossroads and down past the flanking cottages. The road quickly narrowed and occasional passing places appeared on both sides. The tarmac gave way to a mix of gravel and flattened earth. Trees thick with foliage encroached and small bodies of water came into view beyond them. A series of large ponds, or perhaps swampland.

'How far down here is the estate?'

'Well, the whole thing forms part of the estate, but the house is a few miles,' Rowan yelled.

The cage in the back of the van was a riot of noise with the uneven road and I could hardly hear her talk. We splashed along the pockmarked road. The morning rain had given way to bright sunshine, but the surrounding trees kept it at bay. The road veered left and we passed over a small bridge. The roar of the river underneath challenged the din of the van. The short walls forming the side of the bridge were broken and uneven. It once would have had a uniform turreted effect but now looked like two rows of broken teeth. Rowan slowed to a crawl as we crossed. Two deep grooves dictated our path along the centre, as if we were on rails. The drop below was only around fifteen feet, but the progress felt precarious. The swollen river thundered underneath us, and steam rose from the bridge surface where sunlight found a break in the foliage and beat down on it. Clear of the bridge the road took a sharp left and rose uphill. As we crested, we met civilisation. A long row of terraced cottages, ten in total, stretched alongside the road. On the opposite side an equal number of small gardens lay open to the road but fenced off from each other. Clothes hung from lines in a few and one was filled with children's play apparatus, while another was being used as a vegetable plot. But at least half were overgrown and disused. I urged Rowan to keep the pace to a crawl to indulge my curiosity. It was clear that not all the cottages were occupied. Small faces appeared at a few of the windows and a broad-set man, wielding a rake, eyed us from one of the gardens as we passed. A woman in an apron smiled from the doorway of one cottage.

'Staff cottages,' Rowan explained. 'Groundskeepers, the ghillie, house staff, that sort of thing.'

'Ghillie?'

'You really are a city mouse, aren't you? A ghillie is the fish guy. He looks after the stocks, enforces permits on the land, takes people out on the river, or the loch, that sort of thing.'

'Why are so many of them empty?'

'I don't know, I guess the estate doesn't employ as many people as it used to,' said Rowan, leading the van round to the right as we left the cottages, and the curious faces, behind.

The land opened up. A large, lush field encased in high-wire fencing sat to the left, a circle of deer huddled in one corner. A small loch stretched to the right. A few people fishing at its edge and a single rowing boat at its centre.

The house sat between the field and the loch at the end of the long straight in front of us. It was a little smaller than I would have expected given the amount of land surrounding it, but impressive nonetheless. A large turret drew the eye immediately. It sat in the centre of the building, set with a large blue door. It was topped by a slate cone, and a large weathervane lorded over the structure. The rest of the house grew out from this centre pillar in an L-shape. One side displayed a grand bay window, or rather windows, the many panels creating a gentle curve of glass. The opposite side was a more traditional square construction with a great spread of ivy crawling up its main wall.

'How the other half live,' I said, under my breath.

'Money doesn't bring happiness,' said Rowan.

'That's just something poor people say out of envy. I'll take misery if it comes with a mansion, thank you very much.'

The surrounding view was spectacular. Forest stretched back from the left of the house, and a deep glen to the right where we had driven up from the town. In the middle and far distance, the mountains came into view as the cloud lifted; a mix of gentle undulating rises sitting before rugged and imposing Munros behind. As we pulled up to the house, I saw that it wasn't, in fact, ivy climbing up the side wall, rather a tree was growing right out of the building. On closer inspection, as we parked at the edge of the large gravel circle in front of the house, this section of the building was semi-derelict. We left the van and I cleared my throat to catch Rowan's attention, tugging on the brim of my hat. She rolled her eyes and reached into the van for her own, tucking a few strands of hair behind her ear as she pulled it on.

There was an intercom adjacent to the blue door. I pushed the button and waited. After a minute of silence, we agreed it probably wasn't working. Through the door I could hear music playing faintly. I beat the door hard three times with the ball of my fist and almost immediately the door was swung open by an elderly man. He beamed at us through his well-trimmed white beard.

'Sergeant Colyear?' he yelled over the music, which was playing at considerable volume, something classical and uptempo. He propped the framed canvas he was carrying against the wall and wiped his hand on the paint-flecked apron he was wearing. I shook his hand.

'Yes, Mr Ogilvie? Thanks for seeing us,' I said, leaning towards him so I didn't have to shout to be heard.

'Please come in, come in. I almost forgot you were coming. I'm sorry about all this mess.' He swept a hand down himself indicating the apron. He walked to a record player sitting on a small table and lifted the needle, plunging us into pleasant silence.

'No need to apologise,' I said and followed him inside. Rowan instantly whipped off her hat and pushed her hand through her hair. The interior of the turret was a grand affair, polished stone floor and exposed brick walls hung with tapestries and ornate framed paintings, gave an opulent but strangely welcoming feel. A sweeping staircase complete with a beautifully polished dark wood banister sat at the far end. The eye was drawn ever upward to an exquisite wrought-iron chandelier hanging dead centre. It must have been four feet across and its weight would have been astonishing. Rowan gave me a nudge prompting me to keep up with the agile Ogilvie.

We followed him to the left and entered the room with the large bay window, which I was surprised to find was his art studio. His obvious advanced years were belied by his clothes. He wore light grey baggy canvas trousers, flip-flops and a loose-fitting white three-quarter sleeve top under his apron, giving him an aura of a yoga instructor. Three easels of varying sizes sat atop heavy fabric sheets, presumably to protect the parquet floor. More canvasses, both blank and painted, lay propped against the walls. The lack of furniture gave an echo to our voices.

'It's a beautiful room. So much light in here,' I said.

'Yes, this is why I use it at as my studio. It becomes the dining room when it has to be, but otherwise I put it to better use.'

'What are you working on?' I asked. He paused at the centre easel, closest to the large window.

'I'm not sure at this stage, maybe a landscape, or maybe I will put some figures in, or maybe I will take it into the garden and set the damn thing alight, we will see.' There was an accent in his voice I hadn't heard initially, something of a European lilt to the way he said 'sure', Scandinavian perhaps.

'Don't you dare, it's fantastic . . . whatever it is,' said Rowan, studying the canvas. I looked over her shoulder to an abstract piece in cobalt blue and bottle green. If you squinted your eyes and let your imagination run wild you could just about make out a landscape, maybe not one on earth but a landscape nonetheless, and it did have some artistic merit, I think, although I've always been one of those *know what I like* type of guys.

'Aren't you sweet, Miss . . . ?'

'Forbes, eh, Constable Forbes.'

'Of course, *Constable* Forbes, forgive me. A beautiful woman is kind about my work and it is easy to forget you are here on business matters. Though, that is not a reason we cannot be friendly too, no?'

'I'm sorry we had to meet in this official capacity, Mr Ogilvie. I would have preferred it to be otherwise.'

'Charles, please. And yes, it is rather unfortunate. Tell you what, shall we get the unsavoury business out of the way and then pretend we are meeting under better circumstances?'

'Actually, yes, that would be good of you, Charles. Thank you.'

He washed up and showed us to his office, as grand as the rest of the house. A mahogany desk dominated the room while most of the wall-space shelved some very old-looking volumes. The window at the far side looked out over the gardens, impressive though unkempt. Beyond that a series of log cabins could just about be seen through the trees that marked the edge of the grounds.

I could sense that Rowan was uncomfortable about charging the man, so I did the necessary. I took his details and read the charge from my notebook, explaining that as the director of a company he had a responsibility to ensure his driver's documents were in order.

'Yes, I understand,' was his response, which I noted down. 'I suppose I trust too easily. Alistair told me he was fit to drive for me, so I gave him a job. That trust was betrayed and so he no longer has a job, not with me. So, is that it?'

'That's it, yes. Erm, I suppose we should let you get back to your painting.'

'Nonsense, like I said before, let's forget all that official stuff. Now, I'd like to show you around, if I may?'

'Yes, thank you, Charles. That would be lovely,' said Rowan before I could politely refuse.

He led us out to the garden, which was in worse condition than it looked from the office. The grass was knee-high and brown in many areas. The morning rain meant my shoes and ankles were wet by the time we reached a gate at the far end, which was itself needing some attention.

'You must excuse the garden,' Charles said, pulling a spring bolt from the gate and pushing it to swing free ahead of us. 'I have the groundsman doing other things currently, and when it's warm and wet like this it's just impossible to keep on top of everything.'

'Groundsman? You mean just the one?' asked Rowan.

'No, of course not, but our team of staff is smaller than

it used to be; economic downturn. There are now so many sporting estates for people to choose from. At one time we were one of only a few. We are making efforts to keep up with the times, here for example.'

A short forest track had taken us to the line of log cabins I had seen from the office window. Six in total and all brand new judging by the alluring smell of pine and varnish. They were clearly built at some expense.

'We used to offer accommodation in the house, in the east wing, but repairs proved more expensive than we could cope with, and it was actually cheaper to build these. This is a fresh start for us, I hope.'

'They're very nice. What facilities do you offer here?' I asked.

'We were traditionally a shooting and fishing estate. We have over seven thousand acres, the loch, the river, and we're looking into quad bikes, archery, maybe even an adventure playground. It all depends, really.'

'Depends on what?' asked Rowan. She was peering in through the window of the nearest cabin, her hands shielding her face for a better view.

'Investment. Isn't that always the thing? We have lots of land, more than we can put to profitable use, but we need backers to move things forward. Have you ever thought of investment, Sergeant?'

'On my salary? You must be kidding.'

'Well, you are both invited to a little party I'm having next month anyway. It's designed to get rich people drunk and amenable to pickpocketing, but it would be nice to have some other faces there too.'

'Thank you, Charles. I'm not sure we can, but it's very nice of you to offer. I don't know what I was expecting, coming here today, but I have to say it's rare to be received so graciously. Normally we're the harbingers of bad news and inconvenience, and we're not usually made so welcome.'

'I can imagine that is the case. I couldn't do your job, Sergeant. I like to be liked. Confrontation I avoid where I can, but it is an inevitable part of your job, I'm sure. I, too, didn't know what to expect. Stewart has a tendency to paint people with a dark palette, I think. But I am a believer of not sketching people you have not yet met.'

'The inspector and I are still finding our feet, I think.'

'You mean finding your place in the pack, no?'

'I suppose, yes.'

'Stewart is a little stuck in his ways, I think. Like most people in our little town he doesn't like change, and that is what you represent, Sergeant. Tell me, Constable Forbes, how do you react when your superiors start – what would the phrase be? – butting heads?'

'Oh, I've found that when policemen start comparing the size of their truncheons, it's time to make myself scarce, Mr Ogilvie.'

He laughed heartily but stopped as Rowan's and my fingers shot to our ears in sudden synchronicity. As the message from Control ended, she began running. I accepted the call and started walking after her.

'Oh dear, is it something serious?' asked Ogilvie.

'No. No, it really isn't,' I said.

CHAPTER FIVE

Time, Gentlemen, Please

'Relax, it's a vandalism, Rowan, not an armed robbery,' I said, climbing into the passenger seat, my feet only just inside as she threw the van into reverse and carved a wound into Ogilvie's gravel drive. 'We don't even know if it's ongoing.'

'By Stratharder standards, this is major.' As I looked at Rowan it occurred to me that there was something different about her.

'Have you cut your hair recently?' I asked, trying to work it out.

'No, why?'

'I can see more of your face.'

'Hair clasp. I just put it in,' she said, and as she did, I saw it. Her hair, usually falling over her eyes, was kept at bay by a silver clasp near her ear exposing the never-before-seen left hand side of her face.

'It suits you. You should stop hiding behind your fringe.'

She gave me an indignant look.

'Where's the call?' I said.

'Twelve Ochil Drive, near to the hotel.'

'What's been damaged?'

'Not sure. You're going to tell me *that's* important, aren't you?' she said, sternly.

'It might be. I mean if it's an ongoing vandalism to a greenhouse then we would approach quietly from the back. But, if it's to a car parked in the driveway we would go straight to the house, wouldn't we?'

She didn't answer. She flew though the town crossroads, barely slowing. She overtook a Mini too near a corner for my liking, especially with the rain coming down again. I pulled on my seat belt slowly, hoping she wouldn't see. It was barely worth the bother as she took a hard left into a side street and slowed as she scanned the house numbers before finding twelve.

Rowan darted from the vehicle and was at the front door before I had even closed my door. I calmly pulled my hat on and reached for my coat on the back seat and joined Rowan just as the door opened.

'My goodness, you were quick. Come away in, I've just put the kettle on.' The woman, who might have been a hundred years old, led the way down the hall at glacier pace.

'When did this happen?' asked Rowan, still on high alert.

'Just a few minutes ago, dear.'

'Where?'

The old woman stopped and turned, a confused expression on her lined face.

'The kitchen, dear.'

'Are they still there now?'

'Who, dear?'

'Rowan,' I said, 'she thinks you're asking about the kettle.'

She rolled her eyes and seemed to relax a little.

'I'll help you with the tea, Mrs . . . ?'

'Gillespie, dear. Oh, thank you.'

I left Rowan and Mrs Gillespie in the living room while I prepared the pot of tea. I removed my coat as she had the heating turned to Hades. As I did, I felt something crinkle in the side pocket. I reached in and removed a sheet of folded paper. In crude handwriting was etched: 'Sgt'. I returned with a tray to find Rowan scribbling into her notebook and trying to appear interested. Mrs Gillespie was in mid-rant about the youth of today. Rowan leant in and whispered, so as not to talk over her, 'Two broken fence panels. Happened a week last Thursday.'

'Stop the fucking press,' I whispered back.

'Should I even bother noting this?'

'It's still a crime.'

Mrs Gillespie seemed to be of better hearing than I had presumed as she ceased her story and returned to the point in hand. 'I'm sorry to be bothering you with this. I know you have much more important things to be dealing with. It's just that the insurance company wouldn't accept a claim if I didn't have a crime number.'

'It's no problem, Mrs Gillespie, it's our job. Constable Forbes will take all the details and give you a call later with a crime number. After your tea you can show us where it happened.'

As Rowan continued noting, I took the piece of paper from my pocket. I'm not sure why I flinched as Rowan turned her head briefly, but I did. I stuffed it back into the pocket and listened to Rowan note the boring complaint.

'Tell me it gets better,' said Rowan, closing the van door and resting her arm on the steering wheel and then her forehead on that.

'It gets better,' I assured her. 'Although be careful what you wish for. Someday when you're working in the city, stressed out of your head and you're having sleepless nights chasing your tail with calls and enquiries, you might wish you were back.'

'Never gonna happen,' she said and pulled the van out of the street.

'Yeah, probably not.'

'There's no likelihood of ever catching someone for something like this, is there?' Rowan asked.

'A random vandalism? Almost none. I mean if you get a call at the time, or there's CCTV, you have a fighting chance; but a call ten days later? You've pretty much had it.'

'So, what's the point?'

'Well, we still need to record these things. For one, it can help build up a pattern of events which can prove useful. And two, you never know what some idiot might confess to, and if there's nothing on the system there's nothing to pin it to.'

Rowan's face suggested she didn't agree, but she let it go. As we drove back through the crossroads, something caught my eye, something yellow.

'Turn back,' I said.

'You saw something?' Rowan pulled over to allow traffic behind us to pass, then she made a U-turn.

'I think so. Something I've been looking out for. Slow down a bit, pull up behind them.'

We rolled in behind the yellow hatchback pulled up at the side of the road in a bus stop. I was ninety per cent sure it was the one that had run me off the road on my first day in Stratharder.

'You want me to come with you?' Rowan asked.

'Nah, I'll just be a minute.'

There were a few heads hanging out of the passenger side, so I approached along the driver's. There was an animated discussion, which became clearer as I reached the car.

'Come on, show us your tits,' came one deep moronic voice from the back seat.

'Get fucked, ya wee plebs, away and play with each other's tiny wangers,' came the response from the redhead I'd met at the crossroads on my first outing with Rowan.

'Hey, Mhairi, how about a blow job? Oh wait, I've only got a fiver, do you give change?' The front passenger's quip sent the whole car into hysterics.

With the occupants' attention directed at the pavement the driver never saw me coming. I rapped my knuckle twice on his side window. He jumped, turned to see me and jumped again as he clocked the uniform. It had the desired effect. The four acne-ridden pubescent faces turned, horrified.

I gave the universal signal for wind down your window.

'Is that any way to talk to a lady?' I said over the driver to the front passenger. The lad wearing a beanie hat and tracksuit top flushed and looked at the floor.

'We's just havin' a joke, five-o.'

'Is that supposed to be English?' I replied to the driver, sporting a New York Yankees baseball cap and eyeing me disdainfully. He sucked his teeth, I guessed in some derisory manner. 'Ain't no reason for feds to be all up in our shit. Why don't you bounce?'

I looked through both windows at Mhairi on the other side and gave a confused look.

'Did you catch any of that?'

'Not a word,' she said.

The other occupants of the car continued to look anywhere but at me, leaving the driver, the leader I supposed, to be the sole balls-wearer.

'We ain't done fuck all, Fed,' the driver said, giving me a look of utter disgust and that teeth-suck thing again. My temper was wearing thin.

'Take off your hat,' I said, my voice suddenly bereft of jest.

'You what?'

'You heard me, take off your hat.'

The teeth-suck and a head shake. 'What for? You can't make me.'

His accent was Scottish all of a sudden. He looked defiantly straight forward. I bent down to his level and lowered my voice.

'Take that fucking hat off, or I will.' I straightened up. 'I want to get a look at the boy who ran me into a ditch a fortnight ago.'

'Talkin' about, Fed? Trying to frame me.'

Despite his piss and vinegar, he removed the hat. I had to stop myself from laughing. Some people in this world you collectively refer to as redheads, but there is a subgroup that can only be described as ginger; those who are particularly pale and the red a striking orange hue. This guy was ginger. He might even have been some kind of ginger royalty. A great bush of bright red curls was unleashed almost impossibly; it was hard to believe it could have been contained within the cap.

'What's your name?' I asked through a barely disguised chuckle.

'You don't have the right to be askin—'

'Either you tell me your name, or I find out by running your plates while I issue you a ticket for parking in a bus stop.'

Teeth-suck.

'Mick.'

'Mick what?'

'McCloy. You ain't got no right, Fed. Shit, dis is police harassment.'

'Let me just point a few things out to you Mr McCloy. First, you're ginger. Second, you live in Scotland. Third, you live in the north of Scotland.'

'You got a point, Fed?'

'My point, Michael, is that not only are you white, you might just the be the whitest boy who ever lived. So cut the gangsta shit, cos you ain't gangsta, you're nothing but a . . . what was it now?' I looked up at Mhairi, who was chuckling at the pantomime. 'Oh yeah, a pleb with a tiny wanger, and if you think *this* is harassment, just try crossing my path again. Now fuck off the lot of you before I decide that the cigarettes on the dashboard there, sitting alongside the cigarette papers, are grounds to toss this yellow turd bucket for ganga. You feel me?'

Teeth-suck, first gear, ridiculous exhaust growing fainter in the distance.

'You should ask her out. You like her as much as she likes you.'

'How do you figure?'

'Storming in there like Prince Charming. Don't tell me you didn't see her before you got out the van.' Rowan lifted both our drinks from the bar and I followed her to a corner table.

'I *didn't* see her.'

'Yeah, right.'

'It's true, I had no idea. I saw the shitty yellow car and that was all.'

'"Oh, Sergeant Colyear, how can I ever thank you from saving me from those ruffians?" Ha.'

'You know fine well she was joking. Actually, I think she was sort of telling me off.'

'Of course she was, you dizzy twat. Clearly she doesn't need you to fight her battles.'

'That wasn't my intention. Anyway, I think she forgave me. It's actually quite nice in here,' I said, scanning the room and changing the subject. The Stratharder Hotel bar was arranged in a long L-shape, one side kept in a traditional pub style with small round tables and tall chairs at the bar. The other side was set out as a gastro-pub idea, with longer tables set for dinner. Two couples were eating and a few more tables had reserved signs on display – unnecessarily, I thought, as half of the tables were empty. We were sitting in the elbow of the L. The bar itself was gently illuminated by small downlights that reflected off the golden polished wood of the counter. Easy-listening music played quietly from unseen speakers; Tracy Chapman, I thought.

'Do you want to get something to eat?' I asked.

'No, it's my turn to cook. It's a bit late in the day to text my roommate and tell her to sort herself out. The food's quite good here though.'

'Really? Does Odd-Job there double up as the cook?' I nodded towards the shaven-headed, thickset barman with the perma-sour expression who served me.

'I had a burger here a few weeks ago. It was nice.'

'Maybe later. Do you think we should ask him to join us?'

'Who, Odd-Job?'

'No, Brian.' He had spotted us as soon as we entered. He was sitting at the bar nursing a pint of Guinness. Rowan had patted his shoulder as we passed and he had nodded his acknowledgement. He was still stoking the dying embers of the same pint, occasionally exchanging a word with Odd-Job and the equally morose bar fly sitting on the next stool, but otherwise glaring into the slowly depleting glass.

'Maybe just leave him where he is,' said Rowan. 'Hate to spoil a pleasant evening.'

'You don't like him?'

'It's not that.'

'Because he doesn't seem to like me very much,' I said, feeling a little foolish.

'Fuck him, he's not exactly friend material anyway. Your life's not going to improve by adding him to your Facebook.'

'I just don't like to be disliked. He doesn't even know me.'

'Yeah, about that. What is his deal with you exactly? Just an authority thing?' she asked.

'Maybe, I'm young for a sergeant, that seems to piss some people off.'

'I never thought of that. I suppose it would be weird to have a boss who's younger than you. Still, no need to be a dick about it.'

'But most likely it's to do with what happened back in the city. It's probably my reputation he hates rather than me.'

'Why? What happened?'

'You don't know?' She shook her head and watched me excitedly over her wine glass. 'You must be the only person here who hasn't been warned of my arrival.'

'What did you do?' I could see the smile forming on her face.

'Ach, it's not important.'

'Oh, it is. It is important. It's *the* most important thing. Tell me, tell me!'

'Calm down. I'm sure someone else will give you a much more entertaining version than you'd get from me. Right now, I really don't want to go into it.'

'Come on, you can't do that. You have to tell me.'

'Seriously, Rowan. Drop it, please.'

An awkward moment of silence settled. Rowan finished off her glass and checked her watch.

'Staying for another?' I asked, knowing she wasn't going to.

'No, I better be off. Besides I'm driving, and so are you by the way.'

'I think I'll stay for a bit, leave the car here and walk home. Beats television and whatever my landlady might have left on my doorstep.'

'Maybe you and Brian will get chatting and become bosom buddies.'

'I think there's a better chance of hitting it off with Odd-Job.' Rowan followed my gaze. The stocky barman stood, arms folded, glaring at the ceiling, clearly bored out of his mind. She turned back to me and laughed. 'Failing that I have my book,' I said, pulling a battered paperback from my bag. Rowan lifted it as if from a muddy puddle.

'Crime fiction? Really?'

'I know, it's my dad's,' I said. 'He thinks I should be a big fan, because I'm a cop. He's dying to hear what I think.'

Rowan hauled herself off her chair and patted my shoulder in goodbye. I waved and watched her leave, playfully punching Brian on the shoulder as she passed him. He drunkenly looked round over the wrong shoulder.

The bar grew steadily busier over the next few hours, though the restaurant side had emptied. The bar noise had all but drowned out Tracy Chapman, making her fourth or fifth rotation on the stereo. A few couples occupied the other tables and a group of twenty-somethings took up a large table near the door, poring over each other's phones.

I was on chapter six and my eyes were beginning to grow weary, not helped by the three pints, the last of which I was almost finished with. I decided to head home once I'd finished the chapter. I rubbed at my eyes and stretched my back, looking up for the first time in a while. I was suddenly aware of eyes on me, Brian and his new drinking companion, who I hadn't noticed had entered, Alistair Hughes.

Shit, I thought and lowered my eyes back to the book. I didn't know how long Hughes had been there, but I could see from my periphery that he was becoming animated. I could just about see Brian trying to placate him. I finished my pint and was a few lines away from the end of the chapter when the thud of a body dropping itself into the chair opposite made me look up. This was followed by the heavy clunk of his glass on the table halfway between us, stopping dead every conversation in the place. He waited for my response, but I went back to completing the remaining lines.

'I've just finished work,' he said, eventually. 'Thought I'd drop in for a pint on the way home.' His voice was loud and urgent.

I glanced at him. His eyes were wide, and he gripped the bottom of his glass like he might use it for some other purpose than for which it had been designed. His face was smeared black and his blue overalls were sullied likewise. They gave off a pungent chemical smell.

'Wanna know what I do now?'

I ignored him. I stared into my book, looking at the words, but not reading. The general hubbub of the bar was just beginning to return when again the thud came. A slosh of dark beer covered my hand and pages of the book.

'I asked you a fucking question,' he yelled.

A scrape of chairs and rustle of clothing came from the group of youngsters, followed by the squeak of the door and smack of it closing. In the brief meeting in the inspector's office, he'd been clearly livid but had been forced to keep a lid on it. Now, he had no such restriction.

I looked around, rather than at Hughes. Brian, still slumped at the bar, glowered over with faint amusement.

'Porta-fucking-loos,' he spat. 'Chemical-fuckin-cludgies.'

'Shit job?' There was a faint quake in my stomach, the onset of danger but not immediate, if I was reading it right, so I didn't flinch when he snapped to his feet sending his chair skidding back and then toppling.

'There's a stench in here,' he said, screwing his face at me. 'Reeks of fucking bacon. Eh, no offence there, Brian.'

'None taken. But that's not pig you smell, it's a fucking rat,' he said, letting the 'r' roll, taking great delight. He stood, tottered a little on his heels and then waddled towards the door, which was being blocked by two other men, who may, or may not, have been in the bar the whole time. They moved aside as Brian approached. My stomach reacted with a twinge. *There it is*, I thought, *now we're in trouble*.

The remaining patrons had left or were leaving. Brian's departure was no coincidence, I realised. It would take some explaining as to why he didn't intervene when a colleague was outnumbered in a bar fight. There was another door on the restaurant side and I considered making a run for it, but stubbornness, or stupidity maybe, wouldn't allow it. Besides, this was all pretty coordinated.

There was every chance I would find it blocked and have to add humiliation to the situation.

Fuck it, I thought, *let's get this over with*. I shook the beer off my book and slung it into my bag. I stood and looked in Hughes' face, which was wild. He chewed savagely on his bottom lip and backed up allowing me into the centre of the available floor space. *Don't get cornered*. My stomach was churning. I allowed Hughes to circle in behind me. He was going to be the first to strike. They were all taking the cue from him. The two at the door approached slowly and spread out a little. Both men were in their late forties but looked capable enough. I dropped my bag into my hand, making it clear it was now a weapon. I could hear, or maybe feel, Hughes beginning to make his move. My arm tensed to react when another loud thud made us all pause. The swing-hatch of the bar had been allowed to fall. The barman was now approaching. *Stupid fucking idiot*, I thought, *should have run when I had the chance*. The barman was colossal, a man-mountain. There must have been at least a foot of a drop in the floor behind the bar to not have noticed his full size. I backed up, though there wasn't much room to manoeuvre. I would pull one of them on top of me, I decided, anyone but Odd-Job that was, make it difficult for the rest. *Just protect your head*.

The barman shook his big shaven head at me. His arms hung bowed at his sides, the muscles of his arms and chest not allowing them to fall straight. He looked like he was carrying a pair of invisible carpets.

'Is not a fair fight,' he said. His voice was higher in pitch than would have seemed fitting for such a man, his accent thick Eastern-European. 'Three on one is no good,' he stepped forward and looked down at me. I couldn't read him. He turned to face Hughes. 'But now, two against three? This is fair. But not here. We go outside.' My stomach relaxed as soon as he had finished speaking. I had an urge to laugh, and must, at least, have had a wide grin on my face.

The three men exchanged a look and I knew it was over.

'Fuck this,' said Hughes. He spat on the floor by my foot, catching the strap of my bag. 'I'll be seeing you, Colyear.'

'No doubt,' I said.

The two men by the door held it open for their captain's retreat and then followed him out. I waited a few seconds after the door closed, before turning to Odd-Job.

'Thanks,' I said and patted his shoulder, which might also have been part of his neck.

He shrugged. 'Don't mention. They're not friends of mine.' He returned behind the bar and I took up one of the stools facing him. 'So, you're the new sheriff in town?' he said, pouring a pint.

'Sergeant, but yes. How did you know?'

'Yes, I hear about you.'

'Really, what did you hear?' I asked.

'That you're the new sheriff in town,' he said, as if addressing an idiot. 'There are not many secrets in such a small place, I think.' He pushed the glass in front of me.

'I guess you're right. Thanks, can I get you one?'

'Yes, you can.' He began to pour another.

'I'm Don, Colyear.'

'Yes, I know. I am Pawel Nowicki.'

'It's nice to meet you, Pawel. In fact, I don't think I've ever said that and meant it more. You really saved my arse there.'

'Saved your arse,' he laughed as he finished pouring. 'I like these expressions.'

'Where are you from?' I asked.

'Poland, Kraków.'

'How the hell did you end up here?'

'I ask myself this question sometimes. When I arrive with my wife we are in Stirling. I have a construction job and then after two years, I lose this job, economic downturn. Even though I do the job of two men for less pay than one, they let me go. My wife is pregnant, but she wants to stay so I start to look for another job. I do some casual work but see advert in job centre for Stratharder Hotel, restaurant and bar manager, full training given. So, I ask, and so I get.'

'Construction to restaurant manager? How does that work?'

'Strange, yes? I suppose nobody here wants to do the work, and nobody outside wants to live here, so I get the job.'

'How long have you been here?'

'Nearly one year.'

'You like it?'

'Magda, my wife, she likes it. Is very quiet.'

'But you're not so keen?'

He mulled this over, taking a long sip from his glass and wiping his upper lip. 'I don't know about here. Stirling was OK, felt like a real place. Here not so much. Is difficult to explain.'

'No, I think I understand. Just something off about the whole damn town?'

'You say it better, yes. People are suspicious of foreign people wherever you go, I understand, but usually things get better quickly. But here, nothing has changed. One guy even says to me when he was drunk that I am stealing jobs from Scottish people. I say nobody want this fucking job, but he either doesn't understand or it was just an excuse to shout at me.'

'He was a brave man to be shouting at you.'

'People are brave when they are drunk.'

'Dutch courage.'

'Another expression? Why Dutch?'

'Actually, I don't know.' I placed a ten on the counter. 'Thanks again, Pawel.'

'I said don't mention.'

I pulled my bag back onto my shoulder.

'I would give it a while before you leave. Cowards like to hide in shadows. I think I will close up now. I doubt anybody else will come tonight. I'll walk out with you, just give me ten minutes to lock things up, OK?'

'Sure,' I said and took a seat with the remainder of my drink while Pawel disappeared into a back room. I lifted my jacket to put my wallet away and suddenly remembered the piece of paper I'd discovered in Mrs Gillespie's kitchen. I pulled it from the pocket and unfolded it. Inside, a hastily scribbled note read:

Dear Sergeant,
I simply must talk with you about Jennifer. I apologise for the manner of this note, but I will explain if you would meet me.

I will be at church this Sunday. Back row.
K

'Ready to go?'

Pawel's voice appeared out of nowhere and the surprise made me scrunch the letter in my hand. I peered up at him.

'You OK?' he asked.

'I'm fine,' I said. 'Let's go.'

CHAPTER SIX

Revelations

The soft murmurings from behind the large wooden door, in addition to the occasional cough and baby complaint, confirmed that things were in full flow. The plan was to slip inside unnoticed towards the end of the service and then ride the front of the exodus wave. This plan, however, had included a conveniently open entrance. I pushed my weight against the thick wooden door and was relieved to find it unlocked and the hinges smooth and silent. Just as I estimated I had enough of a crack to slip through, it caught the stone floor in its arc and croaked like a mating toad. I screwed my eyes shut for a second, hoping it hadn't caught anyone's attention, but as I opened them, I saw that half of the congregation had turned to see my apologetic grimace. As I released the door it swung back on a strong spring, every bit as painfully audible. Curious faces became vexed ones. Even the priest halted his sermon while I ducked and scrabbled to the nearest pew, stumbling over an elderly gentleman sitting alone at the end of the row. The rest of the pew was empty, and I slid, half-seated, to the far side just as the priest announced the hymn we would be singing and the congregation rose to their feet. I searched around for a hymn book to no avail, then mouthed along to 'Abide with Me' as best as I could remember.

St Dymphna's Parish Church in Stratharder was a fairly new construction but designed to give the appearance of age. The gravestones in the yard, however, were much older, suggesting the place was built on the site of a previous place of worship.

The service was busier than I had imagined. I'd heard accounts of how attendances at church had dwindled dramatically in a single generation, recovering to a small degree by the influx of Eastern European migrants, but still nothing compared to numbers even twenty years ago. I could believe it. Mum was the religious one; she had me suited and booted every Sunday while my friends were devouring cornflakes and cartoons. It's something you inherit, I guess. My dad continued to take me for about a year after Mum passed, but his presence had been under as much duress as mine. One morning, while we were wrestling our ties in front of the hall mirror, me sulking and him struggling with left over right, or right over left, he stopped. He held both ends of his semi-completed knot for a moment and then drew it back out of his collar. We went to Dottie's instead, Dottie's being Dorothy's Pantry, a little cafe in Oban that made the best Sunday brunch. We traded scripture for pancakes and never looked back.

The man next to me had a good voice, deep and sonorous; it masked my own embarrassed mumbling. We sat as one at the completion of the hymn. As the rumble of people taking their seats increased, I looked around the back rows. I spotted a small wave over my neighbour's shoulder. A woman, *the* woman I thought might be here. The awkward hug she had given me was the delivery moment for the letter.

I waited for the next invitation from the priest to rise and I slid past the man. I ducked around the back and slipped in beside the gaunt woman who sat at the furthermost corner of the last pew. I couldn't age her. She might have been forty or sixty. The deep circles under her eyes and her sunken cheeks made it impossible. She wore the same long coat she had worn that day at the crossroads. She shook my hand as I sat.

'Thank you for meeting me,' she whispered. 'And I'm sorry about the note, it's just that—'

'It's fine,' I said, seeing that her hand and bottom lip were trembling with emotion. 'What is it I can do for you?'

'I was just hoping you might be able to give me an update on Jennifer. My husband would be cross if he knew I was here. I know Inspector Wallace says that you'll contact us if there's any news, but it's been weeks since we heard anything.'

I thought for a moment, trying to recall any context where the name Jennifer meant something in my time in Stratharder, but I had nothing.

'I'm sorry . . . erm?'

'Katherine.'

'Katherine. This is a little embarrassing, but I'm not exactly sure what we're talking about here.'

'Jennifer,' she said, perplexed. 'My daughter, Jennifer Mulligan.'

Again, it meant nothing to me. I wanted to nod my head in placating acknowledgement, but I could only shake it slowly, still desperately trying to find some connection.

Katherine turned to me, squarely.

'She's been missing since June, nearly four months now.' A few faces turned to us with the rise in her voice.

I swallowed my surprise. There was nothing at all on the missing persons system. I checked it every day, always in vain, but part of my routine.

'What was the last you were told?' I asked, reading from her that an admission of ignorance would bring about an angry reaction.

A look of resignation came over her. 'I don't doubt you're doing all you can. And chances are she *is* in London with Viv, but it's just so unlike her not to let me know she's OK. She'll know fine well I'll be going out of my mind with worry. Jack, my husband, says not to bother you, and to stop going into the station, but I thought, seeing that you were new, not that I don't trust the others of course, but that maybe you might have some other ideas? That you might be more understanding?' This last sentence she said in an almost inaudibly quiet voice.

'I have to admit, Katherine, I haven't had much involvement,' I exaggerated. 'My inspector has remit over these kinds of enquiries, but I can assure you I'll be looking deeper into it. Tell me about Viv.'

'That's all I ask, thank you.' She paused as we were beckoned to stand for some reason beyond my ken. 'Viv, as you know,' she continued, speaking softly into my ear, 'is Jen's best friend. She went off to London last year. They still messaged on Facebook or whatever, but Jen missed her terribly. Every time she got into an argument with her dad, she threatened to follow her down there, but I never thought she would. She's not as worldly as Viv, you know, more . . . trusting.'

'And we think Jen's down there because . . . ?'

'Of the phone thing. What do you call it now when you get a hit on her position with the phone?'

'A ping.'

'Yes, they pinged it . . .' Some silent and unseen signal caused the congregation to sit again, like a shallow wave hitting a shore in front of me. '. . . a few times before it stopped working and it was in central London. The other officer, the large one?'

'PC Ritchie, Brian Ritchie?'

'Yes, he said that the information was being passed to the Metropolitan Police and that they would be looking into it, but I've not heard anything. I keep up the payments on her phone contract. I try the number every day, but I get nothing.'

'What did Jen and her dad argue about?'

'Och, you know teenagers, they fight about anything. But . . . well, Jack has a bit of a gambling problem, but he's on top of it now, I'm proud of him. But sometimes money would be really tight at home and she would blame him. That reminds me, don't tell Jack I'm still paying for her phone, I told him the police were doing that, as part of the enquiry.'

I wanted to ask so many questions: what about bank accounts? CCTV at the train station? Social media? Other friends? But again these would only highlight my lack of any knowledge or involvement.

'I promise you, Katherine, I will look into it. I'm certain it's all in hand, but I'll make sure. OK?'

She nodded as we were prompted to stand again. Katherine crossed herself then began shuddering. I put an arm around her and rubbed her shoulder and the tears flowed. A few faces were still turning to look in my direction, but my embarrassment was quickly turning to annoyance and I glared back at every nosy enquiry.

'Stupid question, Katherine, but how are you both holding up?'

'Oh, you know,' she said, trying to compose herself. 'We're getting on with it. Nothing else for it, is there? We've got Rachel to think about. We can't be seen going to pieces.'

'And how is Rachel dealing with it?' I assumed this was a sister.

She shrugged. 'In her typical way. She's furious with Jen. Thinks she's being selfish putting us through this. They've both talked about getting out of Stratharder, only Rachel is studying hard to go on to university next year. Jen was never so gifted. She had talked for a while about joining the army. She'd been training up for it, running, weights; the whole thing. Rachel's our scholar, Jen is our little athlete. But Jack would never allow it. So, she said she would wait until she was eighteen when she wouldn't need our permission. The idea sort of faded, though, fizzled out really. She hadn't mentioned it in months. It was still the first thing we checked when she disappeared, but nothing. They hadn't heard from her.'

'Maybe a few months trying to stand on her own two feet in the big city will be good for her. A short, sharp shock?' I said.

'That's what Jack says. Says she'll be home, tail tucked, in no time. Maybe he's right. I pray he is, but it just doesn't feel right to me.'

'Leave it with me, Katherine, and try not to worry. I know it's easy for me to say, but just trust me, OK?'

This brought a fresh flow of emotion. I rubbed her shoulder again as I ushered her to sit, against the tide. She heaved a determined breath to regain the ability to speak. 'Thank you, Sergeant. You don't mind that I came to you, do you? I just didn't know what else to do.'

'Not at all. And I won't mention it to your husband, if that's what you want?'

'Thank you, I'd appreciate that. If you need anything from me, you can come by the house. Maybe best on a Wednesday night, that's when Jack has his card game. OK, I'm going to slip out, the service is about to end.'

'I'll give it a minute, then do the same,' I said, squeezing her arm.

She smiled and wiped her eyes again before shuffling deftly from the pew. I sat and watched her time her exit perfectly and cursed that I hadn't just followed her. The priest was beginning a slow procession down the aisle followed by the congregation.

I was powerless and resigned myself to sitting, pretending to sing along to a hymn I had never before heard while the devout section of Stratharder society gawked at me on their way out the door. I smiled and exchanged a nod of recognition with Margaret as she passed. Pawel passed and did a double-take and pointed me out to his family. Mhairi shot me a wink and others, I wasn't quite sure if I'd met, gave a mix of scrutinous glares and warm smiles.

It was painfully slow progress squeezing through the lingering crowd on both sides of the exit.

'Sergeant Colyear?' The priest was the first to accost me as he stood at the door shaking hands and thanking people for their attendance. I wasn't in the slightest bit surprised he knew my name.

'Hello, Father,' I said, trying to keep frustration from my voice.

The white-haired man in scarlet vestments clutched my hand earnestly. 'Welcome to St Dymphna's. Father McCann. It's so nice to finally meet you. So, you're Catholic, are you?'

'Lapsed perhaps, but yes, I suppose.' I was aware of an audience forming, as two celebrities meeting in public might invite.

'Well, that's all right. I'm a bit of a lapsed jogger,' he said, patting his paunch. 'Only takes a few outings to get back into shape though.' His analogy was limp.

I smiled and nodded. 'I thought it was time to dust off the, eh, running shoes, Father.'

'We'll be seeing more of you, then? I'm so glad. Oh, and one other thing.' He lowered his voice and took my elbow. 'We could use your presence at the local council meetings. You see, we've been inviting the police to come along for the longest time, but other commitments and all that. I appreciate you're very busy, but it would be so lovely to have you there. It would make it all feel somehow . . . legitimate.'

'Oh, well, I don't know, Father. As you say, we're very busy, but perhaps if you—'

'He'll be there. Won't you, Sergeant? There's nothing so urgent we can't get you freed up for a little community interaction.'

'Inspector Wallace, sorry, I didn't see you there.' I really hadn't, it took me by surprise, but shouldn't have. I should have spotted him; out of uniform he looked exactly the same. Shoe-polish-black hair slicked to the side and a stiff black suit. The two women flanking him could not have been more contradictory. His wife, I assumed, shook my hand.

'This is Marjory,' said the inspector, rather resignedly, 'and this is Paula, my daughter.'

'Pleased to meet you.'

Both women looked too young next to him. Too young to have married him and, in her early teens, too young to be his daughter. Both were contrastingly jolly in appearance, wearing broad smiles. The inspector's was a thin and cool one as he ushered them on. 'See you at work, Donald.'

I nodded and turned to Father McCann. 'It's nice to meet you, Father, but I really must run.'

'Of course, of course.'

I ducked out the door and down the steps of the church.

Pawel was waiting for me on the grass that formed a sort of unofficial car park. He was clearly keen to introduce me to his wife. *My God*, I thought, as I reached them, he seemed even larger than I remembered from the bar. Perhaps it was the formal clothes. It might also have been that the blonde, rosy-cheeked woman standing next to him was about my height and seemed dwarfed by him. I said a combined hello. Before Pawel could respond, the woman hugged me with one arm. The baby she was holding in the other was squeezed between us.

'Pawel tells me he *saved your arse*,' the woman laughed, obviously tickled by the retelling. 'I'm so glad my Pawel has a friend.'

'As am I, and handy that he turned out to be an enormous arse-saving one; and Pav, once again, thank you,' I said, trying out a short version of his name. If he minded, he didn't mention it.

'Oh, don't say that, it makes him very grumpy,' she said, reaching up and squeezing his cheek. He grinned awkwardly but affectionately. 'I'm Magda, since the grumpy bear forgot to introduce us. The little one is Adam.'

The strong autumnal breeze had her hair and dress swirling. She swatted at both to keep them under control. She adjusted the woollen hat the baby was wearing so I could get a better look at him. He was his dad's double, although I supposed all babies look a bit like Pav, somewhat out of normal adult proportion, round-faced and bald.

'It's nice to meet you, Magda, I'm Don. And he is

just adorable, congratulations to you both. Are you guys heading out?' I was eager to leave but happy to talk to them. We began walking towards the road. 'Can I help you carry something?' Pav, as big as he was, was laden down with a baby bag so capacious it might carry enough equipment to keep a grown man in comfort for a week. Magda pushed a pram with her free hand.

'Sure,' said Magda, handing me the baby.

'Oh, actually I've never . . .'

'You'll be fine,' she laughed. 'Just hold his head, like this, see? He's four months now, so really quite robust. You won't hurt him.'

A steady stream of cars was passing us from the church as we headed down the hill towards the hotel. As usual, many a face was pointed in my direction.

'What is it makes you grumpy, Pav?' I asked, gently rubbing the baby's hand between my thumb and index finger.

'People saying thank you,' said Magda.

'People being polite annoys you?' I enquired.

'Not being polite. It's hard to explain.'

'He thinks people are too nice in this country.' Magda laughed and I couldn't help but join her.

Pav shook his head 'That's not it. It's just people here spend their lives with saying nice things to each other. They're scared of being not polite. I don't know how you people get anything done.'

'I'm not sure I follow,' I said.

'It's like . . . how many times have you said thanks for helping you in the bar?'

I shook my head.

'Yes, I lost count too,' he said. 'You said thanks in the bar, and that's enough. It's like when someone comes in to order a drink it goes like: *I'll have a pint of lager and glass of wine, please,*' he held up a finger. '*You want this lager or that lager? Oh, I'll have that lager, please, thanks.*' He held up a second and third finger. '*And you want a red or white wine? Oh, red please. Large glass? Please,* he says. I pour the drinks and place them on the bar, *Thank you,* he says.' Unable to use his other hand with the amount he was carrying he went back to one finger again to indicate six. '*That'll be nine pounds.* He hands me ten and says *Thanks.* Why he says thanks when he hands me money I don't know. I give him the change he says *Thanks very much,*' Pav finished, but had given up remembering how many fingers to hold up.

Pav looked at his hands. 'That's eight, or maybe nine, times he says polite things, for one order. Unbelievable. Now in Poland this is how it goes: I go in the bar and I point at the beer and ask for the wine. He pours and I slide the money over, he rings it through till and puts the change on the bar. Now maybe he nods and I nod, like a sort of thanks. Nobody is offended, nobody is thinking *How rude.* I get my drinks, he gets his sale and we have two minutes extra in our day to do other things.'

'Ignore him, Don, he's just a sourpuss. I like that people here are polite, although you have to remember to do it yourself. That takes some time.' Magda's English was exceptional, her accent subtle, mildly European, there was even a hint of the Scottish within.

'I think Pav has a point,' I said. 'We can get a bit fixated on niceties in Britain. I guess we just don't notice it until someone points it out. Where do you guys stay?' I asked.

'We have an apartment attached to the hotel, but we're looking for a bigger place,' said Magda.

'She's looking for a bigger place; I'm happy to have a home for free.'

'Can you imagine living with a little monkey and a giant gorilla in a small apartment, Don? It's crazy. After Christmas we're getting a bigger place.' Magda nudged Pav with her elbow. We reached the section of road that cut off towards the hotel and I softly passed baby Adam, now asleep I was proud to see, back to his mother.

'You're a natural, Don. You can babysit anytime,' said Magda. 'I want to invite you to dinner sometime. Will you come?'

'Oh, well I would need to check my shifts and—'

'Is pointless to say no. Best to save yourself the time and say yes. She is like a dog with a bone with these things.'

'In that case, Magda, I would be delighted,' I said.

On the way home, I stopped in at the station, which was empty. I logged on to the system and opened the missing persons database. Nothing live. No mention of Jennifer Mulligan as a missing person. I interrogated the historical function for Stratharder and Kirkmartin and had two hits: Vivian Jenkins, eighteen years old, being the most recent. Reported missing the previous May. All the standard checks looked to be present and correct. Amongst her known family and friends was Jennifer Mulligan, interviewed and could provide no pertinent details. Search passed to the

Metropolitan Police in the July after bank records returned hits in central London. Traced sixteenth of July safe and well, elected not to have her whereabouts confirmed to parents, as was her right.

The search prior to that was a Richard Naylor, nineteen years old, missing in 2008, traced a month later in Glasgow, with a similar outcome and again all the usual checks completed.

I closed the database and opened my emails with little else to do with my last day off. My eyes scanned the thirty-odd new inbox entries and centred on one in particular. Subject – I'm a bored sergeant, get me out of here. From Inspector Bennett:

Don,

How the hell are you? And how is life in the sticks? I trust the banjo lessons are coming along? Have you bedded a relative yet?

I have good news and bad news.

Good news is – I have a job you might be interested in!

Bad news is – it's the most mind-numbing central admin role going. Seriously, NOBODY is going to be applying for this. Only an idiot would actually choose to oversee licencing applications, so naturally I thought of you.

It's in Edinburgh and carries a high risk of suicide, but it's the best I could come up with right now. Further bad news is that it's not open for applications for another four weeks, and the job wouldn't be starting until January, but, as I say, it's the best I could find.

I understand if it's sort of frying pan into fire territory. It's up to you.

Let me know if you're interested, interview would be in December.

I replied straight away, and kept it simple:
Hell yes!!!

CHAPTER SEVEN

Wardrobe

John never once asked how I knew about the baby that was hidden in the bedroom, and I'm glad. I wouldn't have known how to explain it. Perhaps he didn't ask because it scared him, and to ask was to open a box that could never again be closed.

That's certainly why my dad never once brought this thing up. Enough small things happened as a kid for him to pick up on it, but he didn't want to know. It remains, now, an unspoken tension between us. But that's OK with me, it's not a conversation I want to have.

Shit, if Dad could see me now, he'd enjoy a good old I told you so.

I'm on my knees. I feel a little less queasy, but my head still swims a little. I think it was a low beam I struck. If I move slowly, I can just about find spaces between them, spaces almost high enough to stand; but with my hands fixed behind me, I'm forced to map my environment with my forehead and I am terrified of another blow. The ringing in my ears has eased, another sense returned, but of little use. The only sounds are the ones I'm responsible for. Tapping my foot against the base of a beam sends dust falling from the low ceiling and a hollow echo chimes, which seems to stretch for a distance. Wherever I am may be squat, but it is also long. I think about calling out, but that's as likely to be as dangerous as it to be helpful, so I don't.

I've made my way perhaps ten feet and have found a wall. Cold stone, irregular blocks held together by loose mortar. I sit again and at least now have something to rest my back against.

What was I just thinking about?

Oh yes, this ability? Affliction? Whatever this thing is, this . . . feeling, it's a useful tool as a cop. Well, mostly. I am of course bleeding like a bastard and have no clue where I am, and it's not the first time it's gotten me into a lot of trouble, but generally speaking, yes, useful. When I think about that night with Carly's mum, I have to also think about how things changed afterwards.

The twelve months that followed are a bit of a blur of success. John and I became something of a dream team. Whilst we never spoke openly about it, John suspected there was more to it than good intuition. It unsettled him to the point that it guaranteed there would be no open discussion about it. He just accepted and encouraged it. No questions asked. From that night on I would take the lead; John would trust my decisions, my intuition. If I said something strange, he would go with it. No questions asked. But it was that encouragement that nudged me nearer this dark place and ended John's career. But, if I had to pinpoint one moment when things turned sour, it would be the shift night out in Glasgow. Funny, I had no idea at the time.

'. . . So, there I was, barely a week in the uniform when we gets this call. Some woman, hasn't been seen in umpteen weeks, and you know how you just get a feeling sometimes, well, this was one of those. So, my tutor, he goes in first . . .'

'How many times have you heard this story?' Alyson said in a low yell, which constituted a whisper in this place.

'You mean this week?'

'It wasn't even funny the first time I heard it. And I don't believe a word of it. For a start it involves Terry answering a call, so right there we're into the realms of fiction.'

'How long do you think I have to stay here before I can bugger off and people won't notice?'

'You're going nowhere,' said Alyson, nudging my shoulder and sloshing both our drinks, narrowly missing the back of the girl in front of us, not part of our crowd, who, like others, had meandered over to our corner of the bar to hear the sermon. 'If I have to be here listening to this crap, then so do you.'

I hated the work night out. It happened after every rotation of nightshifts. I think it was designed to help you through that toughest of all weeks by giving you something to look forward to at the end. For me, though, it only added to the sense of dread, but, after John's departure, they became all the more important. I was a confirmed constable, no more handholding. I was tossed into general population. You never really knew who you might be working with on any given day and these drunken, debauched evenings were imperative in maintaining a sense of camaraderie. Alyson had also successfully negotiated her probationary period. For her, this was a triumphant step. Her tutor, Phil, had long since realised she wasn't going to sleep with him and had, from that point, made her life hell.

'I can't believe they put you with him, it's so unfair. Who did you piss off?'

'Shhhh, the walls have ears,' I said.

Alyson was drunk. She was funny when she was drunk, but she was also loud. Alyson had a kind face and gentle demeanour. Once you got to know her, you couldn't help but like her a lot. The first time you met her, however, was a different story. Her physique often intimidated men. Some of the lower lifeforms on the shift didn't know how to take her. At nearly six feet, she cast an imposing shadow.

'Sorry,' she said, lowering her voice. 'It just sucks. We hardly ever get to work together these days.'

'What?'

'I said it's shit we're not getting to work together.'

'I know. But it won't be for ever. Keep this to yourself, but the bosses have Terry on a sort of action plan. If he doesn't improve his figures, they're going to kick him out. I was told to help. So, if I can do that, I can get shot of the useless fucker, and, if I can't, they'll do it.'

'. . . I'm heading up the stairs, sweating like a stepdad at a press conference, and of course the tutor knows fine if she's gonna be lying dead somewhere, it's gonna be upstairs. Naturally he's searching the downstairs . . .'

Terry, immensely incompetent though he was, was a popular member of the shift. One of those brashly confident types who can command a room, he always had an audience when he went into story mode. He had an entire corner of the Glasgow city-centre pub captivated, most of whom must have heard this particular story at least once. Any sensible person would have gone to great lengths to avoid disclosing the fact that you're a cop to a busy Glasgow bar – not Terry.

'How has it been working with him?' asked Alyson.

'Well, luckily, he's still sick half the time. Those are the good days. Otherwise it's a complete nightmare. He's taken it as a personal insult that I've been put with him. So, if at any point I say black, he says white, and any time I suggest doing something proactive, he jumps down my throat. I can't win with him. People like him shouldn't be in the job. If it was up to me, I'd just get rid of him and worry about the tribunal later, but there's protocol. Anyway,' I said with a calming exhale, 'how about you? What's new?'

'Me and Simon split up. Did I tell you?'

'I heard. I'm sorry. Are you OK?'

'I'm fine. It was a mutual decision.'

'Really?'

'I'm choosing to think so.'

'What happened?'

She shrugged and polished off the rest of her pint. 'No one thing. The job didn't help, but I can't blame it entirely. We just sort of liked each other less than we used to. Does that make sense?'

I nodded, finished my drink. I shuffled from our corner, teasing a path to the bar with my elbows and ordered replacements. Even from the extended distance, Terry could be heard in full flow with his homily, his disciples captivated:

'. . . *So, I goes up and start the search. I'm convinced there's gonna be some dead chick on the shitter, but thankfully not . . .*'

'How about you, you guys set a date yet?' yelled Alyson over the clamour of the three-deep bar area.

'No, not yet,' I bellowed back. 'I'm still trying to get my head around being engaged. I think putting actual plans in place would be just too real for me right now.'

'You're not going to be one of those annoying couples who stay engaged for years, are you? I mean you've done the hard bit, the whole getting down on one knee, so just get on with it.'

I laughed and passed over her fresh pint, and we made our way back to our relatively quiet spot.

'Actually, it never really happened like that. I'm a bit annoyed there isn't a cuter story. I should have planned it better, or planned it at all. It was a drunken conversation when Karen and I were on holiday in the summer. It just kinda crept in there, like a hypothetical, which sort of formed into a suggestion and then somehow metamorphosed into a proposal. I remember waking up in the morning with a headache and then a holy-shit moment in the shower when I realised I just got engaged.'

'Just like in a fairy tale. She's so lucky to have you.'

'Yes, I know, I'm quite the catch.'

'. . . *And then I go into the last room, the curtains are drawn, so it's pitch-black, but you can smell someone's in there, you know what I mean? I flick the switch and there she is on the floor naked as the day she was born, except for the massive solid-oak wardrobe covering her top half. God knows how long she's been trapped under there, but she's pissed and shit herself, the way folk do. "Fuck," I says, "what a way to go." She was only forty . . .*'

'Are you sitting your promotion exams this year?' asked Alyson.

'I think so. The inspector's insisting I do and I think he'd be offended if I don't.'

'You should, he wants to fast-track you, doesn't he?'

'I don't know, I'm just trying to concentrate on the here and now.'

'Bullshit,' she said. 'Don't be shy about it. You'd be a great sergeant, and you deserve it. Don't be ashamed of it.'

'We'll see. What about you? You sitting them?'

'Nah, I'm trying to get a placement with CID. I'm concentrating on that.'

'. . . *I want to puke my guts out, but I'm keeping it together as my tutor comes stomping upstairs.*'

The crowd around Terry drew closer as the pub grew busier. Alyson and I slunk back, becoming disjointed from the rabble.

'Have you bought an ill-fitting polyester suit to replace the uniform yet? Or are you waiting until you've been accepted?'

'Shut it. I can't wait to get away from the shift, start doing some proper work. I'm sick of rolling around with drunks on a Saturday night and listening to people whinge ceaselessly about mundane crap, it's driving me nuts.'

'Joking aside, I think you're made for detective work. You'll be great at it.'

'You really think so?'

'Definitely. You're already a sour-faced misanthrope, you just can't teach that.'

'Funnnnnny.'

'. . . *He comes in, cool as you like, takes one look at the poor woman crushed under the wardrobe and says, "Check the fanny on that."*'

'Here it comes,' said Alyson, pausing for the punchline.

'. . . *to which a muffled voice replies, "Never mind the fanny, get this fucking wardrobe off of me."*'

Alyson and I kissed that night. I didn't even feel guilty about it, not really. It was just a thing that happened. We had snuck off when we were confident people were too drunk to notice and headed for the train station. I stopped at an ATM and, when I turned around, she was there. I don't know if she had intended it, and I can't say I had given it any thought. We were just there in that moment alone, and we kissed. Afterward we both burst into laughter. We hugged and I think we both realised it was like kissing a relative. It wasn't going to go anywhere and wasn't likely to happen again; maybe it was like trying a food you already knew you weren't going to like, but you still have to try.

Alyson left the shift a few months later, her obvious potential snapped up by CID and she started her training. We kept in touch though, and it was handy for both of us having someone on either side of the investigation fence to call on when needed.

She was the best friend I had on, or out of, the force. That's why it hurt so much.

CHAPTER EIGHT

Asleep on the Job

'The Mulligan girl? You mean Jenny Mulligan? Yes, of course I know her,' Margaret said.

'Did you know she was missing?' I asked.

Margaret looked at me as if misunderstanding. 'Of course I did. Why? Did you not?' She plucked the second earphone from her head and placed the headset on her keyboard, committing to the chat.

'Not until Sunday.'

Margaret shook her head as if to drive the confusion out. 'How is that possible? No offence or anything, but isn't that something you should probably, definitely know?'

'Yes, my thoughts exactly. There's no trace of her at all on the system.'

'Ah,' she said, comprehension washing over her face. 'The inspector doesn't trust it.'

My turn to shake my head.

'The system, computers and pretty much anything that was invented after the seventies,' she continued, contemptuously.

I pictured the email I received from him shortly after I had accepted the position. It was brief, unpunctuated, and it yelled in block capitals. Every word. Hard to feel WELCOME when being screamed at. I recalled Terry, as well, who carried around a pile of missing persons forms, something that had been gradually done away with over the past couple of years in favour of a computerised system, an advancement that meant greater search possibilities, multiple simultaneous input and cross-border functionality.

'So, someone *is* looking into it?'

'Of course. I think the inspector allocated it to Brian. You can speak to him next time he's up from Oban.'

'I'd like to get a look at the file sooner than that. A missing eighteen-year-old girl? I don't understand why everyone isn't falling over themselves in the investigation,' I said, trying not to sound too accusatory.

'You haven't been in Stratharder very long, so perhaps you haven't really been told.'

'About what?' I asked.

'About the kids here.' She paused, took off her glasses and pressed pause on the video recorder. Two silent faces were locked in passionate argument on the screen. 'It's sort of a tradition, really. There's nothing at all for the young ones in Stratharder, so they tend to get out as soon as they get an opportunity. One or two have been lucky enough to move on to university, a few have joined the forces and some have found jobs here; but quite a few just leave for the city and don't look back. Everyone knows Jenny's in London with her friend. Her dad's a bit of a drinker,' she said, with a sudden lowered voice. 'They don't get on, and that's putting it mildly. It's Kathy I feel sorry for. Did she tell you about Jenny on Sunday, at Mass?'

'You saw?'

'I heard more like,' she laughed. 'You came in like a bull in a china shop. My advice: stick to policing. I think you'd make the worst spy. Is that why you're in today? I wasn't expecting you.'

'Yeah. That and I have this community council meeting later. I'll be up in the canteen if you need me.'

'I'll bring you a tea,' she said, before pressing the button and allowing the on-screen couple to commence silently yelling at one another.

Brian had plenty to say about giving up the missing persons form. Rowan had called from the Oban station to tell me he was point-blank refusing to hand it over, that it was none of my business. When I told her to relay the instruction that he was to either call me or the inspector at his house for clarification, he relented.

Rowan drove it up from Oban and I examined it with meticulous scrutiny. I wanted to find some glaring error, but I was disappointed to find that it was well-managed.

'So?' asked Rowan.

'Everything's as it should be. I don't think there's anything I can add to it.'

'Then what's next?'

I scanned the last updates from Brian and the inspector. Jennifer's Facebook account had been accessed, but there was no activity since she went missing. There were a number of earlier messages between Jennifer and her friend Viv discussing joining her in London, but sadly no addresses or new phone numbers exchanged. It had been confirmed, though, that if messages had since been deleted by either party they could no longer be retrieved. On the day of her disappearance her father found his wallet had been emptied to the tune of two hundred pounds. Jennifer's phone had continued to be checked once per week, but no hits recorded in some time. The last entry was an acknowledgement from the Met that they had received the file and provided a reference number, so the checking of the phone would now be their responsibility. It really was out of our hands.

'Not much. I suppose I could go back round her friends just in case, but there are full statements in here. It's really quite comprehensive.'

Rowan tutted and leant back against the wall of the station. 'He's a lazy bastard, but he's not a bad cop. He knows his stuff all right.'

'It does look like it,' I said begrudgingly. 'What do you mean by "lazy" though?'

'Are you asking me to snitch on my colleagues, Sergeant?'

'No, I didn't mean it like—'

'Relax, I'm just messing with you. You remember that vandalism we went to, the broken fence?'

'Yes, the one you've devoted a bizarre number of man-hours to?'

'Yeah, well I was working with Brian the other day in

Oban and we got a call, the same sort of thing – there's a noise in the middle of the night, caller gets up in the morning and finds the kitchen window cracked, insurance company tells him to call the police so he can make a claim.'

'OK?'

'Only we go and Brian's there for about thirty seconds, hands him an incident number and leaves. I'm like, *Aren't you going to take a note of anything? Do you want me to?* And he's like, *For this? Are you joking? Not a chance.* He calls in and gets Control to change it from a vandalism to an accident; says it must have been a stone flicked up by a passing car during the night.'

'But you don't think that's likely?'

'Not unless it managed to clear the house right in front of it, no.'

'You're right, it's laziness, but it happens. Cops don't want unsolvable misdemeanours in their work baskets. It brings stats down come appraisal time.'

'That's why he changed it?'

'I guess so. If it was left as a vandalism on the system, the bosses would want to see a corresponding crime report, but if you change it and nobody notices, then nobody comes looking.'

'That's sneaky. Clever, I suppose.'

'Don't worry I'm not going after him for a vandalism. I couldn't care less. Speaking of which, you still haven't filed your crime report.'

'I'm still working on it.'

'What could you possibly be working on? Just get it filed and away.'

'Yeah, soon,' she said, swatting the order away with a backhand gesture. 'What are you going to do with this, then?' She snatched the folder from my hand.

'I'll go back over one or two things then hand it back.'

'Are you going to check with the inspector first? Like he said?'

'Of course,' I said with a devious grin. 'I'm a nosy, bored police officer. What else would I do? Are you finishing, then?'

She checked her watch and said with a sigh, 'I've got another hour to go.'

'I won't tell if you don't. Besides, I need to go to this meeting tonight. It's up to you, finish now or come with me to the primary school for the dullest evening of your life.'

She was in her civvy jacket and out of the door in less than two minutes. If it had been a cartoon there would have been a small ring of dust where she had been standing.

I lifted the folder from the desk where Rowan had dropped it. At the very least, I would have to speak to Jennifer's parents, I realised, go back over the information they provided. Not because I thought it would do any good, but because it showed I was trying and that the police had not forgotten. I called the tech-support team in Glasgow and requested a final ping in anticipation of the visit I would have to make, probably the following day. Lynn from the team took the details, explaining she was doing it as a favour. Since the case had been handed over to another force area, they really shouldn't be incurring the cost of the procedure, and said she'd call back with the result. Waiting for her to reply was making me late, but it was a good excuse.

By the time the phone rang I was just beginning to think I was late enough to cancel altogether, but not quite.

'Thanks anyway, Lynn, I appreciate it,' I said, hearing the expected negative response. 'I just wanted something to give to the parents when I tell them that we're handing it over.'

'I understand,' she said. 'These types of cases are never easy.'

'What do you mean?'

'I was looking through the information you sent over. If it's one of these cases where someone just doesn't want to be found, and if she *has* gone off to London, it becomes next to impossible. If she doesn't want to get in contact, there's not much anyone can do. We see a lot of these. And with this being a pay-as-you-go phone it's likely it's already been dumped. I'd be shocked if you get any more pings on it.'

'You're probably right. But I'd just settle for knowing she's safe then leave the family to the politics. Thanks for trying anyway, Lynn.'

Stratharder Primary School was in complete darkness when I arrived. A dense mist had descended off the hill and my bare arms were beaded with increasingly large drops of moisture as I skirted the grounds looking for signs of life. The mist painted a dramatic cone of searching light from my torch and eventually it found an open side gate leading to a back door that was closed but unlocked. I entered and wiped the water from my brow and arms. A faint light shone at the end of the long hall where Halloween-themed pictures adorned the walls; enormous paper and tissue pumpkins grinning menacingly down at me. I checked a mental calendar and realised that yes, we were now just into November. These pictures would now be replaced by ones depicting fireworks and then, incredibly, a matter of weeks until they would lose their place to Christmas.

As I followed the light, I heard animated voices growing louder.

'There he is,' Father McCann sang, wide-armed. A further six faces turned to look at me, not one of them female. The very centre of the gym hall was lit by a single light from above. The rest of the vast room lay largely in darkness. I instantly thought of old cop movies – good cop, bad cop, the light tilted into the eyes of the perp, forcing a confession from him.

I sat in the one empty chair at the far end of the rectangular table. I was going to struggle to remember names, as the six men flanking each side looked strangely alike. Their beards were of differing lengths and hues and their clothes of various, but similar, thick country wear. Each one was entirely interchangeable to my eyes. Any one of them would pass admirably as 'Farmer No. 3' on a cast list.

'So sorry I'm late. Something came up I couldn't avoid. Have I missed much?' I said.

'Not a thing, Sergeant. Now you're here we can get started.' *Started?* I thought. *Damn it.* I had been hoping just to catch the death throes of the thing.

'You don't mind if we dispense with the pomp and ceremony, do you? None of us are particularly interested in that kind of meeting.'

I said I didn't mind at all and Father McCann proceeded to introduce the men around the table. The names and the respective explanation as to how each was related to other members and also persons within the community quickly became an incomprehensible blur. I just hoped I wasn't going to have to refer to any of them by name.

'Do you take water, Sergeant?' Farmer No. 3 asked.

'I'm sorry?'

'In your dram, do you take it with water?' The man held a ceramic jug of water, poised over a very large glass of whisky.

'Oh, thank you, but not for me. I'm not permitted while on duty. But that's kind of you.' The man was dumfounded. He looked around at the other faces all of whom equally befuddled, the jug still poised to pour.

'Do you no' like whisky? I could see about getting you something else.'

'I do like whisky,' I lied, 'but it's against the law for me to drink on duty.'

The men glanced at each other momentarily before exploding into laughter. The man pushed the glass in front of me. 'In that case, boyo, you need put them cuffs on your inspector when you get back. There's no' a meeting he attended he didnae fall oot that door pished as a fart. Remember, you are the law, son, so get it doon ye.'

'Fine, I'll take some water, then.' I wished I had just said I wasn't a fan. Three bottles of single malt, one of which had been well dipped into, sat in the centre of the table, and one other cheap bottle of blend. I felt sorry for whoever had brought that along – his name, whatever it was, would surely be mud.

A sheet of paper was passed down the row of men and my heart sank as I looked at the agenda in front of me. Starting with a prayer and ending on the reverse side were a list of inane agenda items.

I sat back and drained my glass in three long sips, then reached for the bottle and reloaded. It was nice stuff, I conceded, and spun the bottle, taking a mental note of the label. My resolution to stop at two glasses faded as the agenda items grew more and more absurd. There was an objection to the shade of purple the florist had selected for the front of the shop. This, of course, demanded a half-hour debate. Afterwards, there was a heated argument between two members of the council about some convoluted land contract. Something about accessing one field where one Farmer No. 3 had sold a piece of his land to Ogilvie, which meant you had to pass through another piece of land owned by another Farmer No. 3 and, since flats were to be scheduled to be built on the land, it would require services to be piped through said disputed area. Or something like that. I lapsed into a daydream soon after they started talking.

'What's he wanting with flats anyway? Who's going to buy a flat here? Phylida had her hoose up for sale for three years before she got it sold, and even then, it was her brother who bought it. Ogilvie's aff his heed, and so are you if you think I'm letting you churn up my field on a fool's errand.'

And so it went, as did three further glasses of the whisky down my neck. The hall had been cold when I arrived but now was too warm and I could feel myself becoming too comfortable. Once or twice I had to sit myself up with a shake of the head to fend off sleep.

The two men went back and forth over the point, and I had long since lost both track and interest. I quickly became less concerned about unprofessionally nodding off and had settled myself, arms folded, for a quick nap when a thought struck me like a cold slap. The word 'contract' had been said so many times, but it suddenly registered in my mind.

I sat up straight suddenly, trying to tighten my grip on the thought. The men fell silent.

'Everything all right there, Sergeant?' someone asked.

'It was a contract,' I said.

The men looked at one another, wondering who amongst them understood.

'Her phone,' I said, more to myself than any of them. Her mum said she was paying her contract, but the tech lady had said 'pay-as-you-go', hadn't she?

CHAPTER NINE

After the Horse has Bolted

'They're in the inspector's office,' said Margaret. 'Can I bring you some tea?'

'No thanks. What kind of mood is he in?'

'Stressed, so be careful.'

'Roger. Are you still running through the old missing persons forms?'

'Yes, love. Still putting them onto the computer.'

'Have you come across the Vivian Jenkins form?'

'Oh, I don't think so. I could check, but I don't recall coming across it. There's still loads to get through.'

'If you happen to see it could you let me know?'

'Sure thing. While you're here – "His illicit pastimes include"?'

'S-T.'

'Thanks, love.'

* * *

There was a heated conference in the inspector's office. My entrance caused some eyes to deviate momentarily, but it did not halt the conversation. Brian sat guiltily in one corner while the inspector perched on the edge of his desk, arms folded. A woman stood next to Rowan, looking like she wanted to be anywhere but here, her hands tucked into her armour. I guessed this was Claire who, as Rowan had explained, Brian preferred to work with and with whom she suspected there might be a little more going on than on a professional level. Rowan smiled as I closed the door behind me.

'We're just discussing how we proceed with this mess, Sergeant. Is that Jennifer's form?' the inspector asked and reached for the folder I was carrying.

I handed it over. 'There was nothing wrong with Brian's groundwork, from what I could see. I'm confident he collected everything he could.'

'It's like I said, Inspector, this doesn't actually change anything. It was a stupid mistake. I hold my hands up, but it's unlikely that if I'd noted down the right number that it would have made the slightest bit of difference.' Brian spoke with his hands literally held up.

'She's definitely in London if you ask me. Makes no difference.'

'Nobody *did* ask you, Claire. Unless you have something productive to contribute, keep your mouth shut.' The inspector didn't even look at her as he shot her down.

'I just got two of the numbers round the wrong way. It could have happened to anyone.'

'Oh really,' said the inspector, raising his head now. 'Rowan, if you were in the home of someone's parents noting details for a missing person, would it have occurred to you to read back the telephone number they provided to you?' Rowan's face shot an alarming shade of red.

'Well, I . . .'

'It's about what we do now, though, isn't it?' I said as I took the folder back. Part of me couldn't believe I was coming to Brian's rescue, but selfishly it was just unbearable to witness. He would also be reeling from the knowledge that it was me who had figured out he had noted the wrong number. It *was* a simple mistake, but in such cases, it could also be a very costly one. Tech support had been pinging the wrong phone for months. A request had now been placed with Jennifer's phone company, but any useful information from the correct number would probably now be lost.

'Yes, I suppose it is. So, where are we?'

'Well, in one sense Brian is right, we're not necessarily in a different position from where we were. The most likely scenario is the one we've been following anyway. From the interviews in the folder, her friends are convinced she's in London. All evidence supports this, so we just pass over the details to the Met like we had planned to. I've asked Margaret to look out for her friend's form to see if there's anything there we can use, anything that wasn't copied on to the computer system. As we suspected, her actual phone number is non-responsive, no hit at all. Because the previous phone hits were in London, we didn't really push hard for CCTV evidence from bus and rail stations here to confirm. Brian and Claire can get started on that. But that's about it. I could reinterview Jennifer's friends, see if we missed anything?'

'I don't think that's necessary. I sat in on the initial chat; they weren't particularly helpful. But I might give them a ring,' said the inspector.

'What do we tell the parents now? Do we come clean about the mistake?'

'OK . . .' the inspector said, pacing and rubbing at his chin. 'I have some connections with the Met. I'll make sure they expedite anything we send them. When Margaret locates the form, bring it to me. From here on I'm taking over the enquiry. Leave Jack Mulligan to me. I know him well; I'll have a quiet word. Reassure them that everything is being done.'

'See, all in hand. No harm, no foul.' Brian got to his feet and adjusted his radio. 'Shall we?' he said to Claire, moving for the door.

'Where do you think you're going?'

'To get started on the trains and busses . . . like he just said.'

'Claire, you get to work on that, will you? If you have any questions, come straight to me. The rest of you can get back to work. Donald, would you close the door on your way out, thank you.'

We shuffled from the room, all of us trying not to look at Brian, the dead man now sitting again, arms crossed defiantly, awaiting his scalding.

Margaret had located the file I had asked for and I leafed through it. The updates were all completed as I would have myself and there was nothing new. The final entry was the fax confirmation from the Met that she had been traced to Croydon, that she was holding down a steady job at a bookmakers. All this had been copied into Jennifer's form to assist the Met when we passed it down to them.

I took my notebook and copied the details of the officer giving the update – a PC Eric Caruthers 663ZD from Addington police station had spoken to Viv.

I found the police station on Google, dialled the number and was immediately placed on hold, being assured that my call was important and that someone would be with me shortly. In the meantime, I could listen to awful instrumental music.

I sat at one of the desks near Margaret. Rowan was beavering away at a computer terminal and Claire paced uncomfortably like an expectant new father in a hospital waiting room.

'Hello, Addington station, can I help you?'

The cheerful voice of the lady barely registered as Brian entered the room, his face flushed and crestfallen.

'Hello, can I help you?'

I was forced to answer the lady and so missed exactly what was being said. I asked to speak to PC Caruthers and was put on hold again.

Claire was running a consoling hand up and down Brian's arm as they left.

A minute later the inspector likewise departed. I was glad to be on the phone so as to avoid further interaction with him. As the door closed behind him the pressure in the room dropped.

'Sorry, just to confirm it's Eric Caruthers you're looking for?' said a voice, at last. I confirmed it was and she apologised explaining how officers move through offices like a game of musical chairs, and she directed me to central enquiries.

'You're better emailing them. They might need time to find where someone is currently posted Trust me, it's a nightmare,' she explained.

I thanked the lady and hung up.

With nothing else to do I took Jennifer's paperwork to the canteen, or what passed as such. It was little more than a large empty room with a series of mismatched tables pushed together to make a large, uneven one. A fluffy-looking dartboard hung on the far wall surrounded by small holes in the plaster around it, suggesting a general lack of competency of the resident users.

I went through every entry of the missing person form again and thought about any new lines of enquiry. The soft thud on the table made me look up from the file. It was the first I was aware Rowan had entered.

'What's this?' I asked looking at the garish thing in front of me.

'It's for you.'

'What is it?'

'What's it look like?'

'It looks like a cupcake made by a toddler with a ludicrous amount of pink icing on top.'

'And a candle.'

'And a candle,' I agreed.

'Happy birthday, you ungrateful dick. I made that myself.'

I picked the thing up. It was far heavier than any cupcake ought to be. The lit candle began to subside down the molten pink frosting, so I blew it out.

'I believe you. How did you know?'

'I have my ways. You really ought to tighten up the security settings on your Facebook.'

'Ah. I'll go one better and delete it when I get home. Thanks for the cake.'

'You're welcome,' she said, taking a seat opposite me and scooping a fingerful of the frosting. I didn't want to give it to you earlier with everyone around. Sorry it's just the one candle, but I don't think I could have fit all, what? Forty-eight? On there.'

'Thirty-four. I'm surprised your mum let you bake. Did she let you lick the spoon after?'

'Touché!' she garbled through the frosting. 'What are your plans?'

'For my birthday? Oh, big plans, yes. I have a date with a bottle of wine and a giant cupcake.'

'Aww,' said Rowan throwing her arms around my neck and laughing, then instantly drew them back sheepishly as Margaret entered the room.

'Margaret, are you OK?' I asked. She was almost spectral, her pallor disturbingly bleak.

'We just got a call. Or, rather, *I* just got a call, from my friend, Betty. She's a cleaner for Mr Ogilvie. Says they found a body.'

My own face dropped as solemn as Margaret's. I turned to look at Rowan. She was beaming from ear to ear.

CHAPTER TEN

A Little Light Reading

'Take it easy.' I pushed my hand against the dashboard to stop from rolling into Rowan as she took the left out of the car park, wheels screaming.

'What do we do? My mind's gone completely blank.' She crunched between third and fourth gears. I activated the lights but kept the siren off as the traffic in town was minimal.

'Just relax. We won't know anything until we get there. We'll assess it and take it from there – if we get there at all. Slow down.'

My first thought when Margaret delivered the message was Jenny Mulligan. How could it not be? But Margaret's friend had confirmed the body to be an Iain Cooper, a groundsman and odd-job employee of Ogilvie's.

I let loose the siren as we tore through the crossroads, making every pedestrian stop in their tracks and stare.

I wondered if some of them had ever seen the police responding to an emergency in their lives. The van flew down the road towards Ogilvie's, seeming to hover over the bumps and holes, wreaking untold damage to the old vehicle's suspension.

Rowan slowed to thirty for the small stone bridge. My own right foot was close to forcing its way through the floorwell as I pumped an imaginary brake. Once clear, she dropped gear and deftly threw the van round the tight right-hand bend before the staff houses came into view. I cut the lights as Rowan swung the van into the side verge. It wasn't hard to discern our destination. A small crowd had formed at the first cottage. One woman, being consoled by another, waved at us.

'Hat!' I barked as Rowan leapt from the van. She tutted and snatched it from between the seats.

'He's in there,' said the woman who waved. Her hand shook uncontrollably as she pointed at the open door of the cottage. Two men stood in the background looking anxious and a family, complete with two small children, watched with morbid interest from their own doorway a little further up.

'Are you Betty?' I asked the woman.

'That's right.' She dabbed at her face with a tissue.

'We're going to need to speak to you later. Where can we find you?'

'I stay in town. Margaret knows where to find me.'

'Are you OK?' Rowan asked.

She tried to hold herself together, attempted to hold back the emotion. She shook her head as the tears welled and her mouth twisted into a silent sob. The woman with her arm around her pulled her in close.

'OK, let's see what we've got,' I said.

Rowan's enthusiasm left her. She stepped up to the doorway and paused. She glanced through the door and moved aside, prompting me to take the lead.

I was immediately transported to the night with Carly's mother as we stepped into the cottage. The same smell of decay filled my nostrils. Again, the floors were bare. Unlike that night, the low evening sun illuminated the interior.

'Just breathe normally,' I said, looking behind me at Rowan who had the crook of her arm covering her mouth and nose.

The first doorway from the hall was the living room. It contained a once-white leather couch, now beige, and an enormous flatscreen television. A coffee table, complete with a half-smoked joint in an ashtray next to a small bag of weed, amassed the total of the furniture in the room. Nobody there; or no body was there. We moved on to the kitchen, where the smell was almost certainly coming from. Three filled, and badly tied, bin bags lay in one corner with a steady flight pattern of flies circling, waiting for their chance to land and refuel. A pot lay on the stove, containing something brown. It was dotted with the beginnings of spore clusters. Rowan gagged and blew out hard before moving her arm back into place. The images of that night played behind my eyes, seeming to overlap with what I saw in front of me. I knew instinctively he was in the bedroom, just as Carly's mum had been.

The scene that met us, as I pushed open the bedroom door, ended any comparison to that night. As undignified as her demise had been, it was nothing compared to this poor bastard.

'Holy fuck!' said Rowan, my thoughts coming from her mouth. Though perhaps we should have been thinking *Unholy fuck*.

The dead man lying on the bed had a pentacle carved into his massive bared torso. That was my first thought, and all I could focus on for a moment. We stood in the doorway, afraid to go any further. The flies had located a possible new landing site and before long those bin bags would be abandoned for a far tastier meal in this room. They buzzed around the underpants of the man, once presumably white, now less so. The same could be said for the bedsheet directly below.

We stood for what felt like an age taking in the scene. He lay on his back, his right hand bound to a bedpost, the other on his groin. His ankles, too, were tied, all with a soft-looking fabric. He was gagged and blindfolded and there he remained in a surreal pose. Bizarrely, I couldn't escape the thought of how much he looked like he was impersonating Michael Jackson's trademark crotch-grab move. It almost made me laugh out loud.

My focus was so demanded by the dead man it was some time before I realised that what I thought was some kind of hippy art on the wall behind the bed was actually wildlife.

'What the hell *is* that?' Rowan stepped past me as she followed my glare at the thing. She squinted as she tried to establish what the grey fur was or used to be. 'A rabbit, I think. Jesus, it's nailed to the wall. And . . . uh . . . look at this thing.'

At last, I stepped into the room and reluctantly took in the creature which, true enough, had been crucified to the wall by a six-inch nail through the neck. Its tongue stretched from its toothy maw and was itself fixed to the wall by a much smaller nail. Its eyes bulged, as though it had been paused in a cartoon scream. A soft buzz came from somewhere within it.

'Nice,' I said. 'Really ties the room together. Don't touch it.'

'Don't touch it? You couldn't fucking pay me to touch that thing. And what's with this guy? What do you think?'

'I think it's lipstick.'

I approached the bed and confirmed, to my relief, the pentacle had not in fact been carved into the man's chest.

'What is?'

'The pentagram, or whatever you call these things.'

Rowan joined me near the top of the bed.

'Euch, thank God. How do you know it's lipstick and not paint or something?'

I pointed towards the bedside table where a lipstick, worn down to a flat nub, sat beside a pool of black wax. On the opposite side a black candle had guttered out before dissolving like its neighbour. Beside this stood an empty glass and two pill bottles. I walked around and studied the labels. Both were empty and used to contain the same medicine: tramadol. Behind the bed lay a shelf covered in more candles, a mix of black, red and white. All well used. Some strange marks on the wall above the shelf around the rabbit caught my attention. It looked like a clear paste, liberally applied on the white wall. I traced its outline, then something occurred to me. 'Rowan, turn the light out.'

'What? Why? I mean, are you fucking kidding me? You're aware how creepy all this is, right? And you want me to plunge us into darkness?'

'Just for a minute. Put a glove on before you touch the switch.'

The snap of a glove, the flick of the switch, then Rowan's gasp as the massive five-pointed star came to luminous life. It was crudely sketched but impressive in its scale, with the bunny wall art at its centre. Odd markings, too intricate to be accidental, were painted into the five internal triangles created by the overlapping lines of the star.

'What is all this?'

'I have no idea. I'm not really up on my occult practices. But you're not going to like this next bit.'

'What?' she said, menacingly, before flicking the light back on.

'We need to check the body.' I pulled my own latex gloves from the side pocket of my trousers, where two pairs were always stored.

'For what?'

'Life, for one thing.'

'This enormous man could not be more dead,' she said, with a dramatic sweep of her arm across him. 'Look at him, he's white as a ghost on the top, and purple as a . . . purple thing, on the bottom. And if he was breathing that pentacle would be moving.' She was right of course, he was clearly dead, and had been for at least a few days, maybe longer. Post-mortem lividity had set in causing the purple discolouration where the body starts to break down and fluids run internally to the lowest points.

'We still need to check. Can you imagine how embarrassing it would be if he wasn't?'

Rowan huffed and rolled the sleeves of her jacket to the elbows. I dutifully checked his cold wrist and jugular, all box-ticking futility. 'Try not to disturb anything. We're going to roll him towards you so I can see if there are any more holes in him than there should be.'

She lifted his wrist, the one on his crotch, delicately with thumb and forefinger and pulled while I pushed on his shoulder. The body would only roll so far as his tethered left ankle anchored him. His back was a mottled maze of colour. Swirls of lividity, like purple ink dropped into a glass of water covered his skin, but there were no signs of violence.

'OK, move him back.' Rowan simply let go of his arm and I couldn't slow his return roll. Most of his body came to rest immediately but his stomach continued to slosh back and forth between us for a few seconds.

'Do you think it was the tablets?' she asked while peeling the gloves off.

'That's what the scene suggests. There's just something not right about it all,' I said.

Rowan looked at me like I was a moron. 'Something's not right? You mean like the satanic dungeon thing going on here, and the fact that he's trussed up like a turkey? Yeah, something's definitely fishy.'

'Go call it in, smartarse. I'll look around,' I told her. 'Tell them to alert CID, SOCO and a doctor, and you better let the inspector know.'

I was alone with the body. From where I stood, he looked blindly at me with slightly cocked eyes that seemed to challenge me. I fished my phone from my pocket and took some shots. Through his gag, his mouth was pulled into a smile for the camera. I moved away from him, half expecting the edges of reality to begin blurring, it was almost too surreal.

At the far side of the room was a closet, the door of which sat slightly ajar. It was half filled with clothes hung along a rail to one side while on the other was a bookshelf of black wood. The top shelf displayed creepy bric-a-brac. More candles flanked a skull, a cheap resin replica of one. The books on the shelf didn't seem to be in any particular order and were a mix of occult fact and fiction, as well as what looked like some erotica. I took a few more pictures of everything in situ before examining the books more closely. Few of the volumes I recognised, but one or two rang bells. *The Story of O* was one I remembered from my childhood. One of the kids in my class had stolen a copy from his older brother who had left it behind when he went off to uni. Four or five of us thirteen-year-olds pored over it behind the gym hall and found it entirely, and disappointingly, too wordy to be titillating. You didn't have to be a scholar of the occult to know the general themes of some of the books – *The Satanic Bible*, *The Necronomicon* and *The Golden Dawn*, were just a few of the works making up the black magic side of things, while *Demons of the Flesh* and other well-fingered books on sex magic and bondage made up the others.

Taking pride of place in the centre of the top shelf was a name I did recall – Aleister Crowley. *The Book of the Law* and *The Book of Lies* sat alone, propped up by black candles on each side. I took *The Book of the Law* off the shelf with a gloved hand and tentatively opened the hardback.

I'm not sure what I was expecting as I swung the front cover over with a creak of its spine. Rather like *The Story of O* I was left underwhelmed. Mostly gibberish with the odd evocative symbol thrown in, no screaming demons leaping from the pages. The one dark secret the pages did give up fell at my feet as I thumbed to the centre. I replaced the book and reached for the released Polaroids instead. I had to return to poor Mr Cooper to confirm the man in the pictures was him. The version on the bed was heavier and balder than the one receiving sexual favours in the pictures, but it was him all right.

'Wow,' said Rowan, returning and peering over my shoulder. 'I would say how does a man like that ever find a woman willing to do these things to him? But look at the size of that thing, phew, I do declare.' She fanned at her face with her notebook. There were six pictures, any one of them on their own may have looked suspiciously like the sick games of a kidnapper and molester but together they showed the sex games of the old departed Iain, either tied up or servicing one of three ladies in the same position.

'Prostitutes, most likely,' I mused. 'Kinky stuff.'

'Not really,' said Rowan taking the pictures from me for a better look. 'This stuff is run of the mill these days. Tied up and spanked is the new missionary.'

I looked at her with raised brows; she returned my look, shrugged and went back to her inspection of the snaps.

'The inspector's finished for the day, but they've alerted senior officers in Oban. They're going to call you on your radio. A doctor is on the way.'

'What about a crime scene manager?'

'I asked, said they'd call you about that, too. Brian and Claire are on their way up.'

Control refused to call the inspector at his house, telling me it was not protocol, as doing so would effectively put him back on duty. I took his number from Rowan and called. I had been in Stratharder long enough to know he would hear about this quickly, if he hadn't already. I figured if I didn't call him, he'd hang it over me. After an initial taciturn and confused response, he softened and seemed genuinely grateful for the heads-up.

Brian and Claire arrived quickly. They barely looked at me as they entered. I hadn't yet properly met Claire, but she didn't seem at all interested in proper introductions.

'What's the deal? Gave himself a heart attack having a creepy wank?' said Brian, taking in the scene.

'Worse ways to go,' said Claire, chuckling and taking a set of gloves from Rowan.

'If you find me like this, Claire, do me a favour and throw me in front of a train before you call my wife, won't you?'

'After I put the video on YouTube, I will.'

'Listen, guys,' I said, 'we're treating this as a crime scene until we know better, so I need you both gloved up. Establish a common approach and get everything in your notebooks until the photographer arrives.'

Brian muttered something under his breath.

'What was that?'

'Huh?' he said, as if he wasn't sure what I was referring to.

'Spit it out, Brian.'

'Fine. I said "duh". As in duh, I think we know how to do rudimentary crime scene management.' Claire chuckled into the back of her hand. Brian smiled at her and continued. 'Seriously, I was pounding a beat while your mum was still wiping your nose. We've got this.'

'Like you got Jennifer Mulligan's number noted down? Is that how you "got it"?' His face flashed crimson and he was about to retort.

'Fine,' I said, cutting his reply dead. 'I'm going to speak to the neighbours.'

'Need a hand?' Rowan looked eager to come with me, but it was probably more a desire to be away from the other two.

'No, it's fine. You stay and help. Give me call if anything turns up.'

As I left the cottage, I saw them appearing en masse. From the elevated position I watched the ambulance, like a mother duck, lead a line of smaller vehicles up the long road from the town. They approached agonisingly slowly, the ambulance evidently struggling with its dimensions on the small bridge.

I got no reply from at least half of the cottages, albeit they looked uninhabited. The ones who did answer were either nervous and reticent, or forthcoming but useless. Iain Cooper, the cross-referenced reports confirmed, was a divorced loner. The various reports didn't always match, however. He was described as a 'quiet, unassuming man' by one neighbour, and a 'fucking weirdo' by another. When pushed to elaborate on 'weirdo' the response was inconclusive. Coming and going at strange hours, visitors in the middle of the night, but no descriptions of people or vehicles, and no confirmation of dates and times. A co-worker in one of the cottages told me he was clearly an alcoholic. When he did turn up for work, he was often still drunk or too hungover to be of any real use in the grounds – 'No idea why Mr Ogilvie puts up with him.'

The last confirmed sighting had been eight days previously, which did little to establish a time of death. Apparently, if in the middle of a binge, he could easily fall off the radar for a week at a time.

I stepped away from the last interview into the early evening. The light was fading but a glorious orange-purple pastel clung to the horizon. The low clouds skirting the mountains were underlit by breathtaking amber and highlighted the winter's first frosting on the peaks. That white line would, over the next few months, charge down the sides of the crags and glens to devour the colours of the world.

When I returned to Cooper's cottage the inspector was waiting for me, dressed in a retro-style tracksuit that was either strangely fashionable, or he had simply owned it since 1976 and coincidentally it had at last come back in.

'What do you think?' he asked. He stood, arms folded, leaning against the door of his car.

'Have you seen?'

He nodded grimly.

'Did you know him?'

'Iain? Yes, but then it's Stratharder, how could I not?'

'What's his story?' I asked.

'There's not much to tell. Kept himself to himself – you know the sort. His wife died a long time ago, drank herself into the grave in her early forties. He has a daughter, but she left after her mother died. Since then, he would show up now and again in town, but appearances were few and far between. Whatever dark and deviant secrets he had, he kept. That's the first I've seen him in months. What are your thoughts?'

'We won't know anything for certain until the autopsy report comes back,' I said. 'Might be that it was a simple overdose, getting his mix of pills and booze wrong while he was getting busy. And when he dropped into a shallow coma, whoever was with him panicked and ran. The Polaroids add some credence to that. Although . . .'

'What? What are you thinking?'

'It's all the black magic shit. I mean the photos are just your run-of-the-mill bondage stuff, no glimpse of even a candle, never mind the symbols. I just don't know; it doesn't feel right. If it's all part of the fetish, why does it not feature in the DIY porn?'

The inspector didn't hazard a response at my rhetorical question, he just watched me. I realised after a moment I was waiting for his direction, and I had to remind myself that he was not on duty, that this was my scene until someone told me otherwise.

It was then I noticed Brian standing just inside the doorway examining the pill bottles from Cooper's bedroom.

'Excuse me a moment, Inspector,' I said.

I walked determinedly past him and stormed into the cottage. Brian jumped and fumbled the bottles as he saw me. He picked them from the floor.

'Please tell me you're not handling those without gloves on,' I whisper-shouted through clenched teeth.

'These?' he said incredulously holding the bottles up and twisting them.

'Yes, them, the pill bottles, the fucking evidence. And what the fuck is this?' I plucked the line of police tape like a guitar string. It had been strung at head height along the door frame.

'You said you wanted the scene secured.'

'The scene, yes.' My fingertips went instinctively to my temples. '"We've got this", you said. Are you a moron?' My temper cracked.

'Who do you think you're talking—?'

'Take this fucking tape down, take it outside and put a proper cordon up.' I lowered my voice again as the photographer passed us merrily snapping away.

'Should I call the SWAT team too? The helicopters and the army? Maybe throw up some roadblocks? How about a criminal psychologist or a press conference?' This he said more to the inspector than to me, a wry smile attached to his smug face and no attempt to hide his words from the photographer, who was trying hard to pretend he wasn't listening. Rowan shook her head, her lips a thin line.

'How about you apply a little professionalism, instead of fucking up my scene with your childish incompetence?

If you can't do that just get the fuck out, go back to the station, take the rest of the day off and then hand in your equipment and don't ever come back.'

He shot a dismissive glance at the inspector, waiting for him to intervene.

'Don't look at him. I gave you an order; follow it or fuck off. Either way, do it now. And if you think I'm joking just keep testing me and see what happens.' My hands were balled into fists. I'm not sure why I reacted as I did, I guess there must have been some sense of accumulated frustration. I'd had it with being undermined.

'This is bullshit,' he spat. 'Any idiot been in the job more than fortnight can see it's nothing more than . . . either a suicide, or some sex game gone wrong. This is a waste of my time and total misuse of force resources. Piss poor management, if you ask me.'

A tirade was forming in my mouth when the photographer cut in.

'Erm, you might want to have a look at this.'

I pushed past Brian who partially blocked my path through to the bedroom.

I followed the photographer over to the body; the rest crowded around behind me. He reached down and took the ankles of the corpse and hoisted them into the air and showed me his feet. At first I couldn't see what I was being shown. I gave the photographer a puzzled shake of the head.

'The heels,' he said. 'Look, they're both scraped.'

'So?' said Brian from the door.

'So, it looks like he's been dragged,' I said.

The inspector slid through the crowd at the door to see for himself. 'Brian,' he said. 'Get that fucking cordon pushed back.'

It was just after three in the morning when I spotted headlights on the bottom road, slowly winding their way up towards me. With no spare resources available, I had volunteered to stay until a crime scene manager from the city could make an assessment.

'DS Aitken?' I said and extended my hand. The man took it with his right and shielded his mouth with his left as a yawn erupted over his face.

'I'm sorry,' he said. 'I think I could be in this job for a hundred years and I'll never get used to nightshifts. You'll be Don Colyear, then?' I nodded and released the handshake. 'OK. Walk me through this?'

'Uh, sure,' I said, a little surprised. I had assumed I would be standing outside while he did the detective thing. Aitken, tall, thin and with an air of authority about him reached into a pocket in his suit coat and produced shoe protectors and gloves, passing me a set of each. I led the way with my torch into the cottage. There was a series of 'uh-huhs' from him as we passed through the less pertinent rooms and I passed on our observations. A smile curled my mouth as I saw him recoil a little when I switched on the bedroom light. It made me feel better and less like a subordinate to this fellow sergeant. I talked him though our findings and movements as we entered.

'Gimme a hand with this?' he said as he pushed at the body of Cooper.

'This', I thought, as he pushed at the dead man's bulk as I pulled. There's the detached experience I was expecting. How many of these scenes had DS Aitken visited? He worked quickly and methodically around the body and the room, noting the details on the pill bottles and scratching what looked like a layout of the room into a notebook. He finally slowed when he reached Cooper's feet. He brought out a small torch of his own and held each massive leg in the air while he scrutinised each heel and their scratches. 'You're from the city too, right?'

'That's right. You're wondering how I ended up way out here?'

'No, not really. I heard about what happened. It makes sense.' *Dammit*, I thought. I was just beginning to enjoy working with this man. I was about to attempt some kind of justification, or vindication more like, when he said something unexpected. 'From what I heard you got a pretty raw deal.' He didn't look up as he switched from the left foot to the right. 'I thought all that boys' club shit died in the eighties. Listen, any day now some chief inspector will get caught balls deep in a twenty-year-old probationer, or a DI will get rumbled selling confiscated drugs and you'll be yesterday's news. A few months up here might not be a bad thing. Where are the photographs I heard about?'

'Through here, in the wardrobe.' I had stored the Polaroids individually, making each clear to view in the transparent, sealed evidence bags. I left them near the book they had fallen from, in case the context was important.

'I heard there was some personal repercussions after the tribunal? At least that's how the rumour goes,' he said.

He scanned each picture and placed them back on the bookshelf as he did.

'Something like that. Nothing officially noted of course. It is what it is. I just want to work.'

'Fair enough,' he said and laid the last picture down. 'Is there anything else I should know about?'

'Like I say, it's in the past I just want to put it—'

'About this scene.'

'Oh, sorry. No, I think that about covers it.'

'OK,' he said with a heavy breath. He snapped off his gloves and placed his hands on his hips as he looked the room over one last time. 'Tell you what. If you're serious about wanting to work, I could do with some help tidying this one away. I'll be honest with you, there's nothing here that really interests me. We'll wait and see what the toxicology report says, but I think this one will end up being one for you, not me. So, if you're OK with it, I'll let you work the follow-ups. I'm thinking an interview with his doctor once the report comes back and seeing if we can find any of these working girls in the pics; we might get lucky with the prints SOCO picked up. The heels in and of themselves don't worry me too much. If this is a murder, it's ridiculously subtle and extravagant at the same time. It doesn't go together. I'm thinking it's a sex game gone wrong, or even a plain old heart attack and then the paid company for the evening gets herself gone quick smart. What do you think?'

The question again surprised me. I realised how much I didn't feel remotely on a par with this man, despite equal ranking. 'Sure, yeah. I mean that makes sense, it's just . . . I don't know.'

'Weird as fuck, yeah I know. Thing to remember, when you look at a scene like this, is stick to the facts. Forget any gore, decoration or bullshit and look at what you have in a black and white way. If you do that here, you have very little. I mean, who forcibly binds a person to a bed with silk and in neat bows to secure the knot? No ligature marks, no bruises, no apparent attempt to remove him from his compromising position. I'm not worried here. I'll stay in touch, Don, but it's all yours.'

CHAPTER ELEVEN

Little Rascals

Shit!

Well, that hasn't helped, has it? In fact, if anything, it's made matters worse.

I used to lock up this little toerag called Jamie, a serial absconder from a residential school for wayward children. He was capable of being a nice kid, if you got him alone without anyone to impress, but most of the time, a little shit. Not his fault. Product of a broken home, bad habits learnt from institutional care and the lack of stability and positive role models, but yes, a spectacular little turd of a boy.

He simply refused to be shut up all weekend at the home and no measure of vigilance could prevent it. They have yet to build the prison that could hold Jamie Jardine.

We formed a sort of professional understanding with the home; they would pretend to be concerned about Jamie's well-being when they reported him missing, as they were legally obliged to, and we would pretend to look for him, as was our duty. And come the wee hours of Monday morning, when he would return drunk, stoned and sated, they would give us a call and we would put the form back in the drawer until the next weekend. However, when you did cross paths with Jamie in the course of other duties, you had to lock him up and take him back, a liability thing. He'd seldom go quietly, and it was rarely for longer than about an hour before he would shin a drainpipe or finger a staff member's swipe card and the merry dance would begin again.

After one incident, where Jamie somehow managed to free himself from the back of a cell van, leaping from the rear when it had slowed at a roundabout, it was decreed from above that he would be cuffed whenever you got hands on him. That worked the first time, because he hadn't seen it coming, but then he started carrying a cuff key he had somehow managed to acquire. It took a while, and the help of the magic metal-detecting wand at the police station, to work out how he was slipping them off in the back of the cage. But once discovered the decree evolved to handcuffing to the rear, and a more thorough search. The cuffs stayed on for a while, but he soon figured that out too. One evening, when the cage door was swung open, there he sat, dangling the cuffs out like a hypnotist with pocket watch, a ta-dah! smile on his face. I saw how he did it one night when I had him in a car rather than the van. We had been called to a noisy party and there he was in the kitchen trying to charm a girl twice his height. You had to admire the balls on the kid. I think me marching him out in handcuffs might have *sealed the deal for him; at least I like to think it did. He only swore and fought until nobody could hear him any more, then he went back to his normal cheerful self. He sat on the back seat and I watched in the mirror as he pushed one leg behind him, using the seat to punch his toes up, before hooking the centre of the cuffs over, and from there the second foot was folded onto his lap, Aladdin-style, before slipping that through too –* ta dah!

Little shit.

The technique is sound, but I'm now appreciating the additional need for the elasticity of youth. I got one leg through, rather less gracefully than Jamie, but there is just no way I can bend enough to free the other. So now I'm stuck, bent over, one leg either side of the cuffs, like a basketball player paused midway in a through-the-legs dribble.

I take my shoe off and try again, sitting back in the fluffy dirt all around me. I squeeze my leg into my lap and try to make it crawl – toes, heel, toes, heel, towards the cuffs and it's almost there when cramp erupts in my hamstring. Excruciating, adrenalin-inducing cramp that has me kicking out like a mule.

After a few minutes it seems to pass. I'm breathing heavily, my head on the floor amongst this fluff, which is actually quite comfortable, but then everything is comfortable after cramp.

How long do I have before she comes back? Will she come back? Who is she working with? Will they come for me?

This is fucking hopeless.

I am in the dark, literally and figuratively. When did it start, exactly? What did I miss?

I'm not sure it started with Iain Cooper, but that is when things started to change, though not entirely for the worse. For whatever reason the inspector had softened towards me, a little, from that day.

'Mr Ogilvie, nice to see you again,' I said, closing the office door behind me.

'Sergeant Colyear,' he said, getting to his feet and shaking my hand enthusiastically. 'We were just talking about you. Stewart was singing your praises.'

'He was?'

'I was simply saying that you have good instincts, that's all. That I agreed with your assessment, or at least agreed with your scepticism.' The inspector released the clip-on tie from his neck, before neatly folding it and placing it carefully in the top drawer of his desk.

'You really think there was more to it?' Ogilvie asked me. I hesitated, before looking to the inspector for guidance.

'You can speak frankly, Donald. It's Ogilvie's property after all, and it won't go further than this room. Ogilvie has popped in for an update, and you're in a better position than I to give it. So please.'

With reservation I addressed him. 'I'm keeping an open mind, Mr Ogilvie,' I said, trying to pick my words. 'I'm afraid that's all I can really tell you right now.' I couldn't help but frown at the inspector. I was a little nonplussed by his candour.

'Donald wasn't fully in agreement with the assessment of the CID. While they're not ruling anything out either, they're certainly not concerned that Mr Cooper's demise was anything too sinister, despite the scene itself.'

'What happens next?' asked Ogilvie. He was dressed, this time, in a sharp suit. He turned his chair towards me and sat again. 'What can I do to help?'

'Well, we're waiting for the forensic results to come back. There's some follow up and DS Aitken has agreed to let me get on with that. If it's all right with you I'd like to keep the cottage sealed.'

'Whatever you need.'

'How long until we see the lab results?' asked the inspector.

'A few days.'

'If I'm not here, will you call me? You have the house number, don't you?' It wasn't so much a question as an order. He removed the epaulettes from his shoulders and placed them with his tie in the drawer.

'Of course, Inspector, as soon as I hear anything. There's also some follow-up with the Mulligan girl I'd like to oversee. I never expected to be so busy up here.'

The inspector stopped in the doorway. He was trying to make sense of a clamour from downstairs I was just hearing now myself. 'Leave that with me, Donald. Like I mentioned I have links with the Met. That's all in hand. You can concentrate on helping CID making sense of this Cooper situation. What is going on down there?'

Fierce arguing could be heard before we reached the bottom of the stairs.

'Sergeant, you are still attending my little shindig at the weekend?'

'Actually, I'd forgotten all about it, Mr Ogilvie.'

'I do hope you will, I'm getting a little anxious about numbers. I promise you'll have a good time; and be sure to bring your charming colleague, won't you?'

'You should go. It would be a good opportunity to network, and after the Cooper business, people will want to see the police for a little reassurance.'

'I suppose it wouldn't hurt to make an appearance,' I said, but we were both beginning to drift off. The voices coming from the front office were becoming difficult to talk over. We almost collided with Margaret as she jogged through the door.

'Oh, good, I was just coming to get you,' she said. 'You better get in here.'

'The natives are revolting, Stewart,' said Ogilvie, finding some amusement. 'I'll meet you outside. Looking forward to seeing you Saturday, Sergeant.' He slipped through the small crowd.

'What on earth is going on here?' the inspector boomed and the commotion at the front desk ceased instantly. Four embarrassed-looking children, one sporting a well-blooded nose, stood in front of their respective mothers, all of whom were red-faced and furious. There was a moment's silence then they all made to speak at once. Their voices rose incrementally, to be heard over the others before the inspector bellowed again.

'One at a time, ladies, please. Let's start with you.' He pointed at the boy with the red tissue mashed into his face. His mother leant down and tilted his head up to display his injuries more clearly.

'Look,' she said, shaking the boy's chin. 'Look what

that little brute did to my Charlie. His nose is broken.'

'It's not broken, don't be ridiculous,' spat Mhairi, her own boy tucked sheepishly under her arm. 'Besides, your boys started it, Connor just finished it.'

A venomous cacophony of complaint and accusation erupted.

'Right!' the inspector yelled in a throaty schoolmaster voice. The noise ceased once more. 'Sergeant Colyear here will note the incident, ladies, but he will do so only when you are calm enough to take a statement from, so I suggest you compose yourselves or you will be here all night.

'Good luck, Sergeant,' he said in a whisper then left. The second the door swung shut and behind him the debate resumed with fresh malice, pointed fingers and even a bit of a push from Mhairi.

'You see that? That's assault. I want her and her brat arrested.'

'Who're you calling a brat, you old cow? I'm glad Connor popped your boy. And watch your mouth or you'll get the same from me.'

'. . . and threats, Sergeant. I want that little slut locked up.' The woman was backing up in case Mhairi did take a swing, and it was looking likely.

'Who you calling slut, you frumpy old cunt?' There was a collective gasp from the other mothers.

'OK, OK, Mhairi, I mean . . . miss, perhaps this will be resolved more quickly if you come inside. Why don't we have the other ladies take a seat in the waiting area, please. Where is this incident supposed to have occurred?'

'Video store,' all four of the women said as one.

'All right, Margaret, where's Rowan?'

'She's out doing door-to-door for that vandalism a while back.'

'All right, could you maybe organise tea for these ladies out in the public area and I'll have a word with Mhairi in here?'

I opened the door for Mhairi. She gave me an apologetic smile. Connor bore a look of abject mortification. One of the mothers was still muttering about having Mhairi arrested as Margaret did her best to placate them.

I sat Mhairi and her son down in the canteen. 'So, what's all this about, Connor?' I asked.

'The three of them just laid into him in the video store.'

'Mhairi, please, let him talk. I want to hear it from him.'

She folded her arms and heaved a frustrated sigh. 'Sorry, I'm just fed up with this.'

'Connor, did you hit that boy?' He looked up at me and then back to the floor, giving a short nod.

'What happened?'

'Tell him, Con—'

I held my hand up, urging Mhairi to allow the boy to speak, then I gave Connor time to gather his thoughts.

'They were slagging Mum. I got angry,' he said at last.

'How did it start?'

'Well, I was looking at video games after school and they came in.'

'You know them from school?'

'Yeah, they're in Year Six. I'm in Five, but I know them. They came in and looked at the games too. One of them, Duncan, sort of shouldered me, but I ignored them and moved round the other side, but they followed me and started saying this stuff about Mum and I moved round again, but they kept going round and saying stuff and so I says "Shut up" and they were like "Or what" and I tried to ignore them but then that guy blocks me so I can't move round any more and pushed me and the other two come up behind so . . .'

'So, you hit him?' He nodded and looked like he might cry. 'Then what happened?'

'Well, one of the others came up like he was going to hit me, and he tried but he missed so I smacked him too, but I hit him harder than I meant to – he's the one with the nose. The last one sort of pulled them away after that.'

'Did any of the staff see it?'

'There wasn't anyone there. I think the girl that works there was having a cigarette or something.'

I took my phone from my pocket and typed out a text to Rowan.

'Is that definitely how it happened, Connor?' I said. 'Because I really need to know.'

'It was, I swear.'

'Is he in trouble, Sergeant?'

'It's Don, Mhairi, and no, he's not in any trouble, not if I can help it. But do me a favour and let me deal with it. Try not to get involved,' I said, standing and closing my notebook over.

'I'm sorry, they just wind me up,' she said, rubbing her temples. She turned to her son with a smile. 'You hear that, Connor? Don's going to sort it out, so stop worrying, and I'm sorry you saw me losing my temper. Bad old Mum, right?'

Connor laughed. My phone chirped and I looked at the text back from Rowan:

Eh, what the fuck for???

Just do it, and be quick, I returned.

The three women were huddled conspiratorially in the waiting area and I wondered what toil and trouble they were brewing.

'Sorry to keep you. I'd like to get your boys' version of events if I may.' Two of the women made to speak at the same time; one shot another an angry glare as if they'd just discussed this very point.

'Sorry, Audrey, you go ahead.'

'Yes, well, the boys were in the video store Sergeant—'

'I'm sorry to interrupt, but it's the boys' version I'm looking for, not yours. I need you to be here while I speak to them as they're under sixteen. I also need to take a statement from each of them, out of earshot of the other two.'

'Well, I don't see why that's important, it's quite clear what happened. Look at his face, for God's sake.'

'I understand. However, this is how it's done. If you want to make an official complaint, I need to speak to them one at a time. So, who's first?'

Just then, Rowan came through the front door. She stopped when she saw the room full of people, probably more than had been in the station at one time in years. She shot me a confused look. I raised my head by way of enquiry, and she gave a subtle shake of her own and walked through into the station.

'How about you?' I said. 'Charlie, is it?'

The blooded boy nodded.

'Do you still need that hanky? Can I take a look?'

He lifted the tissue. The blood was dark and crusted, nothing fresh. Both of his eyes were beginning to darken nearest his nose.

'How does it feel?'

He shrugged dismissively.

'He's in a lot of pain, officer. He can't breathe properly.'

'How is it now with that tissue off your face? Breathe better?' The boy nodded. 'Good lad.'

Rowan returned holding the evidence bag in her hand.

'Ah, I don't know if you know Constable Forbes, but she's going to help me take statements from you all. Did you get it?' I asked.

'Sure did,' she said, sounding unsure.

I ostentatiously took the sealed evidence bag from her. All eyes were fixed on it.

'Thanks, this'll clear things up.' I popped the bag under my chair. 'Right, Charlie and Charlie's mum, do you want to come with me, please? Rowan, you can take either of the other two and note some details from them.'

'What's that?' asked Charlie's mum.

'This?' I lifted the evidence bag. I smeared the clear plastic flat to let her see the contents. 'It's a video tape, from the store. Not one you rent of course. It's the CCTV footage from this afternoon. I asked Rowan to collect it while I was speaking to the other boy.'

'From inside the store?'

'Yes, so we can see who's doing what to whom, and what sequence it all occurred. Is that right, Rowan? It's all there?'

156

'Eh, yes. All there.'

'Good. You see I wasn't at the video store, and neither were your parents. This helps make things that bit clearer.'

The boys' eyes went collectively wide; they began looking around at one another.

'I'm perfectly happy to note a complaint, but you have to realise that if it's discovered that a malicious accusation has been made, or that events have been embellished or made up, then I have to pursue a countercharge of wasting police time. Again, it's just how it works. OK, ready, Charlie?'

Charlie took his mother's hand and didn't move. She eventually leant down and exchanged a few whispers with him. An awkward pause settled.

'Are you all right there, Charlie?' I said. 'You're looking a little unwell, mister.'

'He's uh, yes, not feeling great. Very stressful all this,' said his mother.

'Listen, why don't we leave this until tomorrow? Maybe the boys have been through enough for today. Why don't we let them get their dinner and sleep on it? We'll be here tomorrow morning if you want to bring them by and we can get the statements noted then?'

'Maybe that would be best,' said Charlie's mum. 'So, we'll . . . just come back tomorrow then?' she said as Charlie was pulling her towards the door.

'Sure, no problem.'

I locked the door behind them as they left and spun the 'Open for enquiries' sign to the 'Closed' side.

'Don't worry, they won't be back. That'll be the last you hear of it,' I said to Mhairi in the office.

'That's a relief,' she said. 'Good thing they had CCTV in the store.'

I drew the tape out of the bag. 'Actually, they don't,' I said spinning the tape round to let her see the 'Margaret's Soaps' label. 'I had Rowan check, but this worked just as well.'

A high-pitched laugh burst from Mhairi. She placed a hand on my shoulder as she doubled over. Rowan rolled her eyes.

'You're a devious bastard, Don,' said Mhairi, once she'd composed herself and slapped me gently on the chest. 'Woops, don't mind Mummy's language, monkey.' She covered her boy's ears and kissed him on the head.

'Do me a favour in future, Connor,' I said, kneeling and prising Mhairi's hands from his head. 'If that happens again count to ten. Try not to lose your temper, OK?'

'OK.'

'Listen, seriously though, I owe you big time. Those bitch—' Mhairi covered Connor's ears again. 'Those bitches have it in for us. I can't tell you how relieved I am to have someone in this town who's not got a bloody vendetta. So, um, I'd really like to say thank you.'

'It's really not necessary, It's our job and we're happy to—'

'I know, but still. It means a lot. How about, um . . .' Mhairi's eyes flicked self-consciously between Rowan and me. 'Maybe dinner? This Saturday? And I'm not taking no for an answer.'

'Actually, we have this thing . . .' I pointed a thumb at Rowan.

'Oh my God, I'm such an idiot. I'm so sorry. Rowan, is it? I didn't realise you guys were . . . a thing or whatever. Such a bloody idiot.'

'Oh no, he's all yours. He's talking about a work thing we need to go to on Saturday.'

'Yeah, some event at the Ogilvie estate. I promised we'd show up.'

'Then I really am an idiot,' said Mhairi. Her face was flashing a similar red to her long hair. 'OK, well I'm busy the week after that, so, shall we say' – she paused while she flicked through her phone – 'the seventh of December? I promise not to be such an eejit.' She searched around and took a piece of paper from Margaret's desk and scribbled her number and address on it.

I didn't know what to say. I felt I couldn't refuse, not in front of her son anyway, and I really just needed her to be gone as the whole thing had become a bit painful. Then words just spilled out of my mouth as if thrown up though my throat by someone else. 'It's a date,' I said.

CHAPTER TWELVE

Domestic

I remove my sock and finally manage to tuck my leg through the bar of the handcuffs. Both hands now in front. From this angle I can let my arms drop properly and get some fresh blood into my numb fingers. I need to figure out what this place is, then I can set about finding a way out. Once the feeling in my fingers returns, I will explore some more. For now, take it easy, Don. You're cold and you have a nasty wound to the head, but nothing to be immediately concerned about. With a bit of luck, we'll find a door and take it one step at a time. A bit of luck, I think and something resembling a laugh escapes my throat and echoes around this place. I haven't had much of that for some time now.

The incident that set all this in motion was as much about bad luck as anything else, I can see that now.

Wrong place, wrong time, although you can't discount the wrong person factor. The irony was that Terry had been doing better; I was even despising him less. He talked passionately about his family, his two wee boys who were destined to play for Celtic. Even at six and eight it was clear they were just that talented, he'd tell me. I learnt that he was capable of talking about something other than himself and people that had crossed him.

Terry had been improving steadily, or at least his figures had increased sufficiently. It meant that in a few short weeks I would no longer have to babysit him and I would be back on the shift rotation, something I was looking forward to like Christmas. Isn't that always the way when tragedy strikes? *Such a shame, he was only a few days from his birthday. Did you hear what happened? He was retiring next month, did you know?*

Late shifts with Terry were the most difficult. On earlies he was happy to follow my lead, too tired to complain. Nightshifts he slept until I found some work to do, but lates were the only time he put any real effort in, and this was to find ways of avoiding work. He was a master of the art. He could stretch a routine call, that might take another officer five minutes, into a two-hour epic, ensuring he was tied up while the pubs and clubs were emptying. You couldn't help but be a little impressed.

I was more or less comfortable with the routine. It felt a little dirty to be complicit in such things, but a working relationship is built on compromise. *What the hell*, I thought, *it's not for ever.*

This particular shift, I had dragged him all over town, taking statements on a bogus workman case and, in fairness to Terry, he hadn't complained. So, I was prepared to allow him to duck and cover in the last hour, as he liked to do. But the thing about this night was that we were still well short of the last hour when the call came, nearly two hours in fact. Sometimes calls are assigned, but often they're thrown out there – who's closest?

'Unit to respond to a possible domestic situation. Concerned neighbour, sounds of a disturbance. Any unit in the Springwood area to respond?'

My stomach pitched. I doubled over in the passenger seat, but I reached for my radio instinctively, my guts screaming at me that something was wrong, beyond wrong.

'Don't you fucking dare.'

'What?'

'Get your finger off that button.'

Terry, driving, put his foot down. We had been in Springwood just a few minutes before, now he was racing from the area. His voice was earnest, he really was warning me. The wipers were turned to full tilt, but the rain lashing the screen had Terry leaning over the wheel and squinting at the road ahead of him. Headlights on the oncoming side were white starbursts in the early evening gloom.

'What are you talking about? We're right here,' I said.

'I'm talking about not getting stuck with a domestic five minutes before we're due to head in. The nightshift will be on soon; they can deal with it. Besides it's probably nothing, noisy party or something.'

I clutched the door handle as my stomach cramped hard.

'Terry, it's hardly five minutes. We need to go to this; it might be serious. Nobody else is responding.'

'Not a chance.'

We slipped through a blatant red light, but then got stuck behind traffic shortly after. Sweat soaked the back of my neck.

'Further call for domestic situation in Springwood. Unit to attend, please.'

'Terry, for fuck's sake, it's clearly genuine. We need to go to this.'

He ignored me. My hand went to the radio. To my horror he actually grabbed my wrist. He turned his head to me, snarling.

'I won't fucking tell you again. I've got something on after work. I am *not* going to this fucking call. And if you touch your radio again, you and me are going to have a serious fucking problem. Do you understand?'

I yanked my wrist free.

'Control, we can attend, but we're some distance away. No one closer?' another unit announced. I felt such shame, but also fear. Terry was absolutely serious, no doubt also feeling some sense of shame but overruled by his indolence.

'There's no one else responding,' said Control. 'If you can start heading, I'll try to get another unit.'

'See, someone's got it,' said Terry.

About thirty seconds passed before Control gave an update:

'Several calls now. Screaming heard from the house. Address confirmed as 9 Scotia Avenue. All free units respond. Repeat, all free units now attend.'

The look on Terry's face was one of tortured ambivalence. He pulled the car over and stopped.

'Roger, from the station.' The sergeant's voice; it was serious when he stepped away from his computer.

'Three-six in attendance. Any update, Control?' another unit. Sirens heard in the background of the message, everyone understanding the seriousness of the call now.

'Negative, we're trying to get one of the callers back on the line. Standby.'

My head was in my hands, my torso was pulling me back through the seat. I knew if we could just turn the car it would be all right, the pain would let up. Terry sat in the layby, watching the rain thunder off the bonnet of the car.

The radio was quiet for a few minutes as we sat idle. I fought to control my breathing. It came in short, hard gulps.

'What the fuck's going on with you?'

'Terry . . . Please let's just start heading—'

'Will you just give it up, others are closer now. Give it a fucking rest.'

Another minute before the first unit announced their arrival at the scene.

We continued to sit in silence, but not for long. A jolt of electrical pain shot through me and I yelled as I clawed for the door handle. Our radios buzzed their emergency setting a few seconds later and a panicked voice was overheard, all professionalism abandoned.

'Echo-Four-Four to Control, get an ambulance here now, it's a bloodbath, more units, get more units.'

'Roger, Four-Four, any update on casualties?'

There was no direct response but struggling could be

heard with the emergency setting opening up the channel for everyone to hear. The odd word coming through here and there:

'Shit, shit . . . get something . . . fuck it won't stop . . .'

My door opened. I fell out onto the wet pavement. My ears were ringing and my mouth filled with saliva. Terry was asking if I was OK. Then a clear message:

'Put it down, put it down right now, get back, stay back—Control—'

The voice wavered in fear.

'Male . . . knife.'

The rest I couldn't hear.

My own heaving took over all senses. I couldn't breathe between bouts of violent retching, white light behind my eyes again as I struggled for oxygen. I was genuinely afraid I might die. My arms trembled, then they failed to support me and my face met puddle . . .

Then peace.

And rain.

That evening, a young mother was butchered by her boyfriend and I might have been close enough to do something about it. That evening my colleague Gavin got there in my place, too late, and was stabbed himself. He bled out on the way to hospital. He'd managed to get his baton out as the blow came and raised his arm defensively only to be struck deep in the armpit. The axillary artery. I hadn't even heard of it, but he was dead in just a few minutes.

CHAPTER THIRTEEN

LMFAO

'Come on, put your phone away. Show a bit of professionalism.' I said.

'Oh my God, are you serious?' She tossed the phone into the glove compartment and slammed the little door shut with an upward slap of her wrist. 'Can we at least drive around a bit? Besides it'll be dark soon.'

'Well, when it gets dark, we'll move.'

Rowan folded her arms across her chest and blew out in frustration. 'Can I explain why this is pointless?'

'If I said no, would you keep it to yourself?'

'The reason this is pointless is because the first person to spot us holed up here looking for people driving while on their phones or without a seat belt tells someone else, and they tell a few others and in less than ten minutes, the whole village knows. Look,' she said, presenting a hand at the windscreen as a car crawled past, 'the limit here is thirty, and no one in the past twenty minutes has passed doing more than fifteen.'

She had a point, a good one. I didn't want to concede it out of pure stubbornness, but I was as bored as she was. 'What time is it?'

She fished her phone back. 'Half seven.'

'It's Wednesday, right?'

'Yes. So? What are you thinking?'

My hand was brushing my chin, as I considered. 'Fuck it.' I turned the engine and pulled out.

'Fuck what? What are we doing?'

'I'm thinking we might do a bit of order-disobeying. At least I will be. Maybe you should wait in the car. You can even play with your phone.'

'No way, I'm in.' She dramatically tossed her phone back into its cave and I laughed.

'All right, but it's between us.'

It took all of five minutes to find the house. I'd looked at Jennifer's file so many times, I had this address locked in.

I had no way of knowing if Jack Mulligan had left for his Wednesday card game. I didn't see the harm in him seeing us at his door, but to avoid any domestic disagreement to follow I decided on an excuse of clarifying a fictional point. The look on Katherine Mulligan's face as she opened the door suggested there was no need for such fibs.

'You have news?' she said. She had a look of simultaneous excitement and trepidation.

'No, Katherine. I should point that out straight away; there's nothing new. I just wondered if we could talk. I hoped to get a better idea of Jenny and I figured seeing where she lived might help. Is this a bad time?' I said in a hushed voice.

'No, not at all. Please come in. Jack will be out till the wee hours. I'll put the kettle on.'

We followed her into the mid-terraced house and made polite conversation while she made tea. I ran through the information from her file and gave Katherine the opportunity to tell us anything she felt we had missed. 'Anything at all, Katherine, even if it seems irrelevant.'

'I really can't think of anything,' she said as we stood sipping at cups in the kitchen. 'Believe me, I rarely think of anything else. If you want, you could take a look through her room again?'

'It was already checked?'

'Yes, when I first reported her missing. But I don't mind if you want to take another look.'

'What is cross-fit?' I asked Rowan. There were three posters showing extremely toned women in various mid-exercise poses.

'It's a sort of exercise regime. I'm not entirely sure what's involved. There's some people go to my gym who are into it. They seem pretty obsessed. I only go so I can eat pizza without a topping of guilt.'

The room Katherine left us alone in was very much what I had expected. I suppose teenage girls' interests vary, but they're largely variations on common themes. Some posters were devoted to the band Muse – at least I'd heard of them and I silently congratulated myself – while others were of army recruitment. A bookshelf in the corner held far more CDs than books and was littered with framed pictures, one of which Rowan was scrutinising.

'What exactly are we looking for?' she asked.

I shrugged and lifted another of the pictures. Jennifer was hugging her sister, I recognised from pictures downstairs, in front of the Greyfriars Bobby statue in Edinburgh. 'I don't know, it just seemed like a good idea, and better than staring at traffic, right?'

Rowan shrugged this time. 'I suppose, but when you mentioned rule-breaking I thought you had something more interesting in mind. What's the problem with being here?'

'No problem, really. It's just that the inspector made it clear he was taking ownership of it and things with him are . . . well, you know. He'd probably have a fit if he knew we were stepping on his toes.'

'Well, I won't mention anything if you don't.' She made a point of covering her mouth with the picture she was holding.

'What have you got there?' I asked.

'Group pic with friends, somewhere warm.'

I took it from her. Jennifer, in shorts and T-shirt, had two pals in a headlock. They looked to be having a really good time.

'That was Paris,' said Katherine, who had appeared in the doorway. 'That's the Moulin Rouge in the background. You can just about make out the red windmill.'

'So you can,' I said. 'Who are the friends?'

'The girl is Viv. The other one is Mark Donnelly. It was a school trip a few years ago.'

'Mark Donnelly?' I said. 'Yeah, I think there is a quick interview with him in the file. He stays in town?'

'Yes, not far. They were school chums, but not friends like she was with Viv.'

I looked to Rowan and raised enquiring eyebrows.

'Why not?' she said. 'If it's a choice between that and what we were doing, I mean.'

'Do you mind if I borrow this?' I asked Katherine.

Sam spun her laptop 180 degrees on the coffee table to show me the screen.

'OK, I'm not great with social media. You might have to explain what, exactly, I'm looking at,' I said.

Sam swapped onto the sofa beside me and drew a finger across the touchpad, scrolling down to a conversation in large speech balloons. Rowan stood behind the sofa, looking over shoulders at the screen.

'This is Mark and Viv chatting last February.'

'It couldn't have been as long ago as February, could it?' asked Mark, still sitting on the other sofa, leaning forward as if he might see the screen over the purple lid of the laptop.

'It says so right here, dumbass.' Sam tapped the screen with a purple-painted nail – 'Tuesday the eighteenth of February.'

I read the short conversation; or tried to. It wasn't in English. 'I'm not sure I can follow this. What's L-M-F-A-O?'

Sam and Mark both laughed. I also detected a snigger over my shoulder.

'Laughing my fucking ass off,' she said.

Of course it is, I thought. 'If I read through this, can you please translate into old-person for me?'

She said she would and I scrolled to the top of the page.

>Hey Mark, sos (sorry) its bn like ages. Things are gr8 m8 (great mate) bn super busy got a job at a bar and its ok, free beer so wooho LMFAO. So you comin down or what? YOLO (You only live once).

>Hey Viv, nice to hear from u. Gr8 news bout d job. Funny you ask bout comin down cos I was totes (totally) ready to but then something happened and I was like WTF? (what the fuck). I'm at this party few weeks back, totes rager n you remember Sam from schl well we hooked up! I've fancied her forever but always figured she thot I was a goblin or sumthn but anyway we're kinda goin out now lol (Laugh out loud – I actually knew this one). So kinda want to see wha happens with that. Where you stayin?

> OMG (oh my God) that amazeballs (No clear definition offered) You n Sam? Didn't see that one comin lols (plural somehow), between places now, was in Croydon sharin, but got weird. Anyway if u chng ur mind hola (please alert me). Viv xx

'Is that it?' Mark nodded as I peeked over the lid. 'How about text messages?'

'Nah, we were never that close, me and Viv. I just thought it would be nice to have a familiar face if I did move down to London.'

'How close did you actually come to moving away?' asked Rowan.

'Really close, wasn't I, Sam?' She nodded in confirmation. 'Like a few weeks. I'd already saved a bit.'

'I don't get it,' I said.

'What?' said Sam.

'The fascination you kids have for, well, not just moving away, that I get, but completely going off the radar. What are you running away from?'

'I don't get it either,' agreed Sam. 'It's like some silly tradition here. It's the cool thing to do.'

'So, you're happy to stay?'

'God no, I was all set for uni when . . . Well, we're not complaining.' She gently circled a hand on her tummy. There was a bump and a definite glow about her, but I wouldn't have guessed had she not highlighted it.

'Congratulations,' I said, wondering if it was the right word. Viv wasn't the only one who was having a hard time believing these two had gotten together. She was way out of his league. He wasn't a goblin, as he had put it, but out of shape, scruffy and a bit lethargic in his demeanour and speech, and really short. Sam, on the other hand, was tall, slender but for bump, and sharp as a tack. Her straightened black hair and impeccable nails suggested a pride in her appearance that just didn't fit with the slovenly, though undeniably likeable, Mark. He said:

'Thanks, a wee surprise, so he is, but we're stoked, eh?'

To be fair Sam did look stoked. Her sardonic grin at Mark softened instantly into a genuine smile.

'You guys are staying put, then?' asked Rowan.

'Only for now. As soon as the wee one's in nursery I'll be going back to my studies.'

I wondered how they would cope, and at how many couples in town had similar aspirations that would be put on hold indefinitely until they had remained in storage long enough for such dreams to become memories so distant, they would deny they had ever existed. In that moment, I wished them well.

'So, you guys knew – sorry know – Jennifer, right?'

'Sam more than me, but yeah, we know Jenny.'

'Did she say anything to you, Sam, about moving to London?'

'Yeah, all the time, that or the army. In fact, if I remember right, it was her who had thought about it before Viv. They were supposed to go together, but I guess Viv got impatient, she always was a bit fly-by-the-seat-of-her-pants.'

'And you think that's where Jenny is now, with Viv?'

Sam's eyes narrowed. She saw straight through me. 'Do you not?'

'Oh, it's not that, it's just my job to be thorough. I know you've both given statements and I'm just going back over old ground here, but I just want to be sure we didn't miss anything.'

'She's with Viv, I have no doubts about that. Where they both are, though, I couldn't tell you. I mean, I don't even know where Croydon is.'

When the Stratharder Police had reported back to

Viv's parents that she had been traced safe and well, they couldn't tell them her location. She was eighteen, an adult in the eyes of the law and therefore had the right to have her location kept confidential.

'How about Daisy Cavanagh? Do you know her?'

They exchanged negative glances. 'Should we?' asked Sam.

'Another girl, went to your school, Mark, a few years ahead of you.' It was another missing person form amongst the files Margaret was transferring onto the new system. The circumstances were similar but a few years previous to Viv and Jenny.

'Aye, maybe,' said Mark, scratching at the stubble on his cheek. 'Daisy Cavanagh. Like you say she was a few years ahead of me. We weren't friends or anything. What about her?'

'Just wondered if you knew her, that's all. Listen, thanks to both of you for your time,' I said. 'I think that about covers everything.'

'Happy to help,' said Sam.

I pushed the laptop over to her and stood, collecting my coat as I did.

'Actually . . .' said Rowan, her face scrunched in thought. 'I'm not sure what the rules are on this, but how would you feel about us using your Facebook to try to contact Viv?'

'It's a good thought, Rowan, but really we can't be using people's personal information like that, it would be highly—'

'I don't mind, really,' said Mark. 'I honestly don't use it.'

'He really doesn't.'

'I'll write down the log-in for you. One thing, if my mum sends another friend request, please don't accept it.'

'I promise,' I laughed.

CHAPTER FOURTEEN

Uniform Dating Dot Com

The doorbell rang, waking me with a start. I must have been dozing as the football match I had been watching on television had been replaced by the news. I had a moment of panic as I went searching for my phone, or anything that might tell me the time. I slapped at the space bar on the laptop and woke it from its own slumber as the bell rang again, held down longer this time.

The screensaver told me it was only four o'clock, so this must be Hilda at the door, bearing some new culinary concoction, I thought. I applied my surprised but grateful face and opened the door. Rowan stood with her baffled face on. She was wrapped in a thick, black full-length coat.

'Nice underpants, goes well with the tie. I didn't realise it was going to be that kind of a party.'

She pushed past me into the house and up the stairs. I cursed myself. I had been halfway through changing for the party when I noticed the game on TV and figured I had started preparing too early anyway and opened a beer. I darted into the bedroom and threw on the rest of the suit.

When I returned to the living room Rowan had helped herself to a beer and was sitting at the table in her little black dress, her heavy coat slung over the back of the chair. Her make-up was subtle but effective, with some light eyeshadow and liner, drawing attention to her already striking green eyes.

'Sorry about that. I thought you were Hilda.'

She looked up from the laptop screen, eyebrows raised. 'Do you normally answer the door to her in your underpants? Whatever keeps the rent down, I suppose. I tried calling, but no answer.'

'You can't get a signal here, and you're early.' I sat back on the sofa and resumed my own beer.

'I was just sitting around the house, so I thought I'd drop by and we could arrive together. How long do you think we'll have to stay?'

'I was wondering the same thing. I guess we stay as long as the inspector does, or until a suitable excuse presents itself.'

'Woof,' she said, suddenly leaning closer to the computer screen. 'Now I see why you're banging your landlady.'

'What?'

'This woman you've been chatting to, seriously fugly. Are you really this hard up?'

I was plunged into a cold pool of dread.

I sprang to my feet and reached for the laptop, but Rowan snatched it to her chest. 'Don't get embarrassed. Almost every couple I know met online. It's perfectly normal, unlike this woman you've been talking to. What is all that shit in her face?'

'I was passing some time. I opened Facebook. Even though it's unorthodox, I decided to try to message Viv on Mark's account, but I couldn't get the nonsense right, so I was just . . . well, browsing, you know?'

'Relax. Look at the colour of your face, that's hilarious. I've done the online thing myself; come on, talk me through what you were thinking here.' She pulled a chair alongside her and I sat, arms folded in a sulk.

'She's actually very interesting,' I said, recalling the conversation I had with the girl with the bright red hair and multiple face piercings on the screen. 'A tattoo artist from Ayr.'

'God, could you imagine going on holiday with her? You'd be there all day trying to get through customs. You do realise she's a big girl, don't you? Which is fine of course, but you're kind of a little guy. Didn't think you'd go for the larger lady.'

'What? No, she's not,' I turned the screen towards me to look. 'How can you even tell? Look her body type is left blank, and all her pictures are from the neck up.'

She turned the screen back towards her. 'I can tell because she left her body type blank and all her pictures are from the neck up. You really are a nube, aren't you? I can't believe you chose Union Station anyway. This site is just full of sex pests and desperados.'

'I don't know, it's free and it was the first one that popped up when I typed in dating. Have you tried this site, then?'

'For about two days, yes. After I opened my third or fourth geriatric penis picture, I decided free dating sites were a bad idea. Let's see who else you've been chatting to.'

'Rowan, that's private. I'd rather you—'

'This is the picture you chose for yourself? You're better looking than this. The point is to choose a picture that's cuter than you actually are, not the other way around; you'll understand what I mean when you meet some of these women.'

The picture was from a weekend trip Karen and I had taken to Barcelona. I was squinting from the sun and feeling self-conscious. It wasn't a great picture, but it was the best of a pretty exclusive, bad bunch. Almost every other picture included Karen. 'Rowan, I'm really not comfortable—'

'Look, let me give you a few pointers, it'll save you the trouble of some extremely disappointing first, and only, dates. Let's see . . .'

I rubbed my eyes and emptied my bottle as Rowan cycled through the conversations on my contact list.

'Ah, rookie mistake here. And you call yourself a cop.'

'What are you talking about?'

'This one, Elaine. She's so not over her last relationship. You'd be wasting your time.'

'Educate me. How can you possibly know that from one picture and almost no text on her profile?' I said, unconvinced.

'Easy. You see how half her arm is missing in the picture?

179

It only just squeezes her face in.' Rowan tapped a finger at the screen. 'And, if you look at the other side, down at her waist, you see this disembodied hand?'

'OK.'

'She's cropped out her ex. She's probably not been single long enough to find any new shots without him. She's eager to get online, fill a gap in her life.'

'You can tell all that from one picture?'

'Yeah. You develop a certain set of skills with this stuff.'

'All right . . . This is actually quite helpful. Excruciating, but helpful. What else have you got?

'What else? What else? Oh, OK, I don't know what it is you're looking for exactly, but anyone who says on their profile that they're up for fun, or says they're open-minded or similar, is just a complete slut.'

'No . . .'

'Yeah, seriously.'

'But every other profile says that.'

'Then your dry spell is over my friend.'

'So, you're a bit of an expert, then? What site are you on?'

She looked up briefly from the screen. 'I never said that I am, only that I was.'

'You're seeing someone, then?'

'Not currently.'

'So, what site you on, then?'

'Forget it.'

'What?'

'I'm not telling you.'

'Oh, it's OK for you to scrutinise my profile but I'm not allowed to see yours?'

'Now you're getting it. Actually, this girl you've been chatting with seems nice.'

'Which one?'

'The nurse from Glasgow,' she said, scrolling over her profile. 'I can't actually see anything wrong here, no alarm bells ringing. Which probably means it's some fifty-year-old guy getting his jollies out of your loneliness.'

I slowly but assuredly turned the laptop away from her. 'That's enough torture for one day.'

'Aw, come on. I was only halfway through your conversation with her.'

'Do you even realise how inappropriate that is?'

'Of course I do, but it's fun. And you're a good sport.'

'That's fading, trust me.'

'Do you think you'll meet her?'

'The nurse? Probably not.'

'Why not? Scared? It's nerve-wracking the first few times, but you get over it quickly.'

'It's not that. She's in Glasgow for a start, and we both work shifts, so windows would be few and far between. I was actually ready to delete that thing. I joined more out of some morbid curiosity than anything else.' I tabbed back to Facebook, opened the message I was struggling with and returned the screen to Rowan. 'Here, make yourself useful. Send a message to Viv, keep it breezy, and you know, in that shitty version of English you lot use.'

'Sure.' She stretched her fingers and began typing. 'Breezy, illiterate bullshit coming right up.'

'Right, since you've had some fun at my expense, I want

you to answer some personal questions of your own. It's only fair.'

She stopped typing and considered for a moment before saying: 'I'm promising nothing. But go ahead.'

'How long have you been single?'

'Almost a year,' she said, without having to think at all. Her face never moved from the screen.

'Tell me about your last relationship.'

'Hmmm, no. Be more specific.'

'Fine, was your last boyfriend a cop?'

She smiled. 'Yes. The first and last police officer boyfriend. We met at the police college.'

'What happened?'

'Be specific.'

'OK, why did you break up?'

She sat back in her chair and sipped from her bottle, her eyes tracing the ceiling. 'It probably depends on whose version you choose to believe. I would say we grew apart and that, as you just said, our shifts were not exactly compatible. If you asked him, and if his texts and emails are anything to go by, he'd say the situation was too intense. I have an overprotective family and I spend a lot of time with them, and he couldn't really get on board with that. The first time he complained about it I warned him never to make me choose as it wouldn't end well for him. In the end, that's pretty much what it amounted to.'

'Overbearing big brothers, is it?'

'Something like that. Do you have any siblings?'

'No, I'm an only child.'

'Maybe a little difficult for you to understand, then.'

182

'No, I think I get it.'

'I'm fine being on my own,' she said with a shrug and went back to typing. 'Maybe once I'm out of my probation and things settle down a bit I'll feel differently, but right now I'm happy with not having that extra distraction in my life. What happened with your marriage?'

'My marriage? My engagement you mean. We never made it down the aisle.'

'All right, what happened to your engagement?'

'You're not shy, are you? I'm definitely not comfortable talking about that with you; besides . . . I'm not entirely sure.'

'What does that mean?'

'It means you ask too many questions.'

'I'm a cop, it's what I do.'

'Yeah, well, right now our job is to attend a garden party in November. Seriously, who has a garden party in November?'

It was freezing, *actually freezing*, as we stepped from the cab onto the drive, illuminated by candle lanterns, with guests' cars parked neatly along one side. A black-shirted lad took Rowan's hand as she stepped from the cab and helped her walk in her heels on the gravel. With a teeth-chattering smile he directed us towards the front door of the house.

Rowan took the crook of my elbow and we wandered up the steps collecting a glass of champagne from another black-shirted teenager. The hallway had been transformed into a sort of gallery, with a mix of technical drawings and artistic impressions on easels showing Ogilvie's plans for his tourism expansions. Groups gathered round each of the displays and Ogilvie would have been pleased to see just how wealthy the majority of them looked. The door to the dilapidated wing of the house had been cleverly hidden away by a large red velvet curtain with one of the larger easels sitting in front of it.

We stopped by one easel showing a colourful summer scene with blurry figures picnicking next to the log cabins, painted enthusiastically, though with little skill, by Ogilvie himself I suspected. We wandered onto the next easel when the middle-aged couple at it ambled on.

'It's all very impressive,' said Rowan, as she scanned the technical drawing detailing a complete remodelling of the estate in three stages.

'You have to admire his ambition,' I agreed. 'It's just that it seems a little . . . I don't know . . .'

'Ill-conceived? Naive?' said a voice from behind.

I turned to see a man leaning over me, looking past my shoulder at the plans. As tall as he was, he was dwarfed by his wife, or girlfriend, or date for the evening; über-blonde and probably over six feet before she slipped the heels on.

'You're not planning on investing, then?' I asked.

'I'm not sure I can avoid it. Hi, I'm Alex Ogilvie.' He held out his still-gloved hand.

'Nice to meet you. I'm Don, this is Rowan.' Rowan grinned over her just-emptied glass. 'You're a relative, then?'

'Nephew,' he said. 'This is Anja.' The blonde stepped forward, slipping a hand from her own black leather glove and presenting it to me with an iceberg smile. I was caught in that awkward do-I-kiss-or-shake-it moment. In the end I gave her limp hand a squeeze.

'He expects you to invest, then?'

'Significantly, yes. His heart's in the right place, I just don't see much potential in all this. Tourism is not my thing. It's not that I don't trust my uncle, I just am sceptical by nature. I'm an investment analyst, you see, and if you were my client coming to me with this . . . I'd steer you down a different course. Am I putting you off? I don't mean to.'

He was older than me. By how much was hard to say. His hair was expensively styled but he made no attempt to hide the grey coming in at the temples, though he had the skin of a young man.

'No, not at all. Well, I mean I don't have anything to invest. I'm . . . we're . . . just cops. On our salary your investments revolve around whether to have a holiday or get the car fixed every other year. I think your uncle just invited us to be polite.'

'And we were too polite to say no thanks,' said Rowan, snatching a fresh glass from a passing tray.

'Rowan.'

'It's fine, I understand entirely,' said Alex. I'd been trying to place his accent, I'd initially thought Scottish, but now heard perhaps Cornish, or similar. 'We travelled from London for this today and we're on the first flight back in the morning. I wish I had the backbone to tell him no, but he's family, so nothing else for it really.'

'Darling, I think we're holding people up.'

Anja was right, a small queue was forming along the hallway behind us.

'You're right. Have a lovely evening you two and watch

your wallets around that uncle of mine, won't you?' Anja placed an arm over his shoulder and led him on. His own hand found its natural height upon her bottom.

Ogilvie's studio had been cleared and the French doors thrown open to a busy garden, complete with a formidable white marquee, spilling out with well-oiled guests. They clutched champagne flutes and revolved slowly anticlockwise around the interior of the tent as if some slow waltz were playing. The garden had been neatly trimmed back and the grass stairs had been carefully re-established with a red carpet rolled down the centre of them.

A large screen had been set up at one end of the tent showing a flashy showreel of the gallery images from the hall as well as an animated fly-through of the proposed plans. At the other end I spotted the inspector and his wife grazing at a long table of finger food. The plate in the inspector's hand appeared to be reserved only for the rejected items he had pushed into his mouth but thought better of swallowing. He was kilted and had his hair slicked back, which looked to have had a fresh application of boot polish.

'I'm going to mingle,' said Rowan, seeing me advance towards the inspector. She headed into the throng, a little unsteadily in her heels.

The inspector spotted me just as I reached the table. He brushed a hand along his chin, removing the debris, then wiped down the side of his kilt before shaking my hand. The shake lasted an uncomfortably long time as he tried to finish whatever was in his mouth and he was pulling me towards his wife.

'Marjory,' he said eventually, 'you remember Donald, don't you?'

'Yes, of course, how are you?'

'Very well, thanks,' I said. 'You look very nice, Mrs Wallace.'

'Oh please, it's Marjory, and thank you. At least someone's noticed.'

'I said so, didn't I?' The inspector froze before pressing a fresh vol-au-vent into his mouth.

'Never mind, Stewart, go back to your pastry. Did he make you come to this, Donald? Or are you looking to make an investment?'

'I was happy to come,' I lied. 'Thought it'd be a good opportunity to get to know my community a little better, but no, I won't be making a contribution to tonight's cause I'm afraid. How about you? Is this where your retirement package is going, Inspector?'

'God no,' said Marjory quietly, leaning forward with a smile. 'We have other plans for Stewart's retirement, including moving somewhere further away from the Arctic Circle.' She gestured to the open end of the tent where large flakes of snow were gliding into the entrance.

The inspector said nothing but gave his wife a look of rebuke, which would have carried more threat had he not had a mouth crammed with sausage roll.

Marjory waved him off. 'I'm just getting excited, Donald. It's getting so close now, you begin to think it'll never happen, or that you'll be too old when it does to properly enjoy it.'

'I saw that you called earlier. I take it you got some

news about Mr Cooper?' The inspector handed his plate to Marjory with a glare and led me to a more discreet spot. 'Well?'

'I thought better of leaving details on the answering machine, Inspector, but there's nothing to get too excited about. I received an email from DS Aitken. We're still awaiting the results of the toxicology and post-mortem. With more pressing cases taking priority, it may be a while before we receive them. They did run the various prints they found in Cooper's cottage, though.'

'And?'

One set came back as a match for a known escort, PNC shows an address in Oban. He's asked if I would bring her in for an interview.'

'That's something at least.'

'Would you like to sit in?'

'That's not necessary. I'm sure Forbes would find it very useful to see how it's done. Just let me know how it goes.'

'I will. DS Aitken did ask if Cooper had any family that we should be informing? It's likely a verdict of death by misadventure will be agreed by the fiscal's office. In which case they'd be releasing the body for burial, but I couldn't find any contact details.'

'Cooper? Not as such, not that I can think of. His wife died, or rather killed herself, twenty years ago, and he had a turbulent relationship with his daughter who disappeared off to the city at the first opportunity.'

'Another one of those kids who couldn't wait to get out of this place?'

'Yes, I suppose. I don't think they had talked since.

You'll struggle to find her details anywhere, and even if you could, I doubt she'd be remotely interested. There's procedures for dealing with unclaimed remains; I'll have to look it up. Listen, you weren't thinking of sneaking out of here early, were you?'

'Actually, I am pretty tired—'

'Nonsense, I know Ogilvie wanted to see you. A few of the boys are sticking around for a game of cards. Charles always opens the good stuff. You'll stay, won't you?'

'I don't know, Inspector. That's kind but I came with Rowan, and something tells me she might need a hand getting home.'

'Charles has taxis booked out all evening. She'll be just fine. Good, it's decided. I'll give you a nod.'

By the time I got the 'nod' I had been ready to go for over an hour. I had tried to convince Rowan half a dozen times that she should call it a night. She had first of all taken to firing finger pistols at people with a cluck from the side of her mouth to indicate the bang. She said she was hunting millionaires. She proudly told me she had gunned down 'two score, my good man' and that I should 'collect their stinking carcases and save the best heads for my trophy room, there's a chap'.

'Is she all right?' The inspector gestured at Rowan, who was standing on the gravel drive spinning in circles with her arms and mouth spread wide catching the thick flakes of snow which had been falling all night, muffling the ambient sound and laying a thick quilt over the landscape.

'Nothing a good night's sleep won't cure. She's off for the next few days, so I think we can forgive her letting her hair down.'

'Hmmm . . . I suppose. You'll put her in a taxi, won't you?'

'Of course.'

'You know Ogilvie's office? It's upstairs. We'll be there when you're done here,' he said, nodding again at Rowan. 'In the meantime, do you think you could get her to stop spinning? She is representing the police after all.'

'I'll try,' I said, without certainty.

I had, in fact, been trying to keep an eye on her all evening, but it wasn't easy as she was like a curious toddler. If someone bored her she unapologetically walked away, something else I admired and envied about her, something Pawel would have liked, no doubt.

'You know something, Sarge?' she said, falling from her spin to throw her arms round my neck.

'What's that, Constable?'

'You're all right. You know . . . for a cop.'

'Well, thank you, Rowan, you're all right too; pissed as a newt, but all right.'

'I'm not drunk, you big liar, I'm just . . .'

'Catching snowflakes in your mouth?'

'Exactly,' she said and straightened up before pointing a finger at me. 'Oh hey,' she continued, 'while I 'member, we're s'posed to be early shift next Friday, bu' can we do late instead, both 'fus?'

'I suppose. Why?'

Her pointed finger shot to her mouth. 'Shhh . . . Isasecret, somethin' I've been working on, but you'll like it.'

'All right, but you'll have to tell me sooner or later.'

'Later.'

I laughed and took her arm as she was swaying again.

'We really need to get you home.' She hung on to my arm and I led her towards the long line of taxis hired for the exodus. Before we joined the short queue of people waiting to be removed from the party, she stopped and turned squarely to me. Her cheerful, inebriated face was suddenly serious.

'What's up?'

'Listen,' she said, searching for sobriety. 'Something I want to tell you.'

'Rowan, you're drunk, perhaps you shouldn't.'

'No, shhh. Let me talk. Listen, you're all right.'

'I think we covered this.'

'Shhh. I need to tell you that I think you're nice and that I think that we should—'

'Rowan, please don't.'

'No, no this is important. If I don't say this now I probably . . .' She pulled on the lapels of my coat causing me to bend down to her height. She put her lips to my ear and whispered: 'You need to know, Sarge, I like you and I don't want—'

I took her face in my hands and kissed her red, frozen cheeks.

'I like you too, Rowan, but trust me, this is not a good idea. Now, come on . . .'

She grumbled her frustration, but I determinedly took her to the first of the taxis and placed her in the back seat.

'You going to be OK?' I asked.

She patted the seat next to her. 'No, I need a-scorting home. I may have con-snumed a lil too much an' you should do the gen-emenly thing and see me home, kind sir, cos I need to e-splain. You should jus' leave too.'

'If only, and I think you'll be just fine. Drink plenty of water.'

I closed the door, patted the roof twice and watched the cab cut trenches in the driveway snow.

CHAPTER FIFTEEN

Party Line

Before long the guests and the vehicles had departed, all but the white vans of the catering company. I trudged towards the house, pulling my coat close around me and slaloming the staff that darted here and there trying to load the vans as quickly as possible in the plummeting temperature. Some of them were busy draining the opened, but not emptied, champagne bottles. The doors to the house had been closed, making it clear it was now off limits to the uninvited. I entered and shrugged snow from my hair and shoulders.

As I slowly climbed the stairs, carpeted in blue tartan and badly scuffed at the edge of each step, I noted a strange mix of traditional and contemporary adornments on the walls. There were some old sepia photographs of hunting scenes, with handwritten dates in the corners, ranging from late 1800s to mid-twentieth century, all showing the house in past glory with proud gun- and game-wielding figures, presenting their kills to the camera. Above each photograph a handwritten title was neatly inscribed, all the same 'The Caley Club' – some little entitled society I assumed. The rich are fond of that sort of thing, I thought. The photographs sat alongside Ogilvie's own paintings, impressionistic, bold, bright . . . bad.

The first-floor landing was barely illuminated by brass reading lamps set on mahogany sideboards. I proceeded gingerly, allowing my eyes to adjust. I couldn't remember which room was Ogilvie's office, but I could hear muffled voices coming from the far end of the corridor.

My hand reached for the brass handle, but I was halted by the temptation to listen. The door was made in that don't-make-them-like-they-used-to robust style so the voices came as if through water and only the odd phrase could be made out. I pressed my ear to the wood. There was some discussion about a pot, the card game they were playing, I realised, and some general laughter and nonsense. My hand gripped the round handle but froze when I heard my name spoken. I strained to hear, but the context and after discussion were lost.

'Don't be shy; they don't bite.' Alex Ogilvie stood in the corridor, arms folded and clearly amused at my shock and embarrassment. 'I can't promise they won't bore you to death, mind you. The trick is to prepare your excuse in advance, you know, put in some groundwork. Here, I'll show you,' he said, moving past me and opening the door to his uncle's office wide enough only to put his head through.

'Alex, my boy,' came Ogilvie's voice, a little slurred so that the 'my boy' formed a single word. 'Come in, come, we'll find you a chair, come in.'

'I found a straggler, Uncle.' Alex pushed the door wider and, with a hand on my shoulder, he guided me in front of him into a room full of men sitting in a cloud of sour smoke.

'Sergeant, ah, your timing could not be better. Save me from this rabble of crooks. Round them up, they have been robbing me blind,' said a red-cheeked Ogilvie.

The office seemed bigger than I remembered from my previous visit. An illusion I saw, with the furniture pushed back to the walls and a shabby wooden coffee table placed at the centre of the room. Six men sat around it.

'I can't stay I'm afraid, Uncle. Remember I told you Anja was feeling unwell earlier? She's no better and I must get her back to the hotel.'

'I thought you were staying. What is the point of a house this size if people don't stay?'

'I'm sorry, I really am, and thank you, but the hotel is closer to the airport anyway and we have a very early flight.'

'Are you sure? Well, tell Anja I hope she is feeling better soon. I had hoped to talk to you more about the plans.'

'No need, we're sold. I'll be in touch, I promise.'

'Cheque is in the post, then?'

'I promise. Try not to lose your shirt, Uncle. Goodnight.'

'Nicely done,' I whispered as Alex backed out of the room with the occupants wishing him goodnight and a safe journey. There was a moment of quiet as the door closed over and I stood feeling self-conscious as the men returned to their game, Texas hold 'em by the look of it. Some of the men I knew – Ogilvie, the inspector and Jack Mulligan, Jennifer's father. The rest I wasn't sure of, although I had the distinct impression that one of the men, tweedy and beardy, was one of the farmers from the council meeting.

Ogilvie's office had a different atmosphere from before. The window, formerly ablaze with sunlight was a treacle black mirror showing me standing in no man's land awaiting instruction. A desk lamp and the under-lighting of the grim portraits looking down at us around the walls were the only light and, coupled with the dry-ice effect of the cigar smoke, the place had a dream-like quality. After a moment the faces turned to me, wondering why I was still standing. The inspector gestured to the far end of the table where a caramel-brown leather armchair sat vacant. I threw my jacket over the back and sunk into it, thinking it was exactly the colour of the flypaper my grandmother used to have hanging from her kitchen ceiling. The eyes of those around the table flitted from their cards to me and back. I had walked in partway through a particularly expensive hand. A pile of coloured poker chips sat in the centre and grew as the hand came to a final round of betting. All those taking part, save the inspector, were still in. From my angle I could see Ogilvie gnawing nervously on his lip behind his cards, probably a tell, but I never was much of a card player. Farmer No. 3, not involved in the game, was leaning a little on a kilted Jack Mulligan and looked ready to drop. Jack was intensely invested in the deliberations of a man I didn't know. Young, in his twenties with wild, wiry hair and shoulders for carrying girders, and he either had a fantastic poker face or one of genuine bewilderment. He was dressed in baggy jeans and T-shirt, clearly not downstairs at the party. To his left another unknown, but I suspected him to be the young lad's father; he was the absolute spit, if you moved the bulk from the shoulders south to the gut. He had a look of grumpy impatience, waiting for the boy to decide his move.

My phone buzzed an alert in my pocket, and I fished it out while I waited for the men to finish their hand. It was a message from Rowan:

Jus got hme, sorrt for talking pish. Xx

I decided against responding. But then I noticed an unread text, it was from Karen:

Still haven't heard from you but still hoping to. K. x

I checked the message details. It was sent the day before but received some time in the early evening. Evidently the phone reception up at Ogilvie's was far better than at Hilda's. It was unfair of me to ignore her, but I locked the phone, deciding the sober Don of tomorrow morning could make the decision whether or not to respond.

Eventually the boy tossed in the remainder of his green chips with Hollywood theatre, spilling some onto the floor, drawing tuts and headshaking from the other men.

'Let's see them, then,' said Ogilvie with some confidence. The men laid out their cards on the table, except for the boy who slapped his down triumphantly showing a pair of fours, by far the worst hand of the lot.

'Eejit,' the man who may have been his father said to him. 'That last raise cost you fifty quid, and that's all you had?'

'I thought yous were bluffin'. You wouldn't spot us some chips, would ye? I'm good for it.'

'All bets must be covered at the end of the night, Craig. No exceptions, you know that. You can't bet what you don't have,' said the inspector, leaning over the table, gathering the cards in.

'Aye, but . . . aw come on, gee's a chance to win ma money back at least. Only fair, eh?'

The inspector looked up from his deft shuffling, his face serious. 'Are you suggesting there was something *unfair* about how you lost your money?'

'Naw, I'm no' sayin' that. I'm jus—'

'Did someone make you go all in with a pair of fours, like a moron?'

Craig was going red now. Some of those around the table were beginning to pretend it wasn't happening. The boy looked around, shaking his head, and made to say something further but he was again cut off by the inspector.

'Are you still here?'

'What? That's it? I've only played three hands.'

'Do you have anything to bet with? No? Because the rest of us are going to spend the remainder of the evening playing cards with the money we have left. What are you going to do?'

Craig's face had turned a startling hue. I thought for a moment he might actually cry. He stared at the inspector, who stared right back. The inspector placed the fully shuffled cards carefully on the table and placed his hands on his knees. Craig looked to the man to his left, who could only have sensed it because he was looking at something on the ground.

198

'Tell your mother not to wait up, and cover your losses before you go,' he said.

Craig rose, slung a jacket over his arm and leafed through a wallet attached to his jeans by a long chain. He dropped a substantial wad onto the table without counting and left without saying a word.

'Introductions,' announced Ogilvie, sitting opposite and leaning over the table, presenting an open wooden box containing the same fat, reeking cigars that sat in a massive glass ashtray in one corner of the table. I shook my head with a mouthed 'no thanks'. He ran through the players to my left and right. 'Stewart you know. Get him a dram will you, Stewart?' he said to the inspector, who got up and went to a side cabinet where a crystal decanter sat half filled with enticing golden liquid. 'Bill here I don't think you've met. He's our ghillie, looks after our river and loch, and your hard-earned wages if you don't keep an eye on him.' The man, who had just dismissed his son, gave a nod while dealing out cards, two apiece, to everyone. 'The old one snoring there is Mac—'

'We've met,' Mac said, without fully opening his eyes. Ogilvie pushed over the green chips the young lad had been using and I began gathering them into piles.

'It's two pounds a chip. There's no limit, but we keep it friendly here,' he said.

I thought about the look on the lad's face as he left. 'I didn't bring much cash I'm afraid.' I had brought a hundred and forty pounds, actually. I had correctly assumed the drinks would be laid on free, but I thought it better to be safe, however I wasn't prepared to lose that much money.

'Oh, just bet what you're comfortable with. And this is Jack Mulligan.' He pointed at Jennifer's father with the cigar he gripped in his knuckles.

'Jack, I actually know, sort of. How are you?' I asked, feeling a little nervous. I wasn't sure what the inspector had said to Jennifer's family since the cock-up, or whether he knew I'd visited Katherine.

'I'm well, thank you, Sergeant. Yourself?'

'Don, please,' I said, picking up my cards – a seven and a three, not of the same suit. I would be folding imminently.

'Stewart says things are back on track with our Jenny.'

'With Jennifer? I, uh . . .'

'I was telling Jack that I had made fresh contact with the Met, and they were on top of it. And in the meantime, you were looking at CCTV and preparing a fresh press release.' This wasn't true, but I assured Jack it was. In reality it was, at best, an exaggeration. I personally had checked the CCTV at both the train and bus stations in Oban on the day she had gone missing, then three days beyond that, just in case, with no sighting, going by the description given. We were waiting for one or two places to come back to us, the council CCTV of the cameras in town, and at a few fast food places, so we could put that side of things to bed, but I had no confidence it would amount to anything. This was the first I'd heard of a press release. The best hope of progress, I estimated, was with the Met. I was still awaiting a response after sending the email to their central enquiries unit, not realising the inspector was doing the same.

'You haven't heard anything yourself, then?' I asked Jack.

'No, but I'm not worried, at least not overly. She'll be

back when she's hungry, so to speak. Once she's got it out her system.' It didn't seem intentional but he blew cigar smoke at me as he answered stinging my eyes. I discreetly fanned my face with my cards before tossing them as the betting started. 'I feel bad that you lot are having to go to all this trouble.'

'It's no trouble, Jack,' said the inspector, handing me a ridiculous dram, three quarters filling the crystal tumbler. 'It's our job, and if it brings Katherine some piece of mind, we're happy to do it.'

'I actually made enquiries with the Met too, Jack,' I said. Although this was more of a confession aimed at the inspector. 'I thought I'd speak to the officer who traced Viv last year, come at it from that angle.'

'I didn't realise you had, Donald. Have you heard anything?' asked the inspector.

I was relieved at his reaction. In essence we were doubling up on work with our poor communication. It could get confusing with multiple enquiries. 'No, it will take a while. These things sit in a pile and since she's over eighteen it won't be prioritised, but they'll get to it and as soon as we hear anything you and Katherine will be the first to know.'

'I have some friends in the Met, Jack. I'll make sure they act on it quickly. Don, if you send me the details of who you sent off to, I'll see it done.' He pushed a tower of chips into the centre and everyone else immediately folded.

'Of course,' I said, and attempted a sip from the glass I struggled to hold with one hand. It was bitter, burned furiously and I fought to keep my face from screwing up like I'd bit into a lemon.

'What we really want to hear about is the business with Cooper,' said Ogilvie. At this Mac sat up and there was a unified turning of shoulders in my direction from the others. I looked at the inspector for some direction, but he was the only one looking at his cards.

'I'm sorry, gentlemen, I really can't say anything.'

'Ach, come away, we're all friends here,' said Ogilvie.

'I appreciate that may be disappointing, but I'm afraid that's the situation. I can't discuss an ongoing investigation.' This was met with a drone of disappointment from the men.

'We realise you can't go into the nuts and bolts of the thing, Sergeant, besides that would all probably be lost on us anyway, but surely you can give us some kind of . . . overview? Current thinking, that sort of thing?' said Ogilvie.

'I really wish I could.' I looked around at the expectant faces. 'Look, when I *can* say something, I will be happy to do so. Right now, I have nothing for you on that particular topic.'

'See, I told you, murder. He cannae talk aboot it because he was murdered,' said Bill, pointing a told-you-so finger at Ogilvie.

'He's not saying that,' said the inspector. 'Between us, there's not much to tell.'

'Away and don't talk pish, man. A'body kens the fat bastard's heart gave oot while he was up to his nuts in some hooer,' was the retort from Mac.

'Whatcha mean a hooer? Like an actual hooer?' said Bill. Something of a side conversation was now going on between him and Mac. 'Where's he getting a hooer roond here? Unless of course it was . . . no, it couldnae have been her eh, that was ages—' Bill received a sharp elbow from Ogilvie, cutting him dead.

'Ach ye can order hooers like Chinese food on the internet noo,' said Mac.

'I've no' got internet.'

'Ye dinae need it, Bill. You've a wife at hame who's daft for the boaby.' The room erupted into laughter, myself included.

'Look,' I said once the room had composed itself, 'nobody's saying that either. This kind of speculation is really not helpful,' I said, but several conversations between the men had already broken out.

'Satanist cult it was', 'face eaten off by the cat', 'what a load of pish, he didnae have a cat ya numpty', 'his heart was cut oot and left between two candles', 'the cleaner found him cock in hand, deid, but with a braw smile on his coupon', 'aye, that's what I heard, worse ways to go I suppose, ha, ha, ha'.

I let it go and checked my cards.

Within half an hour I was down thirty pounds, and still making precious little progress on my whisky while the others threw it back like lemonade. The game had given up on Mac, who was snoring, and had been laid on to his side by Jack, who was quietly amassing a small fortune.

'You're a single man, aren't you, Donald?' asked Ogilvie. It seemed to catch everyone off guard, myself included. All but the slumbering Mac turned to me.

'Yes, that's right. I was engaged once, but it didn't work out.' My fingers brushed the phone in my trouser pocket, thinking about the coincidental text from Karen, the text I decided against responding to.

'I heard you were seeing young Mhairi,' said Jack. He laid out his fanned cards on the table. The inspector looked suddenly irritated. I assumed he'd lost the money, but he then displayed his own winning hand and I saw that the displeasure was aimed at me.

'Hahaha . . . You'd better keep your money, then, you'll need it,' said Mac, surprising me that he was awake.

'Where did you hear that?' I asked Jack.

'It's not true, is it, Donald?' The inspector was leaning forward in his chair, aghast.

'What? No, it's not. I barely know the girl.'

'That's not what's doing the rounds in town, Sergeant. Rumour has it you're quite the hot couple.' Jack handed me the cards, my turn to deal.

'Well, it's . . . pish,' I said. The inspector gave me an are-you-quite-certain? raised eyebrow. 'Honestly,' I assured him. 'Nothing going on, whatsoever!'

I dealt the cards and was delighted that I had given myself two face cards, a king and a queen. The first decent deal of the night.

'Hey Stewart, what was that thing you were telling me, about when you were a young policeman?' asked Ogilvie. The Scandinavian lilt in his accent was becoming increasingly pronounced the more he drank.

'What thing?' The inspector's tone was flat as he studied Jack's silent assessment of his cards. They sat on opposite sides of the table and by now it was becoming a two-horse race, their chips stacked high in front of them like warring children tucked behind play forts.

'That thing you talked about, the thing you were asked. To see what kind of man you were.'

'Oh, that, what about it?'

'Ask Donald here.'

'Ask me what?' I dealt the flop, three cards on the table for anyone to use in their hand. The first was another king followed by a pair of fives. The inspector and Jack studied each other, which was just as well as they would have spotted my grin otherwise.

'Nothing,' said the inspector. 'Let's leave work nonsense out of it; we've got a card game here.'

'It has wider implications than just work, though, does it not?' said Ogilvie. He paid into the pot like everyone else. 'Go on, ask him.'

The inspector laid his cards down and turned to face me. 'It goes like this: you're on duty, foot patrol, and you walk around a corner to find an old lady laying beaten and bloody in the street and a man running off with her handbag. Now, the question is – did you see him do it?'

I thought on it for a moment.

'I don't get it,' said Jack. 'What exactly is the point?'

'Shut up, man. Let the sergeant answer.'

'It's a sneaky pry into a man's ethics and moral parameters, Jack,' I said, a bit pissed off at Ogilvie's overreaction, and the question itself. 'You see, strictly speaking you've seen two separate things; you can't be certain they're connected. It serves to show if a man is more likely to stick to the law and afford a man a fair trial or perjure himself at court to confirm a conviction.

To answer your question though, it would depend—'

'On what? Depends on what, exactly?' Ogilvie had shifted forward in his chair, fascinated.

'On two things actually. One – are you asking as my superior officer or off the record?'

'The latter, of course,' said the inspector. 'There's no reason not to answer honestly, but don't answer at all if it makes you uncomfortable.'

'The second thing, what is that?' said Ogilvie, trying to brush over the inspector's get-out opportunity.

'Two . . .' A small voice in my head was screaming at me from some deep place not to continue, but I couldn't help myself. 'In this hypothetical situation, can it be proved I didn't see him do it? Is there CCTV, or any risk at all of a witness?'

'Ha! I told you, didn't I tell you? He's one of the good ones.' Ogilvie lost the remaining half-inch of whisky from his glass as his hands shot up in delight. 'Of course you saw it. Fuck him and his fucking lawyer, send the bastard down.' Jack still looked confused; he really didn't get it at all. He made to fold his cards but hesitated and decided to match the bets.

The betting round finished I dealt another card and almost fist-pumped the air as another king came out – three of a kind, one of the better hands played all night. I fought to keep a neutral expression. Ogilvie folded but the inspector and Jack paid in. I wanted to raise, but it would have been the first time I had done so all night and I didn't want to scare them off, especially with Jack seemingly teetering on the edge, so I called.

Released from the game, Ogilvie recharged his glass and pulled his chair towards me.

'Something I wanted to discuss with you, Donald.' The last 'd' in my name had become a 't' as his accent continued to relax.

'What's that, Charles?' I delayed dealing the last card while I listened to him. I had the feeling whatever was coming would prove to be the reason I was sitting here. The two eager faces still playing stared at the deck in my hands, waiting to see the destination of the now-sizeable pot.

'An investment opportunity.'

Ah, this again, I thought. 'I am sorry, Charles. It sounds like a very exciting venture, but I honestly don't have anything to invest.'

'No, you don't understand. You wouldn't have to pay a penny.'

'I'm not sure I understand.'

'The venture, the estate and its future; I would like you to be part of it.'

'Why?' I didn't mean to be quite as blunt, but I was anxious for him to get to the point.

'What venture doesn't need smart, capable young men to succeed? I'd like you on the team.'

I sat for a moment, trying to give it deserved consideration, but I had no idea what he was asking me. 'I'm a little lost, Charles, you may need to clarify. What exactly would you need from me?' I peeled the last card from the top of the deck and laid it out in the centre of the table.

A queen, yes!

'Nothing exactly,' continued Ogilvie, 'I would invest on your behalf, you see. I would place fifty thousand in your name within the company.'

I stopped. It was actually a welcome distraction as I was doing somersaults in my head with my full house about to clean up. 'Why . . . would you do that? Give me fifty thousand pounds?'

'Not give, invest. On your behalf. As the estate recovers from some bad luck and the new venture starts to grow, so would your investment; and when the time is right, you can draw down on that investment.'

I looked to the inspector, to see if he was as confused as I was, but he didn't seem to be. He sat back in his chair holding his glass and crunching an ice cube.

'It means the well-being of the estate is in your hands, in *our* hands. A joint responsibility to ensure its success and long-term future,' said Ogilvie.

'OK, why would you do that, then?' To my surprise Jack raised, considerably. The inspector folded, intimidated out of continuing. The raise was more than I had agreed in my mind I could afford to lose, though I had enough chips to cover it, to raise again if I wanted to.

'I want you on board, that's all it is. You're something of a breath of fresh air, Donald. Young and capable and I want good people with me, people who actually give a damn about what we're doing here. It wouldn't interfere with your job; you have my word. You are planning to be here for a while, are you not?' If the inspector had not been sitting to my right, I would have told him that I had an interview for a job I was confident of getting. Instead I avoided answering the question.

'I'll call,' I said, pushing half of my remaining chips into the centre, 'and I'll raise.' I slid the remainder over, then turned back to Ogilvie. 'It all sounds very flattering, Charles, thank you. But I have a job, so I'm not interested. I don't think I'd be of any use to you and, frankly, I have enough on my plate currently.' Jack scratched at his chin for a moment before counting out the required chips to call and dropped them into the impressive hoard. I laid out my triumphant hand and gave Jack an apologetic smile, thinking about his gambling and subsequent money problems. He replied by laying out his pair of fives, four of a kind. He'd had it right from the start. What were the fucking odds?

'Sorry, Sergeant,' he said, trawling the chips into his fort.

'At least give it some thought, Donald. It is a very generous offer and it deserves some consideration, no? Jack, I'll cover this for Donald.' Ogilvie started to rummage for his wallet.

I stood and held up my hand. I fished my own wallet from my pocket. 'All bets must be covered at the end of the night, is that not so, Inspector? No exceptions.' I pulled every note from the brown leather wallet and let it drop onto the few chips Jack had yet to pick up. 'You can't bet what you don't have. Goodnight, gentlemen.'

CHAPTER SIXTEEN

Cross Examination

I hear feet. Not human feet. It's more scrabbling than stepping. It's coming from above me. What does that mean? That I'm underground? Not necessarily.

When Karen and I first got together we stayed in a second-floor flat in the west end of Glasgow. We bought a cat. It seemed like the thing to do, the next logical step. If I'm honest, I think I did it to stave off marriage talk. Karen took moving in together in her stride. Not that I would ever have admitted to her, but it scared the living shit out of me. I did want to, I was twenty-three, time to put away childish things and all that, and I was certain about Karen. It was just a lot to get my head around. A proper job was next on the list, perhaps the scariest aspect of the whole deal. I'd studied business at uni, though I'd never harboured thoughts of actually starting a business or working for someone else's. It was just one of those subjects you select when you have no clue what to do with your life, like sport science or philosophy. The police was Karen's idea. Her brother-in-law was a cop and he loved it – that was her pitch. *You get to work outdoors . . . it's dynamic, exciting . . . no two days are the same . . . early retirement with attractive package . . . blah blah . . . oh, and I downloaded the application, just in case.* Twelve months prior to this point I'd have laughed so hard at her I might have dropped my hash-pipe.

I began the recruitment process, fully expecting at every stage to have my complete and profound unsuitability for such a responsible role pointed out to me. And yet, somehow, bizarrely, it didn't happen. The final stage, the fitness test, turned out to be the easiest part. I'm not particularly strong, but I am particularly light, and since the focus is mainly on your ability to run, it wasn't a problem. The hardest part was posting my acceptance. It was all of a sudden very, very real.

Now, where was I going with this? My head is still fuzzy. Oh, the fucking cat. Archibald, at first, later Archie.

It took us a while to adjust to each other, Archie and I. For one thing, we had to share Karen, which neither of us were particularly comfortable with, but we found our rhythm eventually. When he was on Karen's knee I sat on the other sofa, and when grown-up noises were coming from the bedroom Archie stayed out. God, there was a monumental amount of shagging in those first few months in the flat; it waned after a while of course, as these things do, and Archie eventually found a little niche in between both sets of legs on the bed, but that was a good period. Archie was largely pretty docile, except when you made the mistake of touching his back just above his tail: that guaranteed lacerations. The only other time he could be stirred from his semi-permanent slumber was when the mice, or more likely the rats, were busy fighting, or maybe humping, in the wall cavity and the ceiling space between floors, at which point he would stand on his hind legs and chatter like a demented monkey. If he were here now, he would be going nuts with the sounds somewhere above my head. I miss him. It's a strange thing to admit to myself, but I do. Though maybe it's more about the context than the cat. I miss my life back then: comfortable, predictable, shared. Then I remember the disciplinary hearing and how that seemed to mirror what was to come. It started in that predictable way before taking a dark turn.

My neck was raw under my collar. I had shaved close and against the grain to ensure I would still be smooth no matter how long it might take. I forgot how abrasive the formal white shirt was, even without starch. I ran a sweaty finger around the inside; the salt on my wet finger only made matters worse.

I straightened the epaulettes on my thin shoulders. The uniform was designed with a more robust physique in mind and the insignia had an annoying habit of slipping to opposite sides, ruining the symmetry.

At last, a figure approached from the far end of the corridor. I wiped my slick hands on my trouser legs and stood as the officer reached me.

'Donald?'

'That's right.'

'You're on. Follow me, please.'

I snatched up my hat from the adjacent chair and did, having to shuffle somewhere in between walking and jogging to keep up.

'Are you OK? You look nervous.'

'I'm fine,' I lied. 'I've just never been to one of these before.'

'But you've been to court? I mean, you've been in the box and given evidence before?'

'Yes, of course, many times. So, it's just like that, then?'

'No, not really,' he laughed and held a swing door open for me. 'But the principle is the same: just tell the truth and you've nothing to worry about. There's no judge of course, it's three senior officers. They should keep you right, but they like these things to . . . flow, so just be careful.'

I was about to ask him exactly what he meant by that, but he was holding another door open and I knew it was too late for questions. Through it, to the left, I could see a raised area with a long table and three crisp white shirts behind it. In front of me, behind a smaller table, were two men in grey suits, deep in conversation. One of them was Terry.

I stepped into the room and all faces turned to me. I felt my arm gripped from behind.

'Hat.'

'What?'

'Put your hat on, take it off at the stand,' the officer growled in a whisper.

I looked down at my hand. I'd forgotten I was even holding a hat. I placed it on my head before walking a few steps and suddenly realising I didn't know where to go. Small tables were dotted all around the room, which was filled with bright sunlight beaming in from the large window directly in front of me, adding to my disorientation. I stepped towards the three senior officers but instantly saw the confusion on their faces. I found myself wandering into the centre of the room, searching side to side like a child playing blind man's bluff. Terry smiled with intense satisfaction.

'Please take the stand, Constable.' The female voice was an irritated one. Her arm directed me to the stand, which had been partly hidden behind the opened door. Now that it was closed, it seemed ludicrously obvious.

I stepped up and placed my hat on the small ledge in front of me, but too near the edge. I grabbed at it as it fell, catching it but slamming my arm into the small microphone set into the centre and sending an ear-splitting screech through the room.

Terry looked at me, his thumb on his chin and curled index finger masking his grin. He slowly shook his head in derision.

The three senior officers, the stern-looking woman flanked by two similarly serious men, stirred, and the man closest to me stood and approached the centre of the floor.

'Constable Colyear?'

'Yes, sir.'

'You won't be asked to swear-in here, such as in a court of law. Rather you are bound by the Police Scotland Act of 1967 to tell the complete truth during these proceedings. Do you understand your responsibilities here and accept that to fail in those responsibilities is to commit an offence under said Act and render yourself liable to prosecution and disciplinary procedure?'

Fuck, give me the damn Bible any day over this, I thought. 'Yes, sir. I do.'

The chief superintendent then ran through my evidence, basically paraphrasing the operational statement I had provided a few months earlier. Terry sat shaking his head, less subtly, tutting and laughing at the more damning aspects of my account. The man sitting next to him patted him reassuringly on the arm now and again and whispered in his ear.

My nerves had begun to settle, that was until my evidence was complete and the floor was handed over to Terry's brief. The man took an age to get to his feet. He sat shuffling through piles of paper while I stood secretly picking at the skin around my fingernails behind the stand.

At last he approached, smiling like a shark. His blonde hair was slicked back diagonally, and it was only when he was right in front of me that I saw his beard, the fine, almost white hair, nearly invisible against his pale complexion.

'Thank you for your testimony, Constable. Did it take you long?'

I was thrown. 'I'm sorry?' I said.

'Take you long, Constable . . . to come up with that enthralling piece of fiction?'

'. . . it's the truth, it's what hap—'

'Convenient little story, is it not? I mean, if we were to swallow that version it renders you blameless for the unfortunate events that occurred and places all culpability squarely and exclusively at the feet of my client.' There was a pause. There was no real question, so I waited, refusing to fill the awkward silence. 'A man's career hangs in the balance here, Constable. Have you nothing to say?'

'I'll answer any questions you have for me, sir,' I said. I could hear ire in my voice. I locked my fingers together behind the stand, applying pressure into my knuckles.

'Let me give you an alternative version of events, Constable. A version, unlike yours, which has basis in fact rather than fiction; a version which can be quantified and qualified and I'm afraid doesn't paint you in a particularly good light.

'You claim that my client refused to attend the domestic incident call, that, despite your best efforts, he would not turn the car around and was therefore in neglect of his duties as an officer of the law, correct?'

'Yes, that's cor—'

'You claim that my client, for as long as you've known him, showed serious and consistent failings as an officer. That the night in question, which resulted in a delayed response to what proved to be a grave incident, was just one example of those failings?'

'That's not exactly what I said, but yes, I think you could—'

'My question to you, Constable, is that if my client truly is the miserable excuse for a police officer, that you claim, how do you explain these?' He held a large bundle of the papers he had been shuffling, fanned out for effect. He flashed them to me and then to the panel of three. 'Eighteen. *Eighteen* character references from colleagues,' he said with some theatre. 'Including four officers who have worked directly with him in the past year, and all of whom make no mention of any such failings.' He separated the bundle into three equal piles and handed them to the panel. 'Not only do the references fail to highlight shortcomings in my client's professionalism, they are, in fact, nothing short of commendations. Can you explain this startling contradiction?'

'Look, no one's debating the fact that he's a popular officer . . .'

'"Capable, professional and dedicated, and a joy to work with,"' he read.

'Well, not in my experience.'

'"I would trust him with my life."' He looked up from the sheet of paper, exaggerating a confused expression to me and then the panel. 'Doesn't sound like the officer you describe, now, does it?'

'You're right, it really doesn't.'

'I'm glad you agree.' He placed the sheet he was holding down and picked up a new bundle. '"Constable Colyear, all of a sudden, began to show signs of extreme abdominal discomfort. I was aware of a call requiring response, but my immediate concern was for my colleague." His immediate concern was his colleague. Now, that does fit, wouldn't you agree?'

'That's not what happened.'

He held a hand up, indicating he wasn't finished.

'"He became increasingly distressed and eventually I was forced to pull the car over to the side of the road. As I did, Constable Colyear opened the passenger door and fell out onto the pavement. I attempted to radio for help, but by then the domestic incident the call handler had been requesting attendance to had escalated and the radio traffic had become too heavy to arrange for help. I alighted from the vehicle and assisted Constable Colyear as best I could. He was violently sick for close to ten minutes, convulsing as if having a fit. I placed my jacket under his head and was about to call for an ambulance on my own mobile phone when he seemed to come out of it. I was thereafter subjected to extensive and prolonged verbal abuse by Constable Colyear and would have reported the unprofessional behaviour had I not assumed the verbal attack to be some sort of after-effect from the fit.

'"It was with profound shock, disbelief and disappointment that I later learnt of the allegations made by Constable Colyear and refute them with the sincerest assertion."

'Sirs and ma'am, this is the truth of the matter. This is the true account of the events of the night in question. As I have shown, his actions are in keeping with the character described by his colleagues. Now, I'm afraid I have to bring to light some unsavoury revelations.' The lawyer was speaking to the panel, but he was looking at me. 'What Constable Colyear has reported to this enquiry is not just inaccurate, or some plausible alternative interpretation. It is, in fact, a lie. Worse still, it is a vindictive one.'

'What?' I blurted.

'A lie with *malicious* intent,' he shouted, preventing any further interjection. 'You don't like my client, do you, Constable?'

There was no safe way to answer. 'I don't see what difference it makes. We're here because of what he did or didn't do. Not because I have a personal quarrel with him.'

'Oh, I think it's very relevant, Constable. In fact, I put it to you it's the *only* reason we're here today.' Again, there was a silence. Again, I waited for a direct question. 'There's nothing you would like more than to see my client found guilty here today, isn't that so? See him lose the job he loves, is committed to and which provides for his family? In fact, you want to see that so much that you concocted these lies to ensure that it happens. Isn't that so?'

'No, that's not—'

'This is a personal attack on a hard-working man you simply despise. This is a vendetta, Constable Colyear, and the wrong officer is on trial here today.'

'Utter nonsense,' I scoffed.

'Nonsense? Is that what you said there? I didn't quite catch that . . .' His voice was suddenly and alarmingly level. I didn't answer. Our eyes locked and I could feel beads of sweat running down my back. 'I have one more account for you, Constable and members of the panel, then I'm done here and I will leave you to decide who has the facts.'

He returned to his table and reached into a black folder, producing two single sheets of paper. I used the short break as an opportunity to sip from the glass of water in front of me. My hand shook as I raised it to my mouth. The rim made a drumroll on my teeth. I didn't know what was coming, but it was clearly what his whole bit was leading to; the finale, his coup de grâce. I had been nervous as soon as I entered the building, but I had the reassurance of being in the right, the comfort of knowing that all I would be required to do, as uncomfortable as it was, was to tell the truth. That was before. Now, somehow, somewhere along the road, I was no longer a witness for the prosecution. I wasn't on the stand; I was in the dock and I had no slick lawyer to defend *me*.

He walked slowly to the panel and handed one of the sheets to the female super, the other two leant in over her shoulders to read. He strolled back to the centre of the room. It felt like he was winding up a pitch, or perhaps cocking a rifle. I glanced at Terry; he winked back.

'"I was told to help get his figures up. So, if I can do that, I can get shot of the big useless fucker,"' said the brief. Three sets of officious eyes shot to him. 'Excuse the language, I'm just quoting here. "Working with him is a complete nightmare."'

Oh, shit.

'You do recognise those words, don't you, Constable?' The repeated use of 'constable' was driving a hot knife into my brain.

'Whose account is this?' asked one of the male supers, pushing on a pair of half-lens glasses before my dry mouth could attempt a response.

'My apologies,' said the brief, scanning his own copy or pretending to. 'I seem to have forgotten to properly title this. This is the testimony of a Constable Alyson Kane, but the words are Constable Colyear's.

'Do you recall this conversation, Constable? Do you remember saying these things about my client?'

'I, uh. I'm not sure if I said . . .'

'Well, your colleague was adamant, Constable. Was she lying?'

'No, well, I didn't—'

'If I may, sirs and ma'am, draw your attention to the last sentence on the page, the highlighted and underlined section.' He coughed into his hand, clearing his throat, pulling the rifle to his shoulder. "People like him shouldn't be in the job. If it was up to me, I'd just get rid of him and worry about the tribunal later."'

Fuck. Fuck fuck fuck!

CHAPTER SEVENTEEN

Worse Jobs

'The time is twenty-thirty-seven hours on Friday the twenty-second of November. I am Police Sergeant Donald Colyear of Police Scotland. We are in interview room one of Oban Police Station. I will ask the others present to identify themselves.' I nodded at Rowan prompting her. She leant over the desk as if there was a microphone in front of her.

'Uh, Police Constable Rowan Forbes. Oh, of Police Scotland.' She raised her eyebrows at me. I gave her an affirmatory expression.

'Miss Gladstone is helping with our enquiries and I will ask her to identify herself and to provide her date of birth and address. Please,' I urged.

'Meredith Gladstone,' she said, and I saw her exchange a look with Rowan. 'Eighteen-four-seventy-seven. My address is twelve Culver Court.'

'Thank you,' I said.

'Swanky name for a prozzer, right?' Meredith chuckled.

'No, well . . . It's j-just—' stammered Rowan.

'Your eyebrows nearly knocked a hole in the ceiling, luv.' Rowan cleared her throat, her eyes on her clasped hands. 'Relax, I'm just pulling your leg. Few generations back, there were some right posh ones in the family by all accounts. By the time me mum comes into the world there ain't two pennies to rub together. Some distant uncle or some shit pissed it up a wall, apparently. So here I am, common as muck, but with a name that makes me sound a bit la-di-da. My mum, you see, she figured a posh name might give me, I dunno, opportunities or something. If she could see me sitting in a cop shop now, she'd realise it were a waste of time. If you prefer, you can call me Celeste, like me, um, clients do. Or used to. I've given all that up now. But if we're going with me Sunday name, I prefer Eddy.'

'Thank you for coming in tonight, Eddy,' I said. 'Before we start, I must inform you that you are going to be asked questions about the death of Iain Cooper. I must caution you that you are not obliged to say anything in response to these questions, and anything you do say will be noted, visually and audibly recorded and may be used in evidence. Do you understand?'

'You make it sound like I have a choice.'

'You are here voluntarily, you understand that? You're free to leave whenever you like. That has been explained to you?'

'When the fuzz turns up at your work looking for ya, it sort of takes the voluntary bit out of it, don't you think?'

'I'm sorry about that. I was eager to get hold of you. I hope it didn't cause any problems?' I had attended the address held for her on PNC on three occasions, the last one pretty late at night. A neighbour on the same floor as her flat had swung her door open, ready to give me dog's abuse before spotting the uniform. Embarrassed, she suddenly became most helpful, pointing out Eddy worked at the local Spar shop and that she worked shifts. I wouldn't make a habit of going to someone's place of work, unless to execute a warrant, but I wanted to do a good job for DS Aitken. I wasn't sure why exactly, other than perhaps to counter a sense of inadequacy. Eddy had looked pretty stunned when I approached her. She was sat behind the kiosk looking absent and bored. Her face flushed red when I produced my identification. After a very quick chat, she had agreed to meet at Oban station the following evening.

'Probably not, though there will be questions.'

'Just tell them you're helping with enquiries. That's all you *are* doing after all.'

'Isn't that what you lot say just before you send someone down? *The police are keen to speak to a thirty-four-year-old male to help wiv enquiries?*' she mimicked. 'Nah, it'll be all right. My supervisor's a bit sweet on me, I think. Not really my type, but I might throw 'im a bone.' She winked at me.

The most striking thing about Meredith Gladstone was how unremarkable she was. I wasn't about to admit that I'd never come into contact with a sex worker before. The areas I had policed in my career didn't have red-light districts and I'd never had an enquiry before that had taken me into the underworld of more covert prostitution. Sitting before me was a woman in her early forties, wearing a green waterproof coat and comfortable jeans. Her dark hair was tied back into a ponytail revealing a handsome, though completely un-made-up face. What was I expecting? Bright red lipstick and fishnet tights? There was a confidence about her, though. Her posture was bold, gallus even. She was unfazed by a police interview. Rowan, however, sat with her arms and legs folded.

'I want to be clear before we get into it, Eddy. You're not being investigated in any way for breaching any laws for sex work. We're really not interested in pursuing anything like that, we're just hoping you can help clear up a few points on what we are investigating. I can promise you that there will be no repercussions in terms of prostitution here. We really are grateful for you speaking to us.'

'And if you change your mind on that, I can get a copy of this 'ere tape so a lawyer can hear you say that?'

'Yes, absolutely.'

'All right. Good to know.'

'Your accent, Eddy, London?' I asked.

'Lewisham. I was there till I were fifteen or so, then I did a lot of moving around, sort of gradually north. I reckon I might hit the Arctic by the time I reach fifty.'

'How old are you, Eddy?' asked Rowan. She could have worked it out from her date of birth, but she seemed to be trying to make conversation, get involved.

'Forty-two.'

'Kids?'

'Four-year-old boy.'

'Where is he now?' Rowan continued.

'With me neighbour Kath. You spoke to her. She has a little one 'n all. We sort of help each other out. She's a good one.'

'We'll try not to keep you too long tonight, Eddy,' I said. 'I mentioned that this is to do with the unfortunate events surrounding Mr Iain Cooper.'

At this she crossed her legs. 'I didn't know his name, but know who you mean,' she said. 'Look, I came out of the game a few years back, when I got the job at the Spar. Being a checkout monkey isn't great, but there's worse jobs.'

'Fingerprints we found in Cooper's cottage matched with yours, you see. Now, I'm not calling you a liar, Eddy, but it's unlikely they're that old; they tend to deteriorate fairly quickly.'

'That's what I was about to say. I gave it up a few years back, but there were one or two clients I would still see.'

'You kept Mr Cooper as a client after you stopped? Geez, how bad were your other ones?' said Rowan.

'Don't get me wrong, luv, he were a manky old sod, but he would never lay a finger on ya. Often quite literally.'

'Could you explain that further?' I said.

She heaved a heavy breath and said, 'I don't suppose I need to explain some of the situations us girls can find ourselves in when we're working. If you don't know, you probably wouldn't believe me. But once my little fella come along, my own safety took on a whole new light. It's not like I weren't bothered before I had him, but I just thought about it so much more. Cooper, if that were his name, well, he were pretty repugnant, but harmless at the same time.'

226

Rowan leant forward slightly, about to ask something, but I placed my hand on her arm out of sight. She sat back. 'He couldn't get it up, you see. Well, not often. He was into taking pictures mostly. Occasionally he got worked up enough to take a hand job but it was . . . I dunno, easy money. Safe money, more importantly.'

I'm sure Rowan was unaware, but she looked like she'd just swallowed spoilt milk.

'When you visited, how did you get there?' I asked.

'I drove.'

'When was the last time you visited Mr Cooper?'

She sat back in her chair and raised her eyes. I followed her gaze. There was a dark orange stain originating in one corner of the porous, cork-like soundproof material that covered not only the ceiling but all four walls too. It spread into the centre of the room like an accusing finger, settling at the small fluorescent light tube that cast a harsh but dream-like haze into the room. 'I think maybe three months ago. It certainly weren't any sooner than that.'

'Is there anyone can verify that?' She twisted her mouth at me in a what-the-fuck-do-you-think gesture. 'For the purpose of the tape, please, Eddy.'

'No, there ain't. It's not like me fanny prints receipts.'

Rowan moved to speak again but glanced at me. I nodded and she said, 'Tell us about the last time you saw him. Please,' she added.

'It was a typical visit really. I showed up in a long coat. Underneath I had a schoolgirl outfit, that was 'is favourite. We did a bit of tying up, 'im first then me. He took a few pics. I thought it was going to be one of the times he got excited enough to come, but he went all limp in me hand. We had a quick cuddle and I left. Easy three hundred quid.'

'Where does all the black-magic stuff come into it?' I said.

'Oh, I dunno really. Sometimes when he had me tied up he'd read from one of 'is books. Mumbo-jumbo. I used to imagine he were trying to raise his willy from the dead – never worked, nor anything else. Trust me, as far as kink goes, it's harmless.'

'How about the rabbit?' asked Rowan.

'The what?'

'There was a rabbit nailed to his wall when we found him.'

'Really? I don't know nothing about that. But yeah, sounds like the sort of thing he might do. I'm not saying he weren't a weird sort, just that I never felt like I was in danger.'

'His body was tied to the bed with silk scarves, a star drawn onto his torso in lipstick,' I said and watched her for any kind of reaction. She didn't flinch as she awaited a question. 'Did you ever engage in such things with him?'

She shrugged dismissively. 'Not so much the lipstick, but yes. The tying up stuff was what he was into. And candles, him and those fucking candles. He was into the whole wax dripping thing. I charged him near double if we wanted to do it to me. If there was ever a twitch of his cock, it was usually during that sort of stuff.'

I pulled Cooper's Polaroids from his folder and laid them out on the table. 'Are you in any of these, Eddy?'

'She leant forward on the table and scanned them. 'Yeah, that's me, schoolgirl outfit, like I said.'

'Any others?'

'Just that one.'

'Do you recognise any of the other girls?'

She leant forward again. 'No, I don't think so. But it's not like we all go out and play bingo together on our days off. Listen, you don't think I 'ad anything to do with . . . well, whatever happened to 'im. Do you?'

'What do you understand happened to him?' I said.

She shrugged again. 'Just what you hear. Someone was talking about it at my checkout last week. It's a small place up here; everyone's into other people's business. These two women were talking to one another, talking about black magic and how this guy was found with his heart cut out and all this. That's bullshit, right? I mean, if that were true it would be all over the news. I didn't even think about it until one of them mentions prostitutes and then I start thinking, shit . . . what if it's Iain? Then you come waltzing into the shop and my heart stops beating. I mean, do I need to be talking to a lawyer?'

'That's entirely up to you,' I said. 'But it is bullshit, yes. It's nothing so grizzly as what people around here have been making up themselves. I'm just trying to put together his last movements. You're sure it was three months since you saw him?'

'Positive, yeah. I have a phone I use for work. I used to post an ad in the classifieds, see. He would call when he wanted to see me. I can give you that to check if you like?'

'Thanks, that would be good. Can I ask . . . ?' I hesitated, a little embarrassed. 'Why does a man who can't get it up use prostitutes? I mean when his erection fails, is that not humiliating?'

She shrugged. 'He never seemed that embarrassed. If you're paying for it you expect a certain, professional detachment, I suppose? I mean it's not like I'm there to be pleasured, right? I'm not going home in a sulk if he can't stick it in somewhere. But like I said, sometimes he did manage, just not often.'

'Apart from the tying up and photography, was there anything that seemed to get him particularly excited?' I wondered if I would regret this question. I expected another relaxed response, but she seemed to harden at this.

'All right, look. I will mention something, and it's probably nothing. I said he was into the schoolgirl thing. One night, I went over and I put a bit of effort in, you see. Tied my hair in pigtails, dotted a few freckles on my cheeks with me eyeliner acted a bit coy when I dropped my coat. That seemed to do the trick. We didn't even bother with the tying up. After he come, he asks me . . .' There was a heavy pause and we let it sit. Eventually she went on but had abandoned her thought. 'You know what, it doesn't matter. I mean, it doesn't mean nothing and it's not kind to talk ill of the—'

'Please, Eddy. It seemed important a moment ago. Please finish.'

She scratched at her hair and then at her chin. 'Girls,' she said. 'Do I know any girls on the job I could introduce 'im to. I says, yeah, of course I do. At this point I think he means he wants like a threesome situation, or maybe just watch me with another girl. But then I catch 'is meaning. Young girls, you see. What you want with young'uns? I say. What you need is a woman knows how to make you feel good, I says. You know, trying to make light of it. But I know what he meant.'

'What did he mean?' I said, knowing also, but for the tape . . .

'Kids, like. You know?'

'Did he say that? That he wanted to sleep with an underage girl?'

'Not in so many words, no. I think he realised I weren't going to be party to anything like that and he dropped it. It were a long time before I heard from 'im again, and when I did, I wouldn't put the extra effort in like that time. Just the usual. Look, I should be getting back soon for the little fella. Am in any trouble?'

'No trouble at all, Eddy.' I said.

CHAPTER EIGHTEEN

How to Secure a Confession

The rain had kept up, in varying degrees, the whole day. When I arrived at work at 10 p.m. I was surprised to find Rowan standing in the public area, dressed for a foot patrol and raring to go.

'You do realise it's pissing down, don't you?' I said.

'Come on, a bit of rain never hurt anyone.'

'People say that, but I think you'd find, if you looked, that a bit of rain has killed countless millions since the dawn of time.'

'Oh, grow a pair. I think there's a Dora the Explorer brolly in the lost and found. Should I fetch it?'

'I tell you what, if you let me in on what this is all about, I'll use it.'

'No deal. Now get your coat on, Sarge. We're off to the pub.'

* * *

Outside, the rain was quickly turning to sleet, as the temperature dropped again. The thickening drops stung like tiny whips on the skin and a dizzying wind, that couldn't make its mind up which direction it was coming from, bit and pummelled. The more established snow on the ground was being galvanised as ice and made slick.

Rowan stood with her arms folded, her collar high and a snood covering her face from just below the eyes. She stared intently at the side door of the hotel, the bar entrance, slowly swivelling her shoulders to keep warm. Her hair was sodden, and now and again she would squeeze a gathering drip from the front of her head. I resisted the urge to tell her *I told you so*. I had reluctantly agreed to go with black jackets as opposed to the high-vis which would have been more sensible in the heavy darkness. I had also agreed to allow the hats to be left in the station, partly intrigued and partly unable to bring myself to stymie Rowan's bizarre eagerness.

'It's time, Forbes,' I said, looking at my wrist where a watch would be, had I one. We'd stood for an hour and a half, saying little to one another. The rain had breached my trousers, dampening my thighs underneath. 'Explain, or I'm calling it a night.'

'I will, I promise. Just give it another ten minutes or so.'

'Fine,' I huffed, 'but no "or so". You've got ten minutes, then I'm pulling the plug. You know, if this is some sort of surveillance there are proper channels we need to observe. You can't just take it upon yourself to spy on people,' I added, trying to second guess her.

'We're not spying on anyone. We're looking at public property, aren't we?'

I tried to catch her eye to give her a look, but her gaze never wavered. 'I suppose so,' I conceded.

From our vantage point under an ineffective eave of the hotel, we had a decent view of the entrance. The rain and lack of moonlight meant the distance and shadows were a problem, but it was as close as we could be without standing in the open.

'I think it's him,' she said uncertainly. She smiled at me and side-nodded her head, urging me to follow her. A dark figure I didn't recognise had stumbled from the bar. He stopped to spit, perhaps deciding whether saliva was to be followed by vomit. Reassured that his recently purchased beer was safe for the time being, he continued down the drive.

'I told you, we can't just go spying on people. You need to apply for proper—'

'Shhh,' she said. 'We just happened to be here. Come on, but we need to keep our distance.'

'You're gonna get us both into trouble,' I whispered. 'OK, time to spill.'

'All right,' she said, leaning in close, keeping her voice low. 'You know that vandalism I've been sitting on?'

'Mrs Gillespie's fence? The one you should have returned for filing a month ago?'

We stopped as the dark figure ahead stumbled against the wall of the hotel. For a moment he looked to have lost his bearings, as though he might head back in our direction. Autopilot re-established, he continued on, as did we, cautiously.

'And you remember what you said a while back about patterns?'

I clawed at the memory but couldn't grasp it. 'Not really, no.'

'You talked about investigating minor crimes when there was little evidence. You suggested looking at potential patterns.'

'Right, yeah, I remember. I also remember looking with you at vandalisms, and although there's been a few, it's not enough to establish any kind of pattern,' I whispered, as the figure took a left onto the main road. There was no footpath, and he was walking one foot on the verge, the other on the road. We waited to lengthen the distance between us as there was no cover.

Rowan pulled at my collar, urging me to lean down to her level. 'You also said sometimes lazy cops change the call types on incidents so that the bosses aren't looking for crime reports we can't solve.'

'So I did.'

'That piss artist,' she said with an aggressive point of the finger, 'is Jim McPhee.'

I shook my head dumbly.

'He's the only joiner in the village?'

I smiled, waiting, still not getting it.

Rowan's eyes rolled and she said, 'He is also the only glazer, builder and blacksmith.'

'Talented guy,' I said.

'Oh, come on.'

Jim, if it was this impressive handyman, had turned off the road into a residential street. Rowan's pace quickened as he disappeared out of view.

'I had a look on the incidents system when I was down

235

in Oban,' Rowan said, breaking into a light jog. 'I asked the operator to pull up everything that was initially reported as a vandalism but was subsequently changed to something else. And guess what?'

'You found a few?'

'I found loads.'

Our heads shot left and right in search of the disappeared Jim as we cut along the street.

'Wait,' said Rowan, and slid to a halt. She backed up and pointed down a back lane where two lots of back gardens pointed at one another. From where I was standing it looked like Jim was humping a garden gate. The silhouette pumped back and forward. Rhythmic grunting was accompanied by the occasional crack of wood. Rowan gave me a mixed look of surprise and comical smugness. I couldn't help but laugh. We watched on for a minute until Jim had stopped, or perhaps finished. We approached quietly.

'Hello, Mr McPhee,' said Rowan, but she got no response. Jim was now midstream against the violated gate which hung awkwardly on a broken hinge. 'Jim,' she said sharply.

'Hoozat?' said Jim, and we both shuttled backwards to avoid being pissed on. 'What th' fuck?'

'Police, Mr McPhee.'

'Is it fuck.'

'It is, Mr McPhee,' I said. 'We were just watching you pulling this gate off its hinge. Any particular reason why?'

'Naw you didnae.'

'We did, Jim. Now nip that piss off,' said Rowan.

'Canae. Once it's goin, it's goin.'

We stood, awkwardly, for what felt like minutes as he pissed like a racehorse. He swayed gently, audibly catching his boot every once in a while.

'How did you know?' I asked quietly, though I suspected it mattered little.

'Some of the incidents were a bit random, changed by cops from a reported vandalism to probable accidents or a stone kicked up by cars or suchlike. But every month, the last weekend of the month to be exact, you have an almost uninterrupted run of calls for minor damage. And when you bring the incidents up on the map system you have this lovely straight line from the pub, through these streets for about half a mile and then they stop at Gourlay Crescent, where . . .'

'Mr McPhee lives.'

'Bingo. When an incident was correctly marked as a vandalism, his was the only name attached to the reports when we looked for a cost of repair to complete them. He had a nice little captive market. Why it happens last Saturday of the month I don't know, but I had a feeling we'd get a result tonight.'

'So, what is it, Mr McPhee?' Is that when the bills pile up? When you have to pay an employee or two?' I asked, as he took an age to zip himself up.

'Doh-no what yer talkin' about, laddie. What's the script anyway? I fell against the gate. I'll fix it t'morra, nae harm done, eh?'

'Not that simple, Jim,' said Rowan, cuffing him. 'We'll get you down the road, then when you've had a sleep, we'll talk about all the little falls you've had over the last few years, eh? Thirty-six by my reckoning.'

The ten-minute walk to the station took closer to a half-hour. With our hands planted in his armpits, holding him up, he threatened a few times to fall asleep mid stroll. He came to when we tried to bundle him into the cage at the rear of the van. With no holding cells at Stratharder, we were going to have to process him at Oban.

'Look, come on now, isnoneed fur-at,' Jim pleaded. His passive resistance was exhausting. By allowing his arms and legs to fall dead weight, it was like trying to pour a giant squid into an aeroplane baggage compartment. Rowan, eventually, climbed into the cage and hauled while I pushed, meaning she had to climb over the top of him to get out again.

'Come on guys, isamisunderstandin, 'atsall it is. I've no' done nuthin', just drop us hame will ye?' he managed, before Rowan slammed the door on him.

We sat in the van waiting for the engine to warm up and the screen to clear. Our sodden clothes cast a wall of condensation that the van's blowers made tedious progress against.

'Thirty-six, you think?'

'At least, yeah. Also, you don't know how many weren't reported over the years. You might well double that number.'

'Cheeky bastard. Quite the racket he's been running. Do you have a note of all the incidents?' I asked.

'I have them all printed off in my folder; all the ones I could find anyway. We could look back through the system when we get down there if you like?'

'No, I trust you caught them all. This is really good work, Rowan. *Really* good.'

'I'm going to choose not to be offended by your tone of surprise. You know your problem, Sarge? You just assume everyone around you is incompetent. It might often be the case, but not always.'

I smeared a sleeve across the passenger side of the windscreen in front of me, hoping it might speed things up, but the moisture in my cuff was comparable to that on the glass, so it did little but provide a distorted view of the world outside. 'You're right,' I said, 'that's fair. But take the compliment. It wouldn't have occurred to me to look over those incidents. Are you comfortable taking the interview when we get . . . What's up?'

Rowan was no longer listening. She was leaning forward over the steering wheel craning her neck as she peered through the small patch of clear windscreen above the vent.

'A car sitting outside the front door of the station.'

'What's it doing?' I asked, unable to make out much from my view but a kaleidoscopic blur.

'Nothing, it's just sitting there. It's running, you can see from the exhaust. I can't see into the windows though.'

'Come on, guys, give us a break. I haven't done nuthin',' came Jim's muffled voice from behind, which we chose to ignore.

'I'll go see what they want; they're maybe lost or looking to report something,' I said and opened the door to an icy wet blast of air.

Sure enough, a black hatchback sat facing us, idling by the kerb outside the station door. The windows were tinted and I couldn't make out any identifying badges. Removed, I guessed, which was the cool thing to do with modified cars such as this. I ducked my head and waved, unknowing if I was being observed as I approached. The car's headlamps erupted on full beam, consuming me in light. I shielded my eyes and stepped to the side, out of the glare. A bright spot burned in the middle of my vision. The car's engine wailed into life and I caught sight of an arm dangling from the passenger window. It held a beer bottle which, a split-second later, whizzed by my head spraying me with its sour stink before exploding off the van's bonnet.

Laughter, a roaring engine and screeching tyres followed. I ran back to the van. Rowan was already hammering the gearstick into first as my arse hit the seat. The windscreen on Rowan's side was a little clearer, though she still ducked to get the best view. On my side, though, I had only terrifying obscurity. She wheel-spun out of the car park and onto the main road in pursuit. I updated Control, but my details were pathetic – black car, two or more occupants, unknown make, unknown registration. Current location? Erm, Stratharder. Direction of travel? (fuck knows) Through Stratharder?

The hatchback was quick, but the van was deceptively fast too, and the conditions were a leveller, as were Rowan's abilities behind the wheel. I searched for a dry patch of sleeve and had another go at the glass, a little better, just in time for me to see us approach a corner on the opposite lane before Rowan took a racing line back in to stay within sight of our quarry. We were still within the town centre, approaching sixty, which is not in itself fast, but in a built-up area with too many adjoining roads to take account of, it felt like light speed. Lights flashing and sirens wailing, we pursued as the black car, pulling away from us a good distance, took a left onto Main Street, too quickly for the conditions. By the time we hit the same corner, which Rowan took slower, but better, the car was only just righting itself from an over-correction. A thump was heard from the cage and a moan. Jim, it seemed, was unprepared for a sudden change of direction, probably asleep but no longer.

Directly behind the hatchback now, Rowan rammed through the gears trying to keep up. I strained to read the car's registration as it roared in front of us, trying to regain its distance, rear end fishtailing slightly as the driver applied too much gas. I caught only a few of the last letters, even then I wasn't certain.

The rain had redoubled and the wipers beat a hasty rhythm that echoed my heart rate. The exertions of the engine had finally cleared the windscreen and I had an unobscured view as the hatchback cut into a residential street.

This time it was our own back end that swayed left and right as Rowan tacked into the street, the extra weight in the rear causing our grip to falter.

'Fuckin-ell. Yous trying tae make me puke, or what?' was Jim's remonstration from the cage, as he was thrown back and forth. 'I've not done nothing, you can't do—' Jim was cut off with a slam, as Rowan slalomed between two cars parked on opposite sides of the narrow road. There were a few seconds of silence and I was worried he had been knocked unconscious but, as the van turned back onto Main Street, losing ground, he was again thrown and again complained.

'Ow, fuck. This isn't gonna work you know. I've no' done nuthin', nuthin'. You hear me!' he yelled, and beat the cage with a fist or a foot. He sounded a little more sober.

'Just hang in there, Jim,' I yelled through the wall.

We reached the town limit and the lying lumps of snow grew by the side of the road. The rear lights of the hatchback glowed like cigar ends in the distance. Rowan gave the throttle everything it had, but the sheer weight of the van meant that the lighter car had a huge advantage now that we were out onto the main road with less turns to even the odds.

'Fucker's going to get away,' said Rowan.

'Just keep on him. You're doing fine,' I said, but I knew we only had a few turns before we were out onto the Langie and four miles of straight road for them to press home the advantage.

Rowan cut the siren; it was pointless out of the town. The emergency beacons stayed on, illuminating the lying snow. The patches clinging resolutely to the trees flashed by like fairy lights and the fields beyond became lakes of electric blue.

Rowan's knowledge of the road was better than mine. I would have slowed the van far more for a double bend that came on us suddenly, but she expertly weaved a direct path through with as little correction as possible. The driver of the hatchback clearly did not know the road as well as Rowan as we had regained good ground on them.

'Should we stop?' asked Rowan with a head flick, gesturing at Jim in the cage.

'Fuck that, we're right on them again.'

'Please . . .' wailed Jim, perhaps hearing our debate. 'Look, maybe I did fall on a few gates over the years, but it was just when things got really tough, and it was just once or twice.'

'Bullshit, Jim,' called Rowan. 'Damn, they're really pulling away now.' She was right. We were onto the Langie and the quicker, lighter car was becoming a red speck. 'You all right?' she asked. I had grown quiet as my stomach began to pitch.

'I'm OK. Stay on him.' I pushed a hand under my body armour and groped at my belly. I had had a painful bout of cramps a few days before and I tried to remember if this was the same thing. Was the pain in the same place?

'I think this is as fast as the shit heap will go,' said Rowan, though we were pushing a hundred and ten aided by a slight gradient. The hatchback remained in view but only just. Large flakes of snow had replaced the drizzle. Had we been anywhere else the deteriorating vision would have necessitated more caution, but the unfaltering straight line had Rowan asking everything of the van.

'Fuck,' I grunted, gripping the dashboard. I knew these cramps. 'Rowan . . . slow up, something's wrong.'

'What are you talking about? We'll catch up to them after the Langie.'

'Rowan,' I said, my voice gaining urgency and volume. 'Something is really wrong. Just let them go. You have to trust . . . ah, fuck.' A sickening bolt of pain shot through me. 'Rowan, stop. Now!'

'Fuck, Sarge. OK, OK.' With a face of disappointment and frustration Rowan let up the accelerator and pushed her foot to the brake. There was a momentary forward lean from the van and then nothing. 'What the fuck?' she said, and she began to pump her leg.

'What, what is it?'

'No brakes,' she said. I thought for a second she was joking, that her leg bouncing up and down was just sick humour but the look on her face erased any such thoughts. 'Shit, shit, what do I do?'

I tried to answer but my guts twisted again and my eyes locked shut. It was a few seconds before I could open them again, and as I did, I saw that her hand was gripping the handbrake.

'No. Don't do that,' I yelled, and her hand sprang away from the lever as if it were white-hot. 'We're doing almost a hundred. If you lock up the back wheels we're dead.'

'Well, what the fuck *do* I do?'

'Your foot's off the accelerator?' She looked at me as if I were a moron. 'Are we slowing at all?'

She examined the speedo. 'Not really.'

I looked at the gauge myself. The deceleration was far too slight. 'How long until the road bends?'

'I dunno, about a mile or so. It's a really sharp left and there's trees on both sides. Should I pick a field and just go through a fence?' she asked. Her voice trembled. She gripped the wheel furiously as we both gently bobbed with the imperfections in the road surface. I killed the blue lights; they were distracting my thinking. The hatchback was long gone.

'At this speed,' I said, 'it would be too risky. We could roll and in this kind of vehicle we'd be dead for sure.' We hurtled on in silence for a moment with the needle refusing doggedly to drop below ninety.

'Half a mile, Don. Then we're straight into a tree.'

Death by fucking cliché, I thought. 'OK, let's try something, but you need to be careful. Push in the clutch and put the gear stick into fourth. OK, now release the clutch slowly. If you do it too fast we'll lock up.'

'Shit, can't you do it?'

'By the time we try to change over we'll be out of time. Just do it gradually. The engine will slow us.'

Rowan's face was solid fear and concentration. The engine began to complain wildly as she raised her foot. The van lurched forward and in her panic Rowan reapplied the clutch.

'I can't, I can't. I'll get it wrong and crash into a ditch.'

'Rowan, there's no time. Do it now or we're dead. Do the same again.'

She did and there was a wobble as she finally managed to let go of the clutch completely.

'OK, good. Now, into third.'

Again, the engine wailed and the van's bonnet bowed in reaction, but this time the tail kicked out. Rowan fought with the wheel for control as I braced for impact, but she rescued the traction. The trees around us were building and I knew the corner was fast approaching. I looked at the gauge – still doing over fifty.

'We're still way too fast for the corner,' I yelled over

the engine noise. 'Now, into second, but you have to be even more careful now.' I gave her a you-can-do-this nod and resisted the urge to scream at her to hurry up. She pulled the stick into second and again, I braced, knowing the lower gears were much more likely to lock the wheels if she released too quickly. The engine noise built again and it screamed its fury. The van heaved forward in short bursts as Rowan tried to find the right pressure. The long glistening line of road in front of us had been eaten up to a dark dead end. The van continued to slow, but it wasn't going to be enough.

'Jim, brace yourself!' I yelled and banged hard on the cage behind me. He didn't have time to ask why before the bend was on us.

Rowan did what she could. A lighter vehicle in dry conditions would struggle to take the corner at thirty and we were still north of forty. She angled the van as far to the right as possible and I just prayed fate wasn't about to deliver an oncoming vehicle to add to the mess. At the last possible moment she pulled the wheel left and finally let the clutch out all the way. My stomach convulsed and the wheels locked, sending the tail of the van spinning out. She must have pushed the clutch in again as the wheels began to spin but it was too late. The rear wheels left the road into a ditch, dragging the rest of the van with it. Rowan was thrown towards me as the van threatened to roll, but her seat belt caught her. A branch exploded through my side window. The handle of my door punched me viciously in the ribs and I lost my breath completely.

We came to a stop in the ditch lying at forty-five degrees. I looked over at Rowan. She stared straight ahead, stunned. Her hair sparkled with broken glass and a trickle of blood was beginning to seep from a scratch just below her eye.

'Are you all right?' I wheezed but got no response. 'Rowan. Are you hurt?'

She didn't look at me, but shook her head slowly, still gripping the wheel with pale knuckles.

I unclipped my belt and crawled onto the verge through my blown window onto iced mud. The only sound came from the defeated van, a fan spinning, cooling the overworked engine. I gripped the handle to the cage wondering what mess might spill out when I opened the door. Jim was OK, physically anyway. Yellow vomit ran down his knees which were tucked into his chest.

'OK, look,' he sobbed. 'I did it awrite. I dunnoi how many, but I'll sign whatever. Insurance always covers it. Is victimless, like. Please, no more. I did it.' I closed the cage over and opened Rowan's door. She was still buckled and sobbing into her hands.

CHAPTER NINETEEN

Don't Ask, Don't Tell

'Are you sure you're all right? You're still shaking,' I said quietly. I passed Rowan the glass Pawel had placed between us, unsure who the whisky was for. Perhaps it was because we were in uniform that he had refused to take any money.

'I'm fine. Stop asking. I think I got off lighter than you. You really should go and get those ribs seen to; they might be broken,' Rowan said.

Pawel laid out napkins from his tray and then the beer.

I peeled off my sopping body armour. As I raised it over my head I was struck by the smell of wet dog – my armour saturated by rain and stress-sweat. I dumped it to the floor and brushed an evaluating hand down my side. 'They're not broken. Trust me, I know broken ribs and this ain't it. I'm more worried about your eye. It's still bleeding a little.'

Rowan dabbed at the cut self-consciously, with a tissue.

'You want I can get you something for this?' asked Pawel, looking concernedly at Rowan.

'No. Thanks. Maybe another napkin?'

Pawel handed her one and left us to talk at our corner table. Rowan watched him leave, bursting at the seams to ask the question she wasn't able to while we had walked back from the crash. With no other units handy and the inspector mercifully unreachable at home, I had made a series of executive decisions. The first was to leave the van with the recovery vehicle. The mechanic assessed it would take at least an hour to dig it out of the ditch, particularly as I wanted it retained for forensic assessment and would therefore need to be more delicately extracted. 'Brakes don't tend to fail that dramatically outside of Hollywood,' I said, when Rowan enquired on this point.

The second was to let Jim off with a warning. Not something I wanted to do, as it robbed Rowan of an excellent capture, but it was something I felt I *had* to do. After all, he'd received a certain summary justice in the van's cage. There wasn't too much wrong with him physically. He would have some bruises to explain to the wife but no broken bones. Still, the story was something a newspaper would leap on if he were inclined to tell it. A quiet, menacing word in his ear resulted in a handshake and a gentleman's agreement – I let the charges drop, or rather suspend them above his head indefinitely, Damocles-style, and he doesn't sue or go bleating to a hack.

We set off back to town, the three of us walking abreast on the empty road, in the falling snow, not one of us saying a word. As we reached the crossroads in town, Jim nodded and departed. I could see in Rowan's face that a conversation was not going to wait until the following day. So, seeing the lights still on at the pub, it seemed like the talk might flow better, lubricated.

She threw back the whisky, screwed her face at the burn and said: 'How did you know?'

'Know what?' I said, dumbly.

'How did . . . ?' She stopped, looked around and moved closer. With a lower voice she continued: 'How did you know about the brakes?'

'I didn't,' I said, and took a long, much-needed, draw from my glass. She glowered at me, assuming I was about to put up a wall of denial. 'That is to say, I didn't know it was the brakes, nothing that specific. I just knew we were—'

'In deep shit.'

'Look, Rowan, it's perhaps best we just let this go. I could try to explain it, but it would probably just leave you thinking I'm nuts, or lying, or . . . I dunno, a bit New Age or something.'

'Sarge, I saw what I saw. Whatever that was, it saved our lives. I'm all ears and I think I will believe anything you have to say right now.'

'It was you who saved us, Rowan. You had the wheel.'

'I was just doing what you told me to do. If you hadn't been there, I would have gone for the brakes about three hundred yards from that corner. They'd have been picking me from metal and branches for weeks. Now, stop stalling.' She drank from her own glass and as I was trying to find the words to begin, her eyes shifted to somewhere over my shoulder before they rolled back. 'Shit,' she said.

I didn't have to ask; I'd spotted him when we entered.

'They'll let any old riff-raff in here.' Alistair Hughes sloshed beer as he pulled up a chair at our table.

'This is a private conversation, Mr Hughes. Do you mind?'

'I don't mind, sweetheart. Hey, I'm pretty sure you lot aren't allowed to be drinking while on duty. Maybe I might just have to let your inspector know. Or . . . you can maybe buy us a beer and I might just forget I saw you,' he half said, half spat, inches from my face.

'Not tonight, Hughes,' I said calmly, not looking at him.

'What's that, Sergeant? What, you no' in the mood like?'

'Just shut up and beat it, Alistair. You picked a bad time,' said Rowan. She dropped her own wet body armour to the floor.

'That right? Well, maybe we should just step outside and we'll see who shuts who up, eh?' he said to me, before directing a leer at Rowan. 'Or how about you take the rest of that uniform off darlin'. I'll put some music on and you start shedding the rest of them black and whites, eh?'

There was a clatter as my chair toppled when I pushed it back, standing. Out the corner of my eye I saw whoever constituted Alistair's 'us' at the bar, also getting to his feet.

'Jezus-Maria, how many times? You, out,' said Pawel, flicking a doorward thumb at Hughes. 'We closed ten minutes ago. You too.' Pawel shooed the bar cohort off his stool and guided the pair to the door like a giant sheepdog, dismissing the complaints and accusations of double standards. 'I'll be in the back, if you need something,' he said, after bolting the door.

'Thanks, Pav,' I said.

He ran a deft hand over a line of switches leaving a spotlight over our table, casting the rest of the place into shadow.

Rowan waited until Pav's footsteps had faded to silence. 'So . . . you were telling me how it is you knew we were in trouble.'

'Was I?' I said, and half drained my glass. Rowan tapped an impatient ring on the side of her own.

There was just no plausible lie to tell her; she wasn't going to be fobbed off. Besides I really missed the understanding I had with John, so I tried.

'You know the expression "gut feeling"?' Rowan nodded. 'Well, I grew up thinking that was a real thing.' She looked confused but said nothing. 'It's not easy to explain, but this expression, and others – "gut instinct", "feeling in the pit of your stomach" – well, they pretty much sum up this thing that happens when something is very wrong. Given how common these expressions are, I assumed it happened to everyone. That's why there was such an apt saying.'

'You're saying you have a psychic stomach? And you're saying you thought everyone had one?'

'No. Well, I wouldn't put it like that. It sounds completely mental when you put it like that. It's . . . some heightened sense of intuition, I think. That, for some reason, manifests in the stomach – a "gut feeling", you see?' Rowan had a face like she was enduring a bad smell. 'I know it sounds crazy and I don't expect you to believe me. But you asked. And, so, I'm telling.'

'This happens often?'

I shrugged. 'Often enough. More so since I became a cop and far more intensely. I suppose that stands to reason, given the nature of the job.'

After an awkward spell of silence Rowan said: 'Tell me about the first time it happened.'

'The first time? The first was when my mum died,' I said. I didn't have to think about it; I'd thought about it so many times in my life. 'I was at school. I sort of collapsed and was violently ill, but I didn't know what was going on. She died at work at the same time I was having this convulsive attack. Somehow, I just knew. Sometimes, and I don't know why, this feeling brings images, though not always. I still have no idea how this works, why it works, but I'm beginning to think that the pain is the key. The pain I get in my gut can be overwhelming, but if another source eclipses it, then things get clearer.' I thought about my broken nose the night of Carly's mum.

'You always knew you could sense danger?'

'Not as such. It was years of little instances before I made the connection, that I could string these incidents together, make sense of them and see this stomach thing as the common thread that bound them.'

'When was the first time you began to suspect the connection?'

'It's hard to say.' I thought on this for a minute. 'I remember this incident a few years after Mum passed. It was after school one day. A group of us went down to the river where some older kids had built a rope swing – you know one of these epic deathtraps that parents these days would have a fit over. There was this tree that jutted out over an embankment. One branch stretched out towards the river and someone had manged to loop the rope over it, God knows how. It meant you swung way out over the river and back. When my turn came, I refused to get on because of a queer feeling, an apprehension that was twisting in my guts. It actually had me shitting in my pants a little. It was enough to ensure I didn't get on that swing. I made an excuse to leave before anyone noticed the smell coming from me. As I was carefully wandering off, Callum Brodie, who took my place on the swing, launched himself. I didn't see what happened, I was backing away, too worried about the others catching a whiff of what was making its way down my legs, but I did hear the snap. Then the other snap. He landed in the shallow river with his leg curled awkwardly underneath him, still holding both ends of the short branch that constituted the handle, or the seat. I've never heard someone scream like that before or since. It took hours for paramedics to get him out of there, Callum's leg never fully recovered.

'There were more incidents like these, though a little more trivial. The theme was the same: stomach cramps, then something bad. It wasn't until I joined the police that I fully strung it together though. You think I'm nuts?'

'Have you spoken to anyone about this?'

'You mean like a psychiatrist? That sort of thing?'

'No, I mean who have you told?'

'Nobody really. It's impossible to talk about. My old tutor, John sort of knew. We worked together too long for him not to, but we never discussed it out loud, even after it actually resulted in him getting hurt, badly.'

'What happened?'

'Ach, I don't really want to get into that. I'll never forgive myself for what happened.'

'The gist?'

'The short version is that we were on patrol. We stop this car as part of a winter check thing we were being forced to do. Turns out the guys in the car had a boot full of class As and a deep desire not to go to jail. We were actually ready to send them on their merry way when this thing kicks in. Shortly after all hell breaks loose and John . . . well, he had to retire shortly after. I've barely spoken to him since then.'

'He blames you?'

'No, I don't think so. But sometimes that doesn't matter.'

'You should call him. Who else knows?'

'I tried talking to my dad about it. That didn't go well.'

'How so?'

'I sat him down one day. I would have been late teens, I think. I should have started with the swing story, broke him in gently. I made the mistake of bringing up Mum's death. Well, he was already getting uncomfortable with the conversation before I mentioned this thing. Then he got all upset, so I got upset, and we never spoke of it again.'

Rowan sat back in her chair and looked at me with an unreadable expression.

'You *do* think I'm nuts, don't you?'

'Jury's still out on that one,' she said. 'But I believe that *you* believe it.'

'But you're not necessarily buying it?'

'Maybe, I don't know, it's a bit . . . out there. Still, I saw what I saw.' She folded her arms, a fresh question forming on her face. 'How does it work, then? I mean, can you walk past someone in the street and know they're going to do something bad?'

'No. I don't control it. Also, I have a digestive condition that can present in a similar way, so that adds to the confusion. Often, I just don't know where to look for the danger. Sometimes I'm warned about a person and sometimes it can even be about a place.'

'A place? I'm not sure I understand,' said Rowan, lowering her voice as Pawel reappeared with his jacket on, clearly eager to close up.

'Well, for example,' I said, pulling my own jacket on and lifting my armour from its puddle. 'My stomach's been killing me since the moment I arrived in Stratharder.'

CHAPTER TWENTY

What's That, Bub?

My fingers ferret blindly through the pockets of the dead man.

He was a grim discovery and I recoiled when I first realised what I was groping. Now, he sort of feels like company. I find his keys. A large bunch, like this poor bastard might be a caretaker or something. I finger the teeth of each one carefully. It takes some time and only confirms what I already know. There is no key for the cuffs. Why should there be? He didn't apply them. It would be Bond-baddie ineptitude to throw a corpse in here with me, holding the means of my escape. I'm not sure which of them this one is, or was, or why he was thrown in with me, but, yes, I'm strangely glad he's here.

Still, the cuffs are in front of me now, that's something. I can explore with more care. All I've found are large piles of this strange dust that covers the entire floor . . . and this guy.

I should be freaking out. I should not be calm in this situation. Who finds a dead body and has the peace of mind to search through it for keys? Maybe I'm broken?

You're just in a bit of shock, Don. Use it while it lasts.

It's good advice, I suppose.

My fingers explore the wound on my head.

Probably not wise. They're most likely thick with dirt.

Like a toddler with a boo-boo I find it far too tempting not to have a prod at it. It's pretty nasty, needs stitching.

I set about trying to map the room with my hands, forming a three-dimensional picture in my head. Bub lies somewhere near the centre of the floor; the walls are roughly equidistant from him. This is his name, I've decided. In honour of the tamed headphone-wearing zombie in Dawn of the Dead. *I thought it fitting; he's another dead man I'm not scared of.*

The walls are cold and wet, almost clay-like. I haven't found a door yet. It's hard work trudging through the dust, which in places is ankle-deep. In one corner, where it's particularly thick, I take a break.

'Just catching my breath, Bub,' I say. *Bub doesn't answer. He probably thinks I'm lazy, that I should get my finger out, that my life might depend on it.* Don't end up like me, you bone idle bastard, *he might say.*

'You're probably right, Bub. I just need a minute.'

Perversely, I'm glad he's here. Solitude will mess you up. I almost quit the force for that very reason, perhaps I should have.

It wasn't easy. The most miserable six months I can recall.

I don't blame Terry for the tactics he adopted at the

tribunal, not really. If my back was against the wall, I can't say I'd have done different. If I ever do find myself in that position, I know the lawyer I want representing me, that blonde-bearded bastard.

I'm not sure how close he came to saving Terry's job and I'll never know how close I came to finding myself on a professional misconduct charge. I can only assume that management's already burning desire to be rid of him, coupled with the bravery award John and I received for the gun incident, meant that it was already a done deal, irrespective of how badly I was chewed up on the stand. What galled me was how utterly unprepared I was. Where was my warning, then, stomach? I just did not see that coming at all. Having my private conversation with Alyson thrown in my face, verbatim. Alyson, who I trusted above all others, helped Terry throw me under the bus, a leg and a wing each.

On the shift, I was already persona non grata before the tribunal; afterwards I experienced a new level of shunning. Nobody wanted to know me. Except Alyson, who attempted to explain a few times why she had felt compelled to divulge our damning exchange. She was about the only person I didn't yearn for to speak to me, to at least acknowledge my existence. I even enjoyed the odd shoulder barge in the hallway; it was better than being invisible. Being despised is preferable to being ignored – who'd have thought? I didn't know how to improve matters. I was on the verge of seeing my doctor, playing up on my stomach issues in a bid for long-term sick leave. It was the sort of thing that was commonplace. It was also the tactic I despised seeing utilised by others. The atmosphere was caustic; I was desperate. Every day at muster I would dodge Alyson's gaze and attempt to catch anyone else's. As the shoulder numbers were called and paired off, my number, if called at all, was assigned whatever job could be completed solo – report writing, prisoner watch, some version of glorified paperclip counting – whatever it took to placate the rest of the shift's demands not to work with me.

Then, one morning, I came into to an email from my sergeant, congratulating me on my successful recruitment to the administration department. A job I hadn't applied for. That's all it said, that and 'you start tomorrow'. No 'hey Don, I'm sorry things have been tough for you, how about this job while the smoke blows over?' Just a loosely veiled goodbye and good riddance.

Fuck it, I thought, *can't be as bad as this.* I was right. It was bad, but not *as* bad. I got the cold shoulder for a few weeks from fellow cops in the department, but there were some civilian staff in the office who didn't give a shit, were not afraid of excommunication by association and so I had one or two faces to talk to.

I received emails from Alyson, which began timid and remorseful but grew more frustrated and unrepentant the longer I ignored her. I resisted and resisted, wearing her betrayal like a badge. She explained that she had been approached by professional standards, who in turn had been approached by Terry's defence, stating that she had been overheard on a night out in conversation with me. She was given a choice: deny it and face a misconduct charge, be summoned as a witness at the tribunal and be forced to see my face as she dropped me in it. Or provide a full and frank statement, with a warning to not communicate with me until after the hearing. So, yes, she had no choice, I see that now. And yes, I regret my childishness, but these are products and benefits of hindsight.

Six months passed and the fickle focus of hatred was beginning to unfix, probably due, in part, to my not inconsiderable efforts within the department. There was a backlog of cases to be sanitised before presenting to the court. An overtime fund was allocated, which I gobbled up greedily, often working late and weekends. Overtime was a rarity in administrative posts, but always easy to come by when working on the shift. I had relied on it to carry the anvil of a mortgage we had taken out. It meant I saw Karen seldom in that time. She would often be sleeping when I got home, and her own job kept her working long and unsociable hours too. I would have felt guilty about it, but she seemed content to have this period of time where we just put our heads down and did what we needed to do. The wedding plans were pushed back, something we would look at again when things eased up.

In addition to the extra work available in the office, a new directive had been announced by the chief constable that all office staff would, at least once per month, perform a uniformed patrol. The reason for this was purported to be to keep those officers 'street ready' while they maintained important, though ultimately non-frontline, duties. The real reason, we all knew, was to fudge police figures. By having office staff back on street patrol, albeit fleetingly, the chief constable could boast that he had put hundreds of extra officers back on the street; an obvious PR ploy, but a headline winner.

'Won't it be . . . awkward?' Karen asked as I was leaving for my first of these patrols, a late shift at my old station. They tried to keep you working in your old stomping grounds, local knowledge being a valuable asset.

'It's not with my old shift,' I explained. 'It'll be fine, don't worry,' I lied. It was going to be awkward as hell. 'I'll be home around midnight, unless I get involved in something close to finishing. Don't wait up.'

'You'll probably be home before me actually.'

'You're going out?'

'Yeah, some friends from work are taking me dancing. I'll try not to be home too late.'

She handed me my thermos of hot tea with a kiss. 'Be careful tonight,' she said, suddenly serious. 'It's been a while since you were out there.'

'Like riding a bike,' I said.

It wasn't as bad as I'd feared. There were a few glances and murmurings at muster, but it was a Friday night and those around me were more occupied with the busy evening ahead to pay much attention. I was paired with an older cop, Dan something-or-other. I recognised him from around the office but had never been introduced. He barely gave me a look when our numbers were called together. I wondered if this were a good thing or bad.

In the car we made polite conversation. We answered calls, taking turns getting our notebooks out. It was like the old days and I was loving it. It had been so long since I'd felt like a policeman.

Typical of a clear and mild Friday night, the calls kept pouring in, thicker and faster the later it got. *Policeman's best friend*, John used to say of rain. He wasn't wrong. It was astonishing how inclement weather could clear an incident board.

I checked back through my notebook as we headed in for a meal break and figured I'd accrued enough to keep me in paperwork for the remainder of the shift. As Dan's finger shot to his ear, I knew the fish supper would have to wait a while longer. 'Control from four-six. Roger we're close by, we'll take that,' he said, and threw the car into a U-turn. I pulled my earpiece from my head and checked the connections.

'I didn't hear the call. What have we got?' I asked.

'Potential house-breaking. People seen climbing in through the windows of the old Priory. It's probably just kids as usual. You OK that I took it? We can eat after.'

He was being polite. The older cop outranks the other. Besides, as he lit the car up in a blaze of noise and light, I realised how much I'd missed the adrenalin that occasionally came with the job.

The Priory had been many things in its time, including an impressive estate and a school. In the '50s and '60s it had last been utilised as a mental health facility, before falling into disrepair and abandonment. It was this inglorious incarnation that proved its legacy. It now lay at the bottom of an equally forgotten road as a shell, gutted and unloved. Kids dared each other to walk from one end of the building to the other with ghosts of demented ex-patients running through their imaginations.

Lately, though, the Priory had been plagued by another group – metal thieves. The price of copper had skyrocketed, and the old Victorian heating pipes and drums had become fruitful pickings for those brave and desperate enough to risk their necks crawling through the bowels of the place. It had been going on for a while and the force was beginning to come under pressure from council officials to do something about it. An arrest at the Priory had become something of a, yet unclaimed, trophy.

'Cut the lights and siren,' Dan said, as he turned right onto the disused road. I deactivated the switches; we didn't want to announce our arrival. He sped along the broken road surface, dodging axel-bending potholes and fly-tipped refuse.

'Four-six at locus,' Dan said. 'Confirm if another unit is attending? Over.'

'What channel are you on?' I said, pulling my radio from my shoulder and inspecting the screen. 'I'm getting nothing.'

'Roger, thanks,' Dan said into his own radio, before looking down at mine. 'I'm on five, what are you on?' He slowed the car as the tall, grey spire of the Priory came into view.

'I'm five as well, I think. It's been a while since I've had to use this. I don't know if I might have done something.'

Dan turned a corner and the whole skeletal frame of the building filled the view from the windscreen. He pulled quietly onto a verge and turned off the engine. 'You go left round the side, I'll head towards the front,' he said, but I barely heard him, I with still wrestling with the nobs on my radio, trying to remember how to adjust the various functions.

'Yeh, no problem. I just need a sec.'

'Here, let me have a look. I'll sort it,' Dan said and took my radio with him as he stepped out of his side of the car.

I stepped from my own door and closed it gently. The sun had just set and low clouds were under-lit in a deep pink-purple twilight glow. The wide gravel path, that once circled the immense building, had been reduced to a narrow gap between foliage, I wasn't sure it was even possible to traverse round where Dan had directed me. As I turned to suggest we both just head round to the front, two things happened simultaneously. I noticed Dan was gone and my stomach pitched with foreboding.

'Dan,' I whisper-shouted. 'Dan, where are you? I think something's wrong. Dan.'

I stumbled towards the front of the structure while lava swirled in my gut and threatened to erupt down the insides of my legs. There was no breeze. No sound. Each step in the gravel was a shout in an exam hall.

I reached the entrance. I was still alone, Dan nowhere to be seen. I peered inside the great half-demolished, half-rotted oak door, hanging precariously on a single hinge. There was nothing but darkness. Then, at last, a noise. More feet on gravel.

'Dan . . .' I started, but it was not Dan. My stomach gave a short lurch then eased, as if to say *This is what I was warning you about, but it's too late.* My stomach might have gone on to say *You never listen, do you? You never have, not once. You're supposed to run when I warn you. Damn idiot.*

I drew my baton, slashing it sharply across my body,

effecting its full extension and making a show of the weapon at the same time. The four men in ski masks facing me were neither impressed nor intimidated. They responded by wagging their own weapons. I counted one golf club, one baseball bat, a hockey stick and what looked like a piece of piping. *Seems this guy wasn't invited on the trip to the sporting goods shop*, I thought. *No wonder he looks pissed off.*

Instinctively, I reached to my shoulder for my radio, my hand squeezed empty air.

Then I heard the car start, its wheels spin in gravel and the noise of the engine fade. There was nothing wrong with the radio; there had been no call. Only one person knew where I was, and he had the only means of my summoning assistance, or he had turned it off and launched it deep into the undergrowth. Either way this was happening and there was nothing I could do to stop it. *Where's my phone?* I considered. *Trouser pocket.* With the screen lock and trying to enter my pin without dropping the baton, I would be a piñata before I even got it to my ear.

One of them stepped forward, grinning through the crude slash in his grey, woollen mask, seeing the situation dawning on me.

I wondered in that moment what Dan would tell people. How he would explain getting separated from me. I supposed that had been thought of too. They hadn't thrown this party together.

'So, which one of you is Terry?' I asked. 'Never pegged you as the type to hide behind knitwear.'

It turned out to be Mr Pipe, the one who had stepped

266

forward. He rolled his balaclava up to his forehead then raised the pipe, tapping it into his hand.

'You've had this coming a long time,' he said. 'And when we're done, you can go grass as much as you like. I have twenty witnesses will swear I'm at a family birthday dinner right now.'

'Fair enough. But what are you going to tell them when I drag you in, half beaten to death?'

He laughed, as did one or two of the others. They started fanning out, trying to form a circle around me. I backed up a little. The three cohorts seemed to be waiting for Terry to make his move. Nobody wanted to throw the first punch.

'I also never pegged you as a coward, Terry. World-class prick, but no coward,' I said, trying to keep my voice steady though my heart was pounding so hard it was causing saliva to rush into my mouth in anticipation of vomit. 'How about a fair fight? You and me, no weapons, no repercussions. If you win, I'll take my beating and won't complain to a soul.'

'Thanks,' he said, scratching his head in mock consideration. 'but you'll be taking your beating anyway. No CS spray, Colyear? That was the one thing I was a little worried about,' he said, his pipe pointing at the empty slot on my belt. You were supposed to carry incapacitant spray with you at all times, but when you worked an office job you had to organise a temporary issue from the duty officer and it took for ever to fill out the paperwork, so for these short, occasional shifts, few ever bothered.

'Never needed it. Not before, not now,' I said. I had a last look around, searching for an alternative to what was fast becoming inevitable. Nothing. 'Well, are we going to do this, then? Or are you cunts just going to stand around looking like you've come from an IRA recruitment drive?'

This show of bravado was designed to instil some doubt in my attackers. It might have worked, too, if it had been just one or two of them, but with four I was facing an unshakeable group confidence.

They came faster now, spreading out. It was happening. I switched the grip on my baton. Their weapons were much longer, there would be no point swashbuckling with them. I flattened the bar across the inside of my forearm with the tip pointing at my elbow. Terry swung first. It was a nervous swipe and cleared short. I circled round as best I could, not allowing them to surround me, but doing so I came into the swing circle of Mr Golf. He was expecting me to back away, but I charged and blocked. It meant I connected with the shaft of the club rather than the lump of metal at the end of the 8 iron. The club bent pathetically around the baton, which I then drove into his mouth-hole. I felt the heel of the baton connect with teeth. It wasn't a clean connection, but it was painful enough to put him on his arse. He scrambled to the side clutching his face as Mr Baseball came in for his try.

We had now switched sides. My back to the Priory, theirs to the road out. Mr Golf had bugged out. Disarmed, he wanted no further part.

Mr Baseball swung brutally, trying to send my head into the cheap seats. He clipped the edge of my ear as I ducked. Failing to connect properly, he over-rotated and almost collided with Terry, who was frantically trying to get at me. I took the opportunity to move the baton in my hand to a standard grip and slashed hard and low, as I'd done in training a thousand times, strike through the limb, not at it. Terry's knee buckled and he wailed. A hockey stick rammed into my back, knocking the breath from my lungs and forcing me towards the oncoming baseball bat. He hadn't learnt his lesson from his first fresh-air swing and he wound the bat back way too far for another home run attempt, giving me enough time to take both ends of the baton in each hand and ram it into his chest. There was a hollow thud when I flew into him. As he went down my feet got caught between his legs and I landed on top. My hands splayed on the ground as I bounced off his chest and the baton rolled from my grasp. He was the first to recover, getting to his knees. He reached for the bat and would have got a free shot at the back of my head had I not grabbed at his mask and pulled it up as far as his nose. He dropped the bat instantly, terrified I might see who this person I used to work with was. He rolled out of the way, and out of the fight. It was just Terry and Mr Hockey left.

'I don't get it, Bub,' I say, finally giving up groping at the slick walls. 'I'm pretty sure I've gone full circle around this room, and there's no door. How does that work?' I carefully try to find my dead friend in the centre of the floor without stepping on him or cracking my head against a beam. I sit next to his up-faced body and twist my raw wrists in the cuffs, trying to find some relief.

For a strange moment I am tempted to lay out flat, use his chest as a pillow, find some true comfort.

'You'd probably just end up farting out some horrendous

zombie stench if I put pressure on you, wouldn't you, Bub? With everything just starting to break down in there. Anyway, what was I on about?

'Oh yeah, so that just left two of them,' I say, as if I had conveyed the first part of the story to him, rather than running through it in my head. 'Mr Baseball must have thought I clocked who he was and that changed his mind on the matter. It seemed he was happy to have a swing as long as it came without reprisal, but now he didn't want to know.

'Now this is the part where things get hazy, Bub. I wish I could tell you how I kicked their asses. I really wish I could.

'What actually happened is this: as I picked myself off the ground, I turned just in time to see Terry bringing the pipe down on me. I'm certain I was still conscious for a few seconds after that, because I have this residual image of his great, fat, fucking face, looking down on me, all triumphant, smug and furious and then . . . nothing.

'I wish I could tell you they were satisfied with that, knocking me out. But they were only getting started. I'm just glad I was unconscious for the rest. When I woke in hospital with my arm in a cast and my jaw sitting so funny, I couldn't talk. I was glad I'd missed the show.

'Still, could have been worse. I mean, look who the fuck I'm talking to. No offence, Bub.' I pat his chest, double-cuffed-handed in apology. 'So, what are we going to do? How did you end up in here, Bub? Were you here before me? Or dumped in here at the same . . .' I pause, an idea forming. 'Or were we dumped down here, Bub? Not in? I mean I doubt you moved far when you arrived, not in your condition.'

I'm standing now, feeling at the low ceiling keeping my head down as more of this thick dust falls, making me cough. And there, right above Bub there's some play in the wood.

"Scuse me, Bub,' I say, straddling his torso. I push hard and a hatch lifts a few inches, sending a thin bar of pale light into my eyes. At full stretch I can open it only a few inches and it's way too heavy to throw over. I let it drop back into place, and I think.

'I got an idea, Bub, but you're not going to like it.'

CHAPTER TWENTY-ONE

Overdressed for Dinner

Spanner Tam stood in the pit, his face screwed upward into a puckered squint as if he were inspecting the midday sun. He gave a double tut and shook his head in an expression which in a commercial garage would have the owner thinking, *Shit, here it comes. What's this going to cost me?*

'You'll no' see nothing from up there. You'll need to come down,' he said, flicking his torch from the underbelly of the van to our expectant faces. I examined the edge of the pit, looking for a way to get in without being covered in oil and grease. I dropped down, laying a single hand at the edge. To my surprise the inspector did likewise, fairly deftly, and we both offered Rowan an outstretched hand to help her down.

She curled her lip, thought about it and shook her head. 'I'm good here, thanks,' she said.

I followed the yellow gaze of the torch to the van's underside, heavily caked in mud and vegetation from where Rowan had sent it into the ditch.

'Sorry, Tam, but what am I looking at? I'm no good with cars. It's just a mess to me,' I said and felt my own face scrunch in concentrated assessment.

'Exactly,' he said. 'Look at the state of it.'

'What's your point, Tom?' said the inspector, apparently having forgotten the head mechanic's name in the introductions a few minutes ago, the 'spanner' prefix presumably to identify him against some other Tam who worked in the building.

'It's rotten. All of it, absolutely boggin-rotted,' said Tam. He waved a once-yellow, now less so, screwdriver like an orchestra conductor's baton at the various pipes, wires, lumps, bumps and general indecipherable miracle miscellany that went into making a lump of metal move on roads. The two of us stared upward, no doubt the inspector was also thinking, *Get to the fucking point, will you.*

Finally, the inspector's patience broke and he was the one to take the risk of looking uninformed. 'Tom, were the brakes cut or not?'

'That's what I'm trying tae tell you.' He began tapping at the guts of the expired beast and we all scuttled backward trying to avoid the downpour of rust that followed. 'There's no way to tell for sure. I'm just amazed it ran at all. Any of this could go at any second.' He waved the screwdriver in an arc now. 'What you've got here is a two-thousand-and-two Ford deathtrap. I mean, what lunatic OK'd this shit-heap for active service? We used to use this thing for the civilian

273

driver to shuttle the mail up and down from Glasgow. It hasn't seen a service in about a decade and we were . . . a bit generous when it came time to renew the MOT.' Tam pulled at a pipe which came away almost instantly.

'It was available and Sergeant Colyear needed a vehicle,' said the inspector, defensively.

'Aye, well, I suppose we should have taken it off the road completely,' Tam said, his cheeks probably flushing, but hidden by oil that smeared his grey-bearded face. 'This is what's left of the brake pipe, look at this.' He twisted it between his hands causing it to snap. He rubbed a short section between his fingertips and we watched as it disintegrated, falling to the floor as dust. 'My guess is you hit the pedal hard and it just gave. You're lucky you weren't killed.' I glanced up at Rowan who returned a knowing look.

'Thank you, Tom,' said the inspector, carefully clambering from the pit.

'Aye, no bother,' said Tam. I caught a little eye roll from him and I smiled.

We walked from the service yard at the rear of the Oban station until we reached the inspector's own car.

'Are you happy it wasn't foul play?' he asked. 'We could get a second opinion if you like.'

'I'm not sure "happy" is the right word, Inspector. The ribs still hurt like a bastard. I never was convinced it was a deliberate act, it was just a suspicion. The timing with the black hatchback couldn't be ignored.'

'Here,' he said, handing me a set of company keys. 'You'll use my Panda until I can get you a new van sorted out, and I mean a new one. I feel somewhat responsible for the near miss, giving you that rust bucket. I really had no idea it was dangerous,' he said to both Rowan and me.

'Of course not,' I said. 'And thank you. You sure you won't be needing it?'

'No, I'll be working out of Oban for a while. There's some reorganising to be done with middle management, part of the force's amalgamation restructure. They want me on board to look through it, push some figures around. Actually, that reminds me . . . Rowan, would you give us a moment, please?' Rowan raised her eyebrows in a look of suspicious wonder, then nodded. There was a lingering pause as the inspector waited for her to be out of earshot.

'So, you're leaving us,' he said, at last.

'I am?'

'Are you not?' he asked, looking less assured.

'I'm afraid you've lost me, Inspector.'

'Your interview, for the administrative position in Edinburgh. Did I hear wrong?'

What is it about this bloody place? I thought. *Is it some kind of infection that spreads, eating away at your privacy until you are fully assimilated to the Stratharder hive?*

'Excuse the tone, Inspector, but how the hell did you get to hear about that?'

'They emailed looking for a reference. I suppose that means you're a shoo-in. Particularly as I provided a glowing account of you.'

I imagined the reference, typed by a single finger, all capitals, the inspector yelling my commendable attributes

275

and no doubt having sent it to the wrong person, or twenty wrong persons.

'Ah, I see. Thank you, Inspector. Sorry I didn't approach you about it—'

'Pshhh,' he said, pushing away a dismissive hand. 'I know how these things work. Don't apologise. You *are* taking it, then?'

'Well, as you say, I have an interview in a few weeks—'

'But you'll accept when they offer it to you?'

'I . . . I don't know, Inspector. I guess I just wanted to keep my options open and I wouldn't want to assume they're going to—'

'Of course they will. You've worked in admin before?'

'Yes, as a constable.'

'It's in the bag, lad. You're wasting your talents here. We'll be sad to see you go, but you have to think of yourself.'

Who the hell are you kidding? I almost blurted. 'Thank you. I promise you'll be the first to know when there's anything to tell,' I said, and wondered if it were a lie. 'I'd like to clear my feet here before I decide anything though?'

'Meaning what?'

'Meaning I wouldn't want to hand over any outstanding work. I'd like to see my caseload through.'

The inspector looked puzzled, or frustrated, it was hard to tell with him. 'What could you possibly have to be so concerned about?'

'Well . . . there's the Cooper death for one.'

'What is the state of play there? You had the woman in for an interview?'

'Yes, but more to rule her out than anything else. She

provided her phone which ties in with Cooper's. She hadn't seen him in months. If it was a prostitute with Cooper on the night in question, it doesn't look like he arranged it on his phone.'

'What's next?'

'I think CID are now keen to bury this one. I got an email from DS Aitken. The post-mortem and toxicology came back and they were less than conclusive. The tablets, his prescription for tramadol, were the most likely cause of death, but the amounts found in his system were not what you'd call excessive. The alcohol and general lack of health are all cited as contributory factors.'

'That's disappointing. Not that I want a murder in my backyard, but it would have been good to have something substantive.'

'I've been asked to clarify the findings with Mr Cooper's own doctor.'

The email from DS Aitken had been casual to the point of lazy. It had started with the assertion that urgency was not an issue. It went on in a similar *laissez-faire* tone. They wanted a 'statement from the deceased's doctor', confirming his medical history, his medication and his state of mind. The implication here being suicide. Basically, just kicking the corpse of the investigation to ensure it didn't twitch. I could easily have asked Rowan to note the details, but I just didn't want to hand it over.

'I see. Well, I suppose that makes sense,'

'Also, there's our missing person report.'

'Young Jennifer?'

'Yes, I promised her mother—'

'That's very noble of you, Donald, but I think it rather unlikely there will be any satisfactory conclusion to that one for some time. Also, I told you, I have that in hand. I have the Met looking into things. Really, don't hold your breath. Teenagers in London who don't want to be found can stay under the radar for a very long time. If you like, I can message you with any developments?'

'I know, it's just . . . I wouldn't feel right leaving without being able to give her . . . *something*. But yes, if it does turn out that I've left before anything comes back, I would appreciate being copied in.'

I could see the inspector's eyes drift up and to the left; 'copied in' was probably a term he had heard but had no idea how to electronically piggyback a conversation.

The inspector planted a hand on my shoulder and started walking me towards Rowan, who stood oblivious, thumbs-a-blur over her phone.

'How is this one coming along?' the inspector asked, raising his voice a little, making it clear he was both referring to, and involving, Rowan.

'Ah . . . she'll do,' I said. 'School crossings, parking tickets . . . and she makes a decent cup of tea. A keeper this one.' Rowan's eyes raised momentarily from her screen, long enough to fire a poison glare in my direction. The inspector gave a laugh; the sound was so alien and unexpected that Rowan and I shared a wide-eyed silent exchange.

'Right, come on, you,' she said, putting her phone away. 'I've got work to do and you've got . . . an urgent appointment,' she said, peculiarly hovering over her final words.

'I do?'

'Yes! You do!' she said, as if to a child.

'You've forgotten, haven't you?' said Rowan. She turned in the passenger seat with an odd grin stretched across her mouth.

I pulled out of the yard thinking how strange it was to be in a police vehicle that did not necessitate a conversation to be exchanged at a yell. The faint, but unmistakable, smell of cigarettes clung to the upholstery of the inspector's squad car. 'Are you going to enlighten me, or just sit there torturing me?'

'You've got a hot date, you dozy twat.'

'What? No . . . No, that's . . . Ah shit.' I frantically flicked through a mental calendar and was horrified to confirm, she was right.

'Yeeeessss,' she hissed with glee.

'Shit, Mhairi. Damn it. I meant to leave that a few days and then call and cancel once I'd thought of a good excuse. Shit, shit, I forgot all about it.'

'Well, you can't cancel now. The poor lassie will be blow-drying her mane and shaving her nay-say as we speak.' Rowan was just loving this.

'Shit, shit, shit. How do I get out of this? Come on, you're the dating expert. Think of something.' I turned north onto the main road, staying ten miles an hour under the speed limit, much to the annoyance of the queue of traffic behind me, too afraid to overtake the cops. I needed the extra time to think, to plot. The miles between us and Stratharder were suddenly a countdown.

'Seriously, Sarge, I don't think you can. It's what? Half six now? What time were you to meet her?'

'Eight, I think.'

'So, she probably is getting ready. And if you called with some lame-ass excuse now, it would be a real slap in the face. That's a bullshit move. Don't do it. What are you supposed to be doing?'

'Actually, I'm not entirely sure,' I said, thinking back to the embarrassed conversation in the office. 'Dinner, I think. I never called or sent a text. Maybe she's forgotten too. We never firmed up on anything. Do you think I could get away with just not showing up?'

'I saw the look on her face when you agreed. You never cancelled, so as far as she's concerned it's on. Don't tell me you don't fancy her, at least a little; all that hair and gravity-defying bumps.' Rowan shook her own locks, shampoo-commercial-style to make her point. 'Why not just take her out?'

'Honestly? She kinda terrifies me . . . a little,' I added.

'I think if you stand her up, you ought to be afraid. If I were you, I'd grow a pair, pick her up and take her down the hotel for a thoroughly mediocre evening.'

Rowan's words drifted and hung in the air as an idea was beginning to form. 'I've got it,' I said, taking the turn for Stratharder and seeing a long, relieved line of traffic accelerating in my rear-view mirror. 'I need an excuse she can't be mad at, right?'

'I'm all ears,' said Rowan. She made no attempt to hide the rolling of her eyes.

'Police emergency!'

'What?'

'It's perfect. We'll just swing by now, I'll go to her door in full uniform, she'll see the car and you in it and I'll just explain something serious has happened, the details of which I can't go into until the family have been informed, you know, that sort of thing. I'll tell her I'll call and reschedule. She can't possibly be mad at that.'

'I wouldn't bet on it. But it's your funeral.'

I put my foot down now, realising it would be after seven when we reached her house. If Rowan was right, her preparations would be at an advanced stage. The miles were no longer a countdown, they were a climbing scale of disappointment and ire.

Rowan knew the street and directed me down a road of crammed, terraced, council houses with no off-street parking. Both kerbsides were likewise crowded with vehicles. I slowed to a crawl as we strained out of our respective side windows, trying to find numbers on doors.

'Twenty-seven, there,' said Rowan, tapping glass. I stopped in the middle of the street unable to see a space to pull into, alongside a familiar-looking car.

'Keep the motor running. I'll just be a minute,' I said into Rowan's open window. I resisted the temptation to drag a key along the door of the parked shitty yellow hatchback I was getting to know so well.

I stepped through two short, rotting, wooden posts where a front gate once hung. Along a path of uneven broken paving slabs, flanked with the stripped remains of children's bicycles, to the front door. I lifted my knuckles to knock but paused as I ran through my story one last time, anticipating any queries that might blow my ruse. *Be brief*, I told myself. *Over-elaboration is a tell-tale sign of a lie. And be hurried, don't let her attempt to rearrange*. I turned to check Rowan hadn't seen my hesitancy, my cowardice perhaps. She was leaning out of her window, shooing me to hurry up. I pulled on my hat, *adds to the authenticity of the situation*, and rapped three times on the white PVC door.

The woman who answered, in a harried mid conversation with someone over her shoulder, was Mhairi, only it wasn't. This woman, though still striking, lean and sporting the same dense deluge of red hair, was somewhere in her forties. Her conversation petered out almost instantly as she leant back away from the door to better allow her handsome, freckled face to take me in.

I pulled away myself to look at the number above the door, confirming it was correct, as I had it. 'I'm sorry,' I said, jabbing a thumb back towards the car, 'I think I might have the wrong—'

'Well, you're early,' she said, planting a serious fist on a hip, 'and a bit . . . overdressed. But come in, I suppose.' She reached out and took hold of my forearm, pulling me over the threshold.

'Actually, I can't really—'

'Dinner won't be ready for at least half an hour,' she insisted, and drew me into the hall like a child taken in front of his father for punishment. 'I don't think Mhairi's quite— Mhairi, put some bloody clothes on, your boy . . . your sergeant . . . friend is here.'

'Jesus, Mum,' yelled Mhairi, who I could see in the kitchen area at the end of the hall in jeans and a black bra.

This is who the woman had been conversing with on my arrival. Mhairi grabbed a green top from a radiator and covered her chest as she darted upstairs.

'What are you gawking at?' Mhairi's mother said and I realised I had been staring.

'Oh, nothing. I mean, I just hadn't expected . . . Look,' I said, desperately trying to take control of a situation which was nose-diving spectacularly away from me. I snatched the hat from my head and tucked it under one arm. 'I'm Don Colyear.' I put out my hand and this seemed to force a breath in the exchange.

'Oh, so you're *not* the strip-o-gram we ordered? Ah well, you may as well stay for tea.' She shook my hand firmly.

'Sorry, I'm a bit thrown. I thought I was picking Mhairi up.'

'Dressed like that?'

'Yeah, no. See, that's the other thing—'

'Never mind, you're here now and there's a roast in the oven. I'm Mhairi's mum, Helen. And I *mean* Helen. They'll be none of that Mrs McCloy shit, you hear?'

'Eh, yeah sure, Helen,' I said, my mind quickly trying to place the surname. Then I remembered the yellow hatchback. As if reading my mind, a voice came descending from the hall stairs:

'I don't fucking—'

Believe it, I thought, finishing Mick McCloy's sentiment, since the words were stripped from his mouth by a clatter across the side of the head from Helen.

'This is who Mhairi invited for tea? Sergeant Five-Oh? How come I don't get a say about what people gets to

283

come into this 'ouse?' said the ridiculous man-boy, in some attempt at London street lingo.

'Because you're a lazy freeloading little shit, that's why. Start paying me some rent and you can have some say. Until then shut your hole and go set the table.'

I smiled contently at him as he passed me, giving the stink-eye.

'You know each other?' asked Helen.

'Not really,' I said, detecting a grilling if I dared answering in the affirmative. 'We've bumped into one another once or twice. It's a small town.'

'God, don't I just know it. I've got dinner to finish, but Connor is playing his games in the living room. You should go say hello while you wait for Mhairi. He's a bit of a fan of yours he is.' Helen motioned at a door down the hall, before turning towards the kitchen. I couldn't help a quick appraisal of her figure as she walked away. *Damn good genes this family, man-boy excepted*, I thought. I wondered at exactly how old she was as I sat down next to Connor on the settee.

'What are you playing, Connor?' I asked.

'*Grand Theft Auto*,' he said, apparently knowing I was there, though his eyes never once fell from the television screen.

'Is a good one dat game, yeh. You get to shoot coppers right in their faces an' everything. Mad fun it is,' said Mick, his hands full of cutlery he collected from a drawer in a sideboard.

'He only talks like that when he wants people to think he's tough,' said Connor. I was again surprised he

284

was registering anything that was going on given he was currently racing through city streets on a motorcycle and gunning down pedestrians with an Uzi.

Mick sucked at his teeth as he was leaving the room. 'Mind ya business, little man.'

'I know that's why he does it, Connor,' I said. 'But don't worry, I don't mind, or at least I don't care. I'm sure he's probably a nice guy when he isn't trying to be . . . whatever it is he's trying to be.'

'Nah, not really. He can be funny sometimes, though Mum doesn't think he's funny. But usually he's just angry and sulky all the time. Bit of a knob-end,' said Connor, who for the first time looked up from the screen to check no other adults could hear him as he whispered his last words.

Connor went back to extracting murderous mayhem while I fished my phone from my pocket and sent a text to Rowan: *I'm trapped. Save yourself.*

I stripped off my body armour and laid it next to the coffee table where Connor's feet were propped up. The screen was paused. An unfortunate digital image stuck to the giant television panel: the motorcycle had slammed into the side of what looked like a shopping mall, pinning a woman in fishnet tights and miniskirt to the wall with an extravagant bloodstain halo around her head. Connor's attention had shifted to the trinkets attached to the vest.

'Is that pepper spray?'

'This?' I unhooked the plastic holster from the vest. The small can of spray was still attached by a coil, designed to keep the thing from being lost if dropped during an altercation. 'It's actually not pepper spray. Some American police use pepper spray, stuff extracted from chilli peppers and put into an aerosol, but this is called CS spray. The letters stand for two chemicals that have a similar effect, but I forget the names.' I spun the small cylinder allowing him to get a good look. I never left the station without it these days.

'What does it do? Make you cry?'

'Sort of. It gets into your eyes and your nose and for a little while it's hard to see and to breathe properly,' I said, playing down the effects a bit.

'Can I hold it?' he asked.

'I'm sorry, Connor, I don't think your mum would like that,' I said, thinking that might be slightly absurd given the image of the mown-down prostitute on the screen in front of me. 'It's easy to have an accident with this stuff. How about I let you hold these instead?'

His face was a mask of wonder as I placed the handcuffs on his lap. He began spinning the arm of one of the cuffs with an index finger, taking great delight in the ratchet sound it made. My phone buzzed in my pocket. A reply from Rowan:

Dkhead! Have fun, and if you cnt b good b careful :) x

'Sorry about that. You kinda caught me unprepared.'

I pushed my phone back into my pocket and turned. 'Yeah, I'm sorry. I was really early . . . you look lovely by the way,' I said, and it was true. Mhairi had appeared in tight jeans and the little green strappy top she'd shielded herself with. Her long red curls fell over her freckled shoulders and she looked bizarrely young to have a boy Connor's age.

'Thank you. And you look very handsome . . . in your uniform. Were you expecting trouble?'

'Sorry about this, I came straight from work. I actually thought . . .' I started but had no way to finish the sentence without throwing light on a lie. 'Sorry,' I repeated dumbly. 'I never even got a chance to pick up flowers or wine.'

Mhairi slipped over the arm of the settee. 'Never mind that, your gentlemanly intent is noted. What's that you've got there, Connor?'

'Sergeant Colyear's handcuffs. I've got handcuffs, but they're plastic, and you can get out of them dead easy. Can you put these on me?'

'Just call me Don, and I don't know, we're only supposed to put these on bad guys, Connor. You're not a bad guy, are you?' I said but was looking at Mhairi.

'Oh, this one can be as wicked as they come. I think he should feel what it's like if he gets just *too* naughty.' Connor squirmed with laughter as Mhairi tickled his neck. He lifted his wrists to me.

'I'm gonna show Nanna,' he said, shaking the cuffs on his wrists and ran off towards the kitchen.

'He's a sweet boy. You've done a good job with him.'

'Thanks, he *is* sweet.' Mhairi slid along the settee next to me. My arm was still resting on the back and now she was under it. I felt uncomfortable but couldn't move without making some kind of statement. 'I can't take all the credit though. Mum is brilliant with him and has brought him up as much as I have. I honestly don't know if I could have coped without her.'

'It's nice you have support. Can I ask . . . ?'

'How old I was when I had him?' she read my thought and saw my regret at asking what she must have had to tell

287

a thousand times. 'It's fine,' she said, and slapped my knee gently. She bit at her thumb, thinking. 'I was sixteen when I fell pregnant, seventeen when I had him. Boring cliché, huh? Teenage mum, never left her home town.'

I wasn't sure how to respond. I opted for neutrality. 'Circumstances are circumstances, I guess. It could happen to anyone. Except me of course. I didn't lose my virginity until I was twenty-two.'

'Bullshit.'

'It's true. I was horrific to look at in high school. My acne made me look like I had some kind of medieval pox.'

'Aww, I bet you were cute, even with zits.'

'I wasn't even cute at twenty-two, but alcohol is a great leveller.'

Mhairi laughed and leant into me. 'You're his new hero, you know?'

'Me? Why?'

'Partly because of the uniform and the utility belt. You did, after all, replace Batman as his new idol. But it had more to do with the incident with the other boys.'

'I just did my job.'

She squinted her eyes as she looked into mine, almost like she was searching for something. 'Maybe,' she said, 'but you listened to him. You *believed* him. I don't think you realise what a big deal that was for him, for . . . *anyone* in this family. I'm not sure if you've realised that we're treated like second-class citizens in this rathole of a town.'

'I guess I've noticed some animosity, yeah. Why is that?'

'Oh, take your pick from a number of reasons. Boils down to the general attitude that we're just not as good as other people. People in small towns have small minds and long memories. I dropped out of high school to have Connor and people started looking down their noses at me. It was a really complicated time. I think part of me just started to behave in a way that was expected of me, a sort of fuck you to the sneering bitches in the bank queue and in the supermarket. You wouldn't think it, but I have a bit of a temper.' She mock-scowled at me and balled her fists. Somehow, it made her look extremely cute and it brought a grin I couldn't help.

'What about his dad? Can I ask?' Again, I instantly regretted my question as a darker atmosphere dropped like a blind. Mhairi's thumb was again in her mouth.

'Let's not ruin a nice evening. Just know that he's not in Connor's life, now or ever. OK?'

'OK.'

'Nanna says you've to levitate me and come to the table,' said Connor, rescuing us from the awkwardness.

'Did she maybe say *liberate you*?' I said, and uncuffed him, not needing a key. I'd locked the cuffs at a setting he could slip out of.

At Helen's insistence I was sat at the head of the oval table in the corner of the kitchen. Mick sat glaring at me from under his baseball cap as the others closed their eyes and said grace.

'Smells lovely, Helen. I can't tell you the last time I had a home-cooked meal,' I said as soon as the prayer was ended, and I meant it, I really couldn't recall. The well-meaning, but often indeterminate, contents of Hilda's Tupperware failed to qualify.

'It's pork. Can you have pork? I mean being a pig an' all. Would that be canniba—' Before I even had a chance to return a bored, humourless glower at Mick, his mother hit him with a slap so fierce it would have rendered many a man dazed, if not knocked out cold. His cap skidded across the kitchen tiles detonating his mushroom-cloud of thick ginger hair. As I sat wide-eyed, Connor and Mhairi laughed hard. That Mick was not only still in his seat, but apparently only mildly aggrieved, meant he was accustomed to Helen's right cross.

'You must be bored out of your mind up here, Don,' said Helen, once dessert arrived, a home-made cheesecake, the quality of which had me nostalgic for Dottie's on a Sunday with my dad.

'Actually, it's been oddly eventful since I arrived. Honestly, I might have to get back to Glasgow for a rest.'

'You're not leaving us, are you?' said Mhairi, either not getting the joke or reading too much into it. Either way there was a concern in her eyes.

'No immediate plans, no,' I lied. 'But you never know in my job. Ours is not to reason why, and all that.' Mhairi looked at me blankly. 'I mean, I could be reassigned. I haven't heard about anything, though you seldom do before they decide they're moving you on.'

'You must miss the city, though?' said Helen. 'All the action, the drug busts, gangs and violence?'

'Well, it's not quite like it is in the movies. It can be pretty dull in the city too. Besides drugs are everywhere, even in Stratharder,' I said to Helen, but my eyes were fixed on Mick. I gave him the faintest smile and expected him to start squirming in his chair, but he simply stared right back mirroring the smile.

Helen caught the subtle exchange. 'Has he been at that whacky-backy again with his friends?'

I said nothing. *Here it comes, you little shit*, I thought, *Mummy's gonna skelp that grin right off your smug little face.*

'They're scamps, aren't they, at that age?' said Helen, and ruffled the top of Mick's wild hair. His grin stretched wide. 'We've all been there, haven't we? I tell him the whacky-backy is one thing, but no hard drugs. I catch you with any of that muck and it's your neck, boyo.' She gave his head another pat.

'Yes, just marijuana . . .' I said, and was about to launch into the links with this perceived safe drug and schizophrenia and the strong evidence with it being a bridge to the hard drugs she mentioned, but one look at the ginger unity I was facing made me think better of it.

'You didn't have to nick him, did you? What have I told you about keeping it indoors?'

Mick's grin straightened and he prepared to duck.

'No, I let him off with a warning, though my hands will be tied if there's a repeat of it. I actually didn't realise these two were related, Helen. I suppose the red hair might have been a giveaway, but with the way he and his friends were hanging out the window of the car saying such things to Mhairi, it never crossed my—'

'What things?'

The air in the room suddenly took on a dark hue.

'What were your scumbag friends saying about your

sister?' Helen had Mick by his collar and there was genuine fear in his eyes.

I've got you now, you little shit. 'They were kidding,' I said, 'but it was ugly stuff. Offering her . . .' I drifted off, my words catching in my mouth as a discreetly shaking head caught my eye. Mhairi's face was a study in piteous alarm.

'A lift, Mum. They were just offering me a lift. They were just being cheeky, that's all. Donald, I think, got the wrong impression, a little, but it was sweet of him to come to my rescue,' said Mhairi, breezily, though her flushed face belied her calm. Mick hung his head over his plate, suddenly very quiet.

What the fuck just happened? I thought.

After the plates were cleared Mick left in his yellow shit-mobile, the growling exhaust announcing his departure to the entire street. I helped Helen wash the dishes while Mhairi put Connor to bed.

'I'll leave you two in peace once I get these tidied up.' She handed me another plate to wipe dry.

'Please, don't worry, Helen. I really should be getting back soon.'

'Back? How do you propose to do that? It's coming down in sheets out there, it's pitch-black and I don't suppose a policeman will be attempting to drive after a bottle and half of wine?'

I cupped a hand over my eyes as I peered out of a back window. She was right, it was wild outside. 'I'll maybe just call a cab.'

She laughed. 'Taxis don't come out here, Donald.

292

Mhairi's putting the wee one down in her room. You can sleep in Connor's. It's no trouble.'

Before I could protest, before I could try to find an alternative, a way to get home, Mhairi reappeared. 'He wants you to tell him his story,' she said, waving a book in the air. 'I'm sorry. I told him no, but he's insisting. Would you mind?' She screwed her face in an apologetic grimace.

'I'll finish these up,' said Helen, and took my tea towel from me with a smile.

'So, what are we reading, then?' I said, pulling a chair from the corner to the edge of the bed. I opened the book Mhairi handed to me at the bookmarked chapter. 'Percy Jackson, huh? Where was Percy up to, then?'

It got awkward after Connor's light went out. I agreed to one last glass of wine. We sat in the living room, talking, but saying very little. Every sentence was flanked by painful silences. I felt she wanted me to instigate something. I wasn't against the idea, exactly. In truth I didn't know how I felt about it. My plan to breezily stop by and ask for a rain check, had failed on a dramatic scale. Now, here I was spending the night. How the hell did that happen? The whole situation felt false and contrived and rushed. I sat, nervously sipping at wine I'd already had too much of, waiting for an excuse to call an end to the evening.

When at last Mhairi yawned, following a particularly long lull in the chat, I announced that I was also tired and better hit the hay in preparation for a fictitious early start.

'All right,' she said and slap-grabbed my knee, either in

293

resignation or punishment of my reticence. 'I'll show you to your room.'

I felt a sense of relief, but also guilt, as Mhairi bid me goodnight standing in the doorway of her son's bedroom, having kissed me briefly on the mouth. A kiss that was reciprocated but only just. I knew if I hinted at enthusiasm that it would not end there.

'Goodnight,' I said. 'If I'm gone when you guys get up, will you thank your mum for a lovely meal?'

'Oh, we're up with the lark in this house. We'll try not to wake you. Anything I can get you?' She stood, one hand on her hip, the other pushed out against the door frame. I sat on the edge of the single bed, complete with a Transformers duvet cover.

'I'm fine, Mhairi, really, thanks. I'll see you in the morning.' She lingered a moment and the opportunity she was offering loitered between us, fading, but refusing to die.

'Hmmm,' she said, unconvinced. 'Sweet dreams.' Her voice was an exasperated breath and her hand squeaked down the frame of the door as she turned and closed it over.

The window in the small room didn't quite fit into its frame. Each time I felt myself about to drop off I was brought back to consciousness by a tortured moan, crying through the gaps. I must have found sleep briefly though, because I woke as a shard of light spilt into the room. I shielded my eyes as I sat up, peering at the source of the light. It came from the doorway where Mhairi once again stood, but not as before, this time I heard myself audibly gasp.

Mhairi's hand was again against the door frame, but her other gently held the peak of my hat, resting coquettishly at an angle on her head. This being the only item of clothing on her body.

'Sorry to wake you,' she whispered. 'Only you left this downstairs and I wondered . . . Do you want it?'

Her skin was flawless cream and lit from behind her figure was breathtaking. Her red curls tumbled over her toned shoulders and there was a clearly defined bicep on the arm holding the hat. She leant on one hip atop long legs and I followed the line of her over her stomach hinting at more muscle but retaining a slender curve, on to her ruby nipples proud on her small but perfect breasts.

I pulled back the duvet in invitation.

CHAPTER TWENTY-TWO

Message Alert

My phone rattled on top of the metal bread bin, turning it into an insanely annoying snare drum. I tried to ignore it, almost certainly Mhairi. I would get to it at some point.

I continued with the beans, stirring and waiting for that point where they just start to break up a bit. Beans on toast sounds like the easiest meal in the world to prepare, but there are actually some subtleties that, if observed, really improve the dish. A little butter, for example, thickens the sauce and really—

'Oh, for Christ's sake.'

The phone vibrated straight off the dome of the bin, bounced briefly on the work surface before clattering to the floor. I lifted the thing, about to switch the alert to silent when I saw that it was not a text message I was being made aware of, but rather a Facebook Messenger alert. I turned

296

off the hob and clicked. It was a message, or rather series of messages from Jenny's friend Viv. I scrolled through and considered a response. I wished Rowan had been there to do it, but we were two days into a period of four rest days. Actually, that's a good idea, I thought. I switched to call function and dialled Rowan. It went to voicemail and I hung up. I selected text instead:

Hey, you around? Could use some help.

I let the phone sit on the kitchen work surface and waited for another buzz while I returned to the beans, but I quickly realised I was too distracted to eat. I left the food and went searching for my laptop. While it was booting up I texted Rowan again.

Oi, call me asap.

I sat on the sofa and brought up Facebook. I rattled around within its framework, trying to remember how to look at messages. Finally, I opened up the conversation Rowan had started. Viv was still showing as being online and given it had taken weeks to get this response, I didn't want to waste the opportunity. I checked my phone one last time for a response from Rowan, but no luck.

I read back the responses from Viv, four of them, and considered how to reply.

>Hey Mark, yeah gd to hear from U. U gd 2?

>All gd here m8, u decided to move down or what?

>Cld put u up for a bit if you want?

>Jus leme know

'OK,' I said to the screen, 'how difficult can this be?'

>Thnkin bout it, Viv. What's the situation down there? Where in London are you? Jenny living with u? She gd?

I hit return and sat, staring at the screen. My eyes were fixed on the green circle indicating Viv was online, sure it would suddenly just go off. Five minutes passed, then ten. *Fuck*, I thought. *Way too obvious. Should have eased into the questions, talked shit for a while. Plus, way too much punctuation. But then, the longer you chat to this girl, the more opportunity she's going to have to realise you're not Mark. You were right to keep it brief and to the point. Maybe. No, definitely should have started with small—*

There was a blurry series of dots appearing under the open conversation. That's good, right? Means she's typing? The dots rolled, then disappeared, then rolled again. Finally, they stopped for a full five minutes and again I started looking to the green circle. Then a message flashed up out of nowhere.

>U know. Wrkin, drinkin, usual. Y u ask bout Jen?

This message would have taken a few seconds to type. And yet Viv had been typing on and off for an age. She was suspicious. *Bring it back to breezy*, I thought. I thought for a minute, then Jen's bedroom jumped into my head.

>Jus thinkin, b cool to have the gang back together. U, me, Jen. I was jus thinkin the other day bout that school trip. Gd times, right?

That's better, I thought. *Bring it back. Play the long game.*

Again, there was a long gap before the dots appeared, though this time the message appeared right away.

>Cops bn talkin to u bout her? What u say?

That was unexpected. She was on full defensive here.

>Nah man. Like I say, jus thought about that school trip

298

I was sure this time the green circle would go. But no, a reply came:

>Cool cool. Yeh, mad times.

I couldn't ask about Jen again, that was clear. At best I had one or two messages left and this line was going dead. Fuck it.

>Yeh, we need to get back to Berlin one day

White dots.

>4sure man. Lk, if ur serious bout comin down let me know, yeh?

>Did I say Berlin? I meant Paris, right? Viv? Who is this?

The white dots appeared for a moment. Then stopped again for a long time. I looked to the green circle. It disappeared along with Viv's profile avatar altogether, or whoever the fuck it was.

CHAPTER TWENTY-THREE

Medical History

Fifty quid?

You have got to be joking.

Perhaps if it had been painted by one of those unfortunate people who, through injury or birth defect, need to hold a brush with a foot or a mouth then . . . Actually, no. It would still be shit.

I nudged Rowan with my elbow and nodded at the watercolour sitting not quite centre in its cheap frame.

'Dear God, did someone paint that with their toes?' she said, a little too loudly and tilted her head to one side like a curious dog. 'What is it even supposed to be?'

'Not sure, maybe a landscape? A bowl of fruit? It's actually one of the better ones.' I motioned around the waiting room at the array of paintings dotted arbitrarily around the walls. A caption was written under each, explaining that a local artists' group were the creators of, or were responsible for, the decor, and that the 'suggested' price of each would be donated to a children's hospital, which made me feel a little guilty at my appraisal, a little.

We squeezed into one corner of the room, as far as possible from the lady sat in the middle of the rows of plastic chairs coughing furiously into a handkerchief.

'Where were you the other night when I was trying to get hold of you?' I asked.

'I was . . . out.'

'Out?'

'You mean like a date?'

'Not like a date date.'

'And?'

'And I won't be seeing him again. No more questions.'

'OK. Sorry.'

'Anyway, you're sure that whoever you were talking to was not Viv?'

'Well, I can't be sure, but yes.'

'What do you think's going on?'

'I don't know,' I said. 'But that angle is shut down now. She, or whoever it was, deleted the profile, our conversation with it.'

'Would it have helped if I'd done the talking?'

'I don't think so, don't worry about it. But I'm more keen than ever to have the Met follow this up. The inspector should be able to pull a few favours, I'll talk to him about it.'

'Speaking of dates,' said Rowan, lowering her voice

further. 'You never responded to my text the other day.'

'It wasn't deserving of response,' I said. It wasn't the only text I had failed to respond to since that evening. Mhairi had sent two messages, breezy but keen in nature. I intended to respond to these, I just hadn't found the right tone.

'What, why? it was a perfectly reasonable question.'

'"So . . . did you shag her or what?" is not a reasonable question.'

'Don't be so sensitive. Well?'

'Well, what?'

'Did you . . . end up spending the night with her?' she asked, in a mock-polite voice.

I took a few seconds before saying: 'I spent the night, but only because I couldn't get home. I shall be drawn no further on the matter.'

'Ha, you totally shagged her!'

I shook my head dismissively but didn't bother to deny it. I thought about the awkward morning after. Her watching me with amusement as I gathered my clothes, putting on only what I had to and carrying the rest. Passing Helen as I power-shuffled out of the house with my uniform hanging off me like a molested stripper.

'Officers?' A tired-looking middle-aged woman ducked her head around the corner, peering at us over the top of her glasses.

'We don't mind waiting,' I said, and thumbed at the germ launcher who had been sitting there when we had arrived.

'No, it's fine. Mrs Reynolds is very ear . . . You're very early, Mrs Reynolds,' she shouted at the elderly woman, who only looked up when hearing her name bellowed. 'You don't mind if I see these police officers quickly, do you, dear?'

'Oh no, I'm—' We waited almost a minute for her to stop coughing, but she never finished the sentence, she just waved us away.

Dr Rowse's office was clean, very clean; the least you should expect of a GP's examination room I suppose, but it still had a dirty feel about it. The room was cramped, the furniture was old and badly in need of replacing. The computer sitting on the desk looked like the old Amstrad we used in primary school, complete with a gargantuan monitor that might need two men to move.

'It's not the most modern, but it's efficient,' she said, falling into her own chair at the desk and noticing my inspection of the room. She motioned at another of the uncomfortable plastic chairs that made up the waiting room and I sat. 'Oh, I'm sorry,' the doctor said, 'I should have brought another chair in. She made to get up, grunting with anticipated effort before Rowan pushed out a hand.

'I'm fine, Doctor. We won't keep you long.' Rowan folded over the protective paper on the bed that flowed from a roll at its head and hopped up onto it.

Dr Rowse hammered the return key on the chunky keyboard until a pale green light lazily began to glow from the screen. 'I normally work out of the health centre in Oban. We run a clinic out of here every Wednesday and Thursday. It's not always easy for people to make the journey, particularly in the winter. So . . . Mr Cooper.' She pulled a thick grey-brown folder onto her lap from the desk and slapped her hands on top of it. 'What would you like to know?' She removed her glasses and let them drop to her chest on the thin chain that hung round her neck.

'I just have some follow-up questions from the detective in charge, Doctor. I don't need to take a full statement or anything. Mostly I need a list of his medication and details of when he was last seen,' I said, and pulled out my notebook.

'Well, that's good, because I can't pretend to have known him very well. I'll print you off his meds.'

'Why is that? Did he have another GP?'

'No, he just was never a particularly regular patient.' She slammed the return key again on the keyboard and the dot matrix printer began its infuriating series of digital scratches. She then began leafing through the folder.

'I was led to believe he was quite ill?'

'Terminal bowel cancer, yes. I last saw him . . . let's see, April this year.'

'So, that's seven months until we found him in November. Is that not unusual for someone in his condition?'

'Yes, though he had an oncology consultant too.' She replaced the glasses and scanned a page. 'A Dr Setty at the hospital, but he'd been missing appointments with him. Do you need his details? I think I have his card somewhere.'

'Thank you, yes. Why was that?'

'I asked him that myself. I called him when Dr Setty got in touch, concerned with Mr Cooper's reluctance to follow up his appointments. I convinced him to come in.'

'How did he seem?'

Dr Rowse sat back in her chair. Her eyes drifted up as she considered. 'Sick, but . . . resolute that he was all right.'

'But . . . he had terminal bowel cancer?'

'Yes, so of course he wasn't all right. I guess he had just come to terms with it all. He wasn't interested in treatment, not once he was told all we could really do for him was to try to prolong things and make him comfortable.'

'Mr Cooper appears to have died from an overdose. One thing the detective requesting this information wanted me to ask, is whether you think he was of a mindset to have done this deliberately?'

'Suicide?'

'Yes, I'm sorry to ask.'

'Oh, don't be, perfectly plausible in the circumstances. A man living on his own, no family to speak of, told he doesn't have long to live? If it were me, I think I would be tempted. But if you're asking if I think he took his own life on purpose, I would say no.'

'Why do you think that?'

'For one thing I've seen the results of the PM and the level of overdose would suggest to me that it was unlikely.'

'How do you mean?' I asked, and at this Rowan stopped playing with the model of the inner ear she had found.

'I had Mr Cooper on some pretty strong painkillers, a high dose of tramadol. It was all I could really do for him. The amount that was found in his system was certainly high, but again, if it were me, I'd have taken twice or three times the amount they found. He had a repeat prescription so it would have been easy enough for him. I mean, I imagine you've decided to end it all with an overdose. My first priority would be to ensure I did it right, that there is absolutely no way I would wind up waking in the middle of the night in respiratory distress or other near-fatal state. I'd have thrown enough tablets down my neck to poison an elephant. But that's only one consideration.'

'What's the other?' asked Rowan, now leaning forward on the bed.

'He was a religious man . . . or seemed to be; and really quite positive. No, if you ask me the overdose was probably accidental. He was in a fair amount of pain. It's more plausible to me that he had been upping his own doses and then perhaps forgotten he had already taken his allocation for the day and repeated it.'

'Religious, really?' I asked, picturing the Hammer house of horror we had found him in.

'Yes, I think so. I asked him why he wouldn't follow up his appointments, why he was refusing treatment. I suspected he was depressed and was of a mind to prescribe something. His reply surprised me. He became quite philosophical, talking about . . . *in the absence of a cure, one has no choice but to turn to a higher power*, something like that. He saw my concern and I remember, he said, "Have faith, Doc." He patted my hand like I was the sick one and he smiled. He didn't strike me as suicidal.' She stretched over and began peeling the printed sheet, trying not to tear through it.

'Thanks,' I said and passed the print-off back to Rowan before checking my notes. 'I've also to ask you about his drinking.'

'Ah yes. Well, that was always a tricky issue.'

'How so?'

'Officially . . . he was teetotal.'

'Not from what we saw in the house,' said Rowan. 'Bottles everywhere.'

'It doesn't surprise me. He would never admit it to me of course. Claimed he hadn't touched a drop in years. Part of the reason I prescribed tramadol instead of codeine or something stronger, was because of these concerns. If I'd known for sure he still had a drinking habit, I may not even have prescribed those. I guess sometimes you just have to take people at face value, particularly when they're facing an end of life scenario as Mr Cooper was.'

'It sounds to me like you were really looking out for him, Doctor,' I said, feeling a sense of guilt from her. 'I think you might have been about his only friend. With the poor guy's wife passed away and his daughter having left him to his own devices, I bet he was . . .' I trailed off as Dr Rowse was giving me the strangest look, a look she also flicked at Rowan, though Rowan was again focused on learning the complexities of the ear.

'Mr Cooper was my patient, so of course I would do all I could for him, but friends we were not. You're not from Stratharder, are you, Sergeant?'

I knew it was rhetorical, but I confirmed I was not.

'Nor am I, but I'm surprised that you don't seem to know Mr Cooper's . . . history?'

'Oh, don't be surprised, Doctor, you'd be amazed at what I seem to be unaware of. But what exactly are we talking about?'

'Well, it's not my place to . . . I'm not one to indulge in idle gossip but—' Dr Rowse started.

'But that *poor* old Mr Cooper,' interjected Rowan, 'he killed his wife and was probably fiddling with his daughter.'

'Well . . . exactly,' finished the doctor.

'This fucking town,' I said, under my breath.

CHAPTER TWENTY-FOUR

Previous Convictions

'You didn't think to tell me about Cooper?' I said, back in the car.

'Sorry, it didn't really occur to me. It's all just rumour; besides, I thought you knew. Everyone knows.'

'Everyone knows, except the cop investigating his death. I felt like a complete idiot.'

'Don't worry, I'm sure the doctor doesn't mind that you're an idiot.'

I pulled into the station car park and saw that the inspector's civilian car was parked up.

'So, go on, then,' I said, turning off the engine. 'What *are* these rumours?'

'OK, well, you have to remember,' said Rowan, fishing her hat from the back seat, 'I've only been in Stratharder about a year and a half myself. You may need to find a proper local for the full story. But as I heard it, Cooper was a lousy drunk, a real bastard when he was in his cups. His wife, I forget her name, was an alcoholic too, one of these co-dependency things, I guess. The daughter, Eleanor I think, goes to live with a relative when the parental units are on a heavy binge. I think maybe this is where the rumours of Dad fiddling with her come from. I don't think there's any more to substantiate it, just the neighbours seeing her being whisked away from the family home from time to time.

'Anyway, after a particularly heavy bender an ambulance is called to the house and the wife is brought out dead, having been so for a few days. I'm not clear on all the ins and outs but there's an investigation, an inconclusive post-mortem and Cooper claims he doesn't remember a thing. Cooper was charged with her murder, but the case wasn't strong enough to even see the inside of a court. She died of asphyxiation, but whether Cooper had anything to do with it, or if it might have been some drunken accident, remains fodder for gossip to this day.' Rowan hopped from the car and we started across the car park towards the station. 'I suppose it all has some nice symmetry about it?'

'What does?' I asked.

'Mr and Mrs Cooper, their deaths in that house and the uncertainty attached to both.'

'I suppose it does.'

'Do you still think there was more to Cooper's death?'

'I think there's more to it than a simple overdose, yes. DS Aitken doesn't concur. I don't know where to go next with it. As soon as I email the doc's statement back to CID,

I think they'll draw a line under it all. I can just be like a dog with a burst ball at times, can't seem to let it go.'

'Is it something to do with your . . . you know, your thing?' said Rowan, in an unnecessary whisper.

'No, nothing like that, no twinges or anything. Just an old-fashioned hunch. Which probably means I'm way out. What the doctor said made a lot of sense, accidental overdose, I guess, but it just doesn't sit well with me. There's one or two things I want to check out before I hand it back.'

'Like what?'

'I'm going to keep that under my hat for now. Don't want you getting in trouble.'

'Oh, don't do that. That's like telling someone you know some dark secret and then not saying what it is. Only dicks do that.'

'I'm sorry. I'll let you know when I can. I promise.'

Margaret actually looked busy as we entered. She didn't even appear to notice our arrival. Her desk was a riot of paperwork and the soaps playing on the television screen had been paused, with some altercation in a pub suspended mid flow.

'He has run off four times in the past three years,' said Margaret, without once looking up.

'S-T,' Rowan said, before I had a chance to.

'Thanks, love. If you want tea you'll have to make it yourself, I'm a bit—'

'Busy, I can see that,' I said. 'What's he got you doing?'

'Still transferring the old mis-per forms to the computer. Which reminds me . . .' She began hunting between and underneath the towers of paper on her desk, a system no

311

doubt, though known only to her, until a single sheet of paper was discovered.

'What is it?' I asked and took it from her.

'Someone from the Met called for you. They started trying to leave a message, but it was all too complicated and I'm up to my neck, so I asked them to fax over the details.'

'I'll pass it on to the inspector as I need to chat to him about that anyway. What kind of mood is he in?'

'Sorry, I didn't really notice. He did ask if you were in, though.'

'I'll go see him. Rowan was just putting the kettle on, Margaret. What can she get you?' Rowan flashed an oh-was-I-now? look.

'Oh, thank you, love. I could murder a cup of tea.'

'Coffee for me, thanks.'

'One tea, one spit-latte coming right up.'

The sounds of a one-sided conversation spilled into the hall as I approached the inspector's office. I took the opportunity to have a look at the fax from the Met while I waited for his telephone call to end.

For the Attention of Sgt Donald Colyear:
Subject – Missing Person enquiry – Jennifer Mulligan.
From: Insp. Fiona Perry, Central Enquiries.

Sgt Colyear,
In response to your email enquiry on the above-mentioned subject, I have to report the following: your enquiry has been allocated to an investigating

officer and will be actioned in due course.

Your reference, should you need to contact us is:
CE-NOV08-1132.

The officer allocated to your enquiry is: PC
Rebecca Richardson CO133, Metropolitan Police
Central Enquiries Team.

The investigating officer will respond to you
directly. We aim to complete enquiries within 6 weeks
of receipt, however this is not always possible when
dealing with high demand. Therefore, please allow
10 weeks before contacting the team for an update.

This message has also been emailed for your
attention and records.

Regards,
Insp. Fiona Perry

'Donald,' said the inspector, seeing me waiting through
the crack in the doorway.

'You wanted to see me, Inspector?'

'Come in. Close the door, won't you? Yes, we need to
have a, well, a conversation.'

I couldn't quite place his tone, some mix of trepidation
and sombre intensity. I closed the door over and drew a chair
to sit in front of his desk. The inspector's hand wandered
around his mouth and chin nervously as he appeared to be
searching for words. He was looking everywhere but at me.

'Oh, this came,' I said, unable to endure. I handed
him the fax. 'It seems there's more mistakes with Brian's
missing person enquiries. I actually need to talk to you

about that, something I need to update you with.'

He scrutinised the page. 'I hadn't realised you'd applied for information. What's happened?'

'I asked to speak to the officer who had traced Jennifer's friend last year. I thought it would be a good place to try to pick up the investigation. Unfortunately, the information Brian's scribbled on the form doesn't make much sense. Anyway, I know you were dealing with it now, so I'm really just handing it over, although I'm happy to go and dig out the initial fax we sent them and tidy this up.'

'Goddammit. This really is a balls-up,' he said, and slapped the fax flat on the desk. 'This will take a long time to sift through. Leave it with me and I'll have Margaret dig out the information. You've got an interview to prepare for and it's likely you'll be leaving us shortly after, no?'

'I suppose so. I should also explain something else that came up in regard to Jennifer—'

'You're not sure? You're having seconds thoughts?' he interrupted.

I heaved a heavy breath. 'I don't know. I guess the thought of sitting behind a desk again is a little depressing.' It was something which had been preying on me for a while. I had to admit that as much as Stratharder was a backwards nothing of a place, it had been liberating being back on the street.

'It's the McCloy girl, I suppose. She has you turned around?'

'W-what?' I stammered, completely unseated. 'How did . . . ? What makes you think . . . ?' I forced myself to pause, take a breath. 'Actually, I'm sorry, Inspector, but I'm not sure that has anything to do with—' I was cut off by the phone ringing. The inspector pushed out a hand instructing me to halt, a hand he may as well have pushed in my face. I sat opposite, impatiently tapping the top of my index finger on the arm of the chair.

'Uhuh . . . I see . . . Yes . . . I'm happy to discuss, but I'm with someone at . . . Uhuh . . .'

Ordinarily I would have thought it too rude to reach for my own phone to check messages, but in the circumstances, I decided it was fair. A message from Karen was waiting:

Still haven't heard from u! Bumped into ur dad in town, was lovely. Wld love to do the same with you sometime. Hope ur well. K x

Dad, you old turncoat, I thought, mostly in jest . . . mostly. My thumb hovered for a second before selecting delete.

'Sorry about that. Where were we?' With the phone down the inspector turned to me as I tucked my mobile back into my pocket.

'You mentioned Mhairi?'

'Ah yes.' The pause returned and I resisted the temptation to tell him to spit it the fuck out. Instead, I waited.

'This is what I needed to speak to you about, Donald. Now, I need you to keep calm as I do. OK?'

Calm? I thought. 'OK . . .' I said.

'Your relationship with Miss McCloy has not gone unnoticed, Donald.'

'My relationship?'

'She's an attractive girl, no doubt there, so I get it,' he said, with his palms out in an understanding gesture. 'The thing is . . .' he sat forward uneasily, 'you cannot see her any more.'

My composure was entering a tailspin and I sat in silence for a moment, wrestling an internal yoke to level off before again opening my mouth.

'Inspector, I'm sorry, I have no idea what you're talking about,' I said at last. 'Whatever you may have heard about Mhairi and myself is, well . . . I'm sorry to be blunt, absolutely none of your business.'

'That, Donald, is where you are wrong—'

'You know, Inspector, if you'd had the decency to just ask me what was going on between Mhairi and myself, I may well have been happy to tell you.' It was, perhaps, poor judgement starting with a lie, but here we were. 'But since you come in shooting from the hip like that I'm just inclined to repeat, this is none of your—'

'None of my business. Yes, I did hear you.' His voice was steady, but he began jabbing the desktop with an impatient finger. 'Let me put this another way, since it appears diplomacy has already failed. You will stop seeing that girl immediately. That, Sergeant, is an order.'

'Ha,' I said, and slapped the corner of the desk with a laugh devoid of authenticity. 'You're ordering me? You're not serious.'

'I am perfectly serious.'

'You don't have the authority to—'

'Oh, but I do. This is not personal, Donald. The fact of the matter is, as officers of the law, we may not associate with known criminals.'

'What?' I said, dumbly.

'It's one of the conditions of your station as a member of the police. You can of course look into the regulations governing—' He stopped, realising this was not my query. His tone softened. 'I see. You weren't aware.'

'What could she possibly have done? I mean, if everyone with a misdemeanour was suddenly off limits, it would be a pretty lonely existence for police officers.'

'It's true there is some flexibility on the point, however, we're not talking about a misdemeanour here.'

'What, then?'

He sighed and sat back in his chair. 'You can look it up yourself, but it's serious enough that we had to have this unsavoury conversation.' His phone began to ring again. I shot to my feet and lifted the receiver and placed it straight back down again.

'I will look it up, but come on, out with it,' I said, still expecting some limp infraction which would vindicate my anger. He breathed heavily with resignation, then proceeded to obliterate any such hope.

'She has previous convictions for prostitution and the sale and supply of class-A narcotics.'

An instant retort caught in my throat as his words hit home. 'Bullshit,' I said quietly and after a time.

'You're free to look it up.'

I spun around and swiped the fax from his desk.

'I can deal with that, Donald.'

'Don't do me any favours,' I said, and almost collided with Rowan, who was stood outside the door holding two cups of coffee, probably lukewarm from the time spent eavesdropping.

CHAPTER TWENTY-FIVE

Kick a Man When He's Down

'Thanks, Bub,' I grunt, as I haul myself up through the hatch. Mercifully there's a large exposed nail in the floorboard I can hook the cuff-handle to, or I don't know how this might have worked.

The light here is better, but not much. That is to say, there is some.

The moon shines down through the open roof but it's held at bay by a muslin of low cloud. Still, it's sufficient for me to realise that where I'm standing is the old sawmill. I never noticed the trapdoor when I walked here with Hilda, must be some kind of old storage for timber.

I thought it was cold underneath, but out here it's absolutely freezing. The thick dust, which I can now see to be ancient sawdust, must have been an insulator. Without a jacket I'll perish before long. Looking back down through *the hatch I consider going back for Bub's coat. I have to concede that would be one ignominy too many. He's still balancing in the face down, arse up position I put him in to use as a step-stool. Poor bastard can keep his coat, his red coat I can see now, even if he did try to kill me. I see who he is now.*

I close the hatch on him.

I reach down and gather snow into my wrists where the cuffs are cutting me. Probably not wise given how quickly I might freeze out here, but it feels good, so fucking good. I even carefully drop a small amount onto the wound on my head. This only feels good for a second though, then I regret it as it begins to sting.

'Just leave it alone,' I scald, and start trudging through the snow back to the road. I begin heading uphill towards Hilda's place. I haven't gone far when the noise of an engine can be heard, mingling with the rush of the branches overhead swaying in the bitter wind. I stop, trying to establish if it's getting louder, if it's coming or going.

Coming, but slowly.

I have time to find somewhere to hide, though there aren't many options. The embankment on both sides is steep and sparse with leafless winter branches and stark contrasting snow. I find a ditch and hunker down as best I can. I have some time.

I try again to inspect the wound on my head. It's a small cut, but pretty damn deep. The snow has dissolved the clots holding it closed. I'm bleeding again.

It reminds me of waking in hospital after I was attacked by my colleagues. I don't want to think about it,

but there it is. Perhaps waking isn't the right word? It was
more gradual than that. More an increasing realisation of
circumstance and self, and pain.

'How long have you been sitting there?' I said, or tried to
say. My jaw was sitting at a bizarre angle and 'long' came
out as 'wong'.

Karen smiled, though her eyes were flooding over. She
opened her mouth to speak before shaking her head and
fleeing from the room.

'Kawen,' I shouted after her and wished I hadn't, the
pain was almost too much.

'She'll be all right. Just give her a minute. You're just a
little . . . difficult to look at right now. When she got the
call, she must have feared the worst. I know I did when she
called me.'

'Da, a di'nt hee you there.'

'Maybe best if you don't try to talk.' Dad sat on the
opposite side, the side where my eye was so swollen, I
couldn't see out of it. He patted my hand. He looked close
to tears too.

'You shou hee the otha guy,' I tried to say, remembering
John making the same joke after I finally visited him at
the hospital following his injury.

He smiled. 'You've been in and out for a few hours,'
he said. 'They're taking you for a CT scan, but they think
you're going to be all right. You'll be eating out of a straw
for a while. They say it looks worse than it is. Hard to
believe, but that's what they told us. I think they were trying
to prepare us for the shock when we got here; didn't work.

'There's an Inspector Bennett here to see you too when you're up to it.' Dad leant in close and lowered his voice. 'I hope you're going to tell him exactly what happened, Don. Who was involved I mean.'

Dad knew something was going on. I guessed maybe he'd been waiting for something like this, based on the snippets he'd learnt over the previous year or so.

'Da, it's not 'at sim-hle,'

'Donald, I mean it. You tell him everything, do you hear me?'

I nodded resignedly.

I would go on to tell my inspector what happened, as best I could. He would go on to listen, to look concerned; to then ask me if I wanted to pursue it. I'd like to say I was horrified to have been asked such a question, the inference being all too clear. The truth is I fully expected it. He asked me to consider my decision, to take my time over it. He invited me in for a chat three weeks later while I was still on sick leave. This chat would prove awkward and full of unexpected turns. However, the chat that would come later that day, in my own kitchen, trumped it on all levels.

'I was getting worried. You've been gone hours,' Karen said. She was unloading the dishwasher. She kissed my cheek gently. There was no need for her to be so delicate. The bruising had faded to a dull mustard hue; there was no pain. I looped my jacket around the back of a chair at the small breakfast table. 'How did it go?'

'Come and sit down,' I said. 'We've got a lot to talk about.'

'Sounds serious. Do you wanna cuppa, love?'

'No, leave that. Come and sit down.' I took the dishtowel from her and pulled her towards a chair. I began clearing clutter from the table and reached for her mobile, which was amongst it. She snatched it up urgently.

'Been hovering over this, waiting to hear from you,' she said. 'It'll need charging.' She made to get up again.

'Later, just sit for now.'

'All right. So, are they going to charge those men?'

'What men?'

Karen rolled her eyes. 'The men who tried to kill you. The reason you went to speak to your boss.'

'Right. Well, I don't think they were trying to kill me. I mean there was nothing stopping them if that's what they—'

'Don, focus. Tell me what's going on.'

'You see, that particular matter never really . . . came up.'

'It didn't come up.' A sardonic statement, rather than a question.

'Not directly, but there's this other thing and it kind of came out of the blue and—'

'Don,'

'Right, focus. OK, this isn't how I practised this on the way home. What I meant to say was I have good news and I have . . . well, not so good news.'

Karen's patience was visibly draining from her. She opened both of her hands, beckoning I get to the point.

'I've been offered a promotion,' I announced. 'That's the good news.'

Karen's eyebrows arched their surprise. 'That *is* good news. Sergeant Colyear.' She tried it out on the ceiling.

'Sounds good on you. Now, out with the *but*.'

'Buuut . . . it's a community sergeant's role up in Stratharder.'

'Stratharder?' Her eyes reflected her brain, scanning an internal map of Scotland. 'Nope, I have no idea where that it is.'

'Yeah, I had to look it up too. It's north of Oban. That's the bad news.'

'I see. You're from up there, but you still didn't know where it was?'

I shook my head. 'It's just a wee quiet place. Thing is I would have to be up there six months or so, but then I could start applying for roles back down here.'

'That's what your boss told you?'

I nodded again, slowly this time. Karen's mind was working and I was preparing.

'So, let me get this straight, love. Your boss brings you in, supposedly to discuss whether or not you proceed with a prosecution against your colleagues. Instead, he distracts you with a big shiny promotion. Like a baby grinning at a set of keys?'

I resisted the urge to nod again

'Not only that,' she continued, 'this promotion is to some outer reach of the solar system? You do realise what's going on, don't you?'

'Of course I do; out of sight, out of mind. I'm not stupid. I know when I'm being bought off, but it's a hell of a pay-off. To be honest I was never sure about pursuing a conviction anyway, Karen. You know how miserable I was at work before the . . . incident. If I go ahead with a court case against other cops, I'll have to look for another career because there's no way I'm going to spend the rest of this one being sneered at and avoided. This is a chance to let it all blow over.'

Karen's phone buzzed on the table surface, making it dance. She checked the screen and pushed it into her pocket. 'Sounds like you've made your mind up. Your dad will be furious.'

'He'll understand. But I haven't agreed to anything. I said I needed to talk to you first. I have until Monday to decide. The thing is, and this is the other bad news, we would probably have to put the wedding off for a while—'

'Don . . .'

'We wouldn't have to sell the house, but we might want to think about renting it out for a while—'

'Don . . .'

'Look I know it's a lot to ask and I know you think it's a terrible idea, but I just want you to think about—'

'Don . . . stop.' She reached across the table and took both my hands. Her eyes were glittering with the onset of tears. 'Actually, I think it's a good idea. I really think you should take it, get your career back on track. I do.'

'Really? God, I'm so relieved,' I said, rubbing the back of her hands with my thumbs. 'You know, I think you'll love it up there. Wait until you see it in autumn, it's just—'

'Don . . .' Her voice was cracking at the edges now, but increasingly insistent. 'I think *you* should go.' She paused, trying to compose herself. 'But . . . I think *I* should stay.' The tears were rolling now. She bit at her bottom lip to control its trembling.

For a moment I thought she meant I should commute back and forth for however long I would be up there. *I can work with that*, I almost said. The words were in my mouth . . . and then I swallowed them like bitter medicine as I suddenly understood what was happening. My heart started hammering in my throat. I drew my hands away from her.

'When did . . . What *exactly* are you saying, Karen?'

'I'm so sorry,' she blurted through deep sobs.

Pull yourself together and spit it the fuck out, some furious part of me demanded internally. Her hands were on her head now and she was standing.

'Oh God, is this really happening?' she said.

I waited. I hoped somehow I was still reading this all wrong.

'I meant to talk to you ages ago but . . . Oh God.' Her hands now over her face.

Come on, come on.

'But then you got hurt. And then there you were lying in the hospital. Oh God. And I couldn't; I just couldn't.'

'You were waiting until I was well enough to get back to work,' I said. Not a question.

'Donny,' she said, this particular endearment had been prevalent in our early years, conspicuously missing in the last few, 'I'm so, so sorry.'

I needed her to say it was over, but that was never going to happen. She was always going to force me to draw it out of her. 'Is it someone else?' I said after another torrent of tears.

'I never – meant for – it to – happen.'

* * *

325

Headlights come into view splitting the darkness with hazy white cones, turning the softly falling snow caught in them into tiny shadows. The beams catch me square in the eye and I drop as low as I can. I push the glare out of my eyes with my fingers. My knees are completely numb and soaking. My arms tremble uncontrollably. If I don't manage to get to Hilda's soon, I will probably stop shivering, then I'll know I'm in real trouble.

The car trundles past infuriatingly slowly. The tyres make a dull crunch as they compact the fresh snow underneath them. When it's gone far enough, I'll run to Hilda's and generate some warmth, *I decide.*

The crunch is growing fainter and I raise my head, preparing to spring from the ditch, only to see the red of a brake light turn to the white of a reverse, and I duck down again. The whine of the reverse gear gains volume and I sink low, face almost into the snow. Then brakes and a long skid and the car has stopped right above me.

The groan of an electric window.

'Who the fuck let you out?' she says.

CHAPTER TWENTY-SIX

Babes in the Wood

'Wasn't he a good-looking man?'

'Very handsome,' I agreed, carefully placing the picture back on the mantelpiece and thereby undoing my desecration of the little shrine.

Hilda handed me my tea. I took the cup and saucer from her and sat on the couch opposite the armchair she was settling herself into. I felt a little ashamed that I was only now spending a little time with my landlady and next-door neighbour, just when it looked like I was leaving.

'Aye, my Charlie was a fine figure of a man. You look a bit like him actually, although he wisnae skinny like you; no offence, son.'

'None taken.'

She was right. Looking at Charlie above the fireplace was like looking at a 'before' picture if I was an 'after', in an advertisement for slimming pills. We shared the same short dark hair and high cheekbones, though his were accountable to strong bone structure, whilst mine simply due to lack of flesh.

The little border terrier I had trodden on when I stepped into the house leapt onto my lap, my clumsiness apparently forgiven.

'He likes you. Norman can be funny around men. He's a good judge of character.'

Norman looked up at me, his comical, white underbite contrasting his brown-tan fur. He was urging me to continue scratching his head.

'When did he pass? Your husband, I mean.'

She checked a mental calendar and said: 'Twenty-two years next March. You'd have liked him – real people-person, you know.'

'I'm sure, Hilda.'

The living room had the feel of a log cabin. Wooden panelling covered every inch of the walls and the furniture had a certain arts and crafts charm. Photographs dominated the decor, the mantelpiece devoted to her Charlie, but otherwise there were pictures of kids everywhere.

'Are these your grandchildren?' I sipped at my tea, which was sweet. I wondered whether she'd got our cups mixed up, or whether she'd forgotten I'd said *Just milk*.

'Eight of them I have, and two great-grandchildren. Can you believe that?'

'Do you see a lot of them?' I said.

'Not so much. Our Tony stays in Australia, that's where the great-grandkids are. He bought me this thing so I can

Skype. Have you Skyped before?' She reached down by the side of the chair to a wicker magazine rack. Filed away next to *National Geographic*s and *Woman's Weekly*s was a silver laptop, which she tapped. 'Are you good with computers, Donald? It's just, I think it might have one of them viruses or something. My Peter thinks so too.'

'What makes you think that?' I said, and sipped.

'It goes slower than it used to. And it keeps asking me if I want a bigger cock.'

Hot, sweet tea flooded my sinuses and I cough-snorted into a cupped hand before discreetly emptying it back into the cup.

'You know, adverts like . . . always popping up offering pills and gadgets. You know, things you pop your wotsit into to make—'

'It does, yes. It sounds like you might have a virus, Hilda,' I interrupted. 'I'd be happy to take a look. At the computer I mean.' I was blushing, and I suspected that was the aim of it, but her face was unchanged.

'We're going to miss you around here,' she said.

'Thank you, Hilda. You mean you and Norman?'

'Yes, but also some of the ladies I meet for lunch too. You have a few admirers you know. If you were partial to the older lady, you'd have more blue-rinsed lady-business than you'd know what to do with.'

I'd learnt quickly not to drink hot beverages while Hilda was talking and had paused pre-sip.

'That's . . . sweet. I don't think there's many around here will be crying into their pillows after I'm gone.'

'When do you return to civilisation?' Hilda asked.

'I'm not sure exactly. It sort of hinges on an interview I have this week, but that would appear to be academic. I then need to agree a finishing date with my inspector. That won't be an issue. I think the prick will be only too happy for me to leave immediately. Excuse my language.'

'Stewart? Och, he's a pussycat. If he gives you any trouble you tell him I'll have words. Trust me, that one likes to play the surly ogre, but when you get him alone, he's nice as pie.'

'When you get him alone?' I said, in a high, mocking tone. 'Something I should know?'

'Let's just say he was a source of comfort to me after my Charlie passed.' Hilda winked as she lifted Norman onto the seat next to her. I suspected that should I have pursued her for details, she would have been very happy to provide them. I did not.

There was a sharp knock at the door, followed by Norman's insane barking. Hilda looked confused. She strolled into the hall trying to push the dog behind her legs. She returned a minute later looking especially smug.

'Visitor for you,' she said. 'A lady caller,' she added in a whisper.

Mhairi followed her into the room, wrapped in a red wool coat and large grey scarf. Her face was glowing. I couldn't tell if it was due to the cold or the embarrassment.

'I'm really sorry to drop in like this. I tried your place and didn't get a response, uh, obviously. I saw your car was there, so I thought I'd try here . . . obviously.'

'You're very welcome, dear,' said Hilda. She drew Mhairi further into the room. 'Can I get you some tea? The kettle's still hot. Dear God, you're freezing, lassie.' Hilda had Mhairi's hands and was rubbing at them.

'Oh no, thank you, Mrs Brownhill. I wasn't going to stop. Um, my brother had given me a lift into Oban and I just thought, on the way back, I'd see if Don was . . . well, see if you were in, Don. Sorry, I really should have called first.' Her face blazed.

'It's fine, Mhairi. It's nice to see you,' I said. I could feel my own face burning. 'I'm sorry, I've been meaning to respond to your texts, it's just been such a busy period.' I put my tea down, suddenly realising I looked anything but busy.

'That's all right. Look, I um, I just wondered if you fancied going for a bit of a walk. It's cold out, but actually it's a lovely morning.'

Hilda made no attempt to disguise her interest. She sat grinning at the soap opera being played out in her living room.

'Oh,' I said, and then, 'um.' My eyes searched the floor while my brain floundered for words.

'It *is* lovely, Donald, but Mhairi's right. Best put a coat on; you'll catch your death out there. I was just saying to him, before you came in, pet, that we'll miss him, won't we?' Hilda was trying to rescue me; she was achieving the opposite.

'Miss him?' Mhairi said, looking perplexedly at me. 'I, uh, didn't know you were . . . Are you going somewhere?'

Hilda's smile melted into a grimace. 'Come on, Norman. Let's you, me and my mouth go fix your lunch.'

Mhairi hooked both arms through the crook of my elbow and led me right, down the hill. I hadn't ever ventured any further than Hilda's on the road, so I was curious as to what lay ahead.

The road itself grew sludgy with mud and fallen leaves and its limits were becoming increasingly indiscernible; good-sized tree branches encroached on each side.

'We used to play in here as kids,' she said, as the way cut left into a side road I would probably have missed on my own.

'What is this place?' I said.

'The old sawmill. It closed in the late eighties but used to employ quite a few in the town.'

'Let me guess, another Ogilvie enterprise?'

'That's right. To his credit he did find other jobs for some of the workers. But closing this down pretty much meant the end of Kirkmartin.'

The road opened up into a clearing, or what would have been a clearing but was now being reclaimed by the forest. Three walls of the mill stood on a carpet of green moss. The missing wall had long since crumbled into an offshoot of the river. A large iron wheel still remained with menacing curved blades that once caught the redirected water. A smaller wheel seemed to grow out of the ground opposite its larger neighbour, with only its upper half visible. Within the remaining stone walls were long-rotted benches and a few equally decayed and rusted cutting blades, blunt but still vicious. Most of the roof had long since fallen into one corner.

'Come on,' said Mhairi, and tugged at my arm just as I was preparing to have a bit of an explore. 'This isn't what we're here for.'

'Where are you taking me?' I said.

'It's a surprise, you'll see. Oh, and you'll need this.' Mhairi dug into her coat pocket and produced a toy fire engine. She handed it to me.

'OK, now I'm confused,' I said. 'Intrigued, I suppose, but definitely confused.'

'That's the idea.'

Mhairi led us to a section of metal fencing at the far side of the mill. A small piece of red ribbon marked the place where she climbed over. I followed into dense undergrowth, though the faint idea of a path could just about be discerned. The forest around us grew denser, wetter and colder as the sun struggled to penetrate. The wind carried the smell of winter, that damp scent of decay that's somehow intoxicating.

'If the idea is to murder me and leave my body in a place nobody will ever find, I don't think we need to go any further,' I said, trying to keep up as she zigzagged through thin-trunked trees. The frozen mulch of the forest floor crackled satisfyingly underfoot.

'Oh, I'm not done with you yet, Sergeant; not nearly. It's just up here.'

A series of these small red ribbons were tied to branches every now and then. They led us to a clearing. In the middle lay a large, flat, rectangular stone, littered with trinkets. Four crude posts had been erected at its corners.

'This is it,' said Mhairi quietly into my ear.

'What are we looking at? And why are we whispering?'

'Good point,' she said, returning to a normal volume. 'This is a grave.'

'A grave?' I approached, peering over the thin wire suspended between the posts. The large slab of stone had not fared well over the years. It lay cracked into three large pieces and grass spouted from the fissures. If the stone had been inscribed upon, the names had long since been removed by weather. A thin blanket of frost covered the stone and its adornments. These comprised a blue T-Rex, four toy soldiers and a Barbie who looked like she'd been through some significant trauma in her life. 'Who exactly is buried here?'

'It's a plague grave,' she said, breezily. I couldn't help but recoil back behind the wire. 'I think you can relax. It's been here for hundreds of years.' Mhairi produced a pair of scissors from an inside pocket of her coat and began trimming back some encroaching weeds from the graveside. 'There's the ruins of a small croft about half a mile into the forest. The crofter who lived there lost his three children to the plague as it swept across Scotland in the sixteen-hundreds. They all died on the same day. In his grief he carried their bodies one at a time to this grave he made, far enough from the house to minimise the risk of catching his own death, close enough that he could visit every day.'

'How do you know this?' I said.

'My mum told me.'

'Yeah, but how does she know?'

'Her mum told her.'

'OK, how does anyone know this? There are no markings here.'

Mhairi shrugged. 'It used to be a bit of a tradition. On the last day of school, the kids would all come and lay one toy they didn't use any more for the babes in the wood. It doesn't happen any more, not since I was wee. I guess someday people will just forget and the woods will take this place back. Here, those soldiers have been there a long time, you can replace them with the truck I gave you.'

I reached through the loose wire and exchanged the toys while Mhairi took an action figure from her coat and replaced the dinosaur. PTSD Barbie survived the round of substitutions, I guessed because Mhairi only had Connor's unused toys to give and she wanted to leave a female option.

'It's funny,' I said, looking down at the grave.

'How's it funny? What's funny about it?'

'No, not funny like that, of course it's not . . . I was about to say it's funny, if you'd told me you were taking me to see a children's grave, I'd have expected something really . . . I dunno?'

'Creepy?'

'Maybe not creepy, certainly . . . sad, maudlin, you know? But it's not. Actually, it's very sweet. I love that you still come here.' I looked around at the small clearing, surrounded on all sides by wild forest. A tiny bubble of serenity in a pond of madness.

Mhairi stood and housed her scissors. She took hold of the lapels of my coat.

'Oh, do you? Well, maybe you just love too easily.' She kissed me on tiptoes, first on the cheek and then on the mouth. 'So, what was Mrs Brownhill talking about? Where are you off to?'

My eyes found my feet and I thrust my hands nervously into my coat pockets. 'I have an interview for a job that would take me back down the road. Nothing's certain though.'

'I see,' she said. She mirrored me, her hands finding her own pockets. 'I guess I can't blame you for wanting out of this rat trap of course, but were you going to say something?'

I looked up momentarily, catching her gaze, and quickly looked down again. 'It's not like that. It's a good opportunity. I know the inspector's been here a long time, but I can assure you that's the exception in the police, not the rule. It's likely I'll have all sorts of roles and postings in my career. I won't always have a say in them. I had to tell Hilda, she's my landlady, but as I say, nothing's confirmed yet, honestly.'

'I get, it but were you even going to tell me anything at all? I mean were you ever going to call me or text me back?'

'Mhairi,' I said, the regret in my voice plain.

She backed up a little. 'You know, Don, I'm a big girl. If you don't like me, I can take it. I mean you seemed to like me the last time we—'

'I do like you, Mhairi. It's just . . . it's complicated.'

'Shit . . .'

'What?'

'You're married?'

'What? No.'

'Kids? Girlfriend? . . . *Boyfriend*?'

'No, none of that.'

'Then, what?'

'It's, just that . . . Well, look, Mhairi. Fuck, I don't even know where to—'

'Out with it for God's sake. What is it that stops two consenting adults enjoying each other's company?'

'You, Mhairi.'

A silence settled on us. Mhairi bit at her lip, the way she did. Her arms were folded defensively over her chest.

'Me,' she said, her face was stern granite. 'My past, you mean?'

'Your . . . previous convictions.' Mhairi snorted a laugh that was no laugh at all. 'There are rules in the police about who you're allowed to, I guess, consort with. They really *can* stop you from forming relationships with—'

'Prostitutes and drug dealers?'

'Mhairi.'

She shook her head and looked anywhere but at me. 'So, what?' she said. 'You thought you would check up on me? Do a little background report, see what kind of woman it was you just bedded?'

'It wasn't like that.'

'You know I'm pretty sure you can't just go around checking on people without good cause—'

'The inspector told me, Mhairi. He called me in and said I can't see you. They have rules, like I said. I'm sorry.'

Mhairi's fists were driving into her hips now. 'How much did he tell you, exactly?'

'What do you mean?'

'I mean did he give you a story? Or did he just read out the charges? Did you bother to ask what it was all about? Or did you just hear "whore" and that was that?'

'I guess I didn't ask,' I said and scratched timidly at my head. Her eyes were welling, her face furious.

'So, he didn't tell you about my abusive relationship with Alistair Hughes? That he was the one selling the drugs, had me hooked on heroin, had me doing fucking . . . *favours* for his friends for cash when he couldn't sell enough smack to maintain his own habit? He didn't mention this, no? Or nobody else did? How is it you're a cop and you're the only idiot in this fucking town who doesn't know?' Tears of rage rolled down her porcelain cheeks. I shook my head, unable to speak. 'He didn't tell you how I tried to clean up my act when he got me pregnant with Connor at sixteen, but he just kept dragging me back down, and when the police finally got involved and I finally managed to leave him, how he reported me to you lot, out of spite? Did he tell you how hard I had to fight to keep Connor from being taken away by social-fucking-services? And how they did nothing to help keep Alistair away from me? No. You just heard "whore" and couldn't delete my number from your phone quick enough.'

'Mhairi, I didn't know. You're right, I, I didn't ask. I didn't even know Alistair was Connor's dad. Look, I'm sorry. I feel like a—'

'I don't give a fuck how you feel,' she said, as a tear tumbled to her cheek. She swiped it clear with the back of a hand and spun, her red mane following a split second behind. She strode back through the forest with the grace and determination of a woodland creature.

CHAPTER TWENTY-SEVEN

Loose Ends

It was a street I was unfamiliar with, which was in itself a strange thing in a town as small as Stratharder. It was a continuation of the street Rowan and I had visited to deal with Mrs Gillespie's vandalism call. While hers, and the rest of the street's houses, were unassuming ex-council jobs, these were something of a step up.

What looked like a dead end on the street actually curved right and uphill. A new street sign informed you you had entered Badger Wynd and a series of new-builds looked down upon the grey box-like homes, perhaps figuratively as well as literally.

Karen would have liked this street, I thought. These déjà-vu cul-de-sacs were just her thing; mine too at one point. The only thing that differentiated one mock-Tudor-fronted house from the next was the car sitting in the drive and the water feature in the front garden. I knew now that this was no longer an aspiration of mine.

The man who answered the door at number six looked at me like I was there to sell him snake-oil. 'M'hm?' came the noise through his nose and tight-pressed lips. His arms folded across his broad chest under his red-grey beard.

'I'm so sorry to bother you,' I said. 'This is a little unconventional, but my name is Don Colyear. I'm the community sergeant here in Stratharder.' I pulled my warrant card from the wallet I had been holding, prepared for this introduction, dressed as I was in civilian clothes. I pushed it forward for him to inspect. 'I would have called ahead, but the number we have on file for you doesn't seem to . . .' I drifted off as his arms fell to his sides and he stumbled back into the hall. I tried to grab him as his legs buckled but he was too far from me. He dropped to one knee and his hands found his face as he began to sob.

'Jesus, Paul. What's going on?' A woman appeared from the kitchen, dropping her dishtowel as she crouched next the man.

'Police,' he said through the tears. 'It's our Daisy, isn't it? What's happened?'

'Uh, yes,' I said, quickly catching up. I stepped tentatively into the hall. 'Look, this is about Daisy, but I have no news. I'm not here to tell you anything awful. I promise. I'm sorry, I should maybe have started with that. Maybe we could go into the living room and talk?'

I introduced myself to Mrs Cavanagh and helped poor Paul to a sofa. I explained I was only dropping by to ask a few questions about their daughter Daisy's missing person report from a few years ago.

'You can speak to Paul about that,' said Mrs Cavanagh. 'I'm sick fed up hearing about it. I'll be in the conservatory if you need me.' If she looked at me, I missed it. She kissed her husband on the forehead and left us.

'I'm sorry about that,' said Paul. 'She's moved past all this now, but the very mention of it reminds her of the stress. I'm sorry too about my own reaction at the door, that took me by surprise as well. I suppose I've been waiting for a policeman to appear on my step for some time with some horrendous news. Anyway, what is it I can do for you, Sergeant?'

'I feel bad about bringing all this up again. It's just that I am looking into another missing person report at the moment and I suppose I'm just trying to get my head around a few things.'

'I'll do what I can. Can I get you a tea or something?'

'No thanks. I don't want to keep you long. I appreciate Mrs Cavanagh would prefer that too. But if you don't mind, could you just briefly run through the circumstances leading up to Daisy's disappearance?'

Paul sat back on the sofa and crossed his legs. 'I'm sure you have it all in your file, but it's not too complicated. Daisy had applied to do mental-health nursing at Manchester Metropolitan. She got a conditional offer. But her marks were way short and it didn't happen. She was inconsolable. She couldn't even get a place at another uni and she was facing repeating her exams. The idea of staying another year in this town was too much for her and she left.'

'Just like that?'

He raised his hands in a don't-ask-me gesture. 'It's a thing here.'

'So I hear. I read in the file that there was some tension at home?'

This caused Paul to think for a moment. He leant forward, not aggressively, but there was a shift in his welcoming posture. 'What is it you're asking, exactly?'

'I'm just trying to get a sense of why she would leave without saying a word and then fail to get in touch after. Really, I'm just trying to understand.'

'OK,' he said and sat back. 'You're not from here, are you?' If this was a question at all, he didn't wait for a reply. 'It's the cool thing to do. I suppose when she failed to leave in a productive way, she'd already left in her head and so she took herself off the Stratharder way. I didn't think it would be our Daisy. I mean we had our moments as a family. You look like you're too young to have a teenage daughter, Sergeant, but it's no cake walk. Still, we were pals, you know? I'd taken her down to Manchester twice. I was as excited as she was, sort of living vicariously, you know?' I nodded and let him continue. 'When she didn't come home one night we were in bits. Called you lot straight away. We were told not to worry and we waited to hear.'

'Who took the report?'

He leant forward again, his hands rubbing at his mouth in thought. 'Larger guy, 'bout my size. I forget his name.'

'Brian Ritchie?'

'That sounds right,' he said.

'How long before you heard anything?'

'About a week, I think. Is this not all in the report?'

'It is,' I assured him. 'I just wanted to hear it first-hand.'

He looked at me quizzically. 'Well, then we get a visit and we're told that her phone signal and a cash withdrawal had been traced to Manchester. We're told that the enquiry was being passed down there. Then, I suppose about a week later again, we get another visit. This large cop again, and we're told she's fine. Told that she's going to stay down there for a while and that she'll be in touch when she's ready.'

'But you're not told, where, exactly, or who with?'

'No. She's eighteen and so she's an adult. Ha!' he blurted, and a harsh laugh left his throat. He shook his head. 'You know, maybe at one time an eighteen-year-old was an adult. Before and after the war, maybe. But, seriously, have you spoken to an eighteen-year-old these days? They're still weans. I don't care what the law says.'

'Who did she know in Manchester?'

'Nobody, as far as I'm aware. I was going to go down and look for her myself, but Sal wouldn't have it.' He gestured over his shoulder in the general direction of the conservatory. 'She was furious when she heard she was OK. Relieved, of course, but yeah, she was also livid. What a thing to put a parent through.'

'And this was two years ago?'

'Two years and change, yes.'

'And no contact?'

'No, nothing.'

'What about her social media? Any messages? Who was she chatting to online before she left?'

'No, nothing really. She'd had a bit of bullying online when she was at school. We convinced her to delete it. As far as I know she never went back to it. I was proud of her for that. Why? What's this about? Really?'

I hesitated before answering, picking my words. 'Can I ask, do you think she's in Manchester? I mean, how sure are you?'

'What do you mean? That's what you lot said. Why would I not—?'

'Yes, sorry. Look, as you say, I'm not from here. I just find it hard to get my head around this . . . trend, or whatever you want to call it.'

'If there's something I should know, Sergeant, I think you should get it out.'

'Nothing,' I said and stood. 'I'm just trying to be thorough. Too much time on my hands maybe. It's actually a day off for me, hence the jeans and T-shirt,' I brushed an indicatory hand down myself. 'I'll actually be finishing up here in Stratharder before long, heading back to the big smoke. But I *have* been looking back into this and if anything occurs to me, if there's any info I can pass on, I will, I promise.'

He stood too and shook my hand. 'I appreciate that. I really do.'

'Such bullshit.'

'Don, your voice. Your language, please,' said Pav, collecting my empty glass.

'Huh?' I said. I looked up briefly from the pages of my book, this particular novel stretching the reach of police

344

powers beyond what was remotely plausible. 'Oh yeah. Sorry, Pav. Would you get me another when you're free? Thanks, pal.'

'Don, are you sure you want—'

'I'm *sure*, Pav,' I said, surprising myself with the harshness of the tone. 'Look, I'm not working today, it's fine. Thanks.'

Pav nodded and I turned back to the final chapter.

Detective Inspector Paramour is recapping, like this other guy wasn't aware of everything that's being said. Of course, this is for the reader who will have most likely drifted off through large sections of this table-leg-leveller of a book.

The detective inspector is drawing together the investigation for the fat, rich man who sits, looking mildly amused as Paramour winds up his findings in true Columbo-style. Paramour is explaining that he always had doubts about the victim's convicted boyfriend, that the pieces fell together just a little too neatly. He's also explaining that whenever you're in any doubt during an investigation, there is one true north that will always guide you – follow the money.

'Well, that's about the first accurate thing in this whole fucking book,' I said to Pav, as he dropped a beer mat onto the table, followed by the long, perspiring glass. 'Seriously, Pav, if you ever decide to join the police, come and speak to me about what it's really like, don't ever believe the likes of this piece of fucking fantasy.'

'Don—'

'If you think it would be traipsing around exotic

places and sleuthing out major crimes like Sherlock fucking . . . fucking . . .' I had to stop as the gas from the beer worked up through me into a belch '. . . Holmes, then you're kidding yourself—'

'Don,' Pav interrupted with a punitive whisper. 'For God's sake, can't you see people here are . . . I don't know the word, the thing when you have sadness at a funeral.'

'Mourning?' I suggested, raising my head from the book and feeling a sobering surge pass through me.

I looked around, abashed at the now-busy bar that had grown, unnoticed, around me since I ordered my first beer at midday. The place had filled with sombre black blouses and ties. Most of the people were congregated at the far end of the room where some tables had been pushed together for finger-food. Small groups were formed, engaged in hushed conversations. The bar itself was a mix of the mourners and regulars. A girl, who herself looked too young to drink, was doing her best behind the bar to keep up with demand.

'Sorry, Pav. I was in a world of my own. Probably had a bit too much.' This was an understatement. I'd been sitting in a corner table for hours, having Pav pour me a fresh pint before reaching the bottom of the existing one. I'd taken myself to the pub after leaving Badger Wynd, trying to snatch at some straw that seemed just out of reach. The missing girls, the death of Cooper. Perhaps it was just boredom, some need to throw myself into something as I whiled away the days, weeks and months before getting back to my career. I turned the situation over in my head. The bizarre circumstances of Cooper's death bed. The

Stratharder trend of teenage escape. The Facebook message that seemed to come from some other source than the girl to whom the account belonged. What was that about? Was I hearing hooves and thinking zebras when I should have been thinking horses? To distract myself I'd pulled Dad's paperback from my coat pocket. I'd looked up only a couple of times to go piss, now that my attention required stretching further than my own little microcosm, I realised I would be struggling to walk straight when at last I would have to. 'Who died?' I asked.

Pav shrugged. 'Mr McTear. At least that's what the booking says.'

'I don't think I knew him. That's sad.'

He shrugged those huge shoulders again. 'Not really,' he whispered. 'Ninety-two. We should all be so lucky to get to such an age.'

'I suppose so. I'm sorry if I was being a bit—' A face from the bar made me stop. Margaret came walking towards me, dressed in a black trouser suit, holding two small glasses. She smiled as she passed, but sort of apologetically. Perhaps she'd heard me yelling at my book and was embarrassed on my behalf. I watched as she reached a small group and handed the other drink to an elderly lady, whose shoulders bounced gently as a younger woman consoled her. The widow, perhaps.

'Pawel, a little help, please?' The girl at the bar was beginning to buckle under the weight of demand.

'I'm coming,' said Pav. 'I better go help. You're OK?'

'I'm fine, thanks, Pav. Oh, I'm heading back to the city tomorrow, so I hope you guys have a lovely Christmas.'

'What you mean? You're going back? You're leaving?'

'Um, going home for Christmas, yeah.'

'But you'll be back? After, I mean.'

'I, uh.' I realised in that moment that I had no intention of ever returning to Stratharder, that the decision may have been made some time ago, that I was only now letting myself in on it.

'Pawel, I got two barrels need changing,' said the girl, swatting at a beer pump as it coughed nothing but foam and air.

'Yeah, I'm coming,' he growled. 'You have a good Christmas too. Take care of yourself, Don.' He put out his hand. I shook it. My own hand was like a child's in his massive paw.

'Thanks, Pav; look after that lovely family of yours.' He smiled and squeezed my hand and I resisted the yelp it induced. I watched him struggle his way through the bar crowd and I thought about the goodbyes I wasn't going to say, like this one. The nice ones, Margaret over there, Hilda perhaps? Everything was square with her and I wasn't sure if I would be popping in to see her the following morning, or just pack the car and go. I wouldn't give the inspector the satisfaction of a farewell. He'd get an email. Perhaps I would write it entirely in block capitals, but he wouldn't get the sarcasm. And Rowan, shit, Rowan. She, at least, I would have to find time to talk through my decision in person with. Then there was the goodbye that I simply didn't want to face up to: Mhairi. I didn't have the time to let a cooling-off period pass. I wanted to attempt another apology, but it was too soon. If I had one regret from my time in Stratharder, it was her. Well, not her as such, how I handled it. How I allowed myself to be bullied by the inspector. How I had treated her like this whole town had.

I thrust the novel into the inside pocket of my jacket and supped greedily from my glass before changing my mind about the book. I laid it back on the table. Maybe someone else will give a fuck about how things end for Detective Inspector Richard Paramour. I certainly did not.

I stood and almost had to sit again as my head swam. I gripped the edge of the table for stability and forced my eyelids wide, trying to pull myself out of the ale haze. After a moment my sense of balance seemed to return. I fixed my eyes on the door and began weaving through the crowd.

'How's the new relationship, Sergeant?'

'What?' I said looking around, unsure where the question had come from.

'I tell you, she's a wild one. Needs a strong hand that lassie.' The crowd at the bar parted a little to reveal Alistair, talking into his near-empty pint. He was sitting on a stool with the same cohort he was always with. On the next again stool was a chuckling Brian Ritchie. 'She pretends she doesn't like it,' he continued, spinning around on the chair to face me. 'But she secretly enjoys it. Fucking loves it in fact,' he said, nudging the bar fly with an elbow.

'Don't know how you can afford it on the shit wages we get,' said Brian and laughed hard.

'Hey, that's my Mhairi you're talking about,' said Alistair, seriously.

'Aye, sorry, Ally.'

'But I hope she at least gives you the police discount,' Alistair said, and the three men erupted into laughter, sloshing beer and slapping at each other's shoulders.

'Fine,' I said. It failed to interrupt the hilarity.

'I SAID, FINE.' The entire pub was stunned into silence from my yell. The laughter continued for a moment but quickly succumbed to the dead air in the room.

'What? What do you mean, "fine"?' said Alistair, as confidently as he could manage.

The three chuckling idiots looked uncomfortable with all eyes on us.

'Outside,' I said. 'It's what you wanted, wasn't it? And bring Hoddit and Doddit with you. I don't give a shit.'

Alistair gave a humourless guffaw and turned back to the bar. 'And get done for police assault? Nah, I'll pass.'

'Do you see a fucking uniform?' I spat.

I was aware of two things as the silence in the room seemed to eat away at our very flesh like a poisonous gas: my hands were balled into fists, and I was prepared, in fact excited, about putting them to use.

'I think you better get your pal home before he gets himself into a whole heap of trouble, big yin,' said Alistair with a jovial glance at Pav. Nobody else was laughing. Pav just shrugged. There was the smallest impression of a smile on his face.

'I'll not ask again,' I said. 'If you don't get up, I'll just start swinging, you smug prick.'

Alistair, his back to me, forced another laugh, drummed his fingers on the bar and looked to his friends who were themselves staring straight ahead.

'Go sleep it off—' he started, but my hand was already on his shoulder pulling him backwards off his chair. There was a thud and a scratch of chair legs as everyone was shooting to their feet. My focus, though, was on the beer-drenched Alistair who had failed to let go of his glass as he toppled. I reached down to grab him, to pull him to his feet to begin the beating. He was quicker than he looked. He swung the empty glass at my head. I didn't have time to duck, but my right arm raised with protective instinct and deflected much of the blow. The glass smashed to the floor; it would have been beyond serious had it crashed into my head. My fury intensified and I began raining down blows on him, not allowing him to get up. I batted away his flailing feet and arms with one hand and hurled blows with the other. I threw elbows as his friends tried to grab me and just kept swinging. The flailing limbs stopped as he curled into a ball. I then had both hands free to pound him like dough. The air hissing through my teeth on each strike was the only sound I could hear.

'Gethefuckoffme . . .' I growled, as hands pulled at my shoulders and again, I aimed elbows backwards to repel them. This time they would not be fought off. The cowering Alistair remained underneath me, but I was being raised into the air. I thought both of his buddies had grabbed me simultaneously. As I raised my head, I saw they were still standing at the bar, one of them hadn't even put down his drink.

I stopped struggling.

Pav, like a teacher pulling brawling children apart, placed me back to the floor.

351

Nothing, and nobody, moved.

Pav took a step back, shaking his head and raising his palms in surrender. His mouth was bleeding.

'I'm . . . sorry, Pav,' I said, and looked around. At the far end of the room Margaret was sobbing into her sister's shoulder. 'I'm really sorry.'

CHAPTER TWENTY-EIGHT

As One Door Closes . . .

Professor Hornik was younger than I expected.

It was something aimed at me often enough to make my eyes roll, therefore ensuring I not mention it. It's not just policemen who are looking younger all the time.

Another surprise was the lecture theatre.

I'm not sure what exactly I was envisaging, but it was something with more . . . atmosphere? When you're invited to sit in on a lecture titled 'Cosmology, Magic and Divination in the Classical World' you want dark wood, gloomy lighting and a wizened old sage at the lectern. This lecture hall was bright, clean and clinical enough to perform surgery in. I was most disappointed.

I had managed to follow the lecture, I felt, pretty well, for about the first twenty minutes. After that, I knew I was losing the thread of what Professor Hornik was going on about. His low, monotone voice put me in mind of a psychiatrist soothing an agitated patient. Couple that with my decision to take a seat at the back, next to a radiator and you had the perfect storm for a snooze session. I must have drifted off for a second, as the word 'oracular' had inexplicably slipped into proceedings. If he'd explained what this meant, I had missed it. Now that it had entered, it was here to stay, a rock, upon which the rest of this talk was now sitting. I searched around the faces of the twenty or so students in attendance for a fellow lost expression. If there was one, it was being hidden behind a laptop screen.

It didn't matter that I wasn't following, I was sitting no exams. I did, however, want to honestly and confidently tell the professor that I had enjoyed his lecture. Right now, I was staring at a big, fat fib.

In the end I gave up, or must have. The sudden shuffle of chairs, coats and bags alerted me to the fact that I had properly fallen asleep. Professor Hornik was reminding his students that a webinar – whatever that may be – on Divination and Self Knowledge – whatever this was – was scheduled for that evening.

'Sergeant Colyear?' he asked softly, as I followed the last student down the stairs of the lecture theatre. The student, a long-haired kid, sporting a faded black T-shirt of a band I'd never heard of, turned, eyebrows raised, to look at me, before shuffling out of the hall, giving one more interested glance before he disappeared around the door. I had slipped in with the rest of the students before the professor had arrived and none of them had batted an eyelid. They were masters-degree students and as such spanned a wide age range. I fell somewhere, and unremarkably, in the middle.

'That's right,' I said. 'Thank you for taking the time to see me.'

'Well, I have to admit, I was intrigued. I'm Markus Hornik, but then I guess you wouldn't be much of a policeman if you hadn't worked that out. Your email was a little vague, though as I say, it piqued my interest. Let's grab a seat.'

The professor took his things from behind the lectern and led me along to the end of the first row.

'I didn't know if you would actually take me up on my offer of sitting in today. It felt like the polite thing to do since you were coming all the way down to Edinburgh.'

We sat on the last two available seats, the furthest point from the door.

'I was coming down anyway. I have a job interview directly after this. Besides my father lives here and I'm back for Christmas, perhaps for good if the interview goes well. And I enjoyed the lecture,' I said, releasing the lie.

He smiled knowingly, which made me wonder if I'd snored. Asking to be excused for a moment the young professor tapped away at his laptop for a minute. I took that time to search through my phone.

He was older than me, but not by much. Then again, as I looked at him up close now, I could have been wrong. His hair was thinning badly and contrary to the trend of shaving such misfortune to the bone he had adopted a certain devil-may-care attitude, something that extended to his wardrobe. It was a suit, of sorts, some Frankenstein's monster of an ensemble. Everything was a form of blue, but the shirt, trousers, jacket and tie were independently blue from the others. All of this conspired to age him.

'So,' he said with a satisfying clap of his computer lid. 'How on earth can *I* help Scotland's finest? You have something you want me to have a look at?'

'If you don't mind, yes,' I said. I found the folder in the gallery function on the phone. He leant in eagerly but sat back when I placed my hand over the screen. 'Before I show you this, I think it's fair that I explain a few things.'

'OK,' he said curiously, and crossed his legs. He appeared to be trying to hold back his excitement.

'First of all, you should know that these pictures are pretty . . . graphic. Secondly, they're very sensitive. I could get into a lot of trouble for showing these to you. Where that might leave you . . . I'm not quite sure. So, this is where you should say if you don't want to get involved.'

He gave out a little laugh and removed his glasses, giving them a wipe with his tie. 'After an introduction like that? There is no possibility I'm refusing to look at whatever is on that phone.'

I took a last look over my shoulder to ensure we were alone before finding the first image and handing the phone over.

'What exactly am I looking at here?' he asked, squinting at, and rotating, the phone.

'That's really my question to you, Professor,' I said.

He pushed his glasses onto his forehead and brought the

screen almost to his nose. His mouth twisted as the scene seemed to come into focus.

'Ugh, is that . . . blood? Are these markings actually carved into his abdomen?'

'That's what I thought when I walked in, but no. It's lipstick.'

'Oh,' he said, and I couldn't quite tell if it was tinged with relief or disappointment. 'Still, grizzly business. He's dead, this fella, I presume?'

'Yes, quite dead. Are you OK to continue? We can stop any time.' I made to reach for the phone. He swivelled his shoulder to block the attempt.

'I have a strong stomach, don't worry about me. There's more?'

'Yes,' I said and slid my finger across the screen to show the scene from a distance, then again to show him a close-up of the rabbit nailed to the wall.

'OK . . .' The professor started, and scratched at his chin. 'Some pseudo-occult murder, is that what we have here?'

'Actually, no. At least that's not our . . . the police's findings.'

'And you're not so sure,' he said, a statement not a question. 'And you would like my knowledge of ritualistic practices to shed some light on all of this?'

'Something like that,' I said. 'I'm not even convinced myself about this being a murder. Toxicology and a range of other circumstantial evidence doesn't support it. I just want to understand the scene more than anything. There's twelve pictures in all, just swipe across the screen like this.' I swiped, showing the scene with the fluorescent paint. 'See how the rabbit becomes a part of this pentagram?'

He mumbled something as he thrust the screen back to his face.

'I'm sorry?'

'Pentacle,' he corrected. 'When a pentagram is enclosed within a circle, it is a pentacle . . . It's not important, just semantics. He swiped through the remaining pictures, his face scrunched into painful concentration the whole time. At last, he pulled the phone away and pinched his nose between his eyes. 'I'm sorry,' he said, 'the screen is so small and my eyes are not so clever. You couldn't email the pictures? Much easier to study on a monitor.'

'As I mentioned, Professor, it's more than a little sensitive.' I checked over my shoulder once more and lowered my voice. 'You see these pictures are, well, unofficial. The case is already closed and, really, it's my own curiosity that brings me here. I can't print these pictures out or send them anywhere online, it's too risky. I just want to know what you think is going on here?'

'What is it you hope to achieve?' asked the professor. His face was now studying me rather than the screen.

'I don't like loose ends,' I said. 'I just want to understand.'

The professor sat for a moment, looking and thinking, his lips two solid lines like rail tracks. 'Well, look, I don't think I'm the man to help you,' he said and began gathering his belongings from the chair beside him. 'I mean all of this is pretty dark stuff and I'm a professor of anthropology and sociology. I'm no occultist. It really isn't my area, Sergeant Colyear. You really need to find someone with more specific knowledge.'

I held my hands up. 'Just an educated guess, please, Professor. And I'd be grateful for it.'

'I'm sorry, I really can't. And I'm sorry to have wasted your time.'

As he walked past me, I snatched a guess at his reticence. 'You won't have to go to court. I promise.'

He stopped and turned. 'How can you guarantee that?'

'You're concerned about your reputation?'

'Of course, yes. If I am hauled in front of a court as a so-called expert in black magic, how do you think my employers and, worse, my students will view me? Any sense of professional integrity disappears with the first tabloid report.'

'I can assure you that is *not* what this is about. Like I said, this case, if it ever was one, is dead and buried. This is just my own curiosity.'

He stood there, laptop and coat tucked under his arm. 'I'm still not sure I understand it,' he said. 'Why go picking at this?'

I drew a breath and sighed, putting my thoughts in order. 'Because too many strange things happen in too small a place.'

'This village up north where these pictures are from?'

'Stratharder, yes. Since I arrived in the place, too many odd doors have opened, and I would dearly like to shut at least one before I leave. Please, Professor, help me to understand what I'm looking at here.' I swiped through the pictures once more to find the illuminated pentagram . . . pentacle, and held it up.

He returned his belongings to the chair and beckoned

for the phone, his head shaking and mouth pursed.

'For a start you're concentrating on the wrong picture,' he said. 'Here, this one tells you more.'

He slid his finger across the screen bringing up the picture of the bookshelf in the bedroom.

'This tells us what?' I said. 'That he's a scholar of the occult?'

'No, Sergeant. It tells us the polar opposite.' He tapped at the screen with a fingernail. 'This screams amateur hour. Having a copy of *A Brief History of Time* on your bookshelf doesn't make you a theoretical physicist. I'm willing to bet that not only can you pick up these ridiculous volumes on Amazon, but that if you click on one, you'll see the rest recommended under the "customers who bought this also bought" section. It's like a starter kit for wannabe witches and Satanists; perfectly toothless, if you ask me. Except, perhaps, if you happen to be a rabbit of course.'

'About that, what's going on there?'

'We can only speculate, but there will be some so-called spell, conjuration or spurious incantation amongst these volumes. It looks to be a small sacrifice designed to influence. The tongue being extruded and pinned suggest a desire to make one's words . . . effective. I've seen similar things in Haitian ceremonies. My best guess is that the perpetrator was trying to get the ear of someone, win their favour. It could be for romantic purposes, or it could be financial or something similar. But, as I have said—'

'You're only guessing, yes. All in all, you wouldn't be concerned about this?' I said.

'Maybe. I mean, I'd say that's more your territory. It is a dead rabbit nailed to a wall above a dead man. That has to be worrying, no? Personally, I wouldn't be *overly* concerned about the markings and the rabbit. It's a bit like a kid keeping insects in a jar. A bit cruel and weird but as long as it doesn't progress, it is fairly normal curiosity. I think that's about all I can tell you. I'm sorry I am unable to explain it all fully.'

'No, you've been a big help. Thank you for your time, Professor,' I said and slid the phone back into my pocket. 'And you're willing to testify to that?' His eyes flashed wide in a sudden panic. 'Just kidding,' I said.

The Saint Vincent, nestled quietly in one of Edinburgh's picturesque cobbled New Town streets, was something of a throwback.

When Dad announced that he was selling the family home in Oban and moving to what is a pretty youthful and vibrant, not to mention particularly expensive, part of the capital, I suspected it would be a bad fit. As I descended the stairs and opened the door to this dark and foreboding little pub, I saw that he had found a home from home. The pub was exactly that; there was a noticeable lack of craft beer, hipster beards and hummus. I suspected the barstool on which Dad was perched, half reading the paper and half watching the rugby match on the small wall-mounted television behind the bar, probably had his arse groove by now.

'Faither,' I said straddling the next-door stool.

'Ah, it's yersel', Donald,' he replied and gave my shoulder

an awkward slap-grab – the closest thing to a hug any male would ever receive from him. 'What'll ye have?'

'Just a coffee.'

'The coffee here's terrible. Do you still drink Guinness?'

'Honestly, Dad, it's not even four o'clock. Coffee's fine,' I said and excused myself, scanning the room for the gents. The place actually wasn't without its charms. As dark and uninviting as it was from the outside, it was perfectly comfortable within. The other three men nursing pints and all similarly reading papers, or glancing at the screen, were respectfully ignoring one another at equally respectful distances apart.

When I returned to the bar a pint of Guinness sat settling on the counter in front of my chair. It was pointless to argue. There was probably nothing wrong with the coffee; he just didn't want to feel self-conscious drinking alone.

'I ordered you a burger,' he announced.

'You shouldn't have,' I said, knowing this too was futile. 'I'm not hungry.'

He dropped the paper from his face and inspected me over the glasses perched on the end of his nose. 'You've no' been looking after yourself.'

'I'm fine, Dad.'

'Fine, my arse,' he said and grabbed at my waist just as I was lifting my pint, making me squirm like a child.

'Jesus,' I said, and set the sloshing beer back to the counter.

'Yer stick-thin. I could see it in your face as you came in the door.' His hand, as massive and powerful as ever it was, was now in the collar of my shirt.

'Will you quit that?' I said, swatting him off. The sudden appearance of the barman with our burgers stopped him.

Fuck, I thought. *Do any of us ever get to feel like grown-ups when in the presence of our parents, no matter how old we get?*

'Are you still seeing a doctor at least?'

'Dad.'

'At least get that burger in you. And what have you done to your hands?' He prodded a finger into the plasters which had replaced the bandages in recent days.

'I'm nothing – it's nothing, I mean. Dad, just stop. And I'm not hungry.' It occurred to me, as it had done so many times in my life, how unalike we were. Even in his sixties he was a more powerful man. We had the same nose, but the rest came from Mum, I hoped.

'How'd the interview go?' he said.

I shook my head and wrestled my tie off, dumping it on the bar. 'It wasn't much of an interview, more a when-can-you-start kinda deal.' I undid the top button of my shirt and lifted the lid on the burger to take a look. Blue cheese and mushrooms; it actually looked delicious but it would remain untouched – teenage belligerence.

'Well, that's good, then. When *do* you start?'

'After my annual leave. Sixth of January.'

'Good. You're done up in Stratharder, then?'

'Very done. Just have to collect a few more things from my digs.'

'Good, good. We've been a bit worried about you,' he mumbled, his mouth half full of fries.

'What do you mean "we"?'

He suddenly stopped chewing and began looking decidedly sheepish. He swallowed, wiped his mouth and turned to face me.

'Karen and me,' he said.

'Karen? You mean *my* Karen?' I recalled her mentioning seeing Dad in her text. 'How often are you two getting together to conspire?'

'I don't know; we meet for coffee sometimes. Not often, just once in a while. I bumped into her on the street a while back. She works not too far from here, you see, new job like. Anyway, she said you chatted recently. She was relieved to finally hear from you. I guess she feels terrible about—'

'You and Karen?'

'Is it that weird? I mean you were close to getting married. She was like family.'

'Are you forgetting that she—'

'I know, I know. I suppose that's why I didn't mention it. I felt guilty. She didn't deal with the break well. I was angry too, to begin, but if you sit and talk to her about it, you'd see—'

'I've no bloody intentions of sitting and talking to her.'

'You must want to, at least part of you. Otherwise why did you call her?'

I was pushing fries around my plate, wallowing in a sense of betrayal.

'Look, I'm sorry, Donald. I . . . well, I wisnae trying to upset you. I should have talked to you.'

'Forget it,' I said. 'I suppose you've every right. So, how is she?'

'Aye, fine. She's gettin' big like.'

When I failed to speak, he had a sort of double-take look at my face.

'Oh, for God's sake,' he said. 'I'm sorry. I just assumed, since you'd spoken that she'd told you.'

The Guinness suddenly called to me and I drained half of it.

'Nope. News to me.' It made sense, then, why she'd been so eager to talk in recent months. 'That was quick work. Are they getting married?'

'Look, maybe I should just stay out of it . . . I really don't want to cause any more—'

'Well, it's a bit late for that, Faither. So?'

'I think so, aye. She's wearing a diamond anyway.'

Again, there was a period of silence.

Dad was apologising again; he thought he'd dealt some devastating blow with this most recent revelation, but that's not why I was struck dumb.

It was the television behind the bar. More specifically it was the face on the screen. One I recognised. A young girl in a school blazer.

'Dad, Dad, it's OK,' I said and shouted for the barman. 'Could you turn that up, please?'

The barman slid the remote across the counter. I hit volume up and stretched across the bar to get as best a view as I could.

'. . . discovered in undergrowth near to the Cairn Lodge motor services in Lanarkshire in the early hours of this morning. Police confirm they have arrested a forty-eight-year-old man in connection to the death of the eighteen-year-old from Stratharder but are still appealing for witnesses.*

'*Following the grim discovery, the family of Jennifer Mulligan have been informed and they have asked for privacy while the police investigation is completed.*'

'Where are you going?' asked Dad.

'Back to Stratharder,' I said. 'Help yourself to my burger.'

CHAPTER TWENTY-NINE

Just the Fax

I was surprised to find the station was open.

Perhaps the inspector wanted it that way as a sort of public reassurance thing, in light of Jennifer.

I had driven straight up after leaving Dad in the bar. It had been so late when I arrived, I just pulled in at Kirkmartin and slept. Hilda had already left for Glasgow and her family. In the morning I wrote her a note of thanks, put the rest of my things in the Polo and drove to the police station.

I stood in the car park staring at the building for what felt like an age. I don't know what I was waiting for, exactly. The flakes falling relentlessly robbed all sound beyond the gentle crunch of compacting snow under my boots.

Just as I stepped up to the door a patrol vehicle came rumbling around the corner. Rowan smirked and looked confused through the windscreen.

'What are you doing here?' she said, slinging the van door closed.

I shrugged. 'I saw the news. I had to come.'

'The Mulligan girl, yeah. Fucking horrible. Are you coming in?'

'Yes, of course,' I said and let her lead the way. 'What happened?'

'Uh, not sure. The inspector's been running around daft with the family, so I've not been able to get much information.' Rowan pressed in the combination of the door while I swept snow from my hair and clacked my boots together like a clumsy Dorothy wishing for home. 'Glasgow are dealing with it. Apparently, someone just handed themselves in, led cops right to her; a truck driver.'

'What did he do to her?'

'Again, I'm not entirely sure. Rumour is rape and murder.'

'Shit.'

'Yeah, but we're not going to get any part of it.'

'There's nothing for us to do?' The sound of my voice made Margaret look up from her computer. I smiled uncomfortably, thinking about the scene I'd caused in the bar. For a second, she just continued looking, expressionless, but then came a reciprocated up-turn of the mouth before she returned to her screen.

'Not really. It's just family liaison stuff at our end and the inspector has it covered,' said Rowan. She dumped her armour onto a chair and adjusted her hair. 'So,' she said, 'didn't think we'd see you until after Christmas. How's civilisation?'

'It's still there. Actually, you won't see me after Christmas at all, Rowan.'

'No?'

'No, I had an interview. They want me to start soon.'

'Interview?' The inspector stood in the doorway at the far end of the station holding a thick wad of folders. He might have been there the whole time.

'Eh, yes. I decided to take that admin job after all.'

'What? When did this happen?'

'Just yesterday.'

His tone was odd – was it surprise? Disappointment? Both seemed unlikely.

'Well, we're sorry to lose you, Sergeant.'

'Thanks, Inspector. I'm sorry I didn't give you more notice. I just thought you'd prefer me out of your hair.'

'It's fine. I just didn't realise . . . Anyway, I better get on, lots to do.' He turned to go back to his office, then stopped, apparently realising he'd just come from there. He looked completely lost.

'Yes, I'm very sorry to hear about Jennifer, Inspector. I feel just awful for her mum. Is there anything I can do?'

'I . . . um. No, I don't think there's anything left for you here. Yes, Katherine is in a terrible state, as you can imagine. It's just dreadful for everyone involved. Um, if you haven't already forwarded everything to do with the Mulligan enquiry, please do so before you leave today. There will be a review no doubt, but don't worry, it won't affect you. Rowan, I'll be in Oban all afternoon. This is your last day before the holidays?'

'Yes, Inspector.'

'Then you can finish early. Just tidy up whatever you're doing and you all have a nice Christmas. You too, Margaret.'

'Thanks, Inspector,' said Rowan.

'Donald, all the best. I'd say stay in touch but . . . well.'

'Yeah,' I said and shook his hand. 'You too.'

Margaret swept up her coat and left right behind him. 'Merry Christmas to you both.'

The sound of the kettle was a welcome buffer against the cold silence. I looked around at the ramshackle station and was surprised to feel a certain sentimentality.

'I guess this is it, then?' said Rowan.

'I suppose so.'

She walked over to where I was sitting and looped her arms around my neck, squeezing not so gently. She kissed me on the corner of my mouth.

'I'd say stay in touch,' she said. 'But . . . well.'

I laughed and pulled her in for a better hug.

'I *will* be staying in touch. You need to get out of here. You'll rot if you stay too long. If I see any opportunities, I think you might be right for, I'll let you know.'

'Thanks. Since this is your last day, I'll make tea, and I'll find you a biscuit as you damn well need it.'

'You sound like my dad. Thanks.'

I cleared what was left from my locker, which took all of two minutes. *I guess I never really committed to Stratharder*, I judged.

I gathered together the few pieces of information I had on Jennifer Mulligan and slid them into a folder. The last task was to clear out my emails. Again, not a job that was going to take much time. Twenty-two unread and most of them force circulars – lookout requests, procedural updates and such.

Alyson's email, her somewhat aggressive apology still sat there. I never did get around to finish reading it, or else deleting it. *Too much time's passed now*, I thought. My silence would tell her everything she needed to know. Still, I smiled as I glanced over at the summary panel of the screen showing the first few lines of the message:

Don,
Will you please grow up!
Deleted.

There was one email worthy of note, though now somewhat redundant. *Too little too late*, I thought as I clicked it open. It was a response from the Met Enquiry Team from three days ago. I selected print to place it in the folder with the other information and read it from the screen while I waited for the hard copy.

FAO Sgt Donald Colyear
From: PC Rebecca Richardson CO133, Metropolitan
Police Central Enquiries Team
Ref: Missing Person – Jennifer Mulligan

Sergeant,
With regard to the above referenced enquiry
forwarded to us I regret to inform you that we were
unable to action your request . . .

I stopped reading and again struck delete, the point now being rendered moot. The Met's inability to follow through on a standard request for assistance was just one more failing within this whole mess. Selfishly, I hoped the inspector's assertions that none of this would land on my desk come the enquiry would indeed be true.

In the back room, the timpani of teaspoon on porcelain could be heard. I took the two sheets of A4 from the printer and began looking round the desks for a stapler. As I fumbled with the sheets, trying to line them up, a line of text on the second page caught my eye. It was the conspicuously informal tone, contrasting the all-too-familiar officious opening, that struck me as odd. PC Richardson had continued . . .

> . . . *maybe it might be best if you just gave me a call, Sergeant, as there's just so much I don't understand. I work Monday to Friday until 4 p.m.*
>
> *Regards . . .*

With a crunch of the stapler I sealed the document together and slid it into the Mulligan folder trying to ignore the strange ending. I couldn't help but check the clock on the wall. 3.30 p.m.

Rowan appeared, a mug in each hand and a half-eaten packet of custard creams dangling from her teeth.

'Shit,' I said.

'Wha'?'

'Not you. I need to make a call.' I opened the folder, somewhat disappointed with myself. The curiosity would become an itch I would be unable to scratch later if I didn't do this now.

I called the number for the enquiry team that was on the footer of the email. I was immediately dropped into the centre of an automated-selection spaghetti junction. More than once I teetered on the edge of hanging up.

It took fully ten minutes to reach a living voice, and not the one I needed. Still, the chap I spoke to seemed sympathetic. Another minute on hold and finally I had PC Richardson.

'Hi, Sergeant Colyear? Thanks for calling. You just caught me. I was going to set out what was confusing me on the email, but I thought it would be quicker to just do this over the phone rather than playing email tennis, right?'

'Um . . .' I said, about to disagree and begin a rant on the Met's telephony system, but I figured this would only add to the delay. Every second spent in the station, now that I was no longer obliged to be there, felt like stolen time. '. . . right. Thanks for getting back to me, but I don't know if you've seen recently on the news—'

'Yeah, I did. How awful. You know I didn't make the connection right away. Listen, let me just bring up the email you sent. Two minutes.'

'Sure.'

Rowan was sitting on a desk watching me, chain-munching the custard creams. She pointed the packet at me when she saw me looking back. I shook my head.

'OK,' said PC Richardson. I could hear her clicking away on a mouse. 'So yeah, this whole thing just had me completely confused. Maybe it's my mistake and not yours, but can we just run through this request?'

'It's good of you to be so thorough . . . um . . .'

'Rebecca.'

'Rebecca. But it's all a bit pointless now really.'

'Yeah, I suppose,' she said. I could hear disappointment in her voice. She was obviously a fellow fastidious type who couldn't bear a loose thread.

'OK, well, what was the issue?' I couldn't resist.

'Well, all of it, really.' Her pace and enthusiasm returned. 'I mean first of all I was convinced you'd just sent this to the wrong place, but then you mention this other enquiry and a . . . what was it now . . . PC Caruthers?'

'Yes, I think so.'

'You gave his collar number and station and of course that means it *would* be meant for us, and then there's these areas you mention in this previous missing person enquiry, again should mean us, right?'

'Sorry, Rebecca, you're kind of losing me here. Really I just copied over the information from the faxes we exchanged—'

'Oh yeah, and that was the other thing, see,' Rebecca said, in full excited sprint now. I rubbed at my eyes and pulled the phone away from my ear slightly. Rowan looked at me with a shrug that requested information. Again, I shook my head.

'OK, Rebecca. Look, I don't have an awful lot of time. Maybe you could just explain the problem, exactly?'

'Right. OK, well. PC Caruthers, right?'

'Yes.'

'Well, we have three.'

'Three. OK?'

'Right, but the collar number you give is for a . . . where

is it . . . yeah, a PC Carling. So, I thought maybe you just got the names mixed up, both begin with a "C", but I checked and that's a Samantha Carling, and you were looking for an Eric, so unlikely, right? And she didn't know anything about it. So, I go back for the other names, maybe it's the collar number that's wrong, right?'

'Right.'

'Wrong!'

'What?'

'You see, I checked the other Caruthers . . . or is it Carutherses? Carutherses . . . that's not right, is it?'

'Rebecca, please.'

'Yeah, never mind. The point is none of them are an Eric and none of them work out of Addington. I checked. There was one Eric Caruthers, but he retired ten, eleven years ago and he was an inspector in Ealing – nowhere near.'

'OK,' I said. 'Some other crossed wires somewhere. To be honest, Rebecca, we've kinda dropped the ball with this whole thing on a number of occasions, so this isn't exactly surprising.'

'Well, there's more.'

Of course there is . . .

I sighed and dropped myself into Margaret's great chair pinching the bridge of my nose as if preventing a migraine from crawling up there. 'OK, Rebecca, what else did we manage to mess up?'

'The fax itself.'

'What about it?'

'I can't find it. I checked with Addington and they don't have it. I made them check, twice. I think they were getting a bit annoyed. Some snippy station assistant was like, who sends faxes anyway? And I was like, yeah, I know, right? But it's Scotland, so maybe—'

'Rebecca,' I interrupted pinching harder, my eyes screwed shut. 'I appreciate all your hard work, but do you mind if we skip to the end.'

'Right, sorry. Well, she said I should check with you, confirm what number you sent it to. They keep a copy of all incoming and outgoing faxes. Didn't take her long to check, actually. Like she said, nobody uses them any more.'

'OK, hold on a minute,' I said and fished the fax from Addington from the folder. 'OK, where do I find the number?'

'Yeah, I didn't know either, but this station assistant says it will be printed on the top or bottom corner, depending on your machine.'

I squinted at the sheet in front of me; nothing about the print was sharp. Everything had a black jagged finish, like far too much ink had been used. Except for tiny perfectly printed digits, right there in red where she said it would be.

'OK, the number I have is 01693 . . . Oh no wait, that's Stratharder.'

'Yeah, that'll be the receiving number. The sending one will be in the other corner. Should start 020.'

I flicked my eyes to the other side and right enough, another number. I stared at it before checking the other corners, and then the same on the reverse.

'Hello? You still there, Sergeant?'

'Uh, yes, Rebecca. Sorry. Listen, um. There has been some kind of mistake at our end, but thanks for your help with all this.'

'Sure thing, but look, if you manage to figure out what happened, would you—?'

'I'll be sure to do that, Rebecca. Thanks again,' I said, and laid the receiver down slowly, still staring at the fax.

'What is it? You look like you're about to throw up,' said Rowan, setting the biscuits aside.

'I don't know. Maybe nothing.'

I began frantically rummaging through Margaret's workspace.

'What are you looking for?' Rowan was on her feet, her face full of concern.

'Margaret was still working through putting the old mis-per forms onto the new system, wasn't she?'

'I don't know, I thought she finished those. Why?'

'And the old paper copies, where do they go after?' I said. I pulled a load of old police reports from a drawer and started rifling through them.

'Not sure, sent for shredding I suppose. Are you going to tell me what's going on?'

I threw the reports back into the drawer and started on the next one up. My stomach was cramping.

'If you tell me what you're looking for I can help.'

'This, I think,' I said. I lifted a brown folder strangled by an enormous elastic band. 'MIS-PER – VICKY ALDER' I read. It was from four years ago. I sifted through the pages. Eighteen-year-old, found in Edinburgh. All confirmed by a fax from Lothian and Borders Police. I closed the folder and examined the fax. There were the red digits. The first I recognised, one number out from the station phone line, our fax. The second number I did not. I ran and fetched the file for Daisy Cavanagh. The same thing was there in red ink.

The second number also beginning 01693.

All Stratharder. Exactly the same as the Addington fax.

Rowan was exasperated now, huffing and slapping her legs in frustration. 'What are you doing now?' she said.

I was wheeling Margaret's chair backwards to my computer terminal, barging the existing seat out of the way. My hand shook as I gripped the mouse. I double-clicked the trash can and fished out my old colleague's email, Alyson's awful apology. I quickly made a judgement. There were two options. *Which do I go with? Or which do I go with first?* I had the fax in my left hand and the mouse in the right.

'I'm begging for a favour,' I said. I began typing, but then paused, forcing myself to slow down. This had to be worded right. 'Do you own a suit?'

Rowan looked at me like I'd asked her the most absurd of questions. 'A suit? Not really, why?'

'We need to go on one last road trip.' I said.

CHAPTER THIRTY

The Bowels

She'd cut her hair short. It didn't suit her.

Without the long brown waves to soften her features she appeared angular and serious. In that regard it was effective. There was an instant authority about Alyson. I wondered if she'd wandered into a stylist's and asked for the 'detective constable'.

'Fucking hell, Don. You on hunger strike?' She eyed me up and down as if inspecting a crack that had appeared on the side of a house.

'Don't *you* start,' I said. Rowan sniggered somewhere behind me. Alyson strode up to me, her arms folded tight across her chest, I guessed partly against the icy wind that howled at my back and partly against the tension.

'Tell me,' she said, 'if you hadn't needed this favour, was I ever going to hear from you again?' She passed over the cardboard folder she'd been holding.

'Of course,' I lied. 'I just needed time to stew for a while.'

'Aye, right. Listen, try not to piss this one off,' she said to Rowan over my shoulder. 'The prick knows how to hold a grudge. That's all I could get', she said, nodding at the folder. 'After this we're square, OK?'

'Yes, square.'

'Fuck, you know what. After this, you owe *me* one. This is a hell of a favour.'

'I know, Aly. I wouldn't ask if it wasn't important.' I kissed her cheek and she gave me a hug complete with a few punishing back slaps.

'Alyson Kane,' she said to Rowan and shook her hand. 'I guess this is for you.' She handed Rowan the suit blazer she was carrying. 'It's going to be way too big, but if you roll the sleeves and leave it open, you'll just about get away with it.'

'Thanks. I'm Rowan.' She inspected the jacket. It was a different grey to the trousers Rowan was wearing, but it would work.

'Do you know what he's getting you into?' said Alyson.

'She doesn't know anything,' I said. 'If she doesn't know, then none of this can come back on her. It's all me.'

'And me,' said Alyson. 'I'll get my jotters if you get caught. Are you at least going to tell me what exactly this is about?'

'Probably best if I don't. Plausible deniability and all that,' I said.

'Like that'll work. Don, I've worked really hard to get into CID. Try not to fuck this up for me, eh?'

'I'll try. So, what's the plan?' I said and opened the folder.

Alyson placed her hand over it. 'Well, that's why I wanted to meet you outside here first. Look at that later. How long do you need in there?'

'Not long, maybe ten minutes.'

'Be prepared to cut it short. The good news is, it's going like a fair in there. The run up to Christmas is always the same. Cells are full of shoplifters, drunks and wife-beaters. With a bit of luck, we'll be able to wander through without being noticed.' She turned to Rowan. 'Confidence is key here. You need to march through like you own the place. Try to avoid anyone wearing a white shirt. It's likely to be the DO and if anyone's going to challenge you, it's them.'

'The DO?' Rowan asked, giving me a worried glare.

'The duty officer, the desk sergeant. You'll be fine,' I said. 'Just follow closely and try not to look lost.'

'Gimme a second to check the entrance is clear.' Alyson walked off towards the front door of the McNair Street police station.

Rowan stood, staring at the building, chewing at her gums.

'Bit bigger than you're used to,' I said, trying to read her thoughts.

'This place?' she said, flicking her finger at the great red-brick building. 'Uh-huh.'

'Well, wait till you see inside. I've only ever been here once myself. It's a whole other thing compared to stations up north.'

'You're not helping.'

'We'll be fine. We'll let Alyson do the talking as much as we can. She'll look after us.'

'She's awesome,' said Rowan.

'Of course you think so,' I said. 'That's you in six years' time.'

'God willing.'

Just then Alyson appeared at the front door beckoning us with a flick of the head.

'Here we go,' I said.

Rowan's attempts at appearing confident were failing.

She gawped at all that was going on around us. Her head darted at the seemingly dozens of conversations happening between uniformed and plain-clothed officers, the pairs of cops supporting prisoners in differing states of sobriety. It had been a while since I myself had seen the bowels of a proper police station and I could feel the sweat soaking the shirt under my suit.

The business end of any large police station is an assault on the senses. Once past the clinical public area and through the clandestine combination-lock door, things change fast. You get used to it and stop noticing after a while, but I was so aware of Rowan and how overwhelmed she looked, that these things came back to me as if for the first time. Alyson marched on down increasingly dim corridors, the pace an even, determined stroll. The noise was astonishing. It's something your brain learns to deal with, filters out the soup of background clamour – phones, shoulder radios and voices ranging from whispered exchanges to furious remonstration, all there but somehow not. That filter takes a while to develop though, and from the look on Rowan's flushed face, she wasn't there yet.

Alyson stopped suddenly at the top of a short flight of stairs. I had never been in this particular part of the station before, still, I knew exactly where we were headed: the cells. It either was, or recently had been, feeding time for the prisoners. The air hung heavy with the reek of cheap, foil-wrapped dinners battling with the sour stench of sweat.

'Stay here for a minute. I want to make sure the DO isn't about.' Alyson's face was drained of colour; she kept swiping at her fringe as if it were a bothersome insect. 'Just . . . I don't know, look busy or something.'

She disappeared down the steps and left us looking blankly at one another in the corridor, which was busy, this being the thoroughfare to the holding area. Rowan went for her phone and began tapping away while I opened the folder and began reading, twitching it closed when anyone came close.

The police report within was lengthy. I wouldn't have time to read it through entirely, so I skimmed for pertinent points. The picture attached with a paperclip showed a wild-haired, bearded man whose grin shone maniacally through the hair.

'OK, the coast's clear. Let's go.'

We followed Alyson past the charge bar. Two civilian custody officers behind the chest-high desk clocked us. We walked straight by with apparent purpose; they went back to sorting through prisoner-property bags.

We turned a corner to where I assumed the cells would be, only to be met with something that surprised me: a lift. One of those insanely old ones made up of strips of concertina metal. The door to the ancient-looking lift lay open. I instantly formed the image of a bear trap with its rusted jaws prised open, awaiting victims.

'You're kidding,' I said, stopping at the threshold of the door. I was afraid to touch the thing in case it suddenly started moving and I lost the finger.

'Relax, it's safe. Now come on,' said Alyson.

I stepped inside and moved to the back. Rowan followed, studying the thing top to bottom. Alyson closed the outer swing-door and began pulling the inner door left to right. A rasp of complaining metal, followed by a satisfying crunch confirmed the process was complete.

'Hold, please.' A voice from the corridor, its origin unseen.

'Fuck, fuck . . .' growled Alyson. She tucked a set of keys slyly into her pocket.

A large white-shirted man could be seen through the gaps in the metal.

DO, I mouthed to Rowan.

The door was again wrenched open and we all stepped back with polite smiles as he squeezed in.

'Alyson,' he said, returning her smile.

'Sarge.'

'Sorry,' he said. 'I know it's cramped, but this thing takes for ever. You don't mind, do you?'

A mumbled chorus of 'no' and 'not at all' followed.

The three of us stared at the floor as the door was secured and the button pushed. The steel cage lurched into motion and we began a painfully slow descent.

For a moment I thought we might get away with it. The DO's attention was fixed on some kind of roster he was flicking through.

Then I saw it happen.

His head rose, his eyes went to the ceiling of the cage, which continued its grinding, screeching journey.

His roster fell limply in his hand and he turned, his face screwed in confusion. 'Where are you going? I mean, clearly you're going down to the cells, but why?' He was glancing at the warrant cards on our chests.

'Sarge?' said Alyson. I could hear a slight break in her voice.

'I haven't been informed of an interview taking place, so it can't be that.'

'Um . . . yeah, sorry, Sarge. I couldn't find you when we . . . um. Well, I just wanted to, well . . . And then when we got to the charge bar you weren't there and so—'

'I'm Rowan Forbes, Sergeant. Nice to meet you.' Rowan stepped in front of Alyson and thrust out her hand. She beamed at the DO. He returned the gesture. He couldn't help himself; he never stood a chance. He took her hand and was about to say something, but she left him no gap. 'I want to be a detective,' she said, the *when I grow up* was implied. 'DC Kane is a friend of my sergeant and I begged them for this favour.' He looked over at me, I smiled apologetically. Rowan still had the DO's hand. 'We work away up in Stratharder and not much happens, you see. So, when I found out that the sarge's good friend was a DC here in the city, well, I just had to meet her, get her to show me around and find out what it is, and what it takes, to be a detective.'

'I see. But what are you doing here, exactly?'

'Well . . . I'd never seen the inside of a proper police

station before. I mean what we work out of are like sheds compared to this place, eh, Sarge?'

'What? Yeah,' I said, unexpectedly yanked into the conversation. 'Like glorified Portakabins up north. Thought Rowan here could benefit from seeing the workings of a real police station. It's hard to explain. Better to show her, I thought.'

'It's just so . . . big, Sergeant. How on earth do you handle something so massive?'

You're overdoing it, I thought.

As the lift slammed to a stop and the DO finally managed to wrestle his hand back to pull open the door. I thought we were about to be sent back up with at least a warning. I was wrong.

'It's no' easy, Rowan,' the DO said with a gallant hand sweep, ushering her out of the lift. 'You see the responsibility laid at the feet of a duty officer should not be underestimated. We get a lot of high-profile custodies here in this station and it's my job to make sure we get them to court in one piece. You said you're from Stratharder?'

'Uh huh.'

'Well, for example, that young lassie that was murdered recently, I forget her name . . . all over the news.'

'Yeah.'

'Well, the guy that did it is right here. Or I should say, the guy accused.' The DO winked at Rowan. 'I bet you'd like a piece of that creep. Best keep you clear, eh?' he said with a laugh, looking back at Alyson and I as we watched, agog, still standing side by side in the lift. 'The key is good organisation. Hey, do you mind if I show the lassie – sorry, young lady – here around a bit?'

'No, go ahead,' I said.

Rowan passed me a worried glance as the DO led her off, his hand on her shoulder. I shrugged in response. What else could I do?

'She's too young for you, you know that, right?'

'Yes, I'm acutely aware,' I said as we stepped into the long passageway.

The smell down here was a concentrated version of above, stale and sour. Light grey walls were peppered with dark grey doors that contained miscreants covering a dark spectrum of criminality. Everything from shoplifting to one awaiting trial for the murder and rape of a young girl.

We stopped, still in sight of the lift. 'Have you spoken with this guy?' I said and tapped a finger at his photo. I read the résumé aloud 'Vincent (Vinnie) Taylor, fifty-seven years old, HGV driver. Current address in Birmingham, originally from Glasgow. A handful of previous convictions, mostly road-related, but some petty theft when he was a young man and a few for disorder, nothing of particular note.'

'No, I haven't. Like I said in my email, I'm not involved; very few people are. It really must be Christmas because apparently this one came gift-wrapped, big old bow on top.'

'What do you mean?'

We leant against the wall of the cell passageway. A gentle murmur of conversations behind heavy steel doors prevented our voices carrying too far.

'Read the file. It's a slam dunk. This guy shows up at a small county station, claims he's raped and murdered a young girl. The local officers think he's nuts, but he's invited in and CID informed. Two city detectives attend, thinking they're having their time wasted and find this guy drinking tea and eating biscuits, with the cops. They bring him here, thinking it will be a quick stop before heading on to the psychiatric ward at the Royal, but then he goes on to describe the specifics. A unit's sent out to check the area he describes, and there she is.'

'And he was happy to just put his hands up?'

'Couldn't sleep, he said. Had to come clean.'

'And they're certain it was him?' I was half listening, half skim-reading the file.

'Read for yourself. There's *amenable to interview*, and then there's this guy. Full and frank confession. His DNA's all over the place and he's full of specific knowledge – he describes a tattoo even her parents weren't aware of, so yeah, they're sure. One thing, though. If you go on to the second page, here, it describes the scene. His DNA and prints are all over her including semen, but no signs of rape as such. They've concluded he attempted but couldn't . . . you know, perform. They think he was just too embarrassed to admit it.'

'Embarrassed to admit to an erection failure, but happy with the raping and murdering?'

Alyson shrugged. 'He's just waiting to be transferred. He's to appear at court to submit his plea.'

'Did they charge him with the rape?'

'No, they felt it was too flimsy. He *has* been charged with her murder now though. So, you know that means he can't be questioned any further on it. If they caught you talking to him, it would put the whole case in jeopardy.

'It doesn't look like you're going to get the chance now anyway, but what were you looking for?'

'I'm not sure exactly, Aly. I . . . stumbled onto something, something that stinks. What's this here? There's reference to a medical file, but no file.'

'Ah yeah, he's being treated for cancer of the throat. They obtained medical files in case he decides to somehow use this as mitigating circumstance, or in the event he throws himself at the mercy of the court. But it was too risky to get that information. You don't need it, do you?'

'No, I wouldn't think so.'

Alyson snapped the file shut in my hands as the DO and Rowan turned the corner.

'Some people think you're just a glorified prison guard, but there's a lot more to it,' said the DO. His hand was still on Rowan's shoulder. I wondered if it had ever moved from there.

'Yeah absolutely, Steve. It's a massively important role. I never really thought about it before.'

Steve? Alyson mouthed at me. I hid my grin.

'You've got a good one here,' the DO said. 'She'll go far.'

'I think you're right. Have you seen enough, Rowan?' I said.

'Actually, Sarge,' said Alyson. 'I was wondering . . . since we're here and all, if there might be someone worth interviewing with Rowan, show her how it's done?'

Rowan's face lit up like a child hearing there was ice cream coming.

'Hmm, well, I tell you what. If you don't mind interviewing in the cell, there's a little shit brought in last night, caught climbing out of a window. Stealing Christmas presents, can you believe it? Takes a special kind of prick. The housebreaking team were supposed to come down and speak to him before he goes to court, but they've been delayed. No harm in seeing if he might burst to a few more break-ins. The interview rooms are rammed though, sorry. It would have been good to show her the whole tape-recorded procedure, it's just crazy up there.'

'No, that'll do fine, thanks. What do you say, Rowan? Wanna see if we can clear up a few crimes?' said Alyson. The DO handed her an enormous set of keys.

'He's in fourteen. You know where to print off crime reports and all that?' Alyson nodded. 'Let me know if he suddenly decides he wants a lawyer, or if he confesses to anything. Otherwise just drop the keys behind the bar.'

'Will do, Sarge.'

'Nice to meet you,' he said to me, and then he just had to get his hand on Rowan's shoulder one last time. 'And best of luck to you. Let me know if you ever need anything, Rowan.'

'I will, Steve, thanks.'

We fumbled around outside cell fourteen, still in sight of the lift which took an age to get going. Alyson pretended to be struggling to find the key until the DO's legs rose out of view. Then we followed Alyson to twenty-five.

'I guess you know who we're here for?' I said.

Rowan gave a single nod of the head. Her gaze was fixed

on the door as Alyson inserted the key. With a sonorous clunk, the key twisted. She prepared to pull it open.

'I'd do this with you if I could, but it would mean my job,' she said.

'I know. That's the only reason I brought Rowan. If he does say something it needs to be corroborated. Aly, I really do appreciate this.'

'You'll have to get straight into it. No time for strategies or rapport. You've got ten minutes,' she said.

'Ten minutes.'

The heavy door groaned open and I got my first glimpse, in person, of the monster.

Rowan scrambled backwards as the tiny cadaverous man on the blue mattress jumped to his feet and immediately approached. He was shorter than Rowan, barely clearing five feet. His brown dishevelled hair and wild beard created a bizarre contrast with his frame and height. He looked like a child in an elaborate Charles Manson costume.

'Come in, come in,' he said, as if we just rang the doorbell to his house. We stepped inside and the door was closed with a foreboding thud behind us. I could feel Rowan tucked behind my shoulder, using me as an unlikely shield. At the far end of the cell, as every cell, the concrete was raised about four inches along the back wall. On top of this sat a blue mattress, or what constitutes a mattress in a police holding cell.

'Please, sit,' he said, planting himself at one end of the mattress and ushering us to the remainder.

'Thanks, but we're fine standing.' I stepped further into the cell, trying to edge away from the toilet in the corner nearest the door. Dark brown piss in the stainless-steel bowl was sending out waves of ammonia reek.

'Mr Taylor, I hoped we could ask a few questions. If you don't mind.'

'No, I don't mind. Happy to help, though I thought I was just waiting to be moved now?' he said, his voice had a metallic rasp to it. He beamed a yellow-toothed grin at us.

'I'm Sergeant Colyear,' I said, deciding it was pointless to lie. He had already clocked my warrant card since I'd forgotten to hide it away. 'It was just one or two things for clarification, that's all.'

'Whatever you need.' He sat cross-legged, a picture of relaxed composure.

I realised at that moment that I hadn't prepared a thing. I guess a part of me expected this venture to end in failure a long way short of the cell. 'So . . . um, where were you when, ah.' I flicked the pages of the report but inspiration escaped me. 'Why'd you do it?' I asked, eventually.

He leant back on the mat sucking air through his teeth. Throwing his hands up and letting them drop to his lap he said: 'I dunno. I'm sick, I suppose. Why does anyone do these things?' His words wheezed, like there were two separate voices saying the same thing.

'You've done this before?'

'No, no. I mean I thought about it, sure. But no, never actually went through with anything.'

'What was different this time?'

He shook his head and scratched at his beard, his eyes scanning the ceiling in thought. 'I've picked up hitchhikers before and, like I said, I've had these thoughts. Just pushed them away, like deep down? Then this girl jumps in, she's young, pretty and on her own. She starts talking about how she's going home, that her folks don't know where she is. She's in the passenger seat. She's got her feet up on the dash, listening to her . . . iPod or whatever, those long, thin legs. She smiles at me a couple of times when I look over and before I know it, or can do anything about it, I pull over. I tell her there's something wrong with the truck and then I'm dragging her out. My hand is on her mouth and then I'm on her and I'm—'

'You dragged her out?'

'Huh? Yeah. Like I said.'

'OK, and then what?'

'Well . . . you know.'

'The raping and murdering?'

'Well, yeah.'

'Let's talk about that for a minute.'

'OK, but I already told them everything, and it's sort of getting blurrier as time passes, you know?'

'It's OK,' I said. 'Whatever you can remember. Also, I have everything here to remind you, if you get stuck.' I tapped at the file. The scratching had now moved to his hair.

'Not much to tell, really. You know. I held her down and I, you know, raped her. Then I killed her. After that I drove off.'

It was so matter-of-fact it was in itself shocking.

'Let's break that down a little. How did you get her clothes off?'

'What do you mean?'

393

'I mean, physically. According to the report she was found completely naked. Did you strip her before or after you murdered her?'

'I don't know. I don't really remember.'

'You don't remember?' I said, incredulous. 'If I was in that situation I would take every grizzly second of that to the grave.'

'I took her trousers off before, the rest after, so I could, you know . . .'

'Rape her, yes. But don't you mean skirt?'

'What?'

'Skirt, she was wearing a skirt.' I tapped at the folder again.

'Yeah, that's what I meant. You know, her bottom half.' Both hands now were in his beard as if dealing with an infestation.

'How did you kill her?'

'Look, maybe I should talk to the guys who interviewed me before, or maybe a law—'

'You strangled her, right?'

'Um, yeah, I think, yeah, I strangled her.'

There was a soft knocking at the door, Rowan went to check.

I knelt down beside him. He slid along the mattress away from me.

'What kind of fight did she put up?'

'What?'

'Fight. How did you overpower her? Did she fight back? Scratch you? You don't expect me to believe she just lay there, do you?'

'I don't remember, maybe.'

'Maybe what? Maybe she scratched?'

Rowan was twirling her index fingers, one over the other. We had to wrap this up.

'I-I don't want to answer any more.' He moved to slide further along. I grabbed him by the chin.

'Answer the fucking question, you little shit,' I said.

'No, I don't wanna—'

He was pushing at my arm. I held him by his grubby, greasy beard. 'That girl was eighteen and in great shape. When I spoke to her mum, she described her as an athlete. You're what? Maybe ten stone? Rowan here would kick the shit out of you without any trouble. You expect me to believe you pulled her from a truck, stripped her of her trousers, and it was trousers by the way, not that you have the first fucking clue, and then forced yourself on her? Not a fucking chance. Tell me the truth—'

'Sarge, we need to—'

'Getoff, getoffame.'

'Who put you up to this?'

'Leggo . . .'

'What do they have on you? What do you get?'

'Don, we need to go.'

'TELL ME!' I yelled in his face. I gripped the beard all the harder but then his manky yellowed teeth clamped and sunk into my skin.

'Get off him.'

'Arrghh.'

I couldn't see who was screaming and I didn't realise I was falling until my arse hit the concrete floor, followed by the back of my head a split second later. The pain in my hand was searing.

'We need to go, now.' It was Alyson. She'd stepped into the cell to see what the commotion was.

Taylor was the one screaming. Rowan had him by the hair; that's why he opened his mouth to free my hand.

'Right now, come on. Rowan, let him go.' Alyson pulled me from the floor. Rowan dumped Taylor to the mattress and helped her.

I stared down at my hand as they hoisted me towards the door. It was bleeding, I saw. It wasn't the blood that worried me so much, it was the saliva running down my wrist soaking into my shirt cuff. Disgusting.

'You-you think you're so fucking clever don't you.' Taylor's rasping voice was shaking with emotion. Tears ran down his face. He hugged his knees and sobbed.

'Tell me who,' I yelled. 'You don't need to do this; you don't need to go to—'

'Think'n' you're so clever,' he sobbed and rocked back and forth. 'So fucking clever, don't you?' His voice grew wee and tremulous.

'Come on, we're out of here, now.' Alyson pulled me into the cell passageway and slammed the door. Her hands shook as she twisted the key in the lock. There was shouting coming from the adjacent cells, excited, angry voices wanting to know what was going on, whose rights were being violated.

I was being frog-marched away from the noise. I was still trying to find my legs. I desperately wanted to get back in there, shake or beat the information from him.

The excitement of the prisoners was spreading like fire, one cell catching the next. I was all but thrown into the lift. Alyson was furious.

It didn't matter, I decided. I knew I was onto something.

CHAPTER THIRTY-ONE

If at First you Don't Succeed . . .

It was while crossing the Erskine Bridge that it hit home it was Christmas Eve. The traffic was thin and we had left Glasgow in record time. I'd never managed anything but a crawl along the bridge in the many years I'd driven across it. Flying over it now at a steady sixty-five, it dawned on me why it was possible. A few hours ago, before 5 p.m., it would have been the usual elevated car park, with people desperate to get home to their families and I might have been tempted to fire up the lights and siren to get through, but as I weaved between an HGV and an ambulance, with Rowan silent beside me, gripping the holy-fuck handle above her window, I could see that only people who really *had* to be on the road remained.

I thought about Alyson. What kind of mess had I left behind for her? She'd shuttled us swiftly and discreetly from the building. Entry teams were already forming to quell the small riot we had left in our wake. She'd only shaken her head when I apologised on our way out of the door. What did that mean exactly?

'Where are you going?' Rowan was suddenly agitated as I indicated left.

'Dropping you home,' I said, and pulled off the A82 onto the Glasgow road to Dumbarton.

'Like fuck you are.'

'Rowan, it was stupid of me to involve you in what happened back there. I'm not putting your career at any further risk, no way.'

'Well, that's up to me, and I'm not—'

'No. Not this time. I'm sorry, Rowan. I don't know what's going to happen next, but it's not going to be anything good. I want you as far away from it as possible.'

'And what if something happens to you? How am I supposed to live with that?'

'All the more reason you're out of the way. Now, where do you live? Where can I drop you?' She sat, arms folded, staring out of the windscreen. The wipers threw large flakes of snow left and right. I pulled the car over into a bus stop, in what looked like the town centre. 'Rowan, where can I—'

'I can walk from here.'

She didn't look at me. She grabbed her coat from the back seat and threw Alyson's blazer into its place before slamming the door. She walked off and was soon lost amongst the falling snow.

*　*　*

399

I almost crashed twice on the descent into Stratharder. After the second near-miss, I swallowed back the adrenalin and eased up.

I pulled up slowly to the police station. The snow was fresh and unmarked.

I changed quickly back into uniform, retaining my civvy jacket, far warmer than the police issue. The next leg of the journey would be on foot.

In the station I checked through Margaret's Rolodex and snatched out the card I needed. The maps function on my phone was next to useless in this town, so instead I took a picture of the wall map in the inspector's office.

The weather had let up a little. The snow that had fallen heavy and thick lay as soft powder, making progress slow and wet. Every step invited a fresh trickle over the lip of my boots.

The town centre was a frozen ghost town, like some spell had been cast upon it. At 10 p.m. the odd car or pedestrian could be expected to pass, but nobody was venturing out in this. The occasional light, through thin-curtained windows, was the only indication the place had not been abandoned all together.

I rubbed my hands with a blast of hot breath and checked the picture on my phone. I selected what I thought was the correct road but began doubting myself as I ventured further and further from the town. The street lights ended abruptly and soon I was walking almost blind. Now and again the moon would find itself between clouds and the world would appear in a silver-grey glow, then all too quickly it would be hidden again and I was plunged into treacle darkness. I was almost ready to turn back when a shape caught my attention, like a little piece of night, darker than the rest: a house. The torch function on the phone was useless against anything further than six inches from the screen but it did allow me to check the Rolodex card and confirm I was where I needed to be. 'Netherlea Cottage' was revealed as I dusted off the ornate wooden post at the bottom of the driveway.

I circled the house and was unsurprised when I found no obvious security. There was no alarm, no motion-detecting light, but it was locked up tight and in complete darkness. The irony of working as a cop is that you learn to be a pretty good cat burglar. Years of attending housebreakings will inevitably teach you a thing or two, however a stealthy entry to this house was beyond my capabilities. I dug around the snow of the back garden with my boot until I kicked something solid. The rock was larger than the job required, but it would do. I removed my jacket and wrapped it around the boulder to stifle the inevitable noise. It took both hands to launch it through the bottom pane of the back door. It performed magnificently. It still made an almighty crash, despite the coat, though I doubted anyone was close enough to hear, besides, if they did, and the police were called, well . . .

I ducked into the kitchen, trying not to plant a hand onto the strewn glass. I began flicking on lights, figuring any notion of discretion was long gone. The place was a real home. There was barely an inch that hadn't been adorned by some photograph or sentimental trinket. Someone clearly had some fetish for elephants as countless figurines were set on every available surface.

I almost stumbled backwards in shock when I hit the light switch in the living room. The inspector's face grimaced down at me from the wall above the fireplace. An attempt at a smile, he looked more like someone who had just lost the battle of holding in a fart. It was one of those photographic-studio family jobs, probably taken within the last few years, judging by the daughter who didn't look much younger, flanked by her proud parents and all wearing the obligatory white and beige clothing.

The office I was looking for was upstairs. The door was locked but it only required a half-hearted shoulder to beat it. Crossing the threshold, I felt like I had stepped through time. Dominating the room was a large desk, upon which sat a computer someone from the '90s would have referred to as retro. I hit the switch on the desktop unit and on the enormous tube monitor, complete with a bizarrely tiny screen. I waited the best part of five minutes for the boot-up, only to be prompted for a password. My fingers hovered over the keyboard and I attempted a few family-themed words. Each strike of the keys, which could be comfortably pressed with two fingers, was rewarded with a cathartic ca-lunk, but no luck. I turned it all off; it would only have been an unexpected bonus. What I was really here for sat in the corner, on a little desk of its own.

Again, the thing was unnecessarily massive. It was the same model as the one back at the station. That made sense. Given the inspector's problems with technology, he would be likely to opt for the same one he'd been forced to learn to use. None of the pre-programmed numbers buttons had anything written next to them; the whole thing was blank. I hit the switch at the back and the fax machine began its growling wake from slumber. The drawers of the table it sat on were secured and would require something far more persuasive than a shoulder. I began searching around for something to jemmy the lock and found a brass letter opener with an elaborate thistle design at its handle. It bowed slightly as I pushed into the space between drawer and desktop and felt the latch move a little. With a solid tug the top drawer slid open. The fax headers I was looking for where right there. Bold as brass. Lothian and Borders, Greater Manchester and the Metropolitan Police, amongst others, including a few foreign ones. Blank headers ready for use.

Patterns, I thought, *the lesson you taught Rowan and didn't see yourself here*. This had been the second option I was met with after I spoke with Rebecca at the Met. This is what I had suspected. I had resisted the urge of coming here first. I wanted to be sure. I began gathering the fax headers up when a beam of light scrolled across the back wall. I moved to the window as the second headlight caught me in the eyes. The inspector's car bounced up the thick snow of the driveway, before sliding to an urgent stop.

I was surprised that my stomach hadn't reacted. I felt no twinge at all. There was no chance to get out before he was in the house. I resigned myself to this and moved back to the fax machine which had finally gone silent.

A car door slammed shut.

I scanned the front panel of the machine.

Keys in the front door.

I found 'Print Test Page'.

Footsteps on the stairs.

I pressed the button and sat myself in the office chair.

Doors opening on the upper floor.

I opened my notebook and removed the fax sheet I had taken from the station and unfolded it. I compared the number to the one displayed on the printout.

The office door burst open.

'It match . . . es,' I said, the word stumbling from my mouth, as my eyes rolled from the A4 sheet, to the inspector, to the shotgun he was holding.

He was panting. The left hand supporting the barrel shook, I doubted it was from the cold. 'What do you think you're doing?'

'Collecting evidence.' I pushed the printed sheet along the desk. 'You're obviously not aware, Stewart. But if you send a fax to someone, your own number appears in the top corner. Here, see? It's tiny and actually I'd never noticed it either. But there it is.'

For a moment he said nothing. The look on his face was concerning; I couldn't quite read it. Again, though, my stomach never flinched. I decided to trust it.

'Put it down. Put it all down and get out.' He lowered the gun at me.

'I don't think so. No, you're not going to shoot me,' I said and tucked my hands confidently into my body armour, letter opener secreted in my palm. 'You're up to your neck as it is. Besides, your fax number is registered, just like your telephone. I don't even need this. We both know, since I have no warrant to be here, it's inadmissible in court anyway.'

'It's . . . it's not what you think.' All colour had drained from his face. The gun hung limp in his hands.

'OK,' I said. 'Why don't you explain it to me.'

He snorted a laugh. 'You wouldn't understand.'

'I'm a cop, Stewart. I've seen my share of shit.'

'No, you only think you have.'

'I can't help you if I don't know what's going on.'

'You're not here to help me.' He backed up and slumped against the desk, half sitting on it; the gun rested on his knee. He stared at the floor and shook his head slowly. His eyes began to fill. 'You know what, it's almost a relief. I suppose the cavalry's on its way?'

'I haven't called it in, Stewart. Not yet. I wanted to be sure. Shit, I wanted to understand. Also, I don't know who's in on this. I don't know who to trust.'

'You *should* call it in.' He looked utterly defeated. He sniffed back tears. 'Six months.'

'Six months?'

'Until I retire, until I get away. Six bloody months. Six God damn, shitty, fucking months.' He was suddenly on his feet, tears rolling down his cheeks. He was throttling the shotgun while the words hissed through his teeth.

A ball of fire erupted in my gut.

If I hadn't been seated, I'd have fallen flat. 'Uggh . . . Stewart, take it easy. Put the gun down. Don't shoot—arggh.' I doubled over and cried out. It felt like a hand was inside of me, pulling and scratching. I wanted to shit, throw up and explode; anything to relieve the pressure.

'What?' he said. 'This thing's not even loaded.'

I looked up, sweat was rushing from every pore. The

gun was on the desk and the inspector had no intentions with it . . . what, then?

That question was answered by the sound of tyres on snow outside.

'Shit,' he said, cupping a hand against the window. 'We have to get you out of here, right now.'

He was stronger than he looked. He hooked a hand under my arm and pulled me to my feet. We stopped on the stairs as the knocking began on the front door, then the doorbell and then the banging, a foot by the sounds of it. 'Back door,' he whispered. We rounded the hall and into the kitchen. There were men already crawling through the hole I'd prepared earlier. I would have attempted the armed bluff, but we'd left the gun upstairs. The two men, now on their feet, blocking the back door, had made no such mistake.

'Open the front door,' one said to the other, levelling both barrels. He looked vaguely familiar. Bearded, broad, pissed off.

The inspector propped me against the frame of the door. 'I'm sorry, Donald. You don't deserve this. You know, I tried absolutely everything to get you to leave, did I not?'

'Yes,' I said, planting one hand on the door frame and the other pressed firmly to my stomach. 'I suppose you did.'

'Look, he doesn't know anything, not really,' the inspector said. 'We can let him go after we tidy everything up.'

'He knows enough.' A gruff voice. I lifted my head. It was Ogilvie's man, the ghillie, Bill.

I was quickly flanked by two more black-clad

henchmen-types entering through the front door. Again, they looked vaguely familiar. One of them pressed his shotgun to the side of my neck.

'I don't want any part of this, Bill,' the inspector said, jabbing a thumb in my direction. 'This isn't my role. He knows I won't play any part in this. Now move aside.'

'It's too late for all that, Stewart.' Bill looked somewhat ashamed. He couldn't look the inspector in the eye. The free man raised the butt of his shotgun to his shoulder.

'What the hell are you doing?' Bill said, and pushed the barrel to the floor. 'Not here, you fucking moron.'

'Wait, what? No, we have a deal.'

'The deal was that your family aren't touched. That stands. As for you, well, just too many fuck-ups. I'm sorry, Stewart, we're cleaning house.'

'Who's we?' I said. 'Ogilvie?'

Bill's eyes flicked to me for the briefest second and then to the floor. 'Get them in the van,' he said and twisted the radio on my shoulder, releasing it from its clasp, then unbuckled my belt, complete with baton and CS spray. 'Take their phones and cuff *him* to the rear. No more mistakes.'

'How many, Stewart, how many girls?' I managed, between bouts of crippling cramps.

'Shut up, just shut up.'

I was on my knees in the back of the transit van we'd been bundled into. My hands were locked behind my back. I was trying to brace myself as the back end bounced and fish-tailed in the snow.

'Stewart, we're in deep shit here. When we get to wherever we're going, they are going to fucking shoot us. At least tell me what I stumbled into. What happened to those kids?'

His face was buried in his hands. They hadn't bothered to cuff him; he was no threat.

'The second I retired, I was going to take them to Australia. Furthest point from here.'

'The girls?'

'What? No. Marjory and Paula. Get them out of this place, away from all of this. I was going to write a letter. A long, long letter. No one would believe I wasn't directly involved, but it would be written, I'd have told it. That's the important thing, don't you think?'

He was in shock, or denial, or something. Making no sense. 'Stewart, you need to concentrate. All those missing person reports, Jesus, dozens of them. How many kids, Stewart? How many did you—ugghh . . .' I strained to keep my bowels from emptying. I bit down on my bottom lip and doubled over as tightly as I could.

'It – it wasn't all of them. Young ones genuinely go missing all the time. They can't wait to get out of this town.'

'And what about the other kids?' I said, panting for breath.

'They're not kids. It's not children for God's sake.' The inspector's head was between his knees, both hands full of tight-gripped hair. 'Nobody under eighteen. Not while I was . . .'

'Shit, of course. *Nobody under eighteen.* I get it.'

'You don't get it; you have no idea.'

'No, I think I do. If they're under eighteen, by law, you have to tell the parents where they are, right? But, if they're over eighteen you just have to confirm they're safe and well. As adults they have the right to not have their whereabouts divulged.'

'Just shut up, it doesn't matter now.'

'So, you send a fax from your own house pretending to be an investigating officer from another force area to confirm they've been found, that they don't want the parents told anything else? Case closed.'

'Shut up, shut up.'

'Of course, no investigation had ever been instigated, because the kid was never missing in the first place.'

'They're – they're not kids. Shut up.'

'How many, Stewart?'

'Shut up, just SHUT UP. You don't fucking understand. I had no choice. He could take them any time he wanted.'

'Who?'

'I had . . . no choice. And I had no real part in it. I needed to keep my family safe.'

He was sobbing in deep, convulsing waves. He hugged his head and rocked back and forth. I was waiting for him to compose himself, to continue badgering him until he said . . . something, when the van stopped suddenly. My stomach pitched and I knew without a doubt what was coming next.

I moved onto my knees and shuffled towards him. There was the sound of doors being slammed shut and raised voices coming around the side of the van.

'Listen to me,' I whispered. He wiped tears from his face

and sat back, examining the certitude on my face. 'Those men are going to shoot us the second they open that door.'

'What?'

'Right now, they're probably arguing about who is going to do it. The one who doesn't has to dispose of us and the van.'

'You can't possibly know—'

'Listen . . .'

'Fine, fine. But you're burning the van,' came the muffled conversation from outside.

'We've only got a second. Reach into my armour, somewhere near my heart.'

'How do you—'

'Fucking do it now.' He thrust his hand in and didn't have to rummage long before producing the letter opener.

'Now, get up, move forward.'

Keys rattled.

'When that door opens move immediately to your left. He should miss.'

'Should?' The brass blade hung limply in his hand.

'Then you stick him and we run.'

'I don't, I don't think I can.'

'If you don't, we're dead.'

'Shit, Shit. Donald, listen. If anything happens to me, I've placed a letter with a lawyer. I need you to get my family and—'

He turned to face the door as it was heaved open.

I stood directly behind the inspector and shifted left with him as the blast erupted. My ears rang and I shouted, 'Now,' but wasn't sure if the words even left my mouth.

He grunted in pain as some of the shot caught him. He moved forward, but tentatively, not the charge I wanted.

'Fuck,' the man said as he fumbled in his pocket looking for a cartridge.

'Do it now!' I yelled and pushed my forehead into his back. The inspector moved, his arm came up slowly and I watched as he pushed the blade into the man's neck with sickening slow precision, like he was testing the tenderness of a cooked chicken. The shotgun fell to the ground and the man dropped to his knees, his hands shaking as they explored the foreign object, now slick with blood. It ran through his fingers and down the sleeve of his red coat.

'Shit,' said the other, who was so stunned by what he was seeing that it took him a moment to remember he too was armed. The look of disbelief in his face shifted to one of fury. He raised the barrel at the inspector's face and I pushed with everything I had. Another shot went off as we all tumbled hard to the cold mix of mud and snow.

I flayed around trying to get onto my feet, trying to gain some purchase on the ice, to run. After a full minute of failing to even get to my knees I stopped. I lay on my back sending clouds of hot breath into the cold air, made red by the brake lights of the van. I was going nowhere. The man underneath the still inspector was struggling free.

I turned my head. The one with the red coat lay face up, one hand still at his throat the other by his side, the letter opener lying slick in his palm. The man grunted as he pushed the inspector's lifeless body off himself. There was a scratch of grit as he lifted the gun. I turned away and waited.

The yellow piece of shit came out of nowhere. I barely had a second to look to my right as it flew towards us with a single functioning, blinding headlight. It slammed into the gunman before any brakes were applied. There was an *oof* of breath and a crack of gunfire as he was thrown into a deep bank of snow. The car slid until a tree caught its side. Both front doors opened. Mick ran to inspect the damage, Mhairi ran to me.

'Are you OK?'

'I'm fine,' I said.

'Good,' said Mhairi. Her hand traced the edge of my face. She then struck me with a solid blow with whatever she was carrying. My head rung like a bell. My vision dulled and swam.

'Argh, dammit,' I said.

I tried to focus but before I could she said: 'Sorry.' And she struck again.

The light of the world swung sideways, and went out.

CHAPTER THIRTY-TWO

Present, Tense

'No one let me out,' I say, but have to make two attempts at 'one' as my voice struggles against the shivering. 'I cu-climbed out.'

'Jesus, you're freezing,' says Mhairi, and steps out from the passenger side. She moves to help me from the snow. I scuttle backwards, unsure of her intentions. 'Hey, hey, it's OK. Oh shit,' she says, suddenly getting a look at the wound on my head. 'I didn't mean to hit you that hard. God, I'm sorry.'

'Wu-why did you f-feel the need to hit me at all?'

'Look, get in. It's warm at least.' She takes my arm and leads me into the back seat of the yellow-piece-of-shit. The stench of cigarette smoke is stifling, but it's warm as promised. I slide along the seat and just lie there for a minute. Mhairi slides in at my back and spoons me, rubbing the aching cold out of my arm and dabbing a careful finger at the congealed mess on my head. 'I'm sorry, Don. I was trying to keep you safe.'

'Huh?' I say. 'How does that wu-work?'

'There's men,' she says. 'They're looking for you. They were all over the place when we came to get you. I knew you'd refuse to hide. You would have been caught. So, I thought I'd, you know, knock you out for a little while, like in the movies. Thought I'd put you somewhere safe. It took us ages to get clear of them. The handcuffs were to stop you climbing out of there.'

'They searched the car twice,' says Mick, talking over his shoulder from the driver's seat.

'You nearly took my head off. I might have bled to death. And what men? How did you know where I would be?'

'Jesus, this is Stratharder. There's almost no point in owning a phone. The jungle drums start beating and everyone knows something's going on. We started hearing about the disturbance at your boss's house. Mick went to check it out.'

'Saw you getting thrown into the back of a van,' says Mick, no notable trace of gangsta in his voice.

'He came to get me. It took us a few minutes to catch up to you. But like I say, there were men all over the place, some with guns. They're watching the roads; there's no way out of town without getting stopped.'

'Ogilvie's men, right?'

'That's right. You need my phone, call for back up?'

I lie on the back seat considering this for a moment. Mhairi's head is on my hip, her hand slides up and down my arm. The situation is absurd, especially with Mick right there, squirming in the front seat, but it's so soothing I could just about sleep. 'Mhairi . . .'

'Yes?'

'Why did you throw a dead man into the cellar with me?'

'That's what I said,' says Mick. 'I was like, what the fuck are you doing? We need to get out of here? And she was like—'

'I panicked, OK? I was just trying to tidy everything away. I don't know what I was thinking.'

If I had my own phone, I think, *I would call Rowan or Alyson, someone I trust. But I don't know her number, not even sure I know my own number, that's why you keep all that stuff in your phone, right? It would have to be a call, either to treble-nine, or a general non-emergency call to a station.*

'I can't risk it,' I say. 'If the inspector's involved in all this, there's no telling who else might be. I need to get out of town. Mick, can you take me back up to my car? I'll make a run for it.'

There's a glance between Mhairi and Mick.

'What?'

'Um, I'm guessing you parked it outside Hilda's?' asks Mhairi.

'Yes.'

'It might be out by now, but when we passed it earlier it was a fireball. Besides, you'd never make it. Like I said, they have checks on the road.'

'We could get you close to the road. It would still be like a five-mile walk through the woods, but it's doable,' says

Mick. It's odd to hear him talking normally, and not just that, but with what might be mistaken for compassion.

'OK let's do that. If I can get out to the main road, I'll stop in at the first garage and call a cab, get back to civilisation and figure it out from there. Can you take me back to Hilda's? I need warmer clothes. I left a few boxes in my room.'

Mick turned the car and started back up the hill.

'Here,' says Mhairi and pulls me to a seated position. She takes a cuff key from her pocket and begins trying to unlock my wrists.

'Where did you get that?'

'From your pocket. Before we lowered you into the cellar.' She carefully draws back the arm of the cuff to release my wrist. I give it a roll and there's an initial stab of pain followed by a euphoric sense of comfort. 'Got it.' The other wrist is released and Mhairi rubs at them gently.

'Thanks,' I say. 'Listen, Mhairi, I'm sorry too. After the way I treated you I couldn't have expected your help.'

'Ach, never mind all that. I shouldn't have flown off the handle the way I did. You were only reacting the way everyone else does. It was unfair of me to expect more.'

Her words stung. I had no reply. I just sat as her hands worked down from my wrists to my fingers.

'Don't be long,' says Mick, as he pulls up outside the house. 'If anyone sees us, we're screwed.'

'I'll only be a minute.'

I duck out of the car and start fishing through my pockets for keys, but Mhairi must have taken them, the cuff key was attached. The Polo is a black, smoking skeleton at the edge of the road. The air is filled with the acrid smell of burnt rubber. I am about to go and ask Mhairi, when I notice Hilda's front door is ajar. Hilda left a week ago to spend Christmas with her family. I check the roadway and her little jeep isn't there, however a little further up the road I see a grey car, not so much parked as abandoned.

'Seriously,' Mick shouts, 'we need to get going.'

I step up to the driver window and whisper, 'Just stay in the car for a minute, I'll be back. But stay here.'

'What's going on?' says Mhairi, leaning over the back seat.

'I don't know. Just stay here.'

I lift a rock as I approach the door. The lock's been forced. There's a light on in the living room, I see, as I step into the dark hall. I proceed slowly, listening, but there's no sound other than the chorus of metallic pings and clicks from the remains of the Polo outside.

The door to the living room is open a crack. I pause to peer through. There's a motionless leg visible, the toes of a huge boot pointing straight up. I can't see who it's attached to. I push the door slowly and the huge outline of the man lying on the rug comes into view. His frame is so enormous that it can only belong to one person.

'No . . . no, no, no.' I drop the rock and run to the gentle giant. 'You fuckers, you fucking cunts.' He must have heard I was in trouble and come looking for me. I don't know who walked in on who, Pav or the shooter, but I don't suppose it matters. 'Jesus, Pav.' He lies there atop the shattered remains of the coffee table. I sit on my knees next to him for a full minute, before bouncing a balled fist against his massive thigh. 'What the fuck were you thinking? You have a kid.' I punch his leg again and this time a groan leaves him. 'Fuck, Pav.' I check his neck; there is a pulse, albeit not a strong one. The injuries to his chest and neck would have killed a normal-sized man for sure. I check his pockets for keys and run outside yelling for Mick to give me a hand. I reverse Pav's car to the door. Mick and Mhairi take a leg each while I haul his arms and spill Pav into the back seat.

'Mick,' I say. 'Drive to the hospital in Oban. Don't let anyone stop you. There's no time to wait for an ambulance, even if they let one through. Mhairi, you go with him.'

'But—'

'Please. And Mick, give me the keys to your car.'

'Wait, what? You're no' takin' my car. No way.'

'Mick, don't argue,' says Mhairi and pulls him away. 'You're away to do something stupid, aren't you?'

'I'm afraid so. Thank you for your help, Mhairi. You too, Mick.' She steps up to the window and carefully pushes her fingers into my hair before kissing me at the corner of my eye.

'Try not to get yourself killed, you hear?'

'I'll try.'

'You're no' goin' to damage her, are you?' says Mick in a wee voice.

'Mick,' I say, 'if you have any last words to say to this jaundiced turd of a vehicle, I think now would be the time.'

CHAPTER THIRTY-THREE

Exit Strategies

I can't help but be impressed with the yellow-piece-of-shit; it's frighteningly quick and handles extremely well, even on the snow. I punch the gear stick from third into second and take the sharp left onto the Langie. The tail swings out, but as I hammer the accelerator it rights itself and I am pushed back into my seat. The road surface is thick with slush, the thin tyres carve through like sled-rails.

It's not long before headlights appear on the horizon, square in the centre of the road. I flick the lights to full-beam and bear down on the on-comer. I think back to my first day in Stratharder when this very car I'm driving was doing the same thing, forcing me off the road. Well, not today. The oncoming car's lights begin to flash. I don't let up. At the last moment, it swerves off-road and I catch a fleeting glimpse of two men in the four by four, furious and straining to spot who's driving. They make slow work getting back onto the road and turned around. They're a blurred dot in the rear-view mirror as I hit the outskirts of town.

I slow to a crawl as I descend into the empty streets. A few curtains twitch at the harsh sound of the car's ridiculous exhaust, otherwise nothing is moving.

I turn right onto Ogilvie's road. The surface here is particularly wet where more traffic has carved the snow into pulp. My stomach pulses in constant waves of tense pain, danger everywhere, it's telling me. *Yeah, no shit.*

Progress is slow as the road turns sharply uphill. I end up switching between first and second gears, to find a middle-ground between traction and not skidding or stalling. Finally, the road levels out and I reach the small, stone bridge spanning the gorge.

My path is blocked.

I stop in the middle of the narrow bridge, the engine running, growling through the pimped manifold. The lights of the two Range Rovers at the far end spark into life and I need to shield my eyes. Two men have stepped out, judging by the break in the light. There's no way past them and they're approaching. More light hits my eyes, this time through the rear-view mirror. The other lot have finally caught up. They come to a halt, manoeuvring the small jeep at an angle so as to prevent me reversing out of this situation. The men in front are close now, their shadows are growing smaller as they get closer to me and further from the light. I check the mirror; there's another figure approaching from behind.

There's a harsh tap at the window, not a knuckle, a gun barrel. A face appears, cupping a hand to block the light. Our eyes meet. He's smiling and curling a beckoning finger at me. I smile back and push down on the accelerator. The noise from the exhaust is almost more than I can bear. Two of the three are backing off, only Smiley is now pointing both barrels at me. Without letting up on the gas I push in the clutch, ratchet the gearstick into reverse and release my left foot. For a second there is only the sound of the spinning tyres joining the engine, then suddenly they grip, perhaps having grated the slush from the road surface and I am flying backwards. I push my head back into the seat and wait for the impact. The car slams into the angle of bonnet and flank of the jeep sending it into a spin. The back end swats Smiley off his feet and over the side of the bridge. I have to restart the engine. I pump the gas, but the starter motor just turns and turns. The two in front are looking unsure, but they're still coming. One has a shotgun raised to his shoulder. The engine roars into life, the men stop. I ease down on the pedal with menacing intent. This is enough to have one rethinking. He retreats back to the Range Rovers, the other stops, takes aim.

'Fuck it.' I'm charging again.

There's a blast and the windscreen explodes. I clamp my eyes shut and there's pain, however the sense of fury is stronger. When I open them, the gunman is dropping his weapon and jumping clear off the side. I ram both feet onto the brake pedal, only it's too late. The yellow-piece-of-shit's last act in this world is to test itself against the might of both Range Rovers. The air is forced from my lungs as the seat belt prevents me flying through the open windshield. There is a confusion of smoke, airbag and glass all round me.

I concentrate on my breathing first; without that, nothing else matters. Then, damage assessment. There is pain everywhere, but most of it I can ignore, all but one thing. I look down and see that I am pinned to the seat. A thick shard of metal protrudes from the junction of arm and shoulder on my left side. I am unsure what vehicle it belonged to. The adrenalin is still flowing and so I try to use it. I move to raise both hands to the metal, but the pain in my left arm is too much. I try to pull it out one-handed, but it's going nowhere. I have an idea. I unclip the seat belt and stretch my right hand under the seat and find what I am looking for. I take two deep breaths and grip the seat adjuster. The car must be sitting slightly uphill because the second I pull the lever the seat shoots back and the metal slides free of my flesh. A yell of fury and pain erupts. I pour myself out of the door and onto the wet ground. There is a chorus of clicking and hissing coming from all three vehicles which are now conjoined in a mechanical *ménage à trois*. There are satisfying valleys carved into the bonnets of both Range Rovers while Mick's car has all but lost its front third entirely. Still, it did well; he should be proud. There are noises coming from below the bridge, some painful groans and an angry exchange, both alive it seems. I brush glass from my hair and lift the shotgun from the ground. I squeeze past the marriage of metal, my left arm hanging limp. As I do, I see that the third guy is sitting behind the wheel of one of the Range Rovers. It's Alistair. He's still sporting a magnificent black eye from the bar. A look of terror meets me as he realises I've spotted him. He raises his hands and I walk straight by, inspecting the gun. One barrel fired, one remaining.

I check over my shoulder a couple of times as I walk; I'm not being followed. I stop for a moment and check my shoulder. There is a lot of blood, but it seems to have abated. The pain is astonishing, but if I don't try to use the muscles in my shoulder, I can just about live with it. I continue on. Soon the only sound is my boots breaking virgin snow. The sky has cleared and has become quite brilliant. Were it not for the pain burning through my arm right now, I might enjoy it. The moon, almost full, has turned the lying snow a metal-blue colour. My breath sends up the only clouds amongst the impossible, countless clusters of stars on show.

The estate house comes into view. It sits like an image from a Scottish calendar sold to tourists, with its little loch in front, dead still, a thin layer of ice trapping a single rowing boat close to the shore.

There are a couple of vehicles parked in front of the main house, otherwise little signs of life. As I near, something starts to register in my ears. I have to stop for a moment to silence the crunch of snow to detect exactly what it is. It's music. Classical music.

The front door is lying open and as I push and step through, it's all violins screaming and cymbals crashing. I find the stairs in the near dark and start climbing. The light builds as the stairs turn and before I even reach the top step I am running and yelling and tossing the gun aside.

'No you don't. No you don't, you fucking coward.'

He's swinging by the neck from what looks like an electrical extension cable. It's slung over a beam in the middle of the hallway, a piano stool kicked over underneath him. He's hissing and gurgling through his teeth, spittle collecting on, then dripping from his beard.

I grab Ogilvie's legs as best I can with my one good arm, taking a good kick to the face as I do. Every fibre of him is lashing out instinctively against death. I try to take the weight off his neck, but he's so damned heavy and he can't stay still long enough for me to find a centre of gravity, so now he's just choking more slowly as we spin in an awkward circle.

'Help me, you stupid old fucker.' He either can't or won't straighten his legs. His backside flails around while he croaks and thrashes. My arm is already getting tired. *I could let him go*, I think, *run to the kitchen grab a knife and return; but where the fuck is the kitchen? He'd be dead for sure by the time—*

'Let him swing.'

I swivel Ogilvie's legs to get a look at whoever's talking. I only now realise that the music has stopped.

'Go on. Let him go and move back.' Ogilvie's nephew, Alex. It takes a second to place him; we're standing pretty much where I spoke to him last. He lifts the gun from the top step and flicks the barrel, gesturing me away from his uncle. 'Let him swing,' he says.

'What are you going to do with that?' I say, nodding at the gun. He's opened the barrels, inspecting the contents.

'Honestly? I have no idea,' Alex says, tossing the empty cartridge and snapping the gun closed once more. 'For now, just let him go and back away.' His voice is steady, almost tired-sounding.

I try to release Ogilvie gently. As soon as his full weight is back on his neck, he lets out an agonising hiss and he's kicking with the energy of a young man. I move to take his legs again, but stop as Alex clears his throat and shakes his head. We swivel, slowly, in a circle. He levels the gun at me with one hand and reaches up to Ogilvie with the other, taking hold of his belt.

He begins to pull.

It's almost too awful to watch, and yet I can't look away.

'Don't look at me like that,' says Alex. 'This is a kindness.' His voice is strained as he yanks at the belt. Ogilvie's hiss has turned into a series of tortured clicks that snap from his mouth more and more infrequently.

If you're going to run, I tell myself, *it's now or never*.

I begin backing away as his concentration has moved from me to Ogilvie fully. The gun has drooped to point at the floor and his eyes are all but closed in his efforts. But then, just like that, it's over. Ogilvie is silent. His gums are pulled back showing a bleeding stump of tongue between his teeth. He sways gently.

Alex's eyes open on me and he gives a smile. 'What a mess. What an absolute mess.'

'That's one description, yes.'

'Are the police on their way?'

'Be here any moment,' I lie.

He begins nodding, his eyes to the floor, but the barrels on me.

'Can I ask you a question?' I say.

He shrugs. 'Is there any point?' He pulls at Ogilvie's foot as he passes, sending the old man into a grim spin. His limp body turns in a shallow arc, his head lolled forward, his lifeless red eyes staring hard at nothing whatsoever.

'Why?' I say, nodding at Ogilvie. I have a thousand questions, and that's what comes out.

'I'm respecting my uncle's wishes. If this is how he wants to deal with all of this, then who am I to convince him otherwise. I should warn you, I have no intention of giving up so easily.'

'You won't get far.'

He rubs the back of his head with one hand. 'You'd be surprised how resourceful I can be.'

'I should have realised Ogilvie wasn't at the top of the pyramid. He doesn't . . . didn't, seem to have the mind for something this organised. Tell me, how long did you think you were going to get away with it?'

'He enjoyed playing the big man, lord of the manner, while I took a back seat. I don't know, we had a pretty solid system until you came along.'

'Those girls were never going to stay simply hidden. Sooner or later something was going to slip, even with Stewart there to cover your tracks. How many did you rape? Kill? What is the deal here?'

His face drops. A shaking hand runs through his hair and grips hard. My stomach lurches. I'm pushing his buttons but I don't care. 'And Jennifer. You let her body turn up. Why? Because I was getting too close?'

'Something like that. It doesn't matter now; none of it matters.' He's crying and there is a laugh in his voice, but it is devoid of any humour. 'If you'd done us all the favour of dying in the car crash, we might have avoided all of this.'

'So, it was me or Jennifer? One way or another, you needed me to stop looking into things?'

'OK, that's enough. You know what has to happen here. For what it's worth, I'm sorry.'

'I have more questions.'

'I bet you do, but this isn't a James Bond movie. I need to be gone before your lot get here.' He's composed himself. There is a determination about him. My stomach cramps in response. 'Please,' he says, 'do me a favour and get on your knees.'

He pulls the gun to his shoulder.

I ease down slowly, one knee at a time. 'I want to know how you got the inspector involved.'

'A simple promise. He turns a blind eye and closes things off and in return his family stay safe. Now, enough.'

'And what about Cooper? What did he do to you?'

'Cooper?' he says, looking genuinely confused. 'You mean Iain Cooper? I assure you, it was nothing to do with me. Pentacles and candles? No. Not my doing. It's true I knew the man, a little at least. Years ago, he got wind of what was going on. That's why he was kept on as staff, keep him close in case he opened his mouth. He'd been diagnosed with something awful, I forget what. Anyway, he wanted in. Even turns up at my door with a Polaroid of his own daughter strapped to a filthy-looking bed, wearing only underpants and a rag in her mouth, black magic symbols painted on her. I'm not a monster, Sergeant. I put a knife to that man's throat and promised him that if he ever brought it up again, I'd open him, balls to chin. He knew I meant it.'

'I see. So you're really a good guy, that's what you're telling me?'

'I'm simply telling you that I had no part in whatever that was. But I am sorry for what needs to happen next. You won't believe me, but I am.'

He approaches and my stomach cramps so hard my bowels release instantly. *This is it.*

For just a moment I feel the barrel at the outside of my shoulder and I grab it. *What the hell*, I think, *I'm fucked if I don't try something*. My hand is slick with sweat, but it seems so are his.

'Get the fuck off,' he shouts. I don't stand a chance with one arm, and he wrenches the gun free and swings the butt. The blow leaves my right ear ringing and my brain struggling to identify up from down. 'You're only making this easier for me,' he yells.

He lifts the gun, checks the barrel once more.

I take short breaths and close my eyes.

The barrel is on the back of my shattered shoulder. He's hesitating.

'Come on,' I say, through tears. 'After everything you've done, this is nothing. COME ON.' I can hear his breathing is fast and getting faster. Then, he draws a deep breath and holds it.

'You're penned in,' I say. My head lowers to the floor in exhaustion. He falls backwards to a seated position, his back against the wall.

'It's impossible,' he says. His voice is small, cracking.

428

Something occurs to him and I know what it is.

'Stewart,' I say, and he looks up at me. 'He tried to tell me. He's left something in the event of his death. He was only involved to protect his family, but if he's gone all he has left is what he knows. There's no way out.'

He sits behind me, rubbing his temples. The gun is between us and I consider going for it when his head drops into his hands. My shoulder makes me way too slow. So, I do nothing. I wait for the inevitable. And then, at last, it comes.

'There's always a way,' he says, getting to his feet and lifting the gun.

I watch him stand, then place my forehead on my knees.

My eyes are screwed tight and my hands grip my shins. Ten agonising seconds pass, fifteen. I am shaking, crying. I am about to scream at him to do it . . . and then comes the blast.

For a moment there is nothing, but I am aware of the nothing.

I raise my head. Then I hear a thump and I look backwards. His body has crumpled to the ground, spasming and kicking.

He's fired from under his chin, it's not a clean shot.

'Oh, dear God.' I am moving clear of the kicking and the blood. He's managed to take the right side of his face off, but he's alive. It won't take long, judging by the flow of red, spraying and pooling around him. I slide to the side, away from the blood. His remaining eye, wide and alert, watches me until whatever light is behind it goes out.

* * *

I don't remember getting to my feet. The next thing I recall is stumbling over steps and slamming my shoulder into a door. The pain wakes me. As I enter, I stumble to my right and through the curtain that separates the broken-down wing of the house. I step into a long, dark hallway. The roof is partially exposed and through it the clear night stars can be seen. In the air the sound of sirens, far in the distance. At the end of the hall is a staircase. I cannot go up as debris blocks its passage and so I go down. The stairs are slick. At the bottom is a door.

EPILOGUE

As he descends the steps of Buchanan Street Station, Don is met with a waft of warm air that brings a smile to his face. He's never been to Paris; never been to New York either, and can't say what the Métro or Subway smell like, but he imagines they each have a unique aroma. It could have been a thousand years since last he visited the city, he thinks, you could blindfold him and he would know in an instant that this smell is the Glasgow Underground. It's not a pleasant scent, he couldn't in all honesty describe it as such; it just has that familiar, sentimental quality that brings you instantly back to a time and place in a way only the nose can.

It's been so long he can't recall which of the two directions he needs to take. There's a train already waiting at the platform and he boards. It turns out, looking at the map above the window, that he got on the wrong one, but it's a circular route and he's in no rush.

He disembarks at Hillhead and checks his watch, still early. It was cold in the morning, but the afternoon has arrived with bright sunshine and rising temperatures. He removes his jacket and winces as he pulls his left arm from its sleeve. The two opinions he's received from doctors contrast. One thinks the shoulder may make a full recovery. The other was far less optimistic.

He stands for a moment and allows the world to buzz around him. The average age in this part of Glasgow is markedly younger than others, he's noticed before. Glasgow University being the reason.

Please still be there, he repeats in his head as he walks down Byers Road. It is!

Little Italy. A small cafe-cum-pizzeria was a favourite haunt when he was a student here. Don was never one for hitting the bars hard. He struggled with his studies more than most and could rarely afford the time devoured by a hangover. His intention was to order a cappuccino, however the woman in front is served a slice of pizza and a new favourite smell of the day is discovered. He remembers the woman serving, a solid, dark-haired lady with an amiable aura. Her name escapes him, but he used to know it, and she knew his. Don smiles at her and she smiles back, but it's the smile she will give to everyone; she doesn't know him any more. He orders what the previous customer had and takes it to a seat by the window. The slice is eaten before he's even halfway through the coffee and he debates a second. A check of the watch removes the temptation. He leaves, exchanging smiles again with . . . he wants to say Sheila? Shona?

He thinks he remembers where Cecil Street is but refuses to check his phone, deciding to make an adventure of it, wander the streets. He has time.

He passes a shop window and catches his reflection. The display inside is sparse and dark and with the sunshine outside it creates a good mirror. If anyone's watching, he hopes it looks like he's browsing. In fact, he's looking at where his T-shirt bulges out slightly at the stomach. It's not enormous, but he actually has a belly. He grins and pats it like a proud mum-to-be might.

The street wasn't exactly where he thought it was, but it wasn't too much fuss to find. Another check of the watch confirms he is now bang on time.

He finds the door and checks the piece of paper from his pocket against the names on the buzzer panel. Working his way up, he finds it, right at the top. A smile grows on his face, John's voice is talking to him. *Three certainties in life, Don. Death, taxes, and they're always on the top floor.*

He presses and for a while there's nothing. He's left staring at this black door, waiting. He thinks about that other black door, nearly three months ago now. The descent into that wet darkness. For a moment, when he found the girl wrapped in a filthy duvet on a filthier mattress, he thought, or hoped, that it was Jennifer. That somehow, impossibly, there would be a happy ending to it all. No, it was Viv, the girl purportedly living in London. She was thin and terrified, but otherwise OK. What must she have been thinking to see her rescuer collapse in front of her? When he awoke his head was on the mattress with the girl. Rowan was shaking him. He remembers Rowan's expression, grim with concern, turn bright as she returned his smile. The other police officers busying around him, removing the girl. The messages being sent on her behalf over Facebook are being studied. As Don is not allowed anywhere near the investigation, he doesn't know where they're leading. What is clear is that it's far more likely to be someone relatively young who was faking them so proficiently. Don's guess is the boy at the card game, Craig, the ghillie's son. This also makes Don wonder at what the dive team will find when they get round to dredging Ogilvie's little loch. Don doesn't know what Viv has had to say in her statement. Don's own was cagey to say the least. He told CID what he could without mentioning anything that might result in an enforced chat to a psychiatrist. It meant a lot of little coincidences that made some people in the upper echelons more than twitchy. He did manage to glean a few things before being removed from the investigation. The arrest of Jack Mulligan for one. A payment of three hundred thousand pounds into his account, damning him. *Follow the money*, Don thinks and recalls Detective Inspector Paramour from the novel he abandoned in Pav's bar. Pav, who will never be pretty, but then never was. The surgeons did an incredible job to rebuild part of his throat from other parts of Pav. Selfishly Don had been relieved to hear that they were moving back to Stirling. Had they remained in Stratharder, he knows it's unlikely he would have ever visited his friend again.

Six girls was the last count before Don was locked out. There were plenty of genuine missing person enquiries from Stratharder, but at least six that lead back to Stewart

Wallace's home printer over nine years. Raped countlessly before being disposed of. How many were directly involved and how many were on the books to keep things quiet is really the burning question. As it stands, Don is likely to find out only at the same time as the press do. One satisfying nugget he was told through the grapevine was that Brian burst like a balloon at interview. While he claims he never laid a hand on the girls he's admitted to a perverting the course of justice charge as well as neglect of duty and, rumour has it, he will also be charged art and part alongside anyone else for the rape, abduction and murder of the girls, irrespective of his depth of guilt. A jury will make up their minds on that.

He presses the buzzer once more. He thinks about Rowan. What has she told CID? She's clever, he tells himself. She knows what to say, and what not to say. He will call her when it's all over, but not before.

Don is about to press again when the panel crackles into life.

'Yes, hello?'

'Uh, yeah, hi. It's Don Colyear, we spoke on the phone?'

There's another moment of silence before the shrill buzz of the door lock sounds.

Ascending the four floors has him panting a little. A clunk of locks and rattle of door chains meet him at the top.

The door is opened wide enough to see a face. Long dark hair covers one eye of the girl who answers.

'Miss Darrow?'

'Do you mind if I ask to see some ID?'

'Of course. I mean, of course *not*.' He fishes his warrant

card from his wallet and passes it through the gap. She steps back from the door, still secured by a chain and studies both sides of it. She nods, passes the card back through and closes the door to release the final security chain. The door swings wide and she's already walking back into the flat.

It's a homely little place, lit softly with table lamps. A glance at the pristine-white kitchen as they pass shows a clean and neat existence. She opens the door to the living room and ushers Don inside.

'Thanks,' he says. 'I won't take up too much of your time . . . uh, Eleanor?'

'It's Ellie, and yes, if you don't mind keeping it brief, my fiancé is due home within the hour and if it's all the same I'd rather . . .'

'Yeah, I get it. Don't worry.'

She offers coffee, which is refused. He takes a seat while she makes herself one.

The living room, like the kitchen, is fastidiously tidy. He feels bad about walking on the beige carpet with my shoes on. The bookshelf is more ornaments than volumes, not much of a reader. The ornament theme continues to the sideboard and coffee table. Everything arranged just so.

Ellie returns after a few minutes and ensures a coaster is in place before setting down her mug and sitting into an armchair opposite the sofa Don is occupying. She sits, cross-legged, arms folded and face half hidden under her dark veil of hair.

'As I explained on the phone, Ellie, there will undoubtedly be a thorough reworking of missing person cases from the Stratharder area. The reason—'

'How did . . . ? Sorry,' she cuts in.

'No, it's OK, go on,' he says, allowing her to voice the question burning in her.

'How . . . did you find me?' This she asks while she chews at a thumb. She hasn't once looked at him directly.

'It's . . . well, it's complicated.' And it is. To explain would be to tell her more than she needs to know.

'Did my aunt tell—'

'No. No she didn't. I haven't spoken to Margaret about any of this.'

'You know her? Of course you do, she works at the police station.' She shakes her head, embarrassed at the obviousness. 'What I mean is, you know her well?'

'I wouldn't say well. She's a lovely woman, one of the good ones. But indirectly, it's sort of how I tracked you down. You see when you disappeared from Stratharder, all those years ago, you were traced to Stirling, staying with a friend?'

'Yes. A girl I went to school with, she had left a few years before, for uni.'

'Well, as you were over eighteen you had the right not to divulge your whereabouts to your father, but you asked for an officer to let your aunt know.' This request, amongst the pile of suspicious reports taken from Stratharder over the years, is what made hers stand out. It was confirmed as genuine.

'Yes, I remember. How did that lead you here? To Glasgow, after all this time?'

'Well, I wanted to speak to you and I searched through the various Eleanor Coopers in Central Scotland and that wasn't getting me anywhere, just too many. Then I remembered your aunt. She never married and so has the same maiden name as your mum. A search for Eleanor Darrow brought far fewer hits, then it was just a case of phoning around.'

'So, when you called . . . you didn't know for sure?'

'That's right, I wasn't certain.'

'And when you asked if I was originally from Stratharder, if I'd said no?'

'I might have just given up.' She considers this for a minute, chastising herself, Don thinks.

'I . . . It's just a part of my life I left behind. I prefer not to think about it.'

She's begun drumming the underside of a ring on her coffee mug.

'I won't take up too much of your time.'

'Good, as I say, my fiancé.'

'Yes, sure. Look, the thing is, I can't promise more officers won't want to come and speak to you.'

'Why?'

'Like I said, there is a review of all missing person enquiries from Stratharder about to be conducted. I just wanted to find you before it gets under way.'

'OK,' she says, releasing a long intake of breath and finally moving her hair away from her face. 'What do you need?'

Don is thinking where to start, how to start? The rattle of her ring on her cup is not helping.

'That's a hell of a rock you have there.'

'Sorry?'

'Your engagement ring. It's a stunner.'

'Oh, this?' She holds it up for a second, silver band and enormous rectangular stone. 'I guess he went a little overboard.'

'Can I take a look?' She hesitates. Not wanting to appear rude, she offers her hand. 'What does he do?'

'Oh, he, um, works for the council, something complicated, I don't really understand myself.'

'What's his name?'

'De-eh, David. Why?'

'You're not really expecting David home, are you?'

'You should go,' she says, now on her feet and she's starting to cry. 'David will be—'

'There *is* no David.' Don's tone is consolidatory, as if he's telling her something she doesn't know. 'You use that enormous ring to stop men from bothering you, I think. I mean you just have to look around this flat; there's not so much as a cushion out of place. Two people living together couldn't keep such a pristine house, you'd expect at least a few dishes in the sink, or something. And you're engaged, but there's not a single photograph on display?'

'Please . . .' She's sobbing now, sitting again and rocking slightly in her chair. It's awful to watch; she's so scared.

'You know I'm here about your dad.' At this there is a fresh burst of emotion. She buries her face in her hands. 'I think you were there the night your dad died.'

'No . . . Please . . .'

'Ellie, listen to me. If you don't talk to me, it might be someone else who will be asking you these questions and they will be less willing to understand.'

She's completely broken down now. There are noises coming from her, but nothing remotely coherent. Don drops to his knees in front of her. 'Please trust me,' he says and takes her hand. 'Just tell me what happened. Start at the beginning.'

Don wondered if he might have to try to induce some way of trying to see what happened, though he has no idea how that might work. But, in the end, he doesn't have to. It takes some time, but she begins. Once she starts, it's apparent it's a tale she wants to tell, is desperate to tell. There are a few stoppages where she races ahead and has to be brought back, but she tells everything. The sexual abuse as a child. Then as a teenager, when the physical abuse seemed to stop, there was still the neglect. Then the evening where he came home, hammered drunk, stripped her and tied her to the bed for that photograph, drawing sigils on her naked torso with a magic marker.

She explains that killing him was an ever-present fantasy. She had never been able to have a relationship with a man, couldn't stand the thought of someone touching her. She would have violent dreams, sometimes memories of things he did to her and sometimes of things she would want to do to him, horrible things. She had stayed in touch with Margaret, she explains. She told her that Stratharder had a new sergeant, someone who could be trusted, as Margaret had put it. She'd been too afraid to go to the police, it was an unspoken acknowledgement in the town that the police could not be trusted, that something was going on and they were up to their necks in it. She could have reported it in Glasgow, she continues, but, ultimately, she knew it would be passed up to the local police and they would have access to her address.

Margaret had urged her, then, to speak to Don about the historic abuse and she'd given it a lot of thought. That thought sat too long, she explains, had festered into something else.

'I just lost it,' she says, crying again, but in control. 'Lost the plot completely one night. After I started to think again about speaking to the police it all came back. All the anger, all the shame. I drove to the house that night to kill him. I would kill him, I thought, and then I would stand over his body until you came to arrest me. I would tie him to that bed, the way he did to me and I would cut his throat.'

'But your plan changed? He didn't have a mark on him, except for his heels.'

'When I got to the house, I was absolutely determined. I pushed the door open with one hand, the tyre iron from the boot of the car in the other. I go into the living room where he wakes in his armchair and says "It's yersel, love. Fetch me a drink, will ye?" Like it was that very morning I left. He asks me to fetch his tablets. Like an idiot, that's what I do. I stand in the kitchen, crying, not knowing what to do next. I try to pull myself together and I take some of the tablets and grind them into the work surface with the heel of the glass and sweep it in with a large measure of vodka on top. I wanted him disabled a bit, you know? Make it easier but I've overdone it. I move him to the bedroom, still determined. But he's all over the place. I need to half drag him. But, he's on the bed and I'm going to do it. I want to do it. Do what he did to me and then kill him. I draw the fucking star on his chest, I even use my own lipstick, I don't care. And I'm going to do it . . .'

She's weeping again, her fist balled and bouncing on her knee.

'Go on,' I urge.

'His breathing,' she says. 'It gets so shallow and he's struggling to get air in.'

'Then it stops?'

She nods and wipes at her face.

'Then what happened?'

'Then, like that,' she clicks her fingers and looks Don in the eye for the first time, 'it's like I wake up.'

'A moment of clarity?'

'Maybe. Or a moment of horror, terror. I realise that I've just committed murder. You can't understand the power of that.'

Don considers the bodies that fell around him to get to this point and can relate. 'And you ran?'

She's nodding. The tears are rolling again. 'How long will I get?'

'What do you mean?'

'Pu-prison.'

He takes her hand again and pushes a piece of paper into it. He draws her to her feet. 'Ellie, listen to me. If anyone comes here to ask you about your father, you say the last time you saw him was when you walked out of that house as a teenager and you haven't so much as wasted a second thought on him since. You say that and then you call me.' He taps at the hand now holding his number.

'But—'

442

'Promise you call me. I'll advise you from there.'

'I don't underst—'

'The only reason I came here was to make sure you weren't a danger to anyone else. I'm not here to take you in. Hell, I'm not officially even a cop at the moment.' She looks up him, confused. 'I'm on a six-month career break. It's more like gardening leave, really. You'll have seen on the news, the shootings, the whole mess up there?' She nods. 'Well, they want me out of the way while they try to untangle the whole thing. Let's just say I was less than helpful in the initial enquiry.' Don stands and collects his jacket from the arm of the chair. 'I had to be sure about this and I am. I can't undo what that man did to you, but for what it's worth, you're safe. Whatever was going on up there, it's finished. You have my word.'

She nods. She doesn't really understand; how could she? She gives Don a brief and awkward hug as he leaves.

He checks his phone as he descends the stairs. There's a text from Mhairi, confirming some details about her trip down this weekend, the second visit this month. There's some picture attachment. He'll look at that later in case it's as graphic as the last one she sent.

He doesn't know what's going to happen there but can't wait to see her.

ACKNOWLEDGEMENTS

Warmest thanks to my beta readers: Lindsay, Azul, Seonaid, Rebecca and Sam who I can always rely on for constructive, honest and insightful feedback. Also, to Kelly and Lesley at Allison & Busby who welcomed me into the family and have been looking after me. A special thank you to my agent, Joanna, for her vision, expertise and faith. I am extremely grateful to my team at JD for their support and thereby allowing me to pursue this thing I do. Thank you must also go to all of my previous colleagues in the police service, who throughout my career kept me safe, sane and plied with stories; particularly to John for his guidance, humour and wisdom (not all names have been changed to protect the innocent).

STUART JOHNSTONE is a former police officer who, since turning his hand to writing, has been selected as an emerging writer by the Edinburgh UNESCO City of Literature Trust, and published in an anthology curated by Stephen King. Johnstone lives in Scotland.

storystuart.com   @story_stuart